CE

"Oh, Lord_____nd!" The realization that _____denly burst into the attorne_____ught his clenched right hand up and around very swiftly. Mervyn let out a strangled croak of agony and bowed at the waist like a closing jackknife. Nor was that the end of his misfortunes. The black-gloved hand met the attorney's descending face. Leather-sheathed knuckles smashed the inadvertently offered jaw. Bone snapped as Mervyn was spun around—unconscious before he sprawled limp on the ground.

DON'T MISS THESE EXCITING DELL
WESTERNS BY
J. T. EDSON

THE HIDE AND TALLOW MEN
THE FASTEST GUN IN TEXAS
TROUBLED RANGE
SLIP GUN
THE BAD BUNCH
NO FINGER ON THE TRIGGER
THE NIGHTHAWK

The Justice of Company Z

J. T. EDSON

A DELL BOOK

Published by
Dell Publishing
a division of
Bantam Doubleday Dell Publishing Group, Inc.
666 Fifth Avenue
New York, New York 10103

ISBN: 0-440-20858-0

Reprinted by arrangement with the author.

Printed in the United States of America

Published simultaneously in Canada

March 1991

10 9 8 7 6 5 4 3 2 1

RAD

For W.O.1 "Tom" Netherton, RAVC, although he may no longer be "Tara" and could have moved into James Lambert Drive by the time this book is published.

Author's Note

Because of the unconventional nature of Company Z's duties, the State Legislature of Texas still considers it politic to disclaim all knowledge of Company Z's formation and operations.

We realize that, in our present "permissive" society, we could include the actual profanities used by various people, but we do not concede that a spurious desire to create "realism" is a valid reason to do so. Last, as we do not conform to the current "trendy" pandering to the exponents of the metric system, we will continue to employ pounds, ounces, miles, yards, feet, and inches where weights and distances are concerned, except when referring to the calibers of such weapons as are gauged in millimeters.

J. T. EDSON
Active Member, Western Writers of America
Melton Mowbray, England

INTRODUCTION

"Well, yes sir, Andy," Alvin Dustine "Cap" Fog said, a hard timbre underlying his leisurely Texas drawl. "I reckon you're as right as the Indian side of a horse* when you say that what us good old boys of Company Z did back in the twenties and thirties wouldn't have sat any too well with the kind of 'liberal' bleeding hearts who seem to be running the movies and television shows these days. Fact being, I suppose we'd be what they'd slap a brand of 'fascist' on. Which same to them, strikes me, is anybody who washes, shaves, keeps his hair cut short, wears a suit and necktie, doesn't smoke pot or mainline,** is loyal to his country, believes in having law and order, and is more concerned with the suffering of the victims of crime than

---

* "Right as the Indian side of a horse": Cowhands' expression meaning "absolutely correct." It was derived from the discovery that the Indians mounted from the right side and not, as they did, at the left. *J.T.E.*
** "Mainline": To take "hard" narcotics such as cocaine and heroin intravenously. *J.T.E.*

looking out for the 'rights' of the goddamned son-of-a-bitching criminals who abused them."

The vehement declaration had been made in response to a comment from the fourth member of our party while we were discussing the increasing number of programs apparently intended to discredit the security and law enforcement agencies of the United States of America and Britain being put out—either in the form of "documentary exposés" or as alleged "entertainment"—by the media in both countries. It was a subject in which I shared my companions' misgivings, as I too found the trend very disturbing.

"Language, dear!" Mrs. Rita Fog protested in a mildly reproving tone as her husband's clearly heartfelt tirade ended. "You're not in Company Z anymore."

"Not for a *long* time, honey, more's the pity," Cap admitted, sounding more than a trifle regretful. Then the hard expression on his tanned features softened and a note of affection came into his voice as he continued. "But I swear you still look as young and pretty as you did when you were being 'Rita Ansell' for us back then."

"Did you ever hear such nonsense, J. T.?" inquired the still good-looking lady who was respectfully and fondly referred to as "Miz Rita" by all her friends and associates, showing she was far from displeased by her husband's supplementary comment. The years she had spent in Texas had failed to eradicate all traces of an accent that indicated she had had a well-educated upbringing in New England. Turning to the man whose remark had provoked the outburst from Cap, she went on. "Why, I declare, he's getting to be as big a flatterer as your Uncle Ranse used to be, Andrew."

I was in Boulder, Colorado, attending the 1979 Convention of Western Writers of America, when the invitation to meet Cap and Miz Rita reached me. Having learned from the itinerary for my visit given in the April newsletter of the J. T. Edson

Appreciation Society that I would be spending a few days in Tucson, Arizona, at the same time they were in the vicinity, they suggested we meet for dinner one evening.

You can bet I jumped at the opportunity!

When I met the Fogs as arranged in the bar of my hotel, the Holiday Inn South, I found they had arranged a very pleasant and exciting surprise for me. They were accompanied by Andrew Mark "Big Andy" Counter, for whose grandfather,* son,** and nephew*** I have the honor to be biographer. After an excellent meal, we all went to my room and, over a few cans of Oly, my favorite American beer—imported specially for me by Big Andy from the Olympia Brewing Company of Tumwater, in the state of Washington—we settled down to, as Miz Rita put it, "visit a spell."

In addition to being most enjoyable, the meeting proved exceptionally fruitful as far as my work is concerned.

One of the points raised by members of the J. T. Edson Appreciation Society since the second of the Alvin Dustine "Cap" Fog series appeared in print—although, due to the peculiar workings of this author's mind, the book in question, *You're a Texas Ranger, Alvin Fog,* is actually the first in chronological sequence†—was how closely Cap resembled his paternal

---

* Details of the career and special qualifications of Mark Counter can be found in the Floating Outfit series. *J.T.E.*
** Details of the career and special qualifications of Deputy Sheriff Bradford "Brad" Counter can be found in the Rockabye County series, which also covers the duties, equipment, and operations of a present-day sheriff's office in Texas. *J.T.E.*
*** Details of the career and special qualifications of James Allenvale "Bunduki" Gunn—whose sobriquet is derived from the Swahili word meaning a handheld firearm of any kind—are recorded in Part Twelve, "The Mchawi's Powers," *J. T.'S Hundredth,* and the Bunduki series. *J.T.E.*
† The first appearance of Alvin Dustine "Cap" Fog in print, based on events much later in his career—after, in fact, he had become the youngest man ever to hold rank as captain in the Texas Rangers, hence his sobriquet Cap—was in *"Cap" Fog, Texas Ranger, Meet Mr. J. G. Reeder. J.T.E.*

grandfather, Captain Dustine Edward Marsden "Dusty" Fog, C.S.A.* On my mentioning the matter in the bar, while Cap was taking a telephone call, his wife declared this was hardly surprising. In addition to the physical resemblance, except for his hair being black instead of dusty blond,** he had received a similar education where gun handling and certain Japanese martial arts were concerned.*** Furthermore, he had always idolized the memory of his grandfather and sought to model himself in Dusty's image. However, as Big Andy pointed out, due to having served as a peace officer since graduating from college—first as a deputy in Rio Hondo County, Texas, under his father, Sheriff Jackson Marsden Fog,† then as a Texas Ranger—Cap had acquired only a minimal knowledge of the cattle ranching business and, although equally competent as a gunfighter and arguably the finest combat pistol shot of his

* Details of the career and special qualifications of Captain Dustine Edward Marsden "Dusty" Fog, C.S.A., are given in the Civil War and Floating Outfit series. *J.T.E.*
** Cap's black hair was inherited from his paternal grandmother, who was, prior to her marriage, Lady Winifred Amelia "Freddie Woods" Besgrove-Woodstole. How she met Dusty Fog and their association progressed is told in *The Making of a Lawman, The Trouble Busters, The Gentle Giant,* and *The Fortune Hunters.* She also makes guest appearances in *White Stallion, Red Mare: The Whip and the War Lance,* and Part Five, Belle "the Rebel Spy" Boyd, in "The Butcher's Fiery End," *J. T.'S Ladies. J.T.E.*
*** Cap's instructor in the employment of, among other aspects of the Japanese martial arts, *ju jitsu, karate,* and the *yawara* stick, was a nephew of Tommy Okasi, a *samaurai* warrior who acts as valet for General Jackson Baines "Ole Devil" Hardin, C.S.A. Details of the career and special qualifications of the general and Tommy are given mainly in the Ole Devil Hardin series. More information regarding the history and use of the *yawara* stick can be found in *Old Devil and the Caplocks. J.T.E.*
† Although as yet no details have been forthcoming regarding the activities of Jackson Marsden Fog in his capacity of sheriff of Rio Hondo County, Texas, he makes a guest appearance—based on an incident while he was serving with the American Expeditionary Force in France toward the end of World War I—in Part Two, "Jubal Branch's Lucky B.A.R.," *You're a Texas Ranger, Alvin Fog. J.T.E.*

day,* he was never anywhere near as excellent a cowhand as his grandfather had been.** On the other hand, Miz Rita and Big Andy agreed that circumstances had never required Dusty to use the kind of unconventional methods employed by Cap and Company Z during those periods when circumstances had compelled him to serve as a lawman in the Old West.***

As a result of our visiting a spell, I was granted permission by Cap to tell the whole story of what had happened on the occasion when his grandfather had posed as a schoolteacher.† This included the part played in the affair by Dusty's cousin, Betty Hardin,†† about which I had seen no reference at the time I was writing of it early in my career.††† I also learned enough to expand upon an incident involving the Ysabel Kid,‡

---

* Some authorities give pride of place as the best combat pistol shot of the period to Ed McGivern of Montana, author of—among other works—*Fast and Fancy Revolver Shooting and Police Training* (Chicago: Illinois, Follett, 1938). *J.T.E.*

** One occasion when Dusty Fog proved his excellence as a cowhand in competition with his peers is recorded in *Goodnight's Dream* (Bantam Books, 1974, edition retitled *The Floating Outfit*). *J.T.E.*

*** In addition to the first four titles listed in note **, page xii, which refer to his early association with Lady Winifred Besgrove-Woodstole, further information pertaining to Dusty Fog's activities as a peace officer are given in *Quiet Town, The Town Tamers,* and *The Small Texan. J.T.E.*

† The complete story is given in *Master of Triggernometry. J.T.E.*

†† Although Betty Hardin is generally referred to as being the granddaughter of General Hardin, speculations have been raised regarding their exact relationship. The present-day members of the Hardin, Fog, and Blaze clan decline to comment on it. She appears in Part Five, "A Time For Improvisation, Mr. Blaze," *J. T.'S Hundredth;* Part Four, "It's Our Turn To Improvise, Miss Blaze," *J. T.'S Ladies; Kill Dusty Fog!; Sidewinder; McGraw's Inheritance;* Part Two, "The Quartet," *The Half Breed; The Bad Bunch; The Rio Hondo War;* and *Gunsmoke Thunder. J.T.E.*

††† Told in Part One, Dusty Fog, in "The Schoolteacher," *The Hard Riders. J.T.E.*

‡ Details of the career and special qualifications of the Ysabel Kid are given in the Civil War and Floating Outfit series. *J.T.E.*

which I had covered previously without being aware of all the facts.*

Another welcome bonus was Big Andy supplying me with more information and authorizing me to tell all of what happened during two incidents in which his paternal grandfather was involved with Miss Martha "Calamity Jane" Canary.** Again, these had appeared at the early period of my production of the Floating Outfit series***—in which category they are included on the list of titles in chronological order—but quite a bit more had taken place that I did not know of at the time. I also discovered there were various discrepancies between my original coverage and the actual events, which I have now corrected. However, Big Andy made one stipulation when telling me to go ahead. For some reason he did not explain and about which I saw no reason to ask, he insisted that both lengthened episodes should appear as part of the Calamity Jane series; this has been done.

The biggest breakthrough, however, had been regarding my knowledge of the work carried out by the little-publicized and

* Originally produced as Chapter Three, "Sam Ysabel's Son," in *The Texan*, it has been renamed *Old Moccasins on the Trail*. *J.T.E.*
** Details of the career and special qualifications of Miss Martha Jane Canary can be found in the Calamity Jane series; also Part Six, "Mrs. Wild Bill," *J. T.'S Ladies*, and Part Seven, "Deadwood, August the 2nd, 1876," *J. T.'S Hundredth*. The two incidents are revised and enlarged under the titles *Calamity, Mark and Belle*, and *Cut One, They All Bleed*. Other meetings between Miss Canary and Mark Counter are recorded in *The Bad Bunch*, *The Fortune Hunters*, and *Guns in the Night*. She also makes a guest appearance in Part Two, "A Wife for Dusty Fog," *The Small Texan*. However, although *The Remittance Kid* is included in her series, it stars Belle "the Rebel Spy" Boyd; "Calam" does not appear in the story. It was placed in this category for convenience, as it is in the "prequel" to *The Whip and the War Lance*, rather than being listed as one of the Miscellaneous Titles that cannot be placed in a series. *J.T.E.*
*** Told in Part One, "The Bounty on Belle Starr's Scalp," *Troubled Range*, and Part One, "Better Than Calamity," *The Wildcats*. *J.T.E.*

less-documented Company Z of the Texas Rangers, in which
Cap had served as a founder member. In fact, until the meeting,
I had known nothing about this elite group except the follow-
ing:

In every democracy, the laws framed for the protection of
the innocent have loopholes that can be—and frequently are—
exploited for the benefit of the undeniably guilty. Although
recognizing that such a state of affairs must exist in a free
society, the governor of Texas had grown concerned over the
ever-increasing wave of lawlessness that had followed in the
wake of the well-meant—if ill-advised and difficult to enforce—
ratification of the Volstead Act.* He had concluded that only
unconventional methods could cope with the malefactors who
slipped through the meshes of the legal system. Being restricted
in their actions by governmental and departmental regulations,
ordinary peace officers were unable to take action in circumstances of that nature. While pondering on the situation, he had
met three prominent European criminologists who were tour-
ing the United States delivering a series of lectures on this subject to the heads of the major law enforcement agencies. Acting
upon the advice of George Manfred, Leon Gonzales, and Raymond Poiccart,** the governor had authorized the state attor-

---

* "Volstead Act": The colloquial name for the Eighteenth (Prohibition)
Amendment to the Constitution of the United States of America. This
defined intoxicating liquors as those containing more than one-half of 1
percent alcohol and made illegal the manufacture, transportation, and sale
of such liquors for beverage purposes. Introduced by Representative Andrew J. Volstead of Minnesota, the act was ratified—over the veto of Presi-
dent Woodrow Wilson—on October 18, 1919. By the time it was repealed
in 1933, it had inadvertently paved the way for the rise of organized crime.
J.T.E.
** George Manfred, Leon Gonzales, and Raymond Poiccart were the sur-
viving members of the "Four Just Men" organization, the fourth having
died before their first recorded adventure was published. Although the following volumes do not cover the lecture tour in the United States, see
chronologically: The Four Just Men, The Council of Justice, The Law of the

ney general to select a special group of Texas Rangers to become—without any mention of its existence being made public—Company Z. Every man was picked for his courage, integrity, specialized knowledge, and devotion to the cause of justice. Their purpose was to deal with those criminals who could not be touched by conventional methods, even if the means they employed might be considered as stepping beyond the legal bounds of the law.

My access to the added knowledge of Company Z's activities came about as a result of Big Andy showing us a story in a newspaper. It told how a proven multiple murderer had had to be released from custody without even being brought to trial because the arresting officer had neglected to inform him of his "rights"—as required by the much-abused "Miranda decision" produced by the United States Supreme Court as a means of protection for the *innocent**—and searched his apartment,

---

Four Just Men, Again the Three, and *The Three Just Men* by Edgar Wallace. *J.T.E.*

* Before questioning a suspect, a peace officer is required to carry out the following procedure and say, the exact wording differing slightly between enforcement agencies: In keeping with the Supreme Court's decision in "Miranda versus Arizona," I am not permitted to ask you any questions until you are warned of your right to counsel and your privilege against self-incrimination.

First: You have the right to remain silent if you choose.

Second: You do not have to answer questions asked by myself or any other peace officer if you don't want to.

Third: If you decide to answer any questions, the answers may be used against you. You also have the right to consult with an attorney before or during questioning. If you do not have the money to hire a lawyer, one will be appointed to consult with you.

Between each item, the officer has to ask whether the suspect understands what it means. Should the suspect be of an ethnic origin that does not claim English as its first tongue, an interpreter must be produced to "read the rights" in the appropriate language as they may be ruled invalid on a claim they were not understood. *J.T.E.*

without having first acquired the necessary warrant to do so, to locate the high-powered rifle he had used to kill seven victims.

Cap had commented that nobody other than a dictator or a totalitarian government—whether Communist or "right wing" —wished to deprive the honest, law-abiding citizen of his rights, but he considered the United States to be carrying this to excessive extremes. It went beyond the case we had just read. For one thing, boys and girls up to eighteen years of age could —and frequently did—commit serious crimes with impunity, knowing that being classed as minors put them beyond the reach of the criminal courts. All too frequently when a minor was taken before Juvenile Hall after committing a major felony, the "bleeding hearts" and "liberals" would ensure she or he was not committed to any form of punitive detention. A remark by Big Andy about the differences in the days when Cap was a peace officer produced the exchange recorded at the beginning of the introduction.

"Not that *I* believe for one moment you *should*," I declared, after Miz Rita had finished addressing Big Andy. "But do you ever feel any remorse over the way in which Company Z used to handle their assignments?"

"Like hell I do!" the elderly Texan asserted firmly. As his wife nodded her support for the statement, he pointed to the other guest's newspaper and went on. "Fact being, J. T., I sometimes reckon it's a real pity there isn't a Company Z around these days. And to prove I'm not any way ashamed of what we did, I'll let you write up the notes I kept of the cases we handled, should you be so minded."

As always, Cap kept his word!

The notes I received proved to be so extensive that in one instance, despite having stated in the final footnote of *You're a Texas Ranger, Alvin Fog* that it would appear as "Case One, Friendly Persuasion" of this volume, it upheld the motto of the J. T. Edson Appreciation Society: "Haven't You Heard? It's

All Been Changed!" It expanded into a full-length book, *Rapido Clint,* describing how a dishonest financier was induced to return to the United States to stand trial after he had taken the precaution of obtaining Mexican citizenship and so could not be extradited from that country by legal means.

The same thing has happened with this book. It was originally intended to cover more than one case.

Here then, by kind permission of Alvin Dustine "Cap" Fog, is yet another example of *The Justice of Company Z.*

1

THERE WAS A MISTAKE BEING MADE

Taking everything into consideration, Eric "Side-Wheeler" Heifer was neither the nicest nor the most likable person in Denton. In fact, one might have searched a vastly more populous community than the seat of Denton County, Texas,* without finding anybody so thoroughly reprehensible.

However, it must be stated in all fairness that he had not been born in Denton, nor did he normally reside there.

A combination of having been a political agitator of the most vicious radical kind and finding it was not as profitable an occupation as he desired, plus having sweated out a sentence for arson in a penitentiary with the reputation of being a "man-

---

* One of Denton County's claims to fame is that, prior to his becoming an outlaw in the mid-1870s, it was the "stamping ground" of the train robber Sam Bass. He makes a guest appearance in Part Two, "The Quartet," *The Half Breed.* J.T.E.

killer,"* had led Heifer to conclude that the life of a pimp would be more to his taste than resuming his former activities. Having acquired the necessary contacts while incarcerated, he had achieved his ambition and had become more successful than he ever had been as an agitator. Although his belief that the new occupation could also be less dangerous had proved correct as far as he was concerned, the same was not the case for the prostitutes who were unfortunate enough to come under his control. Even among a disreputable fraternity not noted for its gentleness and chivalry in dealing with members of the "weaker sex," over the past three years his name had become a byword for the severity and brutality of his treatment.

It was that particularly objectionable trait which had brought Heifer to the—as far as his own line of business was concerned—far-from-lucrative small town.

In accordance with his usual habit, Heifer had subjected his latest acquisition to a savage beating. Although only recently recruited to the ranks of the work of a prostitute and therefore inexperienced, Freda Marino had done nothing to warrant the punishment. It was inflicted for no other reason than to impress her with his superiority and the inadvisability of holding back even a small portion of the payments she received for her services. However, being high on "harmless" *marijuana,* he had overdone the lesson and injured her far worse than was intended. Before lapsing into merciful unconsciousness, her screams had aroused a neighbor with whom she had become acquainted and who, after trying to get into the room, began to shriek for the police. Promising to take revenge upon Rita Ansell for her interference at a more propitious moment, he had fled down the fire escape before the peace officers came on the scene. Unfortunately, so far as either continuing his business or

* "Mankiller": Underworld term for any penal institution that imposed an exceptionally strict or brutal control over its inmates. *J.T.E.*

carrying out the punitive retribution was concerned, his conclusion that—because experience had taught them the victim would refuse to substantiate the charge—the police would not put too much effort into trying to find the attacker of a prostitute had proved to be incorrect.

Due to the amount of outraged public sentiment aroused by the newspaper coverage of the events that had preceded a forthcoming murder trial, the members of the San Antonio Police Department—along with those of every other municipal, county, state, and federal law enforcement agency throughout Texas—were being spurred by their superiors, who in turn were under pressure from the state attorney general at the instigation of the governor, to greater activity where the performance of their duties was concerned. Under such circumstances, the anticipated laxness was not as Heifer had anticipated.

Nor had this been the sole source of his misfortunes.

Calling upon an attorney of dubious morals who had acted for him in the past, the pimp had received disturbing news. Concerned over the way in which the public and authorities were reacting, Hogan Turtle had passed the word that there must be a severe curtailment of illicit activities that could add fuel to the flames of outrage. While Heifer was not employed by the current head of a family that had been dominant in the criminal circles of Texas even prior to the establishment of a republic and whose authority had remained undiminished after statehood was attained,* it was a stricture he had been—even

* Information regarding two earlier heads of the family, Coleman and his son, Rameses "Ram" Turtle, can be found in *Ole Devil and the Caplocks*—which, along with the other volumes of the Ole Devil Hardin series, covers various aspects of the Texans' struggle to obtain independence from rule by Mexico: *Set Texas Back on Her Feet* (Berkley Medallion Books, 1978 edition retitled *Viridian's Way*), *Beguinage*, and *Beguinage Is Dead!*; also, by inference, in Part Four, "Mr. Colt's Revolving Cylinder Pistol," *J. T.'S Hundredth*, and *The Quest for Bowie's Blade*. J.T.E.

without knowing it was passed—ill-advised to ignore. Even without the lawyer's warning, he was aware that he had made San Antonio too hot to hold him and must go into hiding until things cooled down. Nor had he wasted any time in putting the thought into effect. After telling the attorney where he intended to hide out, he asked to be informed when it was safe to return, and then left.

On his arrival in Denton, despite having sufficient funds to stay at the best hotel—a precaution he had always taken against the need for a hurried departure—Heifer had elected to use a smaller and less salubrious, albeit fairly clean and solidly built, establishment in the low-rent district. This was one of the suggestions made by the attorney. As he normally occupied the most luxurious and comfortable quarters available, the change in his life-style could serve to throw any searching peace officers off his trail. However, while he had not been subjected to any unwanted attentions by the local peace officers, after a week in the town he was growing increasingly discontented. Missing the creature comforts to which he had become accustomed, he was impatient for his enforced absence from the more lucrative confines of the larger city to be brought to an early end.

Having retired comparatively early through boredom, the pimp was not yet sufficiently tired to have fallen asleep. Just as he was debating whether to get up again, dress and go out in search of some kind of diversion, limited though the facilities of Denton might be in that respect, he heard a slight clatter that caused him to raise his head from the pillow and gaze across the room. Although he had turned off the solitary lamp before retiring, the drapes were not drawn and sufficient light was coming through the window for him to be able to detect the cause of the sound. It had been produced by the key having fallen out of the hole. Nor had this come about by accident. Even as he looked, the clicking of the lock being turned came to his ears. Contemplating the phenomenon rapidly, he began to draw conclusions with commendable rapidity.

Whoever was unlocking the door had no right to do so!

If the surreptitious way in which the handle was turning and the door creeping open was anything to go by, the person outside was not merely making a mistake and entering the wrong room. While there *was* a mistake being made, it was inadvertent.

So far as the occupant was concerned, the wrong room *definitely* was being entered. It was going to prove a most painful error for whoever came in.

Grinning in savage anticipation, the pimp rolled free of the bedclothes and stood up. For almost the first time since his arrival, he found something about the hotel that met with his full approval. As the usual clientele were cowhands or various types of manual workers, few of whom were accustomed to the luxurious surroundings to which his lucrative trade gave access, the furnishings of the rooms were constructed sturdily to receive considerable hard usage. Although he had previously cursed the solidity and hardness of the bed and mattress as being far less comfortable than those he usually occupied, he now conceded that their failings on that account did offer one advantage under the circumstances. He was able to rise swiftly and without any creaking from protesting springs.

Easing his feet into the pair of patent leather slippers he had placed so as to be readily available if he needed to find them in a hurry, Heifer never took his eyes from the door. Specially made for him, the toes of the footwear were more solid than was usual in casual attire of that nature. This had been done on his instructions to render them more potent when delivering a kick, a quality he had not infrequently found useful in his business. Among others, Freda Marino could have testified to their effectiveness as a means of inflicting punishment. However, being of a cautious disposition, he had no intention of relying solely on them on this occasion. Reaching beneath the pillow with his left hand, he drew out a pearl-handled, nickel-plated Colt Police Positive .38 Special revolver that reposed there. After arming himself, he set off stealthily across the room.

Still the door continued to inch open without haste!

Although some light from the passage was already entering, the pimp made his approach in such a way that he was not illuminated by it. What was more, if the slight sounds he had made while rising and walking toward the door had been heard by the intruder, their potential threat was either being overlooked or ignored. No matter which it might be, he was pleased that he had not frightened his unexpected and uninvited visitor away.

Heifer considered that having the element of surprise on his side he could work over an intended "snoozer"* with his fists and feet, and this would save him the trouble of going elsewhere in search of a less enjoyable diversion. Nor would the local town clowns ask too many awkward questions if the disturbance brought them to investigate. Even with the current wave of pressure causing them to perform their duties far more conscientiously than might otherwise have been the case, no peace officer in Texas would worry unduly about the extent of injuries suffered by a thief caught attempting to commit a robbery.

The pimp had no doubt that he was competent to deal with the situation. Despite the unsavory way in which he made his living, or rather because he was engaged in such a highly competitive line of work, he always endeavored to keep himself in reasonable physical shape, and he had a sound knowledge of the more brutally effective methods of self-defense.

Five feet ten inches in height, Heifer was broad shouldered

---

* "Snoozer": Underworld term for a thief who specialized in robbing hotel rooms. *J.T.E.*

and bulky, but not to the extent of being cumbersome. Clad
only in the slippers and a pair of white silk underpants (he
always wore such garments instead of more formal night attire), the body he displayed was fit and hard. The brown hair
on his bullet-shaped head was normally longer, but had been
cropped very short as an aid to changing his appearance. While
not exactly bad-looking or dissipated, his sharp and sallow features were marred by a nose that had been broken and badly
set. Several blows to his right ear had afflicted it with the condition known as a cauliflower. Taken with his nose, this suggested—without any basis—that he had once been a professional boxer. He was not devoid of fistic ability, but any fighting
he did was always outside a ring where he was free from the
restricting rules of sporting conduct. Even then, unless—as at
that moment—he was confident of victory without undue risk
to himself, he fought only when there was no escape.

By the time he was safely ensconced at the hinged side of the
door, the pimp had thought out the safest line of action for him
to take. However, he had to wait for a few more seconds before
being granted his first sight of the intruder. When he did, the
qualms he had felt disappeared and he decided that, as things
had turned out, he could have handled the situation without
even arming himself with the revolver.

As he was stepping across the threshold, framed briefly by
the light from the passage before he closed the door, the man
who entered was a far from menacing sight. Possibly in his
early twenties, he lacked a good four inches of Heifer's height.
Bareheaded, with shortish curly black hair, his clean-shaven,
tanned face was youthful and moderately handsome. There was
nothing about his features to make him noticeable, however, or
easy to identify. If his clothing was any guide, he was employed
as a worker on a ranch—probably in some lesser capacity than
cowhand—and not very prosperous. He had on an ancient and
much-scuffed brown leather jacket that was left unfastened to

display an open-necked and faded dark-blue shirt, but he was not wearing a bandanna. The legs of his patched and washed-out Levi pants were tucked into the tops of such decrepit, flat-heeled riding boots that no cowhand worth his salt would have owned them.

Nothing he had seen or deduced about the intruder during the brief period of illumination was causing the pimp to feel the slightest concern. Rather the opposite. From all appearances, the other was neither armed nor even an experienced snoozer. In fact, Heifer was willing to bet this was almost his first incursion to such a specialized kind of crime. Although his hands were empty, the ease with which he had manipulated the lock suggested he had not employed a pick, but had obtained a pass-key from somewhere as an aid to gaining admittance. Nor had his subsequent behavior implied he was conversant with the tricks of the snoozer's trade. Certainly he had failed to appreciate that the means by which he had unlocked the door could give a warning of what was happening to any occupant of the room.* Furthermore, on entering, he had not taken the basic precaution of ensuring that he was alone. Despite the state of the bed suggesting this could be the case, a competent snoozer would have looked around to make sure. Instead, as soon as he had shoved the door closed with his heel, the young man had continued walking forward. Just about the only sensible thing he had done, in fact, was to have donned a pair of thin black leather riding gloves that would prevent him leaving finger-prints the police could identify.

Not that, the pimp mused as he stepped away from the wall with as great a stealth as when crossing to it, the solitary sensible precaution would be of any benefit. After what he was in-

---

* How Miss Martha "Calamity Jane" Canary benefited from hearing the key pushed from the lock of her hotel room door is described in *White Stallion, Red Mare. J.T.E.*

tending to do, the town clowns would have no need to search for clues to the identity of the intruder. He would be waiting for them when they came, although not in any condition to answer questions.

Step by step, moving faster than his proposed victim, Heifer made his approach.

With the distance decreasing, a sense of gloating anticipation and eagerness to start inflicting the punishment filled the pimp, enhanced by the conviction that he could do so for once without incurring the wrath of the law.

For all that, despite being confident he would have no difficulty in handling the diminutive snoozer, Heifer never believed in taking needless chances. He decided to follow the line of action he had thought out as he was making his way to the door. While he had collected the revolver from beneath the pillow, it was to be employed as a firearm only in an emergency. Satisfied that such an eventuality would not arise, he began to swing the weapon upward diagonally in front of his chest as a prelude to striking the young man on the right shoulder.

A blow of the kind the pimp was intending to deliver would numb its recipient's arm and further reduce his chances of resistance, making the ensuing working over even easier and safer.

2

YOU'VE GOT A REAL MEAN TEMPER, RAPIDO

Suddenly, an instant before Eric "Side-Wheeler" Heifer estimated he would be close enough to launch his proposed attack, the intruder reversed directions and crashed shoulders-first into him with considerable force. Taken completely unawares, the impact drove him backward against the wall. Giving him no time to recover from the surprise, the young man, twisting around with an equal rapidity, lunged and reached out. Two hands clamped around the pimp's left wrist. Then they started to crush with a power that, in comparison with the small size of the person who applied the pressure, was startling and not a little unnerving.

Such was the shock of discovering that his intended victim was far stronger than he had envisaged, Heifer was unable to avoid having the Colt Police Positive revolver shaken from his grasp. Much to his surprise, as it landed, the painful hold on his wrist was released. Stepping back a pace, the small snoozer gave the weapon a swift kick that sent it spinning across the room until it struck the wall and lay, its nickel plating glinting faintly in the light coming through the undraped window.

A mixture of fear and anger provoked the pimp into taking advantage of what he regarded as the intruder's error in tactics. Grateful that his left arm had been liberated, he rammed both palms against the front of the faded blue shirt and shoved. Propelled backward and just missing the bed, the small man was brought to a halt by the dressing table. However, as Heifer started toward him, he proved he was in no way incapacitated by the not-too-gentle collision. Bringing up his fists and adopting a posture clearly intended to allow him to defend himself, he moved forward.

Keeping the left elbow bent, close to the body and behind the near fist, which was held thumb uppermost, the snoozer had his clenched right hand positioned just below his chin. The other elbow was tucked well in and the knuckles of its fist were turned toward the pimp. With his legs comfortably apart, the left being slightly bent and in advance of the right, he lifted his heels. Balancing his weight evenly on the balls of his feet, he kept the left pointing in the direction of his approaching assailant. Having done so, he began to make the type of dancing steps that permitted fast movements when going forward, retreating, or taking a sideways evasion.

Watching the intruder adopting the sparring stance, it was obvious to Heifer that he had done a reasonable amount of boxing. In spite of that, the pimp was more relieved than perturbed by what he saw. Unless he was mistaken, the bouts in which the snoozer had participated were of the comparatively gentle amateur variety. As Heifer was well aware, such training and competition was more of a liability than an asset in a free-for-all roughhouse brawl. In fact, he believed that having a technique of that kind employed against him by an antagonist offered him the kind of edge he liked.

The pimp's conclusions on the subject were drawn from the

meaning of his nickname. Heifer was not called "Side-Wheeler" because he had had some connection with the paddle boats that plied the Mississippi and other rivers. It was bestowed because he was left-handed.*

Having noticed that the intruder's posture and stance indicated he was right-handed, past experience led the pimp to assume he would expect everybody else to be the same. In which case, particularly as he conveyed the impression of being no more than moderately competent as a boxer, finding himself under attack by a southpaw might confuse and render him easy meat.

Shaken and surprised by the shock of being disarmed with such ease, Heifer's conclusions were causing his earlier confidence to return.

There was, however, a possibility that the pimp had overlooked.

Acting upon his assumptions, the pimp shot forward his right fist from a distance at which his longer arms would reach while he was still beyond the intruder's range. Counting on the other expecting the blow to be delivered by his left, he aimed for the center of the tanned young face.

The punch failed to reach its target, but it was not blocked as one would expect from a boxer.

Once again Heifer felt his wrist caught by the powerful hands of the intruder. Just an instant too late, he realized that the snoozer could have drawn the correct conclusions from noticing which hand he had used to hold the Colt. Furthermore, while he found his attack was being countered by a wrestling hold rather than a boxing one, the appreciation came a

* Other sobriquets given to a person who is born with the left hand stronger and more dexterous than the right are "Port-Sider," "Southpaw," "Wrong-Armer," or "Leftie." *J.T.E.*

fraction of a second too late for him to be able to apply counter-measures.

Swiveling around with the alacrity that had characterized his actions when disarming the pimp, the intruder applied leverage on the trapped limb. Given no chance to even think of resistance, Heifer found himself passing over the snoozer's shoulders. He formed a hazy impression that they were far wider than he had realized, but he was not allowed to ponder upon the discovery. Turning a half somersault and being released as he reached the top of the upward curve, he alighted supine on the bed. Such was the impetus with which he was thrown (by what was somehow akin to a flying mare, yet different from that throw) that he bounced across the mattress. When he found he had landed on such a comparatively yielding surface, he was able to thrust himself erect. Compelled to advance a few steps, he started to turn as he came to a halt.

Heifer's relief was short-lived.

What was more, a hope that the pimp had started to nourish came to nothing.

Although the small intruder had been given an opportunity to escape, he made no attempt to avail himself of it. Instead he sprang on to and across the bed. Coming down as the pimp was turning, he attacked.

"This'll teach you to mind what Hogan Turtle says!" the young man declared, his accent that of a well-educated Texan, driving a power-packed right fist against the side of Heifer's jaw.

Sent reeling into the corner of the room, regardless of the pain he was suffering, the pimp was able to appreciate the implications of what he had been told. He derived no satisfaction from learning his assumptions that the intruder lacked the technical knowledge of an experienced snoozer were correct. There was a far more sinister reason for his apparently incautious behavior on entering the room. It had been intended to

lull his intended victim into a sense of overconfidence. Nor did
Heifer need to ponder on why the other had come. Clearly his
actions in San Antonio had aroused the ire of Hogan Turtle and
orders had been given for him to be punished, although he
would have expected somebody much larger to have been selected to carry it out.

The pimp wasted no time in wondering how he had been
located. A man with Hogan Turtle's standing and connections
in outlaw circles would have little difficulty in obtaining the
necessary information. Probably the attorney in San Antonio,
with whom he was known to associate, had been approached
and felt it advisable to betray him. There was not, however,
even a moment to spare on feeling resentment against the lawyer if his suspicions were true.

Seeing the intruder approaching, Heifer's response was similar to that of a cornered rat. Snarling a curse that was three
parts fear, he flung himself into the attack. It was soon obvious
why the small Texan had been chosen to inflict the summary
punishment. To his horror, the pimp found himself in contention with the most skilled fighter it had ever been his misfor-
tune to meet. Not only did the intruder punch with great power
and precision, he could achieve an equally painful effect with
the edge of his hand or by thrusting his extended fingers into
the softer portions of the body. His elbows and knees proved
just as effective weapons, and he seemed able to kick in any
direction required.

Nor was Heifer any better on those occasions when he contrived to come to grips instead of punching. He learned to his
cost that the small intruder was muscled like a Hercules in
miniature. Even his extensive knowledge of wrestling and dirty
tricks was no match for the man he had earlier dismissed as
being an insignificant country hick only recently embarked
upon a life of crime.

Not all the punishment went one way, of course, at least in the early stages.

Once Heifer managed to give a swing that threw his antagonist across the room and over the bed. If the way he landed was any guide, the Texan was a skilled horseman. Rolling like a bronc-buster who had been piled by a bucking horse, he suffered no damage to his capability. After halting in a sitting position, he was able to catch the pimp's left foot as it drove toward his head. Thrusting himself upright and giving the captured limb a twisting heave, he precipitated Heifer headlong into the front of the wardrobe.

Slowly yet inexorably, the small Texan gained the upper hand. Even on the few occasions when the pimp acquired a brief lead, he was unable to take advantage of it. After the first few minutes, in fact, he was being subjected to a beating as savage and punishing as he had inflicted upon Freda Marino. Nor, as the rooms on either side and below were unoccupied, was he offered the kind of succor that had proved her salvation. Such was the sturdy way in which the hotel had been built that no sounds of the far from quiet conflict reached the ears of anybody who might raise the alarm.

At last, feeling as if he had been trampled upon by a herd of stampeding longhorn steers, Heifer tried to open the door and escape. Caught by the right wrist, he was swung and propelled across the room. A collision with the wall prevented him from falling. Seeking some way to flee, his gaze—restricted by the right eye being swollen almost shut—came to rest on the Colt. Struggling to suck air into his tormented lungs, through the blood being emitted from his rebroken nose and mouth with cut lips and some of the teeth shattered, he forced his agony-throbbing body to move in its direction. Moaning what were supposed to be curses, but which emerged as incoherent mumbles, he bent and his left hand enfolded the fancy pearl grips of the butt. Letting out a croaking gasp of relief, he straightened up holding the weapon.

Already darting to continue the onslaught, the small Texan recognized the potential danger posed by Heifer's actions. As on frequent occasions throughout the fight, he produced a highly effective and spectacular remedy for the predicament. Bounding into the air in such a fashion that his body became almost parallel to the floor, he drew up and thrust out his legs with all the force he could muster. Caught in the chest by the soles of the intruder's boots before he could bring the revolver into alignment, the pimp involuntarily snatched at its trigger. The bullet went harmlessly into the wardrobe door and the Colt flew from his grasp as he was pitched backward bodily. After striking the window with great violence, he shattered through. Taking the panes and sash with him in a spray of broken glass and pieces of wood, he was precipitated from the room.

In one respect, although he was in no condition to appreciate it at that moment, Heifer might have counted himself fortunate. A major factor in his choice of accommodation had been that its window overlooked a wooden lean-to attached to the back wall of the hotel, offering an easy exit in an emergency. However, he had not envisioned that it would serve him as it now did. Instead of falling directly from the second floor to the ground, he landed on the sloping roof and rolled down to drop a much shorter distance. Not that he appreciated the slight blessing. By the time he landed, facedown and spread-eagled, he was already unconscious.

Having rebounded slightly after delivering the leaping kick and alighted safely on his feet, the small Texan stood for a moment swaying and gasping for breath. Then he went and peered through the window. There was nobody in sight on the street behind the hotel, nor could he hear anything to suggest that the noise of the window being broken had aroused attention. In spite of that, he knew it would be inadvisable to delay his departure. After climbing out carefully, so as to avoid being cut on the remaining shards of glass, he slid down the lean-to and jumped to the ground.

"That li'l gal down to San Antonio would rest a whole lot easier could she see you now, you son-of-a-bitching mac," the intruder declared breathlessly, standing straddle-legged alongside his unconscious victim. "And I don't reckon you'll be doing any more blacksmithing for a spell."*

"*That's* for sure, way he looks," commented a voice that suggested the speaker was also a Texan, albeit one whose education had been somewhat lower level. The voice originated from the deep shadows beneath the lean-to. "You've got a real mean temper, Rapido!"

"I've heard rumors to that effect," the small intruder admitted, showing not the slightest concern at being addressed; which was understandable as the words had indicated he was known to the man in the lean-to.

Moving in silence, the speaker emerged from the blackness while his remark was being answered. He was not wearing any form of headdress, but there was insufficient light for the color of his hair or features to be discernible. However, his pleasant tenor voice suggested he was young. Like his companion, his clothing in general implied that he worked on a ranch. His footwear, a pair of Comanche moccasins instead of cowhand's sharp-toed and high-heeled boots,** was the most noticeable

---

* "Mac": Another name for a pimp, or procurer. "Blacksmithing," in this context: To live off the earnings of prostitutes. *J.T.E.*
** The sharp toes of the cowhand's boots were intended to permit him to slip his feet into and free from the stirrup irons quickly in an emergency and the high heels were designed to dig into the ground, offering a more secure footing, when he was roping cattle or horses while on foot. Another use to which the heels could be put is described in Chapter Ten, "I'm Relying Upon You-all," *The Gentle Giant. J.T.E.*

deviation. He moved with a long, effortless-seeming stride indicative of there being hard and powerful, if not bulky, muscles in his six-feet-tall, lean frame. A hunting knife with an ivory handle hung in a sheath on the left side of the waist belt. He was carrying a low-crowned, wide-brimmed black J. B. Stetson hat in his left hand and the right grasped the butt of a Colt Government 1911 model .45 automatic pistol. The latter was encased in a thin suede holster instead of the more conventional loop for attaching it to a belt.

"Seems they were close to being true," the tall young man said dryly, hooking a toe beneath Heifer's body and rolling him over so as to be able to look down at his face. Even in such limited illumination, something of the damage it had suffered was discernible. "Least-wise, *amigo,* I don't reckon this son of a bitch would want to argue against them."

"I'd feel I hadn't done right by him if he did," the intruder claimed without any trace of remorse, accepting the offered Colt and tucking the holster inside the waistband of his Levi's so the clip gripped the material but was hidden by his belt.

"Anyways, we'd best get the hell away from here and *pronto,*" the slender Texan warned. "I didn't hear a thing until he came through the window. But when he came, by cracky, he came loud enough to wake half of the town."

"I *tried* to do it quietly, Comanch'," the shorter of the pair apologized, drawing up the zip fastener of his leather jacket and taking the hat from his companion. Donning it, he continued. "And I'll admit that what you said'll be a reasonable sort of thing for us to up and do."

Leaving the unconscious pimp where he lay without so much as a backward glance, the two young men made their way toward an alley between two of the buildings that faced the rear of the hotel. After taking a handkerchief from the right-hand pocket of his Levi's, the one who had been addressed as Rapido —meaning exceptionally fast in the Spanish spoken along the

international border between the United States and Mexico—
dabbed at the blood that had continued dribbling from his nostrils while they were talking. He had not staunched the flow,
nor was he granted an opportunity to do so.

Just as the Texans were entering the alley, they heard hurrying footsteps approaching the other end. Instantly the taller,
who apparently answered to an abbreviation of the word "Comanche," stepped into and merged with the deep shadows
thrown by the wall of the nearer building. Suspecting he may
have been heard, as his footwear did not permit him to move as
silently as his companion, Rapido kept walking.

The decision proved basically sound.

Each of the two men who appeared at the other end of the
alley wore the uniform of the Denton Police Department. It
was clear that they were coming to investigate the disturbance
and would have been suspicious if they had heard somebody
running away.

"Hold it right there!" commanded the taller officer, right
hand hovering over the butt of his holstered revolver. "What's
happening?"

"I dunno," Rapido lied, coming to a halt with the handkerchief still at his nose. His voice had lost its confidence and took
on a worried timbre as he continued. "I saw a feller come
through a window at the hotel and reckoned it was no place for
me."

"Why not?" the second officer demanded.

"I know how you john l—peace officers are with us *cowhands*!" the small Texan asserted, watching the pair drawing
closer and making the substitution as if suddenly realizing the
term "john laws" might be impolitic under the circumstances.
"Any time there's fuss, you allus pick on *us*!"

"What's your name, boy?" the taller officer asked, relaxing

his wary posture as did his companion. "And where'd you hail from?"

"I'm Billy-Bob Washington from Decatur, Wise County," Rapido claimed, with no greater truth than when making his first reply. "Only I'm riding for the Collins' spread now."

"Riding?" The second officer sniffed. "Cook's louse's closer to what you do, I'd bet. And what for you holding your nose with that wipe?"

"I walked into a verandah post watching what was doing," Rapido prevaricated, contriving to convey dislike for being referred to as the helper of the cook—a most menial task. "Set my nose to bleeding."

"Did, huh?" The shorter officer grunted, his attitude showing he expected nothing better. Glancing at his companion, he went on derisively. "Some folks's just natural born awkward, aren't they, Ted?"

"Just so long's awkward is all there's to it," the other man replied, but without resuming his position of readiness. "You'd best come and show us where that feller fell out of—"

Releasing the handkerchief as the officers were almost within reaching distance, the small Texan lunged forward and brought the instructions to an abrupt end. After placing a hand on each man's chest as his right leg passed between them, he pushed with all his far from inconsiderable strength. Taken unawares, hands dangling by their sides and with a foot off the ground, neither could avoid having his balance destroyed. Giving vent to mutually startled profanities, they toppled on to their backs. Almost before they landed, their assailant had leapt beyond them and was racing along the alley. Still keeping to the shadows, Comanche followed close on his companion's heels.

"What the hell?" Ted spluttered, thrusting himself into a sitting position and grabbing for his revolver. "There's *two* of the bastards!"

Before either officer could draw his weapon, it was too late.

The two young men had turned the corner at the end of the buildings and had gone from view.

The pair's escape was not entirely the fault of Ted or of his companion.

Just because they were serving as policemen in a small town did not imply they were stupid, incompetent, or poorly trained in their duties. In fact, compared with the law enforcement agencies in larger cities (which rarely gave their officers training with firearms applicable to conditions that might be met while on patrol), they were probably better able to cope with a situation that might involve shooting. Normally they would have kept at a greater distance from one another and been ready to draw their guns at the first hint of hostility. As had been the case with Heifer, confronted by such an apparently harmless person, neither had anticipated trouble.

"Come on!" Ted commanded, as he and his companion rose.

"Hey there!" called a voice before any action could be taken. The voice spoke in English that had the timbre suggestive of Hispanic origins in the border country of southern Texas. "You've got trouble, *amigos*?"

Swinging around, the officers saw a man at the entrance to the alley. Of medium height, almost as broad as he was long, he wore the attire of a Mexican *vaquero*. However, although he had features of such a villainous aspect that even his mother might have been excused for mistrusting him, he carried a revolver in the open-topped holster of a gunbelt and the silver star-in-a-circle badge of a Texas Ranger was pinned to his shirt, indicating he had the right to be armed in such a fashion.

"You're Carlos Franco, aren't you?" Ted identified.

"That's me, *amigo*," the newcomer agreed. "I've come from San Antonio after a son of a bitch who's wanted by the police down there. Trouble being, a couple of real bad *hombres* called Rapido Clint and Comanche Blood have been sent after him, and I reckon they've beaten me to it. Which I won't lose too much sleep if that is him lying out back of the hotel. All the meanness he's done in the past, no matter what's happened to him, he sure as hell deserved it."

3

IT'S A PACK OF LIES

"Gentlemen of the jury, have you reached your verdict?"

Uttered by Judge Robert J. McCrindle, the words brought an end to the muted rumble of speculative conversation that arose in the crowded courtroom at the sight of the jury returning at the conclusion of almost four hours' deliberations.

Such was the sensational nature of the trial taking place that it had brought newspaper reporters from every major city in Texas and even a few with national connections. Their numbers were swelled by sensation seekers who had also flocked to the generally sleepy town of Marlin, seat of Falls County. So many of both categories had come, in fact, that it caused much resentment among those of the local residents who wished but were prevented from being able to attend.

There were, in addition to the onlookers, more peace officers than would normally have been considered necessary to keep order. While the town was generally law abiding and peaceful, the judge in charge, aware of how deeply feelings were running regarding the case upon which he was sitting in judgment, considered it advisable to reinforce his bailiffs with every member of the small police department and several deputies serving in the Falls County Sheriff's Office. Furthermore—and probably more likely to produce a salutary effect should there be any disturbance—it was known that there were an undisclosed number of Texas Rangers in attendance.

Every eye was on the foreman of the jury as, having glanced around at the other members, he came slowly and almost reluctantly to his feet. The brief hesitation was all the more obvious when taken in consideration with his appearance. A tall, deeply tanned and leathery man in his early fifties, dressed after the fashion of a not-too-prosperous working rancher, his bearing suggested he was not usually plagued by doubt or indecision. Directing a look of undisguised contempt mingled with frustration to both the defendant in the dock and the attorney for the defense, his whole demeanor was that of one who had been asked a question he was far from pleased to answer.

The defendant was lounging against the rail of the raised enclosure, which put him in plain view over the heads of the crowd. Despite the gravity of the charge to which he was answering and the all too apparent animosity shown by the foreman of the jury, he had the relaxed air of one whose conscience was clear.

Or who believed it was a foregone conclusion that the verdict would be favorable!

Six feet tall, broad of shoulder, lean waisted, and with the carriage of a well-trained athlete, Philip Foote was in his midthirties. Parted exactly in the middle, his black hair was so slicked down with aromatic—or, depending on one's point of view, pungent—bay rum that it resembled patent leather.* Al-

---

* "Bay rum": Originally made by distilling rum with the leaves of the bayberry tree, *Pimenta racemosa*, but now consisting mainly of alcohol,

though sallow in a way suggesting he spent little of his time out of doors, there was a regularity to his features that indicated how he had acquired the sobriquet "Handsome Phil." Nevertheless, the hardness of his eyes and slightly sardonic twist to his lips gave a warning—all too often overlooked, particularly by members of the opposite sex—of his true and anything but pleasant nature. He wore an excellently tailored brown three-piece suit with a loud white pinstripe and his shoes were made from alligator hide. A red, white, and green striped necktie was tightly knotted around the collar of his mauve silk shirt. Jeweled links connected its French cuffs, sparkling like the diamond ring that glistened on each pinkie. Giving the impression that all he wore underneath was of the same material as his shirt, which was true, his attire was far more expensive and made of better material than the clothes worn by the jury; or the judge, for that matter.

Of much the same height and build as his client, although some twenty years older, Counselor Reece Mervyn had the appearance of being equally prone to athletic activities; although now he was running somewhat to seed as a result of good living. His thick brown hair was set in a series of precise waves. There was a smug, self-satisfied expression on his tanned and handsome features, and he displayed even white teeth as he smiled reassuringly at the man in the dock. Although more soberly clad, as became a very successful member of the legal profession, he was one of the few present to dress anywhere near as well as Foote. His black coat and vest, white silk shirt, glossy black cravat embellished by a good-size diamond stickpin, gray striped trousers, black shoes, and white spats had come from the best manufacturers. So well cut were they that they concealed the ravages left by his sedentary and occasion-

---

water, and essential oils. It was and still is used for inclusion in medicines and cosmetics but is not intended for drinking as a beverage. *J.T.E.*

ally licentious way of life. From all appearances, he was confident of a verdict that would add to his string of previous courtroom victories attained when everything had seemed to indicate defeat was a distinct possibility.

The case being tried in the courthouse at Marlin had had signs of being less than successful for Mervyn and his client when it commenced.

There had been no doubt of Foote's guilt when he was arrested for the rape and murder of Eloise Charmain, a local girl attracting attention as a member of the chorus playing the Inter-State Vaudeville Theater in Dallas. Having accumulated all the available evidence, those responsible for the maintenance of law and order in Texas had hoped at last to bring his successful criminal career to an end. Alert to his peril, he had considered only one man could save him.

. Reece Mervyn was arguably the Lone Star State's best trial lawyer and certainly, if not provably, the most unscrupulous. Faced with such an obviously strong case for the prosecution, a more honest attorney would have despaired of even being able to save his client from the death penalty. However, having made an exhaustive study of the ways in which the course of justice could be thwarted in a democracy, Mervyn had believed something more favorable could be produced. Once the financial arrangements had been agreed upon, the sum involved being considerable, he had set to work.

With the connivance of a dishonest reporter, the lawyer had caused the crime to receive a vast amount of coverage and much comment adverse to his client. Using the latter as the basis for his argument, he had sought to gain badly needed time by demanding that the trial be held in a more impartial venue than Dallas was likely to offer. The plea had been successful, but Mervyn deliberately made finding an acceptable location difficult. Court after court had either been objected to by him, or had refused to adjudicate. Finally, at the personal request of the state attorney general, Judge Robert J. McCrindle had offered to officiate. Being noted for his absolutely impartiality and honesty, but also for the severity he employed upon those rare occasions when dealing with the type of crimes of which Foote was accused, he had seemed the worst possible person before whom a defense attorney would want to take a client so patently guilty. Regardless of that, Mervyn had agreed to the venue. In a statement to the newspapers, he had claimed he was willing to accept as he could be sure of the court's fair-mindedness and disinclination to be swayed by the antagonist publicity to which Foote had been subjected since being arrested.

Once the trial had begun, the real reason for Mervyn's acquiesence soon became obvious. Although nothing could be proven, the time he gained had been put to good effect by the members of Foote's gang and the even more competent outside help that had been hired. Of the four witnesses upon whose evidence the prosecution had been basing its case, two had met their deaths in what to all appearances was an accident. In fact, it was so well contrived by the imported specialists and the warped criminal genius behind them,* that—despite rigorous investigations by local law enforcement officers and Texas Rangers—the coroner's jury was unable to claim otherwise. The same incident had resulted in the third witness sustaining an injury to his head so serious that his mental state rendered him incapable of attending the court, much less testifying. Having been under no delusion as to what had happened to the other three, the fourth man had written a note asserting his statement to the prosecuting attorney was false and, after elud-

---

* Although no evidence came to light to substantiate his supposition, Alvin Dustine "Cap" Fog believes the British master criminal "Old Mad John" Flack was the organizer of the fake accident. As is recorded in *"Cap" Fog, Texas Ranger, Meet Mr. J. G. Reeder*, he and Flack met at a later stage of his career. Further information regarding Flack can be found in *Terror Keep* by Edgar Wallace. *J.T.E.*

ing the peace officers assigned to guard him, had disappeared without a trace.

While a lesser man might have been willing to rest upon his laurels, Mervyn had not done so. Having had considerable experience where juries were concerned, particularly those selected from the populations of small towns, he had been unwilling to rely solely on the removal of the prosecution's witnesses to gain an acquittal. Instead, he had established an "alibi" by producing two men from whom Foote was supposed to have been purchasing a shipment of bootleg liquor in Texarkana on the night and at the same time as the crime was committed. Nor would he agree with his client's suggestion that the evidence should merely imply the deal was only discussed and had not been consummated, claiming the latter would have less chance of convincing the "rubes and hicks" on the jury. They would, he had asserted, be far more willing to accept an alibi if it was strengthened by his pointing out that Foote and the two bootleggers would face arrest for violation of the Volstead Act as a result of the disclosure. Although the latter would mean either a heavy fine or imprisonment for all of them, the pair of perjurers would be well recompensed for their participation, and the penalty where Foote was concerned would be far less severe than if he was found guilty of raping and murdering the girl.

After lasting far less time than had been anticipated, the trial was approaching its climax. Sent to consider their verdict when the court assembled that morning, the jury had spent almost four hours before returning to announce their decision.

"Well," Judge McCrindle prompted, after almost a minute had gone by without any answer to his question being forthcoming. "Have you reached your verdict?"

"We surely have, Your Honor," the foreman of the jury admitted, spitting out each word as if he hated the taste of it in his mouth. "While we all *know* he did it, like that fancy-talking legal shyster's kept telling us right frequent, he's got himself fixed up with a goddamned alibi and there's been no witnesses brought forward to show it's a pack of lies—"

"Your Honor!" Reece Mervyn shouted, springing from his chair with far from his usual calmly dignified motions. However, the anger that was suffusing his face and speeding up his well-educated Southern drawl stemmed more from resentment at the derogatory reference to himself than on behalf of his client. "I must *protest*!"

"I don't doubt that, Counselor," McCrindle conceded somberly, but with no noticeable sympathy. Turning his gaze to the clerk of the court, and then to the rows of seats occupied by the newspapermen—all of whom were either writing or sitting with pencils waiting expectantly poised over notebooks—he continued. "You will strike the foreman of the jury's comment from the records, Mr. Sawtell. And I trust the gentlemen of the press who are present will refrain from mentioning it in their reports of the trial."

"Is that *enough*, Your Honor?" Mervyn demanded in tones of exasperation, doubting whether the suggestion of restraint would be heeded by more than a fraction of the more conservative newspapermen. "The honor of my client has been seriously besmirched!"

"Come on now, Counselor!" McCrindle interrupted, his tanned and craggy face impassive. "I think we both *suspect* your client's 'honor' may have been seriously besmirched *long* before this trial. However, should my instructions to the gentlemen of the press be disregarded, I've no doubt that you can advise him of whatever legal recourse may be necessary for his protection."

"Yes, but—" the lawyer commenced.

"Now," the judge said, paying not the slightest attention to Mervyn's attempt at extending the protest to include his own "honor" and swinging a coldly prohibitive glare at the cause of the interplay. "Without any subsidiary or supplementary comments, what is the verdict you have reached?"

The warning in McCrindle's apparently even tone was all too obvious to anybody who knew him as well as the man to whom he was speaking. The latter was certain that, although they had grown up as good friends, no further lapses would be permitted to go unpunished.

Born and raised in Falls County, the judge was liked and respected by all its residents—even those who came before him for trial. While on this occasion he was wearing a dark suit, white shirt, stiff collar, and sober tie—none of which were as costly as the attire of the attorney for the defense—there had been other times when, if he was going hunting or fishing as soon as the court adjourned, his judicial robes had covered less conventional attire. No matter what he wore, his straight-forward dealing, intolerance of humbug, underlying good humor, and ability to temper justice with mercy if the circumstances deserved such treatment were what enhanced his popularity throughout his area of jurisdiction.

"Not guilty!" the foreman of the jury decreed with bad grace, although this was not caused by the rebuke from the bench.

"Silence!" McCrindle thundered, bringing an instant end to the chorus of boos and shouted protests that greeted the pronouncement. Exchanging what was obviously a glance of angry resignation with the attorney appointed for the prosecution, he went on in lower yet audible voice. "And is that the verdict of you all?"

"It is!" the foreman affirmed, after a brief look at the other jurors as if hoping to find some indication that at least one of them had had a change of mind. Then he sat down, his whole bearing suggestive of the extreme distaste he felt over the course circumstances had compelled him to take.

"So be it recorded!" McCrindle instructed, but for once he was not entirely successful in keeping a completely impartial timbre in his Texas drawl. Its lack became even more noticeable to everybody who could claim his acquaintance as he continued. "Seeing the jury has rendered a verdict of 'not guilty' in keeping with the *'evidence'* which has been presented, I have no alternative but to order the defendant released from the custody of this court." He raised his right hand and glanced around to silence the rumble of dissent from the people assembled in the room. "And we will not tolerate *any* further disturbance whatsoever. This court now stands adjourned. Bailiffs, clear the courtroom!"

If the defendant felt any concern over the open hostility being directed at him as the judge's order was being carried out, he showed no sign of it. He had not reached thirty-five years of age and attained his present position of importance in criminal circles—along with sufficient money to retain Reece Mervyn's services and the other expenses entailed by the trial—by allowing himself to be perturbed by unfavorable opinions on the part of the public. Under different circumstances, he might have arranged for the insulting remarks made by the foreman of the jury to be punished. However, if he had, it would have been more for the purpose of retaining prestige in the eyes of his underlings and associates than out of any deeply felt resentment over what was said.

Waiting until the spectators and most of the peace officers had left the courtroom before descending from the dock, Foote was on the point of crossing to where Mervyn was placing documents into a briefcase when he noticed two men walking purposefully toward him. One was tall, burly, blond, and Teutonic in appearance, clad in the fashion of a cowhand and carrying the suitcase in which he had packed his belongings prior to leaving his cell in the basement of the courthouse. Shorter and somewhat older, his hair a grizzled dark brown and with features suggestive of Hebraic origins, the other wore a not-too-expensive two-piece gray suit, a white shirt with a sober blue tie, and black town shoes.

For all their divergent appearance and attire, the pair had two things in common. Firstly, slanting down from each's left hip was a *buscadero* gunbelt with a Colt Government model automatic pistol at the right side in an open-topped holster designed to facilitate its rapid withdrawal. Second, indicating they had the official status necessary to be wearing arms in the courtroom, the badge of a Texas Ranger was prominently displayed upon the left breast of the former's shirt and the lapel of the latter's jacket. It was as much due to their presence as to the personality of the judge that there had been so little disturbance when the verdict was announced.

"All right, Foote!" the shorter of the pair commanded without preliminaries, as his companion put down the suitcase, his demeanor seeming more suited to a storekeeper than that of the very tough and competent peace officer the gang leader knew him to be. "Hold out your hands!"

"Really, Sergeant Goldberg!" Mervyn protested, striding forward swiftly and nodding to the handcuffs that the man he was addressing had brought into view. "Are they *necessary*?"

"Well now, Counselor," the Hebraic Texas Ranger replied, making little attempt to conceal his dislike for the lawyer. "Sergeant Soehnen and I reckon it is. And, more important, Major Benson Tragg told us to do it."

"Which, happen it's good enough for the major," the Germanic peace officer supplemented, "it's way past being good enough for Benny and me."

"Counselor!" Judge McCrindle called, his voice holding a note that warned he would brook no argument. "I'd be obliged if you could spare me a moment in my chambers."

"Go ahead, Reece," Foote authorized. Assuming an ingratiating tone, he went on. "These gents are only doing their duty.

But you don't need those bracelets, fellers. I'll come peace-fully."

"Peacefully or not, you'll *come*!" Sergeant Benjamin 'Benny' Goldberg asserted, opening the handcuffs instead of replacing them in the pocket from which they had come. "And you're doing it with them on."

"You're not thinking of trying to stop Benny putting them on, now are you?" challenged Sergeant Hans "Dutchy" Soehnen, almost hopefully, his Texan drawl underlaid with a timbre indicative of his Germanic roots.

"Hell, no!" Foote affirmed hurriedly, noticing that the blond peace officer appeared to have made a complete recovery from the serious wound he was reported to have sustained a few weeks earlier.* Extending his hand hurriedly, he went on in a voice that could not entirely conceal his resentment at being subjected to such an indignity. "It's just that I'm willing to go along peaceably and—"

"I must say it's right satisfying to meet an obliging gent like you," Goldberg claimed sardonically, deftly coupling the of-fered wrists together with the handcuffs. "And while we don't figure you'd be thinking of trying to escape—"

"Even thinking about escape's never crossed my mind and trying it's the last thing I'd do!" Foote stated, speaking suffi-ciently loud to make sure his sentiments reached the ears of the few people who were still in the courtroom. "There's no need for me to do either. Sure, I've got to go and stand trial in Texarkana for buying that bootleg hooch, but the most I'll get's a fine or a few weeks in jail. So why'd I try to escape and chance getting shot for it?"

"Like you say," Goldberg conceded, but in a disinterested fashion. "Why *should* you?"

---

* How the report of the wound came into being is told in *Rapido Clint.* J.T.E.

"Trouble being, though," Soehnen went on, his tone seeming to grow more Germanic and menacing. "Fellers're *always* doing things they *shouldn't.*"

"Sergeant Goldberg!" Mervyn called over his shoulder, having started to follow the judge but halting when he heard what his client was saying. "My clerk will be following you to Texarkana, just in case Mr. Foote should need . . . *anything* . . . between here and there."

"Likely he'll be able to do the same for Chiverton and Schulman as well," the shorter Texas Ranger replied, referring to the men who had supplied the gang leader with his alibi and who were also to stand trial in Texarkana for bootlegging. Showing no concern over having a witness to everything that happened on the journey, he went on. "Let's get going, Mr. Foote. The sooner we've delivered you safely, the happier Dutchy and I'll feel."

Although the lawyer had intended to expand upon his warning that precautions had been taken to safeguard his client, the peace officers set off with Foote toward the front entrance before he could speak. Letting out a snort of indignation, more for the gang leader's benefit than because he believed it would have any effect upon either of the sergeants, he turned and followed the judge.

"Well, Your Honor," Mervyn said, changing his expression from disapprobation to one suggestive of amiable companionship as he preceded McCrindle into the judge's chambers behind the courtroom. "May I congratulate you upon the completely fair and impartial way in which you handled the trial?"

"No!" McCrindle stated, closing the door and standing with his back to it in a manner redolent of disapproval. "I'd rather *you* didn't. I wasn't happy about holding this f—I nearly said 'farce,' but I won't—nor would I have if the state attorney general hadn't asked me to do it as a favor to him and the governor. So I'll be damned if I'll accept congratulations, from *you* in particular, for having been compelled to adjudicate at the biggest miscarriage of justice since Barabbas was set free."*

"Wh—wha—what—?" Mervyn spluttered, taken aback by the ferocity with which he had been addressed. "How dare you?"

"Shut your goddamned mouth, you overdressed son of a bitch!" the judge ordered, speaking with a savage intensity that brought the lawyer's intended protest to a halt. "I think you and all your lousy, law-twisting kind are a disgrace to the legal profess—"

"You're going too far!" Mervyn warned, trying to sound menacing and yet not directly threatening.

"Am I?" McCrindle challenged. "That being the case, happen you want to haul me before the Bar Association, go right ahead and do it. But just bear in mind, it's only *your* word against *mine* and, should it come to 'proving,' I reckon the foreman of the jury will be willing to say I went straight off hunting with him as soon as I left the courtroom."

"H-he wouldn't *dare*!" Mervyn gasped, alarmed and amazed by such hostility from one he regarded as—despite having been appointed to sit in judgment on such an important trial—no more than an insignificant country bumpkin with only a fraction of his own legal knowledge and ability. "Nor would *you*!"

"Wouldn't we, by God?" the judge thundered. "Well, if that's the way you figure, take me in front of the Bar Association and lodge a formal complaint. I know you're Hogan Turtle's man, but I reckon my kin among the Hardin, Fog, and Blaze clan can stack up to a whole heap more pull than he can raise."

"Well!" Mervyn exclaimed, trying to maintain his air of pomposity and indignation despite suspecting that the latter part of McCrindle's statement was correct. At any rate he was disin-

---

* "Barabbas" (Hebrew, "son of Abbas"): The thief whom the people wanted freed instead of Jesus. See Matthew, 27:16–21 (of the Bible.) *J.T.E.*

clined to put it to the test. While he was the senior legal adviser for the master criminal, the members of the clan to whom the judge was related were among the most wealthy, powerful, and influential people in Texas. Not only would they be able to bring pressure to bear on behalf of McCrindle where the Bar Association was concerned, but he felt that Turtle would not approve of him antagonizing them. Trying to put on a bolder attitude than he was feeling, he continued. "I don't see why I should stand here and be insulted in such a fashion!"

"Then *don't* stand there!" the judge answered, in tones suggesting the conversation was at an end and he was issuing an order of dismissal. Stepping aside, he went on. "Get the hell out of my bailiwick and, if you know what's good for you, make good and goddamned sure you *never* come before me again. You got that raping, murdering son of a bitch off when he should have been found guilty and hanged. I only wish there was some way *you* could be made to pay for it. But there isn't under the law, and you'll get off scot-free."

4

NO JURY WOULD BLAME ME FOR DOING IT

Sitting on a chair by the window of the second-floor room he had taken at the Brendon Hotel, the father of Eloise Charmain watched the people who were emerging from the Falls County courthouse. Scanning them carefully, as the peace officers on the sidewalk kept them moving away from the building, he located the man for whom he was looking. It was his cousin, Bill Shelby, who had been present to hear the result of Handsome Phil Foote's trial. A sigh of mingled anger and distress broke from him as he received the signal they had arranged was to be made if, as they had feared would happen, the jury returned a verdict of "not guilty." After coming to his feet, he crossed to collect the Winchester 1876 model Express rifle that was lying on the bed. Throwing its lever through the reloading cycle almost without the need for conscious thought, he walked back to sit down and rested the twenty-six-inch octagonal barrel on the windowsill.

Just over medium height, but with the solidly fleshed, thick-

set build of an outdoor man, Simeon Oakes—Eloise Charmain
had been the dead girl's professional name—was in his early
fifties and soberly dressed in clothes that indicated he was a
fairly well-to-do town dweller. He was, in fact, a successful
accountant and a law-abiding, respected member of his community. There was nothing brutal about his rugged and tanned
face, only the lines of bitter grief mingled with grimly determined resignation. Despite his resolution, however, he was not
motivated merely by a blind desire for vengeance. If the verdict
had been guilty, he would have been content to let justice take
its course without intervention on his part.

As it was, knowing the defendant had raped and murdered
his only child no matter what the findings of the court had
been, Oakes was—albeit reluctantly and without satisfaction—
ready to inflict the death penalty himself.

Raising the adjustable leaf of his rifle's rear sight and setting
it for the something over 440 yards separating him from his
objective, Oakes studied the situation with the experienced eye
of one who had served successfully as a sniper with the American Expeditionary Force in France during what was now
known as the Great War. Although the crowd that had gathered in front of the courthouse had been swelled by those fortunate enough to be inside during the latter stages of the trial, the
whole of Marlin's small police force and several deputies from
the Falls County Sheriff's Office had ushered all of them sufficiently far away for them to be in no danger from his shooting.
There was only one car parked in the vicinity. It was at the
sidewalk, facing the steps leading to the front entrance of the
building, and would be used by the Texas Rangers to transport
Foote to Texarkana where he and the men who had supplied
his alibi would stand trial for the supposed purchase of the
illicit liquor. Even if the other two were with the gang leader,
neither could be mistaken for him. Oakes was confident, therefore, that he could kill Foote before the safety of the vehicle was

attained and without putting the lives of the escorting peace officers at risk.

A keen sportsman, whose love of hunting had encouraged him to keep up the target practice that made him such an efficient sniper during his military service, Oakes was a dead shot and the old Winchester was his favorite firearm. Its ninety-eight-grain charge of black powder might lack the power of the later "smokeless" cartridges, but he knew it would do all he required of it. The load produced a muzzle energy of 1,615 foot-pounds with which to propel the 300-grain, .50 Express-caliber bullet at a velocity of 1,057 feet per second. Using the weapon with which he was most familiar, he not only had the requisite skill to send the bullet where it would best serve his purpose, but there were ten more rounds waiting to follow the first should they be needed.* He did not believe any of them would be. Blunt-nosed, as a precaution against a chance jolt causing the round ahead in the tubular magazine to be detonated, the lead tended to mushroom on impact in a way that would be almost certain to produce a fatal wound when striking any part of the human torso.

Being fully engrossed in watching for Foote to emerge from the courthouse and deeply perturbed by the enormity of what he meant to do, knowing it was a very different matter from the sniping he had performed during the Great War, Oakes was unaware that the key was being pushed from its hole. Nor did he pay any attention to the faint *click* of the lock being operated from outside the room. The stealthy opening of the door went just as unnoticed, and, as when the key fell, the carpet on

* The respective magazine capacities of the Winchester 1876 model sporting rifle—having a twenty-eight-inch barrel; Express—twenty-six-inch barrel; musket—thirty-two-inch barrel; and carbine—twenty-two-inch barrel—were twelve, eleven, thirteen, and nine. *J.T.E.*

the floor allowed the animal that entered to approach silently until announcing its presence in no uncertain fashion.

Hearing the menacing growl that rumbled from close behind him, Oakes looked over his left shoulder. Although what he saw brought him to his feet in a hurry, he made no attempt to point the Winchester as—keeping the chair between himself and the source of the sound—he turned. Even without discovering that the dog confronting him was not alone, he would have known better than to make any threatening gestures.

Possessing considerable experience in such matters, Oakes needed only one glance at the dark bluish-gray coloration—liberally speckled with numerous irregularly shaped black spots—the black head and saddle, to identify the big dog as an exceptionally fine bluetick coonhound.* However, its size implied it had been bred specifically for hunting larger and more dangerous animals than the semiarboreal raccoon that supplied part of the breed's name. Capable of tackling jaguar, cougar, black and even grizzly bear when running in a pack, it could protect itself against a man.**

From all appearances, the bluetick was ready to take immediate aggressive action if this was needed. Having halted just within leaping distance, it was standing stiff-legged and as tense as a tightly compressed coil spring. A ridge of hair bristled menacingly along its back, and, rigid as a poker, its tail rose in a forward crescent. Although it was no longer growling, it was displaying a mouthful of impressive teeth in a lip-curling if soundless snarl.

The man who had effected the unauthorized entry and fol-

---

* A more detailed description of this particular bluetick coonhound can be found in Case One, "Alvin Fog's Mistake," *You're a Texas Ranger, Alvin Fog. J.T.E.*

** Information regarding the various breeds of hounds used for hunting "big game" animals and how they are employed is given in *Hound Dog Man. J.T.E.*

lowed the dog into the room was tall and as lean as a steer raised in the greasewood country. However, apart from implying he could be fairly well on in years, his leathery brown face gave little indication of his actual age. There were wrinkles at the corners of his keen blue eyes and narrow gash of a mouth that were suggestive of a dry sense of humor, but they gave no hint of levity at that moment. In fact, what little expression showed seemed more sympathetic and understanding than anything else.

There was nothing impressive about the newcomer's attire. He wore a battered and ancient-looking Texas-style J. B. Stetson hat that had once been white but was now a greenish-gray, a somewhat baggy brown coat, a gray shirt buttoned to the collar although a necktie was absent, and washed-out Levi pants with their legs hanging outside scuffed black Justin boots. While there was no sign of him being armed in any way, the dully glinting and dented badge of a Texas Ranger was pinned to the left breast pocket of his shirt. In his left hand was a small metal object that resembled a golf "iron" club.

"Put down the rifle, Mr. Oakes!" the elderly peace officer requested, his voice gentle yet commanding, as he walked forward in a leisurely seeming fashion that was nevertheless much swifter than it appeared. "*That's* not the answer!"

"What—who—?" The would-be dispenser of summary punishment gasped. He made no attempt to comply and, despite recognizing the metal object carried by the newcomer, he went on. "How did *you* get in here?"

"It wasn't so all-fired deafer-i-calt," the peace officer replied, and gestured with the object before dropping it into the pocket of his jacket. "Fact being, *anybody* who'd got him a lockpick like this 'n could've done it just's easy's I did and without you knowing until too late."

"But how did you know I was here?" Oakes asked, wondering if there had been something left unsaid in the explanation.

"We've been sort of keeping an eye on you 'most ever since you hit town," the newcomer admitted. "Which you for sure didn't have that old Winchester hid anywheres near so well's you figured and it didn't take too all-fired many brains to figure out what you might've got in mind. So, when you didn't show in the courthouse today to hear the vere-dict, we sort of esterminated what you-all was concluding to do should it come out not guilt-ery and reckoned you'd best be stopped doing it."

Having crossed the room until close enough to do so while speaking, the peace officer halted and reached, without any suggestion of hesitation, haste, threat, or concern for his own welfare, to take hold of the rifle. Even without the menacing presence of the big dog, being a law-abiding citizen, Oakes would not have resisted. In fact, a feeling close to relief assailed him as he allowed it to be taken from his hands. The moment he was relieved of the weapon, he noticed a remarkable change come over the bluetick. All the alert watchfulness left it and, flopping on to its side as if suddenly overcome by weariness, it lapsed into a somnolence that formed a vivid contrast when compared with the appearance it had presented when he first set eyes on it.

"Hey!" Oakes exclaimed, the big dog's behavior having sparked off a memory. "You're Sergeant Jubal Branch, aren't you?"

"That's who-all I've the mis-honory-bull to be," the elderly peace officer confirmed, retreating a couple of steps and holding the Winchester with both hands and at arms' length in front of him. "Which ain't nothing hey-tal to be proud of being. Do you feel like sitting down again?"*

---

* Alvin Dustine "Cap" Fog claims that the mispronunciation of words by Sergeant Jubal Branch was merely a pose intended to make miscreants in particular assume he was far less intelligent than was the case. We are inclined to believe this. Certainly all of Branch's reports that Cap allowed

"God damn it!" Oakes spat out bitterly, glancing through the window instead of sitting as had been suggested and seeing the two Texas Rangers escorting the murderer of his daughter from the courthouse. "That son-of-a-bitching bastard's got clean away with it and been set free."

"Not eggs-hack-shally," Branch corrected, looking in the same direction. "He's still got to stand his trial for buying that bootleg liquor, which same's going against the Pro-hibit-si-cal law—"

"And what will the murdering bastard get when he's tried for *that*?" Oakes demanded indignantly. "A lousy fine that won't even start to make a dent in his bankroll, or at most a few months in jail."

"I'm not gainsaying it," Branch admitted, working the Winchester's lever to extract the round from the chamber and following it with the other ten out of the magazine. "But it'll likely give us time to see happen we can learn the truthfulness about the way he got his-self found not guilt-ery."

"And what can happen to him even should you be able to do it?" the bereaved father challenged in an angry voice. "I might not be a tophand legal shyster like that fancy-talking bastard who got the son of a bitch off, but I've read enough about the law to know a man can't be tried twice for the same crime, no matter how he got away with it the first time. Which's why I was figuring on—"

"Hold hard there!" Branch commanded, taking his left hand from the rifle and raising it in a prohibitive gesture that brought the other's tirade to a halt. "I'm not saying's how we 'n's could haul him back in front of a judge should we get proof this trial was rigged all ways, on account of that'd double jeopard-isical him against the Constitution of the good old U.S. of A. Only

---

us to examine were written in a far more legible hand than our own. Furthermore, the grammar and spelling is impeccable. *J.T.E.*

your way, *should* you have had it in mind, isn't the answer
neither. What I've heard tell about you when you was in France
with the A.E.F. and as a hunter, you could likely've made wolf
bait of him from up here.* But, *had* such been your intenter-
ations and you'd gone ahead 'n' done it, one of us peace
officers'd've had to haul you in to stand trial for his murder, no
matter how much we could understand why you'd thrown
down on him."

"No jury would blame me for doing it," Oakes asserted, but
his whole demeanor showed he was ill at ease. "Not after what
he'd done to my li'l gal."

"They wouldn't *blame* you, but they'd sure's sin's for sale in
Cowtown** have to find you guilt-ery of doing it," the elderly
sergeant pointed out, despite feeling sure this had occurred to
the disconsolate man. "And, even should they go against all the
heavi-dense 'n' let you off, do you reckon your good lady—or
your *daughter,* comes to that—would want you with his blood
on your hands?"

"I know my Martha wouldn't," Oakes admitted, taking another look out of the window. He found that the peace officers
had already set off in the car with Foote and realized the suppli-
ers of the alibi could not be traveling in the vehicle. Seeing his
cousin approaching hurriedly, he gave no thought to the omission. Returning his gaze to the peace officer, he went on with
what he believed to be the truth. "She didn't even know I was
fetching along that old Winchester of mine, but she begged
Cousin Bill and me not to do anything loco should that son-of-

---

* "Make wolf bait": "To kill." The term was derived from one method used
in the Old West for dealing with carnivores, not necessarily just wolves,
that preyed on livestock. An animal would be killed and, having been
injected with poison, the carcass was left on the range to be eaten by the
predators. *J.T.E.*
** "Cowtown": The colloquial name for Fort Worth, seat of Tarrant
County, Texas. *J.T.E.*

a-bitch Foote get away with it. Well, I'm ready to go with you and I won't give you any trouble. But I'll be obliged if you'll take me out the back way."

"There's plenty's might say's how your good lady gave you some right smart had-vice-erables," Branch drawled, paying no attention to the other's last two sentences and refraining from mentioning that Mrs. Martha Oakes had notified the sheriff of Falls County of what she suspected upon discovering her husband's favorite rifle was missing from the gun rack in his study. "You-all should ought to've tooken it."

"There've been plenty of other times when I should have and didn't, then came to wish I had," Oakes confessed. Hoping to save his cousin from sharing the consequences of his thwarted attempt to take revenge, he continued as he stepped forward. "Well, like I said, I'm ready to go with you."

"Who-all's going any place just yet?" Branch inquired, as—apart from raising its head slightly—the big bluetick gave no indication of knowing the other was moving. "Sit down again. You look like you need to."

"God damn it, this was all *my* idea!" Oakes protested, slumping dejectedly into the chair. "Do you have to take in Cousin Bill as well?"

"As well's *who*?" Branch asked.

"Me!" Oakes answered, jerking his right thumb toward his chest.

"*You?*" the elderly sergeant queried. "Now what makes you reckon's how I'd be wanting to take you in? Or needing to, comes to that?"

"Blast it, man!" Oakes barked angrily, his temper rising as he was subjected to what he considered must be some form of cat-and-mouse game by the peace officer. "You caught me getting ready to—"

"I caught you sitting over by the window holding this old Winchester is all," Branch interrupted. Thrusting the rifle's lever down and up, he pressed the trigger and, as the hammer fell with nothing more than a dry *click,* continued amiably. "Which, looks like to me, it's empty. And, so far's my hex-perry-mence of such goes, that's not again' the legal law in this-here great 'n' sovereign State of Texas."

"Gracias, Jubal!" Oakes breathed, exuding genuine contrition, as his gaze dropped to the eleven cartridges that had been ejected by the peace officer prior to making the experiment and remembering the significant way in which some of the other's previous comments were worded. Letting out a long sigh of relief, he went on. "I reckon you and that fool old hound dog of yours stopped me doing something which I reckon I'd have regretted for the rest of my life."

"I'm not about to ask what *that* might be," Branch declared, and there was a timbre in his voice that warned he had better not be told.

"Whatever you say," Oakes assented, drawing the correct conclusions and far from displeased by the way in which the potentially precarious situation was developing. For all that, he was unable to prevent himself from taking yet another look out of the window and remarking, "But it surely goes against the grain to think that that murderous son of a bitch should get off so lightly when we both know he was guilty as all hell."

"I'd like to be able to come right on out and tell you's maybe he won't," the elderly sergeant said somberly, going to lay the rifle on the bed and sitting alongside it. "Only it wouldn't be right of me to—"

The words came to an end as the door was thrown open.

"Why the hell didn't you—?" began the man whose hurried arrival had caused the peace officer to stop speaking and who, on becoming aware that the person he was addressing was not alone, sent his right hand swiftly beneath the left side of his jacket.

Neither the question nor the gesture was completed. Instead, the newcomer skidded to a halt and stood as if suddenly turned to stone. There was a *very* good reason for the cessation of activity.

Although its master continued to sit apparently at ease on the bed, shedding its posture of somnolence, the big bluetick had come to its feet in a rapid bound. Almost instantaneously, it returned to the menacingly alert attitude of readiness to attack it had displayed on its arrival.

"Well now, Mr. Shelby," Branch drawled, employing the same tone as when warning Oakes against making any incriminating statements. "I wouldn't say's *anything* was going to be done, nor even conter-perlated."

"Hey!" William Shelby gasped, staring at the badge of office worn by the elderly Texas Ranger and allowing his empty right hand to swing back to his off side without provoking hostility from the watching dog. "You're *not* Butch Cope!"

"I can't mind ever saying's how I was," Branch replied calmly, despite knowing the man in question was Foote's second in command and had been in the courthouse during the earlier stages of the trial. "Fact being, we don't look nothing alike, I'm right pleasure-abled to say."

"But when I remembered he wasn't in court this morning and you hadn't—" Shelby commenced, directing the words at his kinsman.

"Could be said Mr. Cope had something to 'tend to otherwheres," Branch interrupted, before the new arrival could make an indiscreet disclosure with regard to his cousin's intentions. "Shut the door and sit down, Mr. Shelby. And, happen you gents don't reckon's how I'm taking a libert-ical, seeing's how this-here's your room 'n' all, I reckon I'll just stay and visit awhiles with you."

"We're not figuring on taking out after Foote, happen that's what's worrying you!" Oakes asserted, watching the bluetick settle down once more and, apparently, fall asleep at once. "But you're welcome to stay just as long as takes your fancy."

"*Gracias,* that's right neighborly of you," Branch answered as Shelby closed the door and went to sit on the other chair in the room. "Anyways, I wasn't figuring's how you'd got the notion to take out after him. But feelings've been running kind of high and, folks being the way they be, somebody else might figure on doing it."

"Who would that be?" Oakes put in, frowning in genuine puzzlement.

"What we've heard, there's some of the other owlhoots haven't been any too pleasure-abled about the fuss he's caused to be stirred up," Branch explained. "Trouble being, should somebody try to do meanness to him over it, you'd strike some folks's being the most likely suspect. So, like that fancy legal-spouting shyster showed was the case with good old Handisome Phil, there's nothing so comforti-ficating as having a real good strong ally-biceral to show's it couldn't've been you's did it."

Coming almost like an echo to the cryptic—if puzzling—comment, several shots were fired from somewhere outside the hotel.

Springing to his feet, Oakes made for the window. Rising and hurrying in the same direction, also without producing the kind of response from the big bluetick that his impetuous arrival had elicited, Shelby joined his cousin. Looking toward the courthouse, he drew a similar conclusion from what he saw.

If the way in which the crowd was behaving offered a guide, the shots had *not* been discharged from the direction taken by the car carrying Foote.

However, if the two men had been less engrossed in trying to discover the cause and location of the disturbance, they might have noticed something strange closer at hand. Instead of rising to join Oakes and Shelby at the window, or leave and investigate the incident, Branch remained seated on the bed!

5

HE'S NOT TAKEN WITH YOUR COMPANY

"Do you reckon's how there might be something in it, Colin?" inquired Sergeant Aloysius Bratton in his broad Irish brogue, as he and a second Texas Ranger strolled to where the deputy sheriff on duty as turnkey was unlocking the door of one of the cells in the basement of the Falls County courthouse. "Sure and it's not often that Major Tragg gets the wrong of things."

"Not so all-fired often it's got to be noticeable, Paddy," Sergeant Colin Breda agreed and, despite being a second-generation Texan,[*] his voice retained a strong suggestion of his ancestors having come from the Highlands of Scotland. "But I sort of hope he is this time. I'd hate to have to lay my life on the line for the likes of them."

"And me," Bratton seconded vehemently, darting a far from

---

[*] As is recorded in *.44 Caliber Man* and *A Horse Called Mogollon*, Tam, paternal grandfather of Sergeant Colin Breda, had preceded him as a peace officer in Texas. *J.T.E.*

friendly glance at the two men in the cell. "But that's the worst of being a peace officer. You're always having to do things you'd sooner be leaving undone."

Six feet tall, black haired, ruddy faced, and in his mid-thirties, the Irish sergeant was barrel chested and solid-looking. Wearing a pearl-gray derby hat at a jaunty angle, a salmon-pink shirt with a bowtie that clashed against its hue, a somewhat loud brown-and-white check suit, and oxblood red shoes with white explosions on the toes, he looked more like a carnival side show's talented talker than a peace officer. He did not wear a gunbelt, but the butt of a Colt Army 1917 model revolver—carried in a spring-retention shoulder holster—showed from beneath the left side of his jacket, and he was carrying a Winchester 1897 model trench gun across the crook of his right arm.*

Matching the other Texas Ranger in height, a few years younger, Breda was less heavily built—which did not make him puny—and had a tanned, craggily handsome face. Dressed in cowhand's clothes, he had on a gunbelt with a Colt Civilian model Peacemaker in its well-designed fast-draw holster.** His

* The Winchester 1897 model twelve-gauge, five-shot, tubular magazine, pump-action shotgun, as modified for use in the trench warfare of World War I. The barrel was reduced to a length of twenty inches, given a radiating cooling sleeve to permit a rapid rate of fire and equipped to take a bayonet. The trench gun proved to be an exceptionally effective weapon for use at close, or in confined, quarters, particularly when loaded with buckshot. After such weapons were used to break up a mass infantry attack, the Germans—who had already employed poison gas, including the especially vicious mustard variety—complained it was "an inhumane and barbaric way of waging war." As is told in the Rockabye County series, classified as "riot guns," firearms of this kind are still used by modern law enforcement agencies. J.T.E.
** Information regarding the different types of Colt 1873 model "P" revolver, commonly known as the Peacemaker, can be found in those volumes of the Floating Outfit series that follow The Peacemakers in the chronological sequence. J.T.E.

left hand gripped a Winchester 1894 model carbine by the wrist of its butt, with its barrel resting on his shoulder.

"Come on out!" the turnkey ordered, with no suggestion of courtesy, opening the door of the cell. Then he looked at the approaching peace officers and continued. "They're all ready for you, Paddy, Colin."

"Sure and isn't it the goodness you are, Barney," Bratton replied, but the note of amiability left his voice as he went on. "Let's be having you out here, darlin's!"

After looking past the two men they sensed were to be their escort to Texarkana, Seth Chiverton and Irvin Schulman exchanged puzzled glances as they walked from the cell. Prior to having become small-time operators in the bootlegging of illicit liquor, they had been a moderately successful "cross-talk" act traveling the cheaper burlesque circuits. They still dressed much as they had in their former occupation.

Tallish, slim, moderately good-looking, Chiverton had been the straight man of the team and still tended to act as its spokesman. He wore a smart light-gray three-piece lounge suit, the jacket of which had a two-button fastening and the single-breasted waistcoat was cut high with a V opening. As he was always one to keep up the current fashion, the legs of his trousers were tailored with the wider legs that were becoming increasingly popular and would soon develop into the extremes of the so-called Oxford bags.

Short, chubby, and, apart from having a naturally dark tinge around his jaws that was incongruous with such innocent-looking features, Schulman was dressed less stylishly as became the comedian of the team. His derby hat was a size too small, the loud check sports jacket too large and long, and his trousers looked a touch too tight. However, the reputation he had where members of the opposite sex were concerned—a trait he shared with his more presentable partner—suggested he was far less ingenuous than he appeared on the surface.

"Where's Handsome Phil?" Chiverton asked, his rasping voice having an East Coast timbre and registering puzzlement.

"He's gone already," Breda replied.

"Without us?" inquired Schulman, in a tone much like that of his partner instead of employing the childish squeak he used on the stage.

"Well now," the Scottish sergeant drawled sardonically. "Seeing's he's not here and you're not with him, I'd say it's closer to yes than no to that."

"Why's he gone without us?" Chiverton wanted to know.

"Seems like that's the way he wanted it," Breda explained, and the Irish sergeant nodded concurrence.

"Why?" Chiverton challenged, his bearing indicative of suspicion.

"Neither he nor that fancy legal shyster of his told us when they brought word from Major Tragg for him to go alone," Breda elaborated. "Only it seemed to me like, now he's in the clear, he's not taken with your company."

"So you noticed that as well, did you, Colin?" Bratton inquired, leaning his trench gun against the bars of the cell and bringing two sets of handcuffs from the right side pocket of his jacket. "And here's me thinking it's just imagining I was that he looked real eager to be quit of them."

"Might just be's how he didn't want to ride along with them in case they started in to doing that lousy act of theirs," the turnkey suggested, making no attempt to conceal his dislike for the pair whose testimony had played a major part in securing the acquittal of Philip Foote. Without mentioning that he too had not been informed why the gang leader was being permitted to travel separately, he went on. "Do you reckon that's what it was, Paddy?"

"Sure now and isn't that just what it might've been, Barney," Britton conceded, then turned a gaze filled with mockery to the prisoners. "Anyways, darlin's, 'tis gone already he is and without you. So you'll have to be making do with just Colin and me for company."

"And pleasant company you'll find us," Breda promised, but with reservations. "Just so long as you don't start doing your act for us."

Disregarding the Scottish's sergeant's remark, but digesting the information they had gleaned from the rest of the conversation, the two perjurers remained in the cell and once again traded worried looks. Stemming out of their own far from reliable, loyal, or trustworthy natures, Chiverton and Schulman each possessed a wary skepticism where the motives of other people were concerned. Because of this trait, they were disinclined to put too much faith in anybody, and the discovery that Foote was apparently desirous of avoiding their company during the journey to Texarkana, added to the exchange of comments they had overheard as their escort arrived, was filling them with disconcerting speculations and misgivings.

Being realists, the pair accepted they were neither the most intelligent nor influential members of their illicit chosen field of endeavor. They also had no doubt this had been the reason they were selected to supply the gang leader with his fake alibi. Despite having allowed themselves to be persuaded by Reece Mervyn's confidential clerk that performing such a service for Foote would be beneficial to their future activities, and having received adequate recompense for the consequences of their falsehoods in the witness box, they had a good idea of how things stood. Neither believed they were regarded as friends, or even as social equals, by the man they had helped save from the gallows. Remembering that he had made no mention of his intentions before leaving for the courtroom to hear the verdict of the trial that morning, they were both surprised and perturbed to discover he had made arrangements to travel separately.

"Come on now, will you, darlin's!" Bratton commanded, his

voice taking on a timbre of impatience close to asperity as the
prisoners continued to stand in the cell and stare at one another. "Colin, Barney, and me've got better things to be doing
than standing around here all day waiting on your convenience.
Sure and you don't have Counselor Mervyn to be looking after
your interests."

Although the prisoners would have liked to ask questions
about the points that were causing their perturbation, they decided that to do so at that moment might be unwise. It was
clear from the burly Irish sergeant's demeanor that he was no
more enamored of them than were the other two peace officers.
They had no doubt that the part they had played in Foote's
trial was creating the hostility. Taking a warning from the reminder that the attorney did not represent them, neither
wished to try the patience of any of the trio, as this could offer
an excuse for punitive action to be taken against them. For all
that, neither was easy in his mind as Bratton coupled their
wrists together behind their backs with the handcuffs—which
would not be comfortable when riding in a car, to say the least
—and ordered them to start moving.

Passing the turnkey, with the sergeants close on their heels,
Chiverton and Schulman ascended the stairs leading from the
cellblock to the ground-floor passage at the rear of the courthouse. The back door was wide open and, beyond the low perimeter wall of the judicial building's parking lot, they could
see the pleasant and moderately expensive houses at the opposite side of the street. Both the lot and the surrounding area
appeared to be deserted as they went through the door side by
side. However, if they had glanced behind them on leaving the
building, they would have seen something calculated to increase rather than diminish their misgivings.

Instead of following their prisoners, the two peace officers
had stepped apart so that each was standing behind the wall on
either side and not in line with the doorway. The precaution,

inexplicable as it appeared on the surface, proved to be justifiable. Two heavy-caliber rifles crashed from an upstairs window of the building directly opposite the rear exit of the courthouse.

The house in question was owned by Judge Robert J. McCrindle, although it was now empty as he was in court and his family on vacation.

The bullets missed Chiverton and Schulman by such a narrow margin that each felt the wind as they passed close to his head. Then the bullets flew onward to shatter harmlessly against the floor of the passage behind the prisoners.

Even as they were yelling in fright—but before either could so much as think of trying to retreat into the safety of the courthouse—the two Rangers plunged through the doorway. Their movements were so smoothly coordinated that, combined with the fact that Bratton had leaned the trench gun against the wall an instant *before* the shots were fired, it seemed they might have anticipated such a contingency was going to take place.

While Breda sprang to one side, swiftly snapping the butt of the Winchester carbine to his right shoulder, Bratton reached for Chiverton and Schulman. Taking hold of the pair who were nearly panic-stricken, he flung them behind him with all the strength he could muster, and he was noted for the power of his muscles. Traveling in an uncontrollable twirling rush, they were propelled to safety. As they were hurtling across the threshold, they heard the Scottish sergeant commence firing with all the rapidity allowed by the lever-action mechanism of his weapon. They were unable to see at whom he was shooting, or whether he was meeting with any success, but no more bullets came in their direction.

Despite having been removed from the potentially dangerous location, the prisoners found their position something of a mixed blessing. They had been flung into the shelter offered by

the building with great force. As their wrists had been secured
behind their backs by the handcuffs, they were unable to use
their arms as a means of regaining control of their movements
or retaining their equilibrium. First Schulman and then
Chiverton, who was the lighter, lost his balance. Each crashed
to the floor in a most painful manner. Nor was their suffering
relieved to any great extent by hearing Bratton yelling exult-
antly that the Scottish sergeant had "got" one of their would-
be assailants.

"That's what I was figuring on doing, Paddy," Breda pointed
out, lowering his carbine and gazing across the parking lot.
" 'Cepting that I was hoping to make it both of them. I'll get
that old corn-sheller of yours, then go and see if I can make it
two straight while you take care of Chiverton and Schulman."

"The devil a bit of that I'll be having, Colin!" Bratton protested, turning around. "*I'll* get the little darlin' and come with
you." After stepping into the courthouse, he picked up the
trench gun and looked to where the turnkey appeared from the
cell block. "Take care of these two for a spell, will you, Barney?" he said.

"What happened?" the turnkey asked, his leisurely arrival
indicating that he had been unaware of the shooting.

"Seems I must have heaved them back inside just a little mite
harder than was good for them," the Irish sergeant replied.

"Well, yes, it sort of looks that way," the turnkey admitted,
also glancing at the recumbent and squirming pair. "Only,
without wanting to sound nosy or nothing, how come you-all
heaved them back inside?"

"Seemed like the right thing to do," Bratton asserted, gesturing with the trench gun toward the hollows left in the stone
floor by the bullets. "Seeing's somebody tried to make wolf bait
of them as soon's they went outside. And, though we'd sooner
not, Colin 'n' me're going to take out after them's was figuring
on doing it."

6

I WASN'T DOING AS YOU PROMISED

"I say there, Officer," Reece Mervyn called, introducing a note of amiability he was far from feeling into his voice. "What's going on?"

Ever since he had been a child, being subjected to severe stress or violent emotions had had a detrimental effect upon the actions of the attorney's bowels.

Feeling the usual pangs assailing him as he was leaving Judge Robert J. McCrindle's chambers at the conclusion of the unpleasant and most disturbing interview, Mervyn had hurried to the lavatories adjacent to the side door of the courthouse. While he was sitting in one of the cubicles, he could not prevent himself from contemplating various ways in which he might take revenge for the affront to his dignity, although he was aware that he had no way of implementing such plans.

All the attorney's considerations on the subject of vengeance achieved was to prolong his stomach spasm. As a result, almost a quarter of an hour elapsed before he could compose his churned-up emotions sufficiently for relief to come. He had been alone in the lavatories all that time and, such was the sturdy way in which the building was constructed, he had not been able to hear the shooting in the parking lot. He was, therefore, unaware that anything out of the ordinary had taken place. Nor was there anybody in sight who might have informed him as he emerged from the lavatories and went through the side exit. Turning toward the front of the courthouse, he found some of the local peace officers were forming what was clearly a cordon across the areaway between it and the next building. Although his thoughts were mainly on how quickly he could leave Marlin and Falls County, he was curious enough to try and discover what was happening.

"Huh?" exclaimed the man to whom Mervyn had addressed the question, swinging around quickly and acting as if surprised to hear a voice from his rear. Big and burly, he wore the uniform of a sergeant in the Marlin Police Department. Although he clearly recognized the speaker—or, more likely, because he did—a frown came to his face and there was no suggestion of a matching amiability in his voice as he inquired, "Didn't you hear the shooting?"

"What shooting was that?" the attorney asked.

"Seems like somebody took the notion to put blue windows in those two jaspers of your'n," the sergeant replied.

"Which two men do you mean?" Mervyn wanted to know, being aware that the term "put blue windows in" meant "to shoot." He was genuinely puzzled as he had only one member of his staff with him.

"Those two no-account burley-cue comics you brought in to give Handsome Phil the alibi that got him off," the peace officer elaborated, making no attempt to conceal his doubts with regards to the veracity of the men in question.

"They aren't *my* men!" the attorney protested, always alert to the possibility of having his manipulations of evidence exposed. "It was my client who told me of their connection with him. I even had to have them brought here on a subpoena before they would agree to give evidence."

"Whatever you say," the sergeant answered, showing no indication of being impressed or even convinced by the explanation he had received. "Anyways, somebody threw lead at them just now."

"Was Mr. Foote hurt?" Mervyn inquired, having deduced from the peace officer's first comment that neither Seth Chiverton nor Irvin Schulman had been hit.

"I shouldn't reckon so," the sergeant declared sardonically, "seeing's how he wasn't with them when it happened."

"He wasn't with them?" the attorney repeated.

"Nope," the sergeant confirmed. "Benny Goldberg and Dutchy Soehnen took him off with them in their car as soon's they fetched him out of the courthouse. What I saw, they didn't go around the back to pick up Chiverton and Schulman afore heading out of town."

"Why didn't they?" Mervyn challenged.

"I don't know and didn't ask," the peace officer admitted, his attitude indicating he considered the matter was none of his business.

"Who did the shooting?" Mervyn asked.

"I don't know nothing about that, neither," the sergeant replied, displaying no greater interest than he had throughout the previous conversation. "We heard the shots, then Colin Breda yelled for us to keep everybody away from the parking lot while him and Paddy Bratton went after whoever had done it. The chief of police said for us to do it, which's good enough for *me*."

Nothing the attorney had heard was making the situation any clearer. He had not known that the Texas Rangers intended to transport Philip Foote and the two bootleggers separately to Texarkana. Nor was he able to think of any reason why this should have been done.

Unless . . . !

Provoked by a memory, a sensation similar to that of being touched on the spine by an ice-cold hand struck Mervyn. He remembered how his client had reacted to being informed of the fake alibi he was organizing. Foote had objected to being placed under such an obligation to Chiverton and Schulman. Nor had he been entirely satisfied with the attorney's promise that they would be unable, even if they were brave enough to try, to exhort any more than the agreed payment for the service they would render.

Although Foote had finally and reluctantly given the appearance of yielding to Mervyn's wishes on the matter of the fake alibi, long experience with criminals had taught him how little they could be trusted. It was possible that the gang leader had only pretended to accept his assurances and decided to take steps to ensure the two bootleggers would be unable to create problems after they had served their purpose. In which case, he could have persuaded the Texas Rangers to take him to Texarkana in a separate vehicle. Provided they were offered something in return, they might agree.

The price, Mervyn felt sure, would not have been money. Neither Goldberg nor Soehnen had ever taken bribes. Nor had Major Benson Tragg, for that matter, and he alone could have authorized the change in the arrangements. However, he might have been agreeable if he was offered a suitable inducement, such as being given information that could help bring about the arrest and conviction of somebody who was wanted by the law.

Considering the possibility, Mervyn was confident that the victim could not be Hogan Turtle or himself. Foote was unlikely to know anything sufficiently incriminating about the master criminal, and the attorney had taken such care in covering his own tracks that the gang leader would be unable to offer more than unprovable suppositions. On the other hand, if the victim of the betrayal was of some importance in the underworld—as would almost certainly be the case if it was to be the reward of such a concession—Mervyn might also benefit. On being arrested, a person with any standing among the lawbreaking fraternity was sure to seek his services as attorney for the defense.

"Are you-all figuring on going to see them?" the sergeant inquired, breaking into Mervyn's train of thought as he was drawing his partially satisfying conclusions.

"Who?" the attorney asked, momentarily puzzled by the question that had jolted him so abruptly from his reverie.

"Chiverton and Schulman," the peace officer supplied.

"No!" Mervyn answered definitely, having no intention of allowing himself to become involved if his suspicions regarding Foote should prove correct. However, knowing how peace officers operated when seeking to acquire information, he decided it would be advisable to expand upon his instinctive brief negative response in case his reactions should be reported to the two bootleggers. "Were either of them hurt?"

"Not so far as I know," the sergeant replied.

"Then I don't think there's any need for me to go and see them," the attorney declared. "After all, it's not as if they were my clients, and I'm sure Sergeants Breda and Bratton are doing everything possible to catch whoever did the shooting. They'll have more than enough on their hands without me bothering them. Besides, I have to be setting off for Fort Worth. I've business there demanding my attention as soon as possible."

"So you'll soon be pulling out, huh?"

"Just as soon as I've collected my bags and car from the Palace Hotel."

"*Bueno!*" the peace officer stated, making no attempt to conceal his feelings. While he despised the two bootleggers for what they had done, he had nothing but contempt over the way in which Mervyn—who had hired them, even though this almost certainly could not be proven—was now obviously casting them aside. "It'll save us good old boys keeping an eye on you."

"Keeping an eye on *me!*" the attorney repeated indignantly. "Do you mean that you've been keeping *me* under surveillance?"

"Not the way you're figuring it was," the sergeant corrected. "It's just there's some around town who weren't took kindly with how you was set to get Foote off, and the chief didn't want anything to happen to you in his bailiwick."

"Tell him there's no need for him to worry any more on my account," Mervyn ordered rather than requested. "Even if I wasn't leaving his bailiwick, as you call it, in the very near future, I'm quite capable of taking care of myself."

"He'll be right pleased to hear it," the sergeant asserted dryly. "And so will all the boys in the department, seeing's ain't none of us had a day off watch since the trial started."

Annoyed by the peace officer's attitude of open animosity and derision, the attorney decided to bring the conversation to an end. Without saying another word, he started to walk forward. The police and deputy sheriffs had made the assembled people move away from the entrance to the areaway and, as Mervyn came from it, some of them started booing. Feeling a red flush come to his cheeks, he was starting to turn in the direction of the Palace Hotel—a more expensive establishment than the one in which Simeon Oakes had taken a room—when he heard a voice he recognized calling his name. Looking over his shoulder as he came to a stop, he frowned as he saw his confidential clerk emerging from the crowd and hurrying toward him.

"What's wrong?" Mervyn demanded, only just remembering in time to hold down his voice. He was aware that his employee should have set off to carry out the precautionary supervision about which he had warned the two Texas Rangers who had collected Foote from the courtroom. "Why are you still here?"

"It's the car, sir," the newcomer replied, his nasal Midwest accent filled with a suggestion of whining apology. "I can't get it to start!"

When Wilfred Plant was addressing his employer—or anybody else in a position that he accepted as being superior to his own—although he did not go so far as to refer frequently to his "humble" origins, there was invariably much in his demeanor to suggest from whom he was descended on his mother's side.*

Tall, gaunt to the point of being almost skeletal, and with rounded shoulders, Plant had a lean and miserable set of features, which his thinning mousy-brown hair did little to enliven. During working hours, he always dressed in somber black clothing more suited to an undertaker than the senior clerk of a successful and wealthy attorney. Sidling in a furtive fashion rather than walking, he rarely met the gaze of anybody with whom he was talking for more than a few seconds at a time. All in all, unless he was dealing with a person over whom he was confident he could assert a measure of authority,** he conveyed an impression of nervousness and downtrodden subservience.

"Why the hell can't you?" Mervyn challenged angrily.

The irascibility with which the attorney reacted was caused more by the memory of his far from respectful or pleasant

---

* The researches of fictionist-genealogist Philip Jose Farmer—author of, among numerous other works, *Tarzan Alive: A Definitive Biography of Lord Greystoke* and *Doc Savage: His Apocalyptic Life*—have established that Wilfred Plant was descended from an illegitimate daughter of a scullery maid and Uriah Heep, self-professed "humble" clerk, peculator, and blackmailer, details of some of whose career are recorded by Charles Dickens in *David Copperfield. J.T.E.*

** An example of how Wilfred Plant behaved when communicating with a person he considered to be of a lower social status is given in Case Three, "The Deadly Ghost," *You're a Texas Ranger, Alvin Fog. J.T.E.*

treatment at the hands of Judge McCrindle and the peace officer than out of any forebodings over the possible danger to Foote. He was already starting to discount the gang leader as a former and not entirely satisfactory client to whom he was no longer under any obligation.

"I—I don't know, sir," Plant confessed, being able to drive without having taken the trouble to learn anything about how and why the vehicle functioned. "The engine wouldn't start when I—"

"When you *what*?" Mervyn said with a growl, his suspicions aroused by the way in which the clerk brought the explanation to an end.

"W-when I tried to start it so I could follow them," Plant replied, deciding it was not advisable to mention he had left the vehicle unattended while he took an attractive young woman—to whom he had offered a ride to Texarkana—for a drink in a nearby tavern. She had gone off in a huff when it became apparent that there was something wrong with the engine and he did not know how to rectify it. "I tried everything I could, but it wouldn't start."

"Did you go to the service station and have them send somebody to take a look at it?" Mervyn inquired, feeling sure there was something he had not been told.

"Yes, but there was nobody there," the clerk answered, with just a trace of defiance apparent to anybody who knew him as well as his employer did. "I waited for a while. Then, as nobody came, I thought I'd better come and let you know what had happened in case Mr. Foote should telephone and ask why I wasn't doing as you promised."

"You did the right thing," Mervyn conceded just a trifle grudgingly, being aware that he could not adopt too highhanded an attitude with an employee who knew so much about his frequently illicit activities. However, in spite of his disinclination to become further involved in the affairs of the gang leader, he realized he could not dismiss the matter and must at least make a show of having kept his promise, or word of his having failed to do so might reach other potential clients, making them reluctant to pay for his specialized services. With that in mind, he went on. "Go and see if they've opened yet. Then, if they can't fix it, hire another car. I don't think those Rangers will chance doing anything to Mr. Foote, but he might complain if he finds out you didn't follow him."

7

WHO TOLD THEM TO TRY TO SHOOT US?

"Well, how'd it go, gents?" asked the turnkey, looking around as the door that he had closed when the two Texas Rangers left was opened. When he saw who was entering he relaxed. "Did you get them?"

Something over twenty minutes had elapsed since the bullets had narrowly missed Seth Chiverton and Irvin Schulman.

After the other peace officers had set off in search of the men who had done the shooting, the deputy sheriff had given his attention to the prisoners. On examining them, he had ascertained that—although each had been hurt by landing on the hard stone floor of the passage—neither was seriously injured. Their wrists had been grazed by the handcuffs. Having lost his hat while falling, the "straight man" had a lump raised on the back of his head where it had come into contact with the floor. Some skin had been torn from the heels of the comic's hands, but his fears of having broken his back had proved groundless.

Satisfied that neither prisoner required more qualified medical attention, the turnkey had collected the means to perform first aid. While he was attending to them, despite being curious, he had refrained from asking any questions about the shooting. Nor, each being more concerned with his own suffering than in talking, had Chiverton and Schulman offered to discuss it between themselves when he had completed his task and ordered them to sit on the floor until their escort returned to collect them. For all that, they were clearly ill at ease. He had considered this was only to be expected after they had had such a narrow escape.

"Sure and though Colin had put down one of the varmints, it was a clean pair of heels the other showed us," Sergeant Aloysius "Paddy" Bratton answered. Then he nodded to where the two prisoners were sitting with their backs against the dividing wall glowering resentfully at him and continued. "And is it any trouble this pair of darlin's 've been giving you, Barney?"

"Nary a bit," the turnkey stated. "They're neither of them hurt too badly either."

"It's no goddamned thanks to you that we weren't!" Chiverton protested, glaring indignantly at the burly Texas Ranger. "You could have made us bust our necks, or backs, the way you threw us in here!"

"Could I have, now?" Bratton inquired, but with a noticeable lack of contrition or sympathy, leaning his Winchester 1897 model trench gun by the door as he had prior to the shooting. "And wouldn't that've been the pity if I had?"

"They're not showing what I'd call a whole heap of gratitude, Paddy," Sergeant Colin Breda stated, exhibiting a similar dearth of sympathy as he studied the prisoners sardonically and placed his Winchester 1894 model carbine alongside his companion's weapon. "Maybe they'd sooner we didn't do anything at all that might help to save their hides the next time somebody starts throwing lead at them?"

"Next time!" Schulman repeated, having noticed the emphasis placed by the Scottish sergeant on the two words and employing a tone close to his high-pitched stage voice in his agitation. Ignoring the pain caused by his hurried movements, he forced himself to his feet. His pudgy features registered a growing alarm as he went on. "What do you mean by '*next time*'?"

"Like Sergeant Bratton told the turnkey, one of them's lit a shuck and's still on the loose,"* Breda explained, refraining from saying Paddy as he was addressing a person for whom he had no liking. His whole demeanor expressed what the prisoners considered to be far greater satisfaction than sympathy over the information he was imparting. "Could be he's the kind of jasper who takes pride in his work, or maybe even *enjoys* doing it. Which being, might be he'll take the notion to make another stab at doing what he's been told to do."

"Where do you come off with that mother-something 'what he's been told to do'?" Chiverton wanted to know, also having accepted the suffering caused by standing up quickly and displaying just as much consternation as was being shown by his partner. "Who told them to try and shoot us?"

"I wouldn't say that anybody asked them just to *try*," the Scottish peace officer corrected dryly. "Fact being, I'm willing to bet's they were *told* to do it."

"You'd be advised to take heed of what Sergeant Breda says, darlin's," Bratton went on in a confidential tone. "Sure and I've never the once known him offer to bet on *anything* at all unless he was certain he'd be the winner. I reckon it's his Scotch blood that makes him so cagey."

---

* "Lit a shuck": Old West cowhands' term for leaving hurriedly. It was derived from the habit in the night camps of trail drives and roundups on the open range of supplying "shucks"—dried corn cobs—for use as extemporary lanterns by anybody who had to leave the firelight and walk in the darkness. As the "shuck" burned away quickly, the user had to move fast if he wished to benefit from the illumination it offered. *J.T.E.*

"Scottish blood, Paddy," Breda objected. " 'Scotch' is a whiskey they make—"

"God damn it!" Chiverton snarled, glaring furiously from one peace officer to the other. With his partner nodding vehement concurrence, he went on just as heatedly. "You know something-well what I mean!"

"Yeah!" the chubby former comic supported. "Who done it?"

"Well, I'll be damned if I don't think neither of them *know*, Colin!" the burly Irish sergeant exclaimed, sounding as if he could hardly believe such ignorance was possible. "And what do you think of *that*?"

"Well now, Paddy, it just *could* be," the second Texas Ranger assessed, eyeing the two disconsolate prisoners with what might have been commiseration and pity for their lack of comprehension, although neither believed this to be his true feelings. "After all, it's likely been done by somebody they might figure is more than somewhat beholden to them for what they've done to help him—even if he isn't a feller's they'd claim as being a real close friend."

"You mean it was—?" Schulman commenced.

"He *wouldn't*, God damn it!" Chiverton spat out in the same breath, but his tone was far from being convincing.

"You'd likely know him a whole heap better than we do, having done business with him pretty regular according to what you said in the courtroom," Breda countered. He looked over his shoulder, then, turning his gaze to the front, he gave a shrug redolent of what could have been resignation and continued. "Anyways, you don't have to take just our word for it. Go and take a look out of the door there. They're bringing in the jasper I downed. Could just be you know him from someplace."

"I wouldn't be going right outside to take a look, though, was I you, darlin's," Bratton warned, as the prisoners began to advance hurriedly with the intention of confirming their suspi-

cions over who was behind the attempt on their lives. "Like
Sergeant Breda and me told you, the other miscreant gave us
the slip and, though I wouldn't reckon it's overlikely, he might
have figured we wouldn't reckon he'd have the spunk to try it
and's sneaked back to have another go."

Concluding without debate between themselves that they
had received a piece of very sound advice, Chiverton and
Schulman halted as they arrived at the door instead of going
through it. Standing in much the same positions as—unknown
to them—the two sergeants had occupied immediately prior to
the shooting, they looked cautiously outside. Although they
could detect no sign of life on the street or in the houses beyond
the perimeter wall, they saw two men carrying a loaded and
blanket-covered stretcher across the parking lot.

Showing no concern for the possibility of a would-be assassin
lurking in the vicinity, Breda strolled past the prisoners and
toward the newcomers.

Slightly taller and more heavily built than Bratton, the leading stretcher-bearer had on the general attire of a working cowhand. His high-crowned white straw hat was thrust back to
show black hair. Although this was cut short, his coppery
bronze features were those of a full-blood Indian. He had on
Kiowa moccasins, and a Colt Civilian model Peacemaker rode
in the open-topped holster of his *buscadero* gunbelt.

Slightly shorter than his companion, slender yet wiry and a
few years younger, the other stretcher-bearer was swarthily
handsome in a Gallic way. However, nothing of his attire suggested he might be involved in ranching. He was clad in a
jaunty white straw boater hat, a dark-blue blazer with a crest of
some kind on its left breast pocket, an open-necked white shirt
of some glossy material, a multihued silk cravat, gray flannels
even closer than Chiverton's trousers to being Oxford bags, and
mottled alligator hide shoes. For all his somewhat dandified
raiment, like the man in front of him, he wore a gunbelt—

although the Colt in its holster was a Government 1911 model automatic pistol—and displayed a badge indicating he too was a Texas Ranger.

Having frequently been in contact with various law enforcement agencies throughout Texas even prior to becoming involved in bootlegging (they had in fact indulged in confidence tricks to boost their earnings as a cross-talk act), Chiverton and Schulman recognized the approaching peace officers. Despite realizing that Sergeants David Swift-Eagle and Alexandre "Frenchie" Giradot were far from the regions in which their respective companies operated, the prisoners spared not a thought to the reason why they should have been selected to help at the trial in Marlin. Nor did the two perturbed men wonder where the stretcher upon which Breda's victim was being carried had come from at such short notice.

At that moment, Chiverton and Schulman were solely interested in discovering the identity of the blanket-covered shape on the stretcher.

"Who the hell is it?" the former straight man demanded, gesturing with his right shoulder as his hands were still manacled behind his back and beating his companion to the question by a fraction of a second, as the Scottish sergeant reached the other two peace officers and they all came to a halt a short distance from the door.

"Well now, that's not for me to say," Breda replied. Drawing back the blanket just sufficiently to expose the head of the shape it was concealing, he went on. "See happen one or the other of you can tell us who he is."

"Well, I'll be damned!" Chiverton spat out, at the same instant as Schulman with equal fury was making an identical identification. They glared at the uncovered face of Philip Foote's second in command and started to move forward. "It's *Butch Cope!*"

"Go right ahead, if that's the way you want it, darlin's,"

Bratton offered, as the couple moved forward. "It's not real likely he will have, but if it's so minded he is to do it, that other feller will've had time to sneak back and be waiting for you by now."

"Wha—" Chiverton began, pausing and looking over his shoulder as he was on the point of leaving the building.

"He might aim straighter next time," Bratton pointed out. "Happen he's there, that is."

Realizing what had been implied by the Irish sergeant's first cryptic comment, the straight man was already reversing his direction hurriedly. No less quick on the uptake, Schulman had also changed his mind about going outside in order to make a closer examination of the motionless figure on the stretcher. After returning to the shelter offered by the walls on either side of the door, they both avoided showing more of their heads than was necessary as they resumed looking outside with caution.

"Something told us you just might know him, gents," Breda claimed dryly, replacing the blanket. "Will you tote him down to the sheriff's office for us now they've seen him please, Dave, Frenchie?"

"Be a real pleasure to do it," Swift-Eagle assented without hesitation, his English fluent and suggestive of his having had a college education. "Or, the way he looks, it might save time if we take him straight to the undertaker's parlor."

"You do it any old way you've a mind, *amigo*," the Scottish sergeant authorized in a disinterested fashion. "Likely we won't see you again afore we leave for Texarkana, so say howdy you-all to all the boys in Company A and Company D."

"We'll do that," Swift-Eagle promised, and Giradot nodded concurrence. "Don't take any wooden wampum along the way, paleface brothers. Are you ready to move, Frenchie?"

"Any time you are, *mon ami*," the second stretcher-bearer confirmed.

"It looks like I owe you an apology, Paddy," Breda declared, returning to the passage as the other two sergeants were carrying away their burden. "They *were* being laid for out back of here."

"There's devil the bit of need for you to be apologizing, Colin," Bratton objected. "Sure and didn't I think you'd called it right when you said they'd be holding off until we was well clear of town? I wasn't expecting anything to happen *this* soon, either."

"God damn it!" Chiverton wailed, staring in an accusative manner from one peace officer to the other and back. While his partner was gobbling a similar complaint almost incoherently, he continued with considerable heat. "You *knew* that son of a bitch was gunning for us and you still let us go walking out there to get shot!"

"Well now, I wouldn't go so far as to say we *knew* what was coming," Breda contradicted, but not in any form of an apology. Rather his tone was sardonic and grew even more so as he elaborated upon the exculpation. "Word *did* get to Major Tragg that maybe Handsome Phil wasn't *entirely* overjoyed by thinking about having a couple of longhorns like you boys with such a strong hold over him, on account of you just having happened to be selling him some bootleg liquor on the night he was *supposed* to be raping and killing that li'l chorus girl up to Dallas." He paused for a moment, as if wishing to allow his audience time to digest the information he had already given, then went on. "There was even some talk that he could be thinking about how that same hold ought to be pried loose a mite. But there wasn't anything *definite,* which Counselor Mervyn kept saying there *must* be all through the trial, we could use as an excuse to pick up and hold Butch Cope on."

"And isn't that the rights of it, darlin's?" Bratton supported, clearly sharing his companion's thinly disguised pleasure over the disturbing and alarming news they were delivering. "There wasn't *nobody* at all went to the major and said outright, 'Excuse me, sir, but I thought you ought to know's Handsome Phil's told Butch Cope to gun down those two good old boys from Texarkana when they get fetched out of the courthouse without him.' Now if that, or some such similar, had been said, we could've took steps to stop it happening and saved you both some grief."

"Why, that goddamned, mother-something son of a bitch!" Schulman yelled, having been staring open-mouthed from one peace officer to the other all the time they were talking. The enormity of the possibility that Foote had ordered the assassination of himself and his partner filled him with such rage that it drove every other consideration from his head and he continued, "He tried to have us killed after we lied—"

"Bag your head, you stupid bastard!" Chiverton interposed savagely, pushing across the space between them and ramming his shoulder into the chest of the former comic. He was alert to the danger posed by the indiscreet comment Schulman had been making, and, as the other was silenced by being jolted backward a couple of steps, he resumed speaking in a voice charged with warning. "They can't try that son of a bitch for what he did again now he's been found not guilty, but they could sure as shit nail *us* for perjury!"

For a moment the pudgy man glared at his assailant and seemed to be on the point of retaliating. Then a realization of why Chiverton had spoken and acted in such a fashion came to him and he relaxed.

"Anyways, we stopped *them* nailing *you*," Breda drawled, having watched the interplay, his attitude suggesting he considered the matter was closed. Picking up his Winchester carbine, he went on. "Now we'd better be making a start for Texarkana."

"That we had, darlin's," the Irish sergeant agreed as he was retrieving his trench gun, also making no attempt to induce the comic to enlarge upon the interrupted admission or to question the straight man's statement. "Sure and haven't we wasted enough time already."

"How about that bastard who sided Butch Cope?" Schulman asked, staring worriedly at the open door. "He could be out there waiting for us!"

"Shucks no, he's not likely to have come back," Breda replied. "And, even if he should have, it won't be with a rifle. He dropped his when he lit out, and I reckon that, between us, Sergeant Bratton and I can hand him his needings happen he should come close enough to try and get you with a belt-gun."

"I didn't see you fetch back no goddamned rifle!" Chiverton objected as the Irish sergeant nodded agreement.

"Or me!" the comic seconded, showing no greater sign of being reassured.

"And no more we did, darlin's," Bratton admitted. "Sure and didn't Sergeant Swift-Eagle and Sergeant Giradot offer, out of the goodness of their two hearts, to tote it and the one Butch Cope used back on the stretcher for us along with himself?"

Catching his partner's eye as he noticed the other was about to speak, the straight man shook his head in a prohibitive signal.

While considerably relieved by the suggestion that neither Breda nor Bratton appeared interested in seeking enlightenment over the potentially incriminating admission he had prevented Schulman from completing, or from his own almost equally ill-advised declaration that implied they had committed perjury, Chiverton was drawing conclusions regarding the omission. Having learned something of the means by which peace officers sought to obtain information, he guessed what had been happening.

Suspecting that their prisoners had lied in the witness box, the sergeants had been using the attempt on their lives to try to acquire confirmation. What was more, due to Schulman's ill-considered remark and—although Chiverton preferred to gloss over this aspect—his own words, they had almost succeeded. With that in mind, he wanted to avoid prolonging the conversation. If Breda and Bratton were willing to oblige, instead of trying to make the most of the opportunity they had been offered, it was all right with him.

"Come on, Irv," the straight man commanded. "I reckon we can count on these gents to look out for us."

"Huh?" Schulman grunted, staring at his partner. Then, accepting that the other knew what he was doing, he swung his gaze to the two sergeants and asked, "Hey, are you going to make us ride all the way to Texarkana with our hands behind our backs?"

"That wouldn't be neighborly of us, Paddy," the Scottish peace officer drawled. "Now would it?"

"That it wouldn't, Colin," Bratton agreed, grasping the trench gun in his big left hand and reaching into the side pocket of his jacket with the right to bring out two keys. "Turn round, darlin's, and I'll put them on the other way."

Once again, Chiverton silenced whatever comment his partner was obviously on the point of making by delivering a warning shake of his head. Taking the hint, Schulman allowed the transference of the manacled wrists from behind to in front without speaking. With the change made for both of them, the prisoners were escorted from the courthouse. Constantly scanning the area beyond the perimeter wall, they were guided to an uncompromisingly angular, somewhat ugly, black 1922 Hudson Essex Coach four-door sedan. After they had taken the backseat as instructed, their escorts also climbed aboard. After starting the engine, Bratton drove them from the parking lot and, reaching the main street clear of the still-assembled crowd, set off along it toward the edge of town.

Having watched the vehicle pass through the window of the Last Chance Tavern, which—as its name implied—was on the outskirts of Marlin, the only customer went to the public telephone. After picking up the receiver, he gave an out-of-town number and, on being connected, said, "They're on their way in one of those Hudson Essex Coaches, *señor*. You can't mistake it, it's a black, four-door sedan. Unless something happens to delay them, they ought to be reaching you in a couple of hours or so."

8
NOBODY *WOULD DARE TRY IT!*

"Hey there, feller!" greeted the man who was coming through the door inscribed "MANAGER, Private," his voice indicating disapproval. "Sounds to me like you're in one all-fired hurry."

"I am!" Reece Mervyn confirmed, having found the lobby of the Palace Hotel deserted on his arrival and having sought to attract attention by pounding several times upon the bell on the reception desk. "I want to check out! Where's the clerk?"

"He's like 'most everybody else in town," the man replied. "Down to the courthouse seeing what's doing."

"Then send for him *immediately*!" the attorney ordered with considerable asperity, having much the same kind of attitude as his senior clerk when dealing with those he regarded as his social inferiors. "And have a couple of the bellhops come up to my suite to help me with my bags."

"I can't do neither," the man stated flatly.

"Do you know who I am?" Mervyn demanded.

"Sure, I know who you are, *Counselor*," the man admitted,

FLINT
IF HE HAD TO DIE, AT LEAST IT WOULD BE ON HIS TERMS..

Get a taste of the *true* West, beginning with the tale of *FLINT* FREE for 15 Days

Hunted by a relentless hired gun in the lava fields of New Mexico, Flint *"settled down to a duel of wits that might last for weeks...Surprisingly, he found himself filled with zest for the coming trial...So began the strange duel that was to end in the death of one man, perhaps two."*

If gripping frontier adventures capture your imagination, welcome to The Louis L'Amour Collection! It's a handsome, hardcover series of thrilling sagas by the world's foremost Western authority and author.

Each novel in The Collection is a true-to-life portrait of the Old West, depicted with gritty realism and striking detail. Each is enduringly bound in rich, Sierra-brown leatherette, with padded covers and gold-embossed titles. And each may be examined and enjoyed for 15 days. FREE. You are never under any obligation; so mail the card at right today.

Now in handsome Heritage Editions

Each matching 6" x 9" volume in The Collection is bound in rich Sierra-brown leatherette, with padded covers and embossed gold title... creating an enduring family library of distinction.

although the way he emphasized the honorific and his tone in general suggested the knowledge did not please him. "But that don't make no never-mind. All the bellhops are with the clerk and, afore you say it, *I* don't aim to leave the desk untended to go chasing after them."

A red flush of annoyance suffused the attorney's features as he studied the speaker.

Big, well made, and in his middle-fifties, the man was bare-headed, with short-cropped grizzled hair and a deeply tanned face in need of a shave. His attire—a well-worn brown leather jacket, an open-necked tartan shirt, and corduroy trousers tucked into calf-high untanned boots that laced up the fronts— seemed more in keeping with a hunting camp than the elegant entrance hall of the best hotel in Marlin. Nor was his laconic Texas drawl anywhere near as polite as that of a menial employee should be when speaking to an influential client, and that was all he struck Mervyn as being, a menial employee, despite having come from the private office of the manager. Obviously, as he was aware to whom he was speaking, he shared the general animosity that had been displayed by other officials and citizens of the town.

Being used to a fair amount of deference on account of his legal skill, which gave him considerable power and authority, as well as through his connection with Hogan Turtle, Mervyn was already in a far from amiable mood due to the treatment to which he had been subjected since the end of the trial. Ordinarily he was far too thick-skinned to worry about how his triumphs in the courtroom might be regarded by others. However, on this occasion, he had become increasingly perturbed by the open hostility directed at him. This had not been restricted to his unsatisfactory interviews with Judge Robert J. McCrindle and the police sergeant.

No other trial in which the attorney had participated had ever aroused such depths of animosity on the part of the public.

Although there had been no attempts at physical abuse as he was talking with Wilfred Plant before returning to the hotel, he was aware this was due solely to the presence of so many peace officers. For all that, the police and deputy sheriffs had done nothing to prevent him being assailed by boos and shouted insults. These had ended and the protestors were diverted by the arrival of the judge on the steps of the courthouse to give the press interview he had promised.

For once Mervyn had no desire to speak with the reporters. Having seen the hostility created as a result of the outcome of the trial, he sensed that he would not be given the kind of favorable publicity that had greeted many of his earlier defenses. With that in mind, and considering that to linger would be injudicious to say the least, he had grown firmer in his resolve to leave Marlin and Falls County with the least possible delay.

The reception he was receiving at the hotel was doing nothing to cause the attorney to change his mind.

"I don't care for your attitude, my man!" Mervyn warned, adopting a demeanor that had never failed to quell any hotel employee who incurred his displeasure.

Until this time.

"Well, now," the tanned man replied calmly. "Happen I figure on selling it, I'll know there'll be no use offering it to you."

"By God!" the attorney barked, putting on all the awesome dignity and threat his years in the courtroom had taught him to attain. "That's enough from you. Within two minutes of my reporting your insolence to the manager, you'll be fired."

"He's not here either, *Counselor*. And, even if he was, he couldn't do spit about firing *me,* seeing's how I *own* the hotel."

"*You* own it?"

"*I* own it."

For a moment Mervyn was on the point of dismissing the claim out of hand. Then, realizing that such a challenge would be tantamount to calling the speaker a liar, an appreciation of the possible consequences caused him to refrain. To do so outside the sanctity of a courtroom where he would have the protection offered by the law against physical reprisals would be ill advised and could even prove dangerous. There was an aura about the man that implied he would resent most strenuously— but might, under the circumstances, welcome—having his veracity impugned by a person for whom he clearly had no liking.

"In that case, *sir*," the attorney exclaimed, contriving to retain a timbre of menace in his voice, "having seen your attitude, I consider it is only fair by my friends to warn them against *ever* coming here."

"I'm right pleased to hear *that*," the proprietor answered, showing no sign of being perturbed by the threat. "Fact being, should they be friends of yours, Counselor, I'd sooner not have them under my roof, and I'm real pleased to hear that you'll soon be out of here, comes to that."

"You know what you can do with your hotel?" Mervyn asked, in what he hoped would be a parting shot.

"I reckon I've a notion what you've got in mind," the proprietor countered blandly. "And, happen you can do the same with your bags after *you've* packed them, you'll be able to tote them out of here without needing the bellhops."

"Hey!" Philip "Handsome Phil" Foote exclaimed, realizing that Sergeant Benjamin Goldberg was driving the dark-blue 1922 Templar four-door sedan in a southerly direction. "This isn't the way to Texarkana!"

"Well, now," Sergeant Hans "Dutchy" Soehnen answered laconically, sitting on the backseat of the vehicle at the right side of the prisoner. "That could be 'cause we're *not* taking you to Texarkana."

"What's the game, damn it?" Foote demanded, staring at the burly Germanic guard in a mixture of challenge and anxiety.

"You know what it is," Soehnen claimed.

"Like hell I do!" the gang leader contradicted.

"I don't believe you do," Soehnen conceded. "Hey, Benny, it looks like Counselor Mervyn hasn't told him."

"That's just what it looks like, Dutchy," Goldberg agreed.

"What didn't he tell me?" Foote asked, swinging his gaze from one to the other of the sergeants and showing more alarm.

"Seems like you're not what could be called popular with some folks—" Soehnen began, sounding as if he was surprised by the need to explain.

"Who the hell cares what that bunch of small-town hicks think?" the gang leader exclaimed with a disdainful snort.

"It's not *them* I'm talking about," the blond sergeant warned, clearly far from displeased by being able to deliver such disturbing information. "There's been so much whooping and hollering in the newspapers since you were arrested about how owlhoots are being allowed to get away with breaking the law, it's got peace officers all over Texas running the owlhoots on the loose ragged. Which same's got *them* more than a mite riled at *you*."

"That's the living truth," Goldberg seconded. "Fact being, there's even talk that some of them sort of figure you should be taught better."

"Hah!" Foote snorted, but there was a strong suggestion of perturbation under his truculent demeanor. "*Nobody* would dare try it!"

"I can name one feller who would," Goldberg asserted.

"And me," Soehnen supported. "Even though you've been using his tophand shyster, you're only small potatoes to him."

"*Hogan Turtle?*" the gang leader guessed, trying without any noticeable success to sound disbelieving. Then he went on, but it was more in the fashion of one who was trying to reassure himself than make a statement. "It can't be *him*. He wouldn't've let Reece Mervyn defend me if that was how he felt."

"Could be he hadn't reckoned on how things would turn out when he gave the word for it," Soehnen countered. "Comes down to a right sharp point, though, nobody's come right out and said it's him who's figuring on doing the teaching."

"They haven't, Dutchy," Goldberg agreed. "But they do say he's real riled about the way things have been stirred up. Look at what happened to that longhorn up to Denton. Maybe he's a friend of yours, Mr. Foote. His name's 'Side-wheeler' Heifer."

"He's nothing but a mother-something pimp and no friend of *mine*!" the gang leader protested indignantly, but his curiosity was too aroused for him to let the matter drop. "What happened to him?"

"Seems he worked over one of his tail-peddlers a mite too enthusiastic down to San Antonio and lit a shuck to hide out in Denton when he heard Hogan Turtle had passed the word for everybody to keep things soft and easy," Goldberg explained. "Do you know Rapido Clint and Comanche Blood?"

"I've been hearing some talk about them just recently, but our trails haven't crossed," Foote replied, then a memory came to him and he directed his gaze at Soehnen. "Hey! Wasn't it Clint who put—"

"Yeah!" the burly blond interrupted, his whole manner prohibitive. He clearly had no wish to be reminded of how he had been shot by the man in question who had then escaped from his custody.

"What'd they do, Sergeant Goldberg?" the gang leader inquired, taking the hint and having no desire to antagonize Soehnen.

"Found Heifer and worked him over so bad he's still not out of the hospital," the older sergeant replied.

"Did the Big *Hombre* send them after him?" Foote wanted to

know, employing the respectful sobriquet by which members of
the underworld referred to Hogan Turtle.

"He's been passing the word that he didn't and they must
have done it for personal reasons," Goldberg answered. "And,
much as I hate his guts, I don't think he's lying. There's no
reason why he should be."

"Could be they did it hoping it would put them in good with
him, them being so bad wanted around Texas and all," Soehnen
suggested, then gave the impression that a thought had just
struck him. "Hey though, I don't recollect having seen Butch
Cope in court this morning, waiting to find out what had happened to you."

"I told him to watch her father," Foote explained, concluding the blond wanted to change the subject for some reason and
that it might be politic to oblige. "Oakes wasn't there either
and, thinking how I'd heard he was a pretty fair sniper in
France, I reckoned he might have it in mind to gun me down
when he heard I'd been found innocent."

"So you sent Cope to down him first?" Soehnen suggested
coldly.

"No!" the gang leader contradicted vehemently. "Just to
take his rifle away from him, if that was what he had in mind."

"And that's what you reckon he's been doing?" Goldberg
inquired, a sardonic note having entered his hitherto not un-
friendly voice.

"That's *all* I told him to do!" Foote asserted, wondering
whether his second in command had been caught either while
or after carrying out the far less innocuous orders he had given.

"Then it seems like somebody else must have told him to do
something different," the older peace officer declared. "Major
Tragg figured on the same lines as you about Mr. Oakes and
what you might do. So Jubal Branch was dogging Cope to
make sure he didn't try to do the stopping permanently. Which
he didn't. Fact being, Jubal didn't even need to follow him for

long. He came from the hotel with his gear, went straight to his car, and lit a shuck out of town."

"He wouldn't *dare* run out on *me*!" Foote claimed, once again with a discernible timbre of uncertainty. "God damn it, I know too much about him for that!"

"Be that as it may, he *would* dare—and *has*," Goldberg countered. "Which could mean he's counting on you not being able to tell what you know about him. Anyways, to make sure nothing happens to you before you stand trial for the bootlegging at Texarkana, the major told us to take you to the State Prison Farm at Jonestown for safekeeping."

"Was I a suspicious man," Foote remarked, after having lapsed into silence for a few seconds during which the peace officers had refrained from speaking as if respecting his desire to consider what he had been told, "I'd think you were trying to throw a scare into me so I'll get riled and give Butch to you."

"Think any old thing you like," Goldberg authorized, showing no offense at the suggestion. "But we told Counselor Mervyn what was doing while the jury was out."

"God damn it!" the gang leader muttered, half to himself. "He never said anything to me about it!"

"Didn't he, though?" Goldberg asked, and glanced over his shoulder briefly, yet pointedly, at the other sergeant before continuing. "And there I was thinking he was just playing along with us after the trial when he acted like he still thought we were taking you to Texarkana."

"He never told me anything about it!" Foote commenced. Then an expression of consternation came to his face and his voice became charged with indignation overlaid by alarm as he protested, "You told *him* where I was being taken?"

"Why not?" Goldberg challenged. "He was your attorney."

"God damn it!" Foote almost wailed. "Didn't you know he's the Big *Hombre*'s mother-something man?"

"Well, yes, we have heard *rumors* that he might be," Goldberg confessed dryly. "Which's why we just told him there'd been a change to the plan. He wanted to know where we were taking you, but I said it would maybe come out better for all concerned if only Sergeant Soehnen and I knew."

"I thought he gave up on it too all-fired easy, though," the burly blond peace officer commented. Then, as he had done on a number of occasions since setting off from the courthouse, he gazed for a few seconds through the rear window. Turning to the front, he went on. "Anyways, *nobody's* following us."

"Nobody?" the gang leader queried.

"Not even that miserable-looking son of a bitch who does Mervyn's dirty work for him," Soehnen affirmed. "And the counselor told us he would be."

Twisting around hurriedly, Foote also studied the road behind the vehicle. He found, as the blond sergeant had claimed, that it was completely deserted as far as he could see. Furthermore, there was not even a trace of dust rising above the horizon to suggest it was being stirred up by a traveler beyond his range of vision.

Returning his gaze to the front, the gang leader ran the tip of his tongue over lips that had suddenly become very dry. He realized that, providing the instructions given for his protection by the attorney had been carried out, Wilfred Plant should be following the Templar despite the alteration to its destination. Discovering this was not the case did nothing to decrease the sense of foreboding that had begun to assail him as the conversation with the peace officers progressed.

Conceding to himself that Goldberg had been correct regarding his lack of importance as far as Hogan Turtle was concerned, Foote forgot his suspicions over the remarks about Butch Cope's activities. He could envision how adversely his future could be affected as a result of the other things he had been told. Learning he had aroused the animosity of someone so powerful in criminal circles and suspecting that his liberty would be curtailed for an indefinite period as a penalty for the supposed bootlegging, which was likely to be stiffer than usual as it had helped him obtain a verdict of "not guilty" at the trial, Cope might have decided the wisest course was to follow the orders received from the Big *Hombre* and leave him to his own devices. What was more, if he was to be punished at the instigation of Turtle, Reece Mervyn would have been instructed to refrain from further involvement in his affairs. This, in turn, would explain why the clerk was not following him as had been arranged.

All in all, the gang leader concluded he was in a most precarious situation!

Slumping worriedly on the seat of the car, Foote drew some consolation from remembering he was in the safekeeping of two very competent members of the Texas Rangers. What was more, he possessed sufficient knowledge of other criminals' activities to use in bargaining for his salvation. Until this could be done, no matter what their personal feelings on the subject might be, Goldberg and Soehnen would have to do their duty as law enforcement officers and give him their protection.

That was, the gang leader told himself with something of his usual smug self-satisfaction, another of the advantages of being a lawbreaker in a democracy.

9
WHAT WILL YOUR WIFE SAY?

"My, what a *magnificent* car!"

"It isn't bad," Reece Mervyn conceded as he looked around, employing the kind of mock understatement that suggested he felt much satisfaction where the object in question was concerned.

The comment about the vehicle had been made by a feminine voice and in tones redolent of much admiration. Its accent was that of a Bostonian—although not one who hailed from that city's wealthy and elite Back Bay district—and came to the attorney's ears as he was straightening up from placing his matched set of pigskin suitcases in the trunk of the car. The way in which he had replied indicated that the compliment and the sight of the person who made it were causing his mood to take a turn for the better.

Conceding that he was having the worst of the exchange with the man who claimed to be the proprietor of the Palace Hotel, Mervyn had repeated his warning that he would be checking

out shortly. When this had evoked no greater display of help-
fulness, or even contrition, he had stalked up the stairs to his
suite with what little dignity he could muster. There was no
need for the two bellboys he had requested to help with his
packing—he had done most of it before leaving for the courthouse that morning. After having relieved the distress caused
to his bowels by the latest affront to his pride, he had removed
his formal attire and placed it in one of the suitcases. After
donning an open-necked white silk sports shirt, a navy-blue
blazer bearing the crest of an exclusive Austin country club on
its left breast pocket, stylish flannel trousers, and brown shoes,
he had gathered his belongings ready to leave.

Being compelled to perform the menial task of collecting and
carrying down his baggage personally had done nothing to improve the attorney's temper. However, he had drawn some
slight consolation from discovering that the parking lot at the
rear of the hotel was unoccupied and the high walls surrounding it prevented anybody who chanced to be passing on the
street, or looking from the windows of the rooms, witnessing
his humiliation.

Until Mervyn had heard the voice, he was unaware that he
was no longer alone in the parking lot. Much to his relief,
however, the tone had been friendly. On turning, he had run his
gaze over the speaker with considerable interest and approbation. Even discounting the amiable and admiring attitude being
exhibited, which he found vastly more satisfactory than almost
all of the treatment he had received since the end of Philip
Foote's trial, he would have liked what he saw.

Although possessing a keen eye and a well-developed taste
for the pleasures offered by members of the opposite sex, the
attorney was not enamored of the current trend in feminine
fashion. It called for a trim, "boyish" figure, and he preferred
something more substantially curvaceous. The speaker could
not be termed buxom, but neither was she slender and willowy.

Nor, despite carrying a suitcase in her right hand, was there anything even remotely suggestive of masculinity about the way she walked. Rather the opposite, in fact. She had the kind of gait that—combined with her build—would have caused him to look after her if they had passed on the street and give thought as to how he might make her acquaintance.

About five feet six in height, pretty without being classically beautiful—although her face was made up just a trifle excessively—the woman appeared to be in her mid-twenties. Hanging to shoulder level and immaculately coiffured, her platinum blond hair was considerably longer than was currently regarded as *à la mode.* Made of mauve satin covered by an overdress of pearled orange tulle, with a matching silk hip sash, her dress showed off a curvaceous figure to its best advantage and left bare her arms. They were clearly strong without losing femininity. The low-cut, square neckline indicated she did not follow the current trend of seeking a flat-chested look with the aid of a device on the lines of a Poiret-designed "flattening brassière." In fact, the back was at such a level it suggested she wore little by way of undergarments above her slim waist and certainly eschewed an unboned knitted elastic girdle, a frequently employed aid to attaining a fashionable shape. Encased in sheer black stockings, her sturdy yet shapely legs ended in silver-colored shoes with very high heels. Like her clothes, the jewelry she had on—fair-sized gold loop earrings, three thin bangles of the same precious metal on each wrist, and a long pearl necklace—were fairly expensive. Grasping the neck of a silver lamé vanity bag, her left hand was devoid of any rings to establish whether she was married or engaged.

"Why, you're *far* too modest, sir!" the young woman declared as she halted her sensually motioned advance in front of the attorney. "Why, I've *never* seen such a magnificently *dashing* car. In fact, I've never seen one like it at all!"

Bending to put down her suitcase while speaking, the blonde

allowed Mervyn to see sufficiently into the neckline of the dress to be left with no doubt that the firm mounds of her well-developed bosom were natural and not produced by artificial means. On straightening up, she made no attempt to adopt the so-called debutante slouch—with hands on hips and pelvis thrown forward that many of her sex were currently adopting to help increase the "flat-chested" appearance. Instead, clearly aware of its appeal to members of the opposite gender, she stood in a way that was calculated to exhibit her well-endowed curves.

"That's not *too* surprising, my dear young lady," the attorney replied, still exuding a blatant false modesty and, as his lascivious gaze roamed slowly over the blonde's figure, trying to estimate just how little underclothing lay beneath the well-filled frock. Deciding it must be minimal, he elaborated, "When I bought it, I was told this is the first of its kind to reach Texas. None of the oil barons, nor even the governor himself, has one of this model."

There was considerable justification for the pride Mervyn was displaying over his car. It was a new 1923 Packard Single-Eight convertible coupe with a dashing red and black trim. In addition to possessing all the style and standards of excellence in workmanship that had already given its manufacturers pre-eminence in the international luxury-vehicle field, he had spent lavishly upon several items of the kind a later generation would refer to as "optional extras." The seats and steering wheel were covered in leopardskin instead of leather. Shining chromium plate sheathed the frame of the radiator, the mascot in the shape of a rearing horse on its cap, the lights, bumper, and the rearview mirrors attached to the holders of the spare wheels on the forward end of each side's runningboard. All the tires were "whitewalls," these being more costly than the usual variety.

"My, now isn't that just *something*!" the young woman exclaimed, sounding as impressed as the attorney had hoped—

even expected—she would be. Then she gave a deep sigh that caused the swell of her magnificent bosom to become even more pronounced and went on in a voice that held more than a hint of suggestive promise, "I'd just dearly *love* to be taken for a drive in such a *magnificent* car. It would be so *romantic.*"

"It is quite an *experience,* I can assure you, my dear," Mervyn answered, continuing to feast his eyes upon the generously displayed feminine pulchritude in front of him and wishing circumstances were such that he could exploit the situation to its full potential. "What's more, if I didn't have to leave Marlin straight away, I'd be honored to take you for a ride in it."

"Are *you* leaving too?" the blonde inquired. Glancing pointedly at the suitcase she had set down, she added hopefully as she looked back at the lawyer, "But I don't suppose you're going anywhere near Austin by any chance?"

"Is that where you're going?"

"I'll be spending a few days there. At least, I will providing I can find some . . . *suitable* . . . accommodation. That's why I've come here. That terribly *coarse* man who owns the Palace also operates a bus line, and I want to make reservations for this afternoon."

"Well, now, my dear," Mervyn said solicitously, his hopes rising with the possibilities that had been opened up by what he had just heard, and sharing the speaker's point of view as far as the proprietor of the Palace Hotel was concerned. "I must say you don't strike me as being the kind of young *lady* who would want to ride *anywhere* in something as cheap as a *bus.*"

"I don't *usually* ride on them and I'll admit I'm not exactly *thrilled* over the idea of having to do so *now,*" the blonde replied, showing considerable distaste for the prospect. "But there just isn't *any* other way for me to leave, and I can't *wait* to get away from this *terrible* little town. It's always so *dead.* Nothing *ever* happens here!"

"I know just how you feel about wanting to leave, my dear," Mervyn claimed truthfully and with considerable feeling. However, his ego caused him to continue. "But *something* has been happening here over the past few days."

"What was it?"

"The trial at the courthouse. You *must* have heard about it?"

"Oh, *that!*" The blonde sniffed, making no attempt to conceal her disinterest. "The people I've been staying with could talk about little else. Which only goes to show what a more dead than alive dump this town is. Was the trial what brought *you* here?"

"No," the attorney lied, not entirely displeased by the question. "I've just stayed overnight visiting with some business associates and, by a most fortunate coincidence, I'm going to Austin myself."

"You *are?*" The blonde gasped. Looking eager, she said, "Why, isn't *that* a coincidence. Do you live there?"

"No, but there are a few meetings I have to attend in the capital," Mervyn asserted. Putting on his most charming and gallant manner, he offered, "Perhaps you'd like to come in the car with me?"

There was no greater truth in the attorney's explanation of why he had to visit Austin than there was when he disclaimed any connection with the trial. He had only made the decision to travel to Austin on learning that this was the young woman's destination. Drawing conclusions aided by his experience of reading emotions gained in the courtroom, he guessed she would find the invitation attractive. Being of a most lecherous disposition, he was eager to take advantage of the opportunity he felt sure was being presented.

"Oh, *could* I?" the blonde inquired, her demeanor suggesting a blend of hope and willingness. *"Please!"*

"I'd be only too delighted to have your charming company during the drive, my dear," Mervyn declared, and continued in what seemed to be a matter-of-fact tone, so as to help pave the way for acquiring the benefits of his generosity. "From what you said just now, I assume that you don't know *anybody* in Austin and haven't arranged to stay anywhere in particular?"

"I don't know a soul there and, as this will be my first visit, I haven't the slightest idea of where to stay," the voluptuous young woman confirmed, as the attorney had hoped she would. "But I'm sure there must be some . . . *suitable* . . . hotels there in which I can find a room?"

"There most certainly are, my dear," Mervyn confirmed, having noticed the slight pause and emphasis on the word "suitable." "And, unless you feel I'm being too *forward,* perhaps you will allow me to suggest the most . . . *suitable* . . . when we arrive?"

"Why, that's most considerate of you, sir!" the blonde enthused. "I'm sure a *gentleman* like yourself will know all the *best* places."

"I most certainly do, my dear," Mervyn affirmed, once more drawing a most satisfying conclusion from the way in which the answer to his suggestion had been phrased. "And you can rely upon my recommendation. In fact, the hotel I have in mind is so . . . *suitable* . . . I'll be staying there myself."

"Oh, I'm so *pleased* to hear *that!*" the young woman declared. "I don't know about you, sir, but I've *always* hated being in a hotel, or town for that matter, where I don't know *anybody* to show me the sights."

"One should never miss seeing the sights, particularly in such an attractive and historically interesting city as Austin," Mervyn conceded. "And, unless you have other plans, I'd be delighted to show them to you."

"I haven't any plans at all and I'd be grateful to you if you would," the blonde stated. Then, studying the attorney's left hand speculatively for a moment, she continued. "But what will your wife say?"

"My *wife?*" Mervyn repeated, in a tone that suggested no such person existed.

"Yes," the blonde replied. "I mean, she might not *understand* if she was to hear that we'd arrived together and you were spending your time showing me the *sights.*"

"Don't let *that* cause you the slightest concern, my dear!" Mervyn suggested with—as he never allowed his marital status to deter him from indulging in the kind of association he was envisioning—such sincerity that he might have been speaking the truth. Exhibiting the left hand and silently blessing his habit of always removing his wedding ring when away from home, he continued. "I'm *not* married."

"You're *not?*"

"No. The right girl just hasn't come along so far."

"I know how you feel, neither has the right man for me—yet." The blonde sighed, but with an expression of calculation coming to her face. After a moment granted to let the attorney absorb what she had said, she put on a winning smile and said, "And, as we're both single, everything is quite proper!"

A growing sense of satisfaction was doing much to remove the final rumblings of the attorney's bowels. He considered that his affairs had definitely taken a turn for the better since his arrival in the parking lot.

Not only was the young woman attractive in the way Mervyn preferred, he felt sure she would be forthcoming sexually. What was more, while she might not have been born and raised in the Back Bay district of Boston, she had the bearing and demeanor that would make her passably acceptable at a certain *very* discreet hotel in Austin which catered to the kind of clandestine visit he was anticipating.

There was, Mervyn concluded, an added bonus. As the blonde was unaware of his true identity, providing he took a few precautions during their brief association, he was confident he could prevent her from finding out who he was and being able to name him as the father if she should become pregnant.

"Then it's all settled, my dear," the attorney announced, gesturing with the small bunch of keys he had taken from the right side pocket of his flannels. "And, just as soon as I've put your suitcase in the trunk, we'll be on our way."

"And just where the hell do you-all reckon you're fixing to take my *wife*, duhhh?" demanded a deep—if somewhat slurred —voice that throbbed with anger, before the loading of the young woman's solitary piece of baggage could be carried out.

"Oh, Lord!" The blonde yelped, her right hand fluttering to her bosom and her tone becoming filled with fright. "It's Joe, my *husband*!"

10

THE GENTLEMAN'S TELLING THE TRUTH

Looking around quickly as he heard the menacing words and the young woman's reply, Reece Mervyn lost all his feelings of licentious anticipation.

Having succeeded in crossing the parking lot of the Palace Hotel so quietly that his presence had remained undetected until it was announced, the cause of the change in the attorney's attitude was already passing in front of the Packard Single-Eight convertible coupe. Even without the substance of the question he had asked, his physical appearance was every bit as threatening as the words had sounded. Furthermore, the response from the blonde and her all-too-obvious fear suggested there could be grave cause for concern over his arrival.

Standing some three or four inches over six feet in height, despite being built on massive lines, the newcomer conveyed an impression of unhealthy corpulence rather than hard-fleshed fitness. Well worn and far from clean, his clothing implied that he might be a cowhand. However, the material of his grubby gray flannel shirt was stretched tight and his bulging paunch hung over the waistband of his patched Levi pants in a way that indicated he was little used to strenuous activity. Furthermore, he was bareheaded and his shaggy, coarse-looking brown hair was far longer than considered acceptable by members of that hard-riding fraternity. Nor was the kind of bushy and unkempt beard he sported any more favored by them.* Apart from concealing enough of it to prevent his exact age and looks from being determined, beyond a general implication that he was not old, the untidy hirsute appendage did nothing to improve his sweat-dappled and scowling face. The most prominent feature of it was a large and bulbous nose reddened by either the sun or, Prohibition notwithstanding, frequent consumption of copious quantities of hard liquor. Covered by black leather riding gloves, which were the newest items of his attire, his big hands dangled loosely by his sides. Rather than walking in an agile or sprightly fashion, he shambled as cumbersomely as a grizzly bear on its hind legs.

If the newcomer's demeanor was any guide, he was in no better mood than a male member of the species *Ursus horribilis* when freshly emerged from a winter's hibernation. For all that,

---

* The author has a strong suspicion that the trend in most Western movies made since the mid-1960s to portray all cowhands as long-haired and filthy has not arisen from the producers' desire to create realism. This kind of appearance was considered to be the "in" thing among the "liberal" element who were becoming increasingly influential in the film industry. Consequently, few clean-shaven and short-haired actors were available, particularly to fill supporting roles. Our extensive reference library does not contain a dozen photographs of cowhands—as opposed to mountainmen, army scouts, or gold prospectors—who had long hair and bushy beards. Furthermore, our reading on the subject and conversations with some of the older members of Western Writers of America—to which organization we have the honor of belonging—have led us to the conclusion that the term "long hair" was one of derision and opprobrium throughout the cattle country during the Old West and Prohibition eras, just as it still is today. *J.T.E.*

although Mervyn was momentarily far too disconcerted to give the matter any attention, it was surprising that one who appeared so ungainly could have approached without his footsteps being overheard.

In exculpation, however, the attorney had been far too engrossed in the conversation with the curvaceous blonde and too busy contemplating the possibilities it suggested to have paid any attention to what was going on around him.

"Well, you goddamned, fancy-dressed city slicker!" the bulky man rumbled in a Texas drawl with much the same kind of intonation actors frequently employed when portraying the role of a dull-witted country bumpkin, as he came to a halt just beyond reaching distance. His blue eyes were fixed on Mervyn's face and he never so much as glanced at the young woman. He went on speaking without waiting for a reply. "Didn't you hear me, duhhh?"

"I—" the attorney commenced, but was not allowed to go any further.

"So just where the hell've you talked this li'l gal of mine into going with you, duhhh?" the newcomer interrupted.

"You appear to be laboring under a serious misapprehension, my good man!" Mervyn declared, making an effort and forcing himself to adopt the kind of superior tone and demeanor that experience in the courtroom had taught him was most likely to produce the effect he was seeking when trying to overawe and quell a truculent, if poorly educated, witness for the prosecution. "The young lady merely stopped to ask if I could tell her the correct time, that's all."

"Just stopped to ask you for the time, duhhh?" the newcomer challenged, glowering in obvious disbelief. "What do you reckon I am, duhhh, stupid?"

"Now, Joe!" the young woman put in placatingly, if without any great conviction. "The gentleman's telling the truth!"

"Then what you all dressed up and got your suitcase with

you for, duhhh?" the burly man countered, showing not the
slightest sign of being mollified or convinced by the explanation
and pointing almost lethargically at the object in question.
"You're figuring on running away *again*, that's what you're
doing. And this duded-up, mother-something city slicker's
helping you."

"I'm not!" the blonde contradicted.

"You for certain sure ain't, duhhh!" the bulky man rumbled,
before Mervyn could add an equally untruthful disclaimer to
the accusation. Reaching out clumsily with his right hand, he
grabbed the young woman by the right wrist and continued.
" 'Cause you're coming back home where you belong, see!"

"Let me go!" the blonde yelped. When the request was ignored, she turned her gaze to the attorney. "Don't let him
make me go with him, sir. I do so want to go and see the sights
in Austin with you!"

"So that's the way of it, duhhh?" the newcomer growled, in a
tone suggestive of having had his suspicions confirmed. He gave
his captive a shove and released his hold on her wrist as he was
speaking, so that she was propelled toward the back door of the
hotel. With this done, he swung to face the attorney. Lifting his
big fists, he announced in a threatening fashion, "Now see what
it gets you, duhhh. Here I come, ready or not!"

Regardless of the indication given by the blonde that she was
still willing to accompany him to Austin, which he had thought
to be most ill advised and inconsiderate under the circumstances, Mervyn had had no intention whatsoever of intervening. It was, however, not the discovery that he was in error
where her marital status was concerned that was causing him
to refrain from taking her off, for he possessed the kind of
mentality which found an additional erotic satisfaction from
having sexual intercourse with a woman he knew to be married,
considering such an act to be a demonstration of his superiority
over the husband he was helping to cuckold.

But in this case, even though the affair had not been consummated, the attorney realized he could be facing grave danger.

Nor did Mervyn believe that, where such an obviously dullwitted and antagonistic hayseed was involved, he would be able to *talk* himself out of his predicament.

Watching the bulky newcomer lumbering closer and commencing such a slow and clumsy roundhouse punch he might as well have announced verbally how he intended to attack, the attorney felt relieved. While the situation was still not entirely free from peril, it was clearly less serious than Mervyn had anticipated.

Mervyn had been a boxer of more than average ability during his days at law school, adding as a precaution a knowledge of roughhouse tactics that would have caused his immediate disqualification if he had employed them in a formal bout. Despite having given up the kind of rigorous training schedule required to ensure complete physical fitness when he had become well established as a lawyer, because it called for an abstinence from the pleasures of the flesh to which he was growing attracted, he still worked out in the gymnasium often enough to feel confident he could cope with such an unscientific adversary.

What was more, the attorney concluded that—in addition to gaining some satisfaction for the various humiliations he had suffered recently without being able to retaliate—beating the hulking brute to a pulp for what would pass as self-defense might produce another benefit. He believed the blonde would be so grateful for her salvation that, particularly if she was offered the protection of his legal prowess, she would present herself to him all the more readily as recompense for his services.

Such was the utter lack of competence being displayed by the enraged newcomer that Mervyn not only found time to draw his satisfying conclusions, but was able to decide upon the most suitable tactics for dealing with the situation.

Ducking under the blow without the slightest difficulty, so slowly was it approaching, the attorney shot forward his left fist. He was aiming for what his instincts as a fighter suggested would be the target best suited to his needs. That bulging belly would be so soft it could not absorb or stave off the kind of punishment he was intending to inflict. Being struck there would render the recipient incapable of fending off the continuation of the attack that Mervyn was intending to deliver. He would be able to carry out the battering without risk of reprisals.

Filled as he now was with a rosy glow of self-assurance and confidence, all Mervyn's earlier misgivings had left him. When the burly man had arrived, he was perturbed by the knowledge that they and the blonde were alone in the parking lot, even though the presence of witnesses would be at the best a mixed blessing. For anybody who came on the scene would almost certainly have taken the part of the newcomer, particularly if they had been present at the courthouse and shared the general trend of public sentiment. Even if the arrival had been a policeman or a deputy sheriff, he might have favored the local resident; or used the "enticement" of the wife as an excuse not to intervene if he tried to avenge himself upon the person supposedly responsible for her defection.

But now, as he saw the situation, the attorney had no doubts about his delight at the lack of witnesses. He considered this meant he would be able to work off the animosity he felt toward the people of Falls County without interference and earn the gratitude of the voluptuous young woman. Unless he was mistaken, the latter was going to prove even more enjoyable than inflicting a savage beating on her husband.

Up to a point, the intentions of the attorney were faultless in their conception and delivery.

Driven with all the strength, weight, and precision Mervyn

could muster, his knotted fist flew straight to its assigned and unprotected target.

At which point, things began to go wrong.

On making their contact, Mervyn's knuckles did not sink deep into the expected flabby and yielding flesh. Instead, the impact was against something beneath the tightly stretched material of the big man's grubby shirt that had a similar consistency to the dummies packed with coir used for tackling training in the game of football.

While the recipient took a long and rapid pace to the rear, that was the only noticeable effect. He did not gasp, grunt, wince, or gave any other discernible indication that the retreat was caused by pain from the blow.

Although a realization that something was radically wrong suddenly burst into the attorney's head, it arrived just an instant too late for him to be able to avert the continuance of the line of action to which he had committed himself. Mervyn's other fist was already rising with the intention of meeting the victim's jaw after the first punch had caused him to bend at the waist and present it as a target. Unfortunately, despite the follow-up blow having been thrown with a similar skill to that of its predecessor, the anticipated presentation of the chin failed to materialize.

Not only had the big man contrived to withdraw in an erect posture, he proved he was in no way incapacitated.

Swaying his torso to the rear a trifle with a deft ease that was surprising when compared with his earlier lethargic movements, the newcomer caused the second blow Mervyn launched to miss. Carried onward by its impetus, the fist flashed by a couple of inches in front of his face and continued to rise. Having carried out the evasion successfully, still showing not the slightest trace of his previous clumsiness, he brought his clenched right hand around and up very swiftly.

Once again an apprehension of impending peril had begun to

bite into Mervyn. The sensation was only momentary, being driven away by pain.

Hurtling into the attorney's exposed and unguarded solar plexus with an even greater force than he himself had been struck, the burly newcomer's fist produced the kind of effect that had eluded his assailant. Feeling as if his whole stomach was being driven through his backbone, Mervyn let out a strangled croak of agony and bowed at the waist like a closing jack-knife. Nor was that the end of his misfortunes. Although driven backward, he was not granted sufficient time for him to be beyond the reach of the other massive fist as it was aimed in his direction.

Seeming to grow rapidly larger until it filled his entire range of vision, the black-gloved hand met the attorney's descending face. Torment erupted through him as, with blood gushing from his nostrils and mouth—accompanied by his false teeth, the top plate broken—he was compelled to straighten up. He was in no shape to put up resistance, but this did not bring an end to his suffering.

Still proving to be vastly more competent than had been suggested by the apparently inept way in which he had launched his first blow, the big man continued the attack. Stepping forward and—by accident or design—crushing the undamaged portion of the dentures underfoot, he directed his leather-sheathed right knuckles against the side of the inadvertently offered jaw. Bone snapped as Mervyn was spun around and crashed against the hood of the car. Rebounding helplessly from it, he was unconscious before he sprawled limp and supine on the ground.

Taking into consideration the alarm she had exhibited on the arrival of the massive newcomer whom she had identified as her husband, the behavior of the young woman following the commencement of the attack would have puzzled Mervyn if he had been in any condition to make an observation. Although she had regained control of her movements without falling after being pushed aside, she had neither fled nor tried to summon assistance by screaming. Instead, on the thud of the first blow reaching her ears, she had done no more than glance over her shoulder. Even the discovery that the attorney's attack had failed did not provoke her into what might have been considered positive action. Still standing with her back to the men, she returned her attention to the rear entrance of the hotel.

As the door opened, the young woman quickly slipped her right hand into the mouth of the reticule.

"Why, hello there!" the blonde greeted as Wilfred Plant came into the parking lot. "Just fancy meeting you here. Have you fix—"

"You!" the clerk exclaimed. "What are *you* doing he—"

Although he recognized the speaker as being the attractive and—he had anticipated—sexually obliging young woman with whom he had dallied prior to discovering the car in which he was to follow Philip Foote and the Texas Rangers would not start, Plant did not complete his question. His words died away as, chancing to glance past her, he became aware that all was far from being well in the parking lot.

The clerk had arrived with the news that he had been unable to obtain alternative transport in which to carry out the escort duty promised to the gang leader. From what he saw beyond the blonde, however, he concluded this would be of no interest to his employer, under the circumstances. Raising his startled gaze from where Mervyn was lying bleeding and motionless, an expression of alarm came to his unprepossessing features as the big man looked in his direction. Being of a far from courageous disposition, unless in contention with somebody over whom he was convinced he could exert authority—which most certainly was *not* the case at that moment—he decided his safest course would be to fetch help. With that aim in mind, he began to turn hurriedly toward the door through which he had emerged.

As soon as the clerk started to swing away from her, the blonde brought her right hand from inside the reticule. It appeared grasping a short, leather-wrapped billy which she swung with deft ease and speed. Given an added impulsion by the coil spring that formed its handle, the weapon struck Plant on the top of the head. His flat cap offered little protection and he crumpled in midstride. Going down as if he had suddenly been boned, he fell against and pushed shut the door.

When the big man saw that the young woman was preventing the new arrival from raising the alarm, he gave no indication of being surprised. Instead, nodding with satisfaction, he went and bent over her suitcase. There was still no trace of his former ungainly motions as he opened it and removed the two small cloth bags that were its sole contents. After stepping over the recumbent body of the attorney without giving it so much as a glance, he raised the hood of the Packard and placed the bags on the engine.

"Can I do anything to help you?" the blonde inquired, but in a different accent and with none of her previous tone suggestive of promiscuous sensuality.

"Just make sure nobody else comes out of the back door before I get through," the big man requested, unscrewing the cap and pouring the contents of one sack—which were metallic and *not* liquid—into the oil sump. While his voice still had the drawl of a Texan, it no longer employed the slurred timbre suggestive of wits that were less than sharp. "It won't take me long to fix things, although I surely hate to do it to such a fine car."

"Well, it's all gone off smoothly enough," the blonde commented, after having watched the burly man replace the cap of the sump and make an addition—which was *not* gasoline—to the fuel tank from the second bag. Crossing to pick up the keys dropped by Mervyn at the commencement of his abortive attack, she went on, "And thank heavens you won't need to keep saying 'duhhh' like some stage mooley." *

"It took in the city slicker there though, duhhh!" the man answered, tossing the now-empty bags into the suitcase and closing the hood of the Packard, resuming the manner in which he had spoken on his arrival.

"You look the part too," the blonde claimed. "Shall I drive?"

"I will," the man declared, reverting to what was clearly his normal voice and holding out his right hand. "That way, if the engine seizes up before we reach our car, it'll save us changing places so you can do the pushing."

"I'll say one thing," the blonde asserted, in either real or well-simulated disdain, surrendering the keys. "Chivalry might not be *dead,* but where *you're* concerned, it's sure limping badly."

* "Mooley": A theatrical term, probably derived from the supposed lack of intelligence of a mule, for an actor portraying an uneducated and stupid person. The characterization is frequently enhanced by deliberately slurring or mispronouncing words and frequently inserting the sound "duhhh" during a speech. The cartoon character Goofy produced by Walt Disney is probably the best known example of a "mooley" throughout the world. *J.T.E.*

11
YOU'LL BE BREAKING THE LAW IF YOU DO

"Look there, Colin," Sergeant Aloysius "Paddy" Bratton requested as he steered the black 1922 Hudson Essex Coach four-door sedan around a blind corner of the road. "Sure and going by the way that feller there's acting, I'm thinking he's wanting us to stop."

"It looks that way to me too, Paddy," Sergeant Breda confirmed. "You know him?"

"I can't be saying's I do," the Irish peace officer confessed. "But I didn't come down this way to stop off there for a meal, so I wouldn't be knowing if that's where he's from. How about one of the other of you two, darlin's?"

"I've never seen him before," Seth Chiverton asserted, peering ahead between the shoulders of the sergeants on the front seat. "How about you, Irv?"

"I couldn't say from here," Irvin Schulman replied. "Anyway, coons are the same as Chinks. They all look alike to me."

Having kept the vehicle moving at a good speed, Bratton had

already transported his party over the boundary between Falls and Limestone counties. Since leaving Marlin, neither of the prisoners had offered to open a conversation with each other or their escort. Nor had the two Texas Rangers done more than exchange the odd remark between themselves, and they had shown no inclination to talk with the handcuffed pair sitting behind them. They were still some five miles from Groesbeck, seat of Limestone County, when the Irish sergeant broke the silence.

The man who had provoked the remark from Bratton was a tall, lanky, and cheerful-looking young black. Although clad in a collarless blue shirt with the sleeves rolled up above the elbows, new Levi pants, and cowhand's boots, he had on an apron speckled by food stains, and a no-cleaner white chef's hat was perched on his head. The latter two items of his attire suggested he was employed, probably as fry-cook, in the kitchen of the small and not overimpressive diner at the left side of the road. Standing in the center of the thoroughfare, he was waving his hands over his head in the criss-cross fashion, which was one way of requesting a vehicle to halt. It was, in fact, a way indicating considerably more urgency than when merely soliciting a free ride.

"What's up, friend?" Bratton inquired amiably, looking out of the open window as he was bringing the Essex to a stop, despite having transferred his right hand to the butt of the Colt Army 1917 model revolver.

"Is you gents Texas Rangers?" the black man asked, having stepped aside when the vehicle drew near. "And, if you is, would you-all be taking them two fellers in the back to the pokey in Texarkana?"

"I reckon's you might say we're Texas Rangers," the Irish sergeant answered, gesturing with his left thumb to the badge of office he was wearing. "And it's not wrong you are in thinking we're taking these two fellers to the pokey in Texarkana."

"That being so," the man declared, "your boss wants to speak to you-all on the telephone."

"And what'd the name of this boss of ours be?" Breda challenged, also sitting with his right hand on the butt of his sidearm although his Winchester 1894 model carbine and Bratton's trench gun were resting between them.

"He allowed's it was Major Benson Tragg, or some such," the black man supplied. "And's how you two gents is Sergeant Bleeder and Sergeant Pattern. Least-wise, that's what it sounded like."

"Sure and it's close enough," the Irish peace officer asserted, relaxing and removing his hand from the weapon. "Shall I take it, or do you want to, 'Sergeant Bleeder'?"

"Sure and seeing's how it's yourself who's such a fine pattern of an Irish boyo," Breda countered with a grin, employing a broad parody of his companion's brogue. "I'm thinking 'tis yourself's should be doing the honors."

"Your boss allowed's how he wanted to talk to you both, gents," the black man warned, before Bratton could reply. "Reckoned it was something mighty important and so urgent you'd best both be on hand to hear what he'd got to say."

"Hey!" Schulman put in, as the two peace officers exchanged glances and seemed on the verge of speaking. "Seeing's we've stopped, I could do with going to the restroom."

"And me," Chiverton supported, "I'm damned near ready to piss myself."

"Sure and we wouldn't be wanting you to be incriminating yourself any the worse by doing such in an official vehicle," Bratton said dryly. "Would we, Colin?"

"Not so long as we have to ride in it," Breda seconded.

"Then you can go while we're seeing what the major's wanting to tell us, darlin's," the Irish sergeant authorized, his demeanor indicating he considered he was conferring a favor. Returning his gaze to the bearer of the information, he went on in a less bantering and more amiable fashion. "Go and tell the major's it's coming directly we'll be, will you, friend?"

"Sure, boss," the black man assented, and turned to walk away with a gait that was gangling but swift.

The black man moved with such rapidity that he was going into the diner before Bratton brought the Essex to halt in front of it.

While leaving the road and approaching the diner, the two sergeants had been alertly gazing about them. From all appearances, business was far from flourishing. There was no sign of activity from the building, nor any other vehicles to be seen in the vicinity. Apart from a small grove of cottonwood trees about a quarter of a mile to the rear and the slope around which the road curved and disappeared, the surrounding terrain was fairly open and seemed equally devoid of human life.

However, in spite of the deserted nature of the area, Breda climbed from the sedan holding the carbine, and Bratton carried the Winchester 1897 model trench gun as he emerged from behind the steering wheel.

"Hey!" Schulman yelped worriedly, glancing at the weapon held by the Scottish sergeant, as the rear door was opened and he received a signal to come out. "Are you expecting trouble?"

"Not 'specially," Breda denied. "What makes you think we might be?"

"Then what you carrying them guns for?" the former comic challenged, instead of answering the question directly.

"You don't reckon we'd leave them in the car, do you?" Breda asked sardonically, studying the scared expression on the other's pudgy features with undisguised amusement. "Get going inside and leave Sergeant Bratton and me to do any worrying that's needed."

"Sure and isn't that the good advice you're getting?" the Irish peace officer interjected, showing no greater concern than his companion over the possibility of danger to their prisoners.

"Get on in with you, darlin's. And it's hoping I am you can do what you have to do with the handcuffs on, because they're not coming off when it's out of our sight you'll be being while you're doing it."

Although far from convinced by either sergeant's comments and actions, the call of nature proved too strong for Schulman to continue the discussion. Being equally affected, despite sharing the misgivings of his partner, Chiverton also refrained from expressing his point of view. Instead, with the former comic close on his heels and their escort bringing up the rear, he led the way toward the front door.

If the way in which Bratton and Breda were carrying their shoulder arms cradled across the left elbow while following the prisoners into the diner was any guide, they were genuinely satisfied that there was no cause for alarm.

The building into which the party entered was little different in general appearance from thousands of similar establishments catering for the needs of travelers on the roads of Texas. There were a few booths along two of the walls, offering slightly more privacy and seclusion than the tables and chairs scattered around the room. Neither booths nor tables were occupied. Nor was anybody sitting on the stools at the counter.

For all that, the building was not deserted.

Nor was the black man who had stopped the car and now leaned against the wall by the telephone—the receiver of which was *on* the hook—with his right hand hidden behind his back, the only occupant.

Standing at the kitchen side of the serving hatch were two men clad in nondescript range clothing.

There was, however, nothing nondescript about the double-barreled, ten-gauge shotgun each man was lining in the direction of the new arrivals.

What was more, the pair and the cook were not alone.

Two men dressed in the same inconspicuous fashion stepped

swiftly through the swinging double doors of the kitchen. The shorter and more thick-set of them was carrying a well-used Winchester 1873 model rifle. Although a riding quirt was dangling from the right wrist of the other, he was unarmed as far as could be seen.

Proving that he belonged to the group and had not been an innocent, or coerced dupe, the young black man brought his right hand into view. He was grasping a cocked Colt Artillery model Peacemaker, and he handled it with the confidence only acquired by long experience.

It was impossible to tell whether the other four men were also black. Each was wearing a hood made from a flour sack that concealed his face and hair, and riding gloves covered every pair of hands.

"Stand still, you Rangers!" ordered the unarmed man, his voice that of a well-educated Southern who was used to commanding obedience. "We don't mean any harm to you!"

No matter what action the peace officers had intended to take, they were being hindered by their prisoners. Letting out exclamations of alarm, Chiverton and Schulman sprang backward. Instinctive though the movements had been, or rather inspired by panic, the frightened pair were acting against their own best interests. In retreating they collided with the men behind them, preventing either the trench gun or the carbine from being brought to a position of readiness.

"Set down your weapons, please!" the unarmed man continued, but—for all their apparent politeness—the words were as much a command as their predecessors had been. "As I said, we don't mean *you* any harm. It's those two lecherous, *girl*-despoiling bastards we want, and we intend to have them."

"You're supposed to be guarding us!" Schulman wailed, having been shoved aside by Bratton. Turning hurriedly, he saw the officer was not offering to move the barrel of the trench gun forward. "Why aren't you doing something?" he cried.

"We don't *want* to shoot, Rangers!" the unarmed man reiterated, his tone showing not the slightest lack of resolution. "But, if we have to, the Wisenheimer and the Dummy will be the first to go."

"Well, darlin's," the Irish sergeant said dryly, knowing the names that had been given were those used by the prisoners for their act when they were performing in burlesque and not merely terms of derision.* "And what would you be wanting us to do for you?"

"Why, sure," Breda supported. Having thrust Chiverton aside, he was also refraining from anything that might be construed as a hostile or threatening movement with his carbine. "Just tell us what we can do and, hot-damn, we'll make a stab at doing it."

"D-don't do *anything*!" Chiverton almost pleaded, and Schulman mumbled just as hurried concurrence.

"You mean we should surrender?" the Scottish peace officer inquired.

"Yes, God damn it!" the former straight man confirmed vehemently. "If you try anything else, you'll get me killed!"

"And *me*!" the erstwhile comic put in, darting a glare at his companion and clearly not enamored of the omission. Then he swung his gaze to the two men at the kitchen door and his voice took on a timbre of whining ingratiation. "You don't need to do nothing to us, fellers. Tell Handsome Phil we'll keep our mouths shut!"

"I'd say they're not after you for Handsome Phil, was I asked," Breda commented, still standing motionless apart from glancing at his companion. "How about you, Paddy?"

---

* According to the summation of entertainers in burlesque and vaudeville, a good "straight man" was worth three comics. So—as in the case of Bud Abbott and Lou Costello, or Dean Martin and Jerry Lewis, for example—the straight man was generally given billing ahead of the comic. *J.T.E.*

"Sure and I'm thinking you've got the rights of it, Colin," the Irish sergeant agreed, being just as careful to avoid movement. "I'd be saying this's more likely to be a personal thing between you and them, darlin's."

"That's how I see it too, Paddy," Breda asserted. "So it's *your* choice, *Wisenheimer and Dummy.* We'll play it the way you want."

The experienced eyes of the peace officers noted certain hints that had helped them reach their conclusions regarding the intentions of the party who had waylaid them. Despite his cheap clothing, the one who was doing all the talking carried himself with the erect bearing of a professional soldier. His tone and general demeanor were those of a person who was capable of exerting authority and having his wishes respected by others. While this alone would not have ruled out the possibility of him being a criminal or even a professional killer, other signs suggested such was not the case.

The most noticeable indication was the way in which the other members of the ambush party were armed. Shotguns were not infrequently included in the armory of the underworld, but they were invariably sawed off to increase their concealability and lethal qualities at close quarters. Those held by the pair at the serving hatch had not been subjected to such treatment. Each still retained barrels a full thirty inches in length, making them more suitable for pass shooting at migrating ducks or geese* than paid assassination. Nor was a Winchester 1873 model rifle generally included in the weaponry of modern outlaws. Furthermore, as more compact and easily hid-

---

* "Pass shooting": A variety of wild fowling in which, instead of being lured to close quarters by decoys or calls simulating their cries, the ducks or geese are taken as they fly overhead. As ranges of up to seventy and eighty yards are common, the shotgun needs a lengthy barrel. This is to ensure the load reaches its target with the pattern still sufficiently restricted to offer the chance of enough shot hitting to bring down the quarry. *J.T.E.*

den handguns were available—including the "Storekeeper" model—the sturdy and reliable Colt Peacemaker was now only rarely used by criminals in the commission of crimes.

"Do what the feller tells you!" Chiverton ordered, and once again his partner gave instantaneous agreement.

"Like Colin said, darlin's," Bratton remarked, his attitude signifying that the onus of responsibility for the surrender rested entirely upon the prisoners, and bending so he could place the trench gun gently on the floor. "It's *your* choice."

"Now your handguns, gentlemen," the spokesman ordered, after the Scottish sergeant had laid his carbine with equal care alongside the weapon of his companion.

"I'll not be dropping this, if 'tis all the same to you," Bratton stated, extracting the double-action Colt—using only the thumb and forefinger of his left hand—from the retention springs of his shoulder holster. "As you may be knowing, us Texas Rangers have to *buy* our own weapons and pay for any repairs they get to be needing."

"You can put them on the nearest table," the spokesman authorized, as—duplicating his companion's actions with an equal care—Breda was lifting the Peacemaker from its holster. "But please don't try any tricks. Those two aren't worth you getting injured to protect them, and we aren't going to kill them."

"Sure and we never thought you were," the Irish peace officer claimed, strolling unconcernedly to do as had been suggested. "What with the length of them shotguns and all, we didn't figure you was professional killers."

"We certainly are *not*!" the obvious leader of the party confirmed. The man by his side uttered an equally vehement agreement. "As you guessed, our interest in those two is purely personal. Take them out back, men."

"Y-you can't let them—" Chiverton protested, being disinclined to accept the declaration of intent and swinging to face the peace officers.

"It was *your* idea for us to give up our guns," Breda pointed out, stepping away from the table and leaving behind his revolver. "Now we have, there's not a whole heap we can do to stop them."

"And leave us not forget what was said about *you two* being the first to get gunned down if it's resisting we were, which wouldn't have let us get you to Texarkana alive as we're under orders to do," Bratton elaborated, also moving clear of his handgun. Then, looking past the prisoners, he continued in a somewhat harder voice. "Where're the folk who run this place?"

"There weren't any customers when we arrived and, as he'd sent his wife into Groesbeck to pick up supplies, there were only the owner and his black fry-cook here," replied the spokesman, to whom the question was directed. "We bound and gagged them, then put them in the storeroom so they couldn't raise the alarm when you came in."

Having left the serving hatch as soon as the sergeants discarded the revolvers, the two men came from the kitchen. They no longer held the shotguns that had been a major factor in quelling any desire to resist the peace officer felt, having exchanged these for, respectively, a Colt Peacemaker and Government model automatic pistol. While the third hooded man and the black man continued to cover the sergeants, they crossed the room. Each took a frightened, but unresisting, prisoner by the jacket collar and, using the weapons as an added inducement, ordered them to start walking.

"You'd best come with us, gentlemen," the leader suggested as Chiverton and Schulman were being escorted into the kitchen.

Obeying the politely given yet obvious order, the peace officers accompanied the hooded men and prisoners. While they were doing so, the fry-cook went to the front door. After closing and locking it, he turned around the sign in the window so it would read "Closed" to anybody outside the diner. After completing these tasks, he collected the weapons discarded by Breda and Bratton, then followed the rest of the party.

Taking the lead as the party left the diner by its rear door, the spokesman neither halted nor spoke until they reached a small clearing roughly at the center of the cottonwood grove. It was obvious that preparations for their coming had been made. A length of rope was fastened, at slightly over shoulder height, around the trunks of each of two adjacent trees.

"I'll trouble you gentlemen for the keys to the handcuffs," the leader commented.

"Do you mind if it's asking what for?" Bratton countered.

"They're to strip to the waist," the spokesman explained, indicating the clearly terrified prisoners with a contemptuous gesture from his quirt. "It will be easier on their clothes if they're free to do it, rather than having us cut them off."

"That sounds reasonable to me," the Irish sergeant conceded, and did as he had been requested. "Only, at the risk of sounding nosy, it's wondering I am why you'd be wanting them stripped that way."

"I'll tell you when everything is ready," the spokesman promised.

Having been liberated by the keys Bratton supplied, working as fast as their fumbling fingers would allow, Chiverton and Schulman divested themselves of all their upper garments. While this was being done, the two men from the serving hatch gave their handguns to the black man. Then, working with a commendable coordination, they grasped the comic by the arms. Despite being strong and a rough handful in a fight, his stage personality notwithstanding, he was in too great a state of terror to resist as he was dragged forward and secured between the trees by the ropes being tied to his wrists.

"W-what's this all about?" Chiverton croaked, watching what was happening with an expression of horror.

"You pair of lecherous bastards took out a couple of girls, neither of whom had reached her eighteenth birthday, got them so drunk on gin-spiked lemonade they didn't know what they were doing, then had your goddamned way with them," replied the spokesman, accepting the Winchester he was being offered and passing his quirt to its owner. "One wound up with a baby, which was bad enough. But the other one lost the child she was carrying, and, as a result, she may not be able to have any more children."

"They were *my* daughter and niece, you goddamned sons of bitches!" the man who had surrendered the rifle went on, his accent also Texan—if one of a lesser social status—making the lash of the quirt hiss viciously. "I aimed to kill you both, but the boss said no. Which being, I'm still aiming to make you both pay for what you've done."

"W-who are you?" Chiverton gasped, being aware that there could be a number of girls who might qualify as his victims as he and his partner had a penchant for subjecting girls in their teens to such treatment.

"Think about it while you're watching that fat bastard being handed his needings," the man with the quirt suggested. " 'Cause it's your turn next. But you can both count yourselves goddamned lucky. When the boss told me I wasn't to make wolf bait of you, I reckoned I'd 'Goodnight' the both of you."*

* We suspect that, as to "Goodnight" a bull produced a less detrimental—in fact, even a beneficial—effect, the man meant "castrate." The term came into being as the result of a discovery made by a famous cattleman of that name. He established that the chance of injury to the testicles of a well-endowed bull could be reduced by pushing the "seeds" up against the belly, cutting the empty sack, and stitching the skin together over them. It was estimated that doing so almost doubled the period of the bull's useful life. Colonel Charles Goodnight makes guest appearances in *Goodnight's*

"Hold hard there!" Breda barked, as the outraged father started to walk toward the trees between which Schulman was suspended. "Are you aiming to use that quirt on him?"

"Nothing else but," the stocky man confirmed, while the pair who had done the tying lined the Colts they had retrieved from the young black man up on the sergeants.

"You'll be breaking the law if you do," the Scottish peace officer warned, without moving apart from spreading his hands from his sides as an indication of his pacific intentions.

"Sure and isn't that the rights of it?" Bratton seconded, doing the same as his companion. "It's committing assault you—or *anybody else*—who does it will be."

"By God, yes!" the spokesman exclaimed, having turned his gaze to the Irish sergeant on hearing the emphasis given to the words *"anybody else."* "If *you* do it, J—you *will* be breaking the law!"

"Likely, boss," the vengeance-seeking father replied. "But I still aim to!"

"Not *you,*" the spokesman contradicted firmly, and pointed with his right index finger as a look of incomprehension mingled with annoyance came to the face of the man he was addressing. *"Him!"*

"Him?" the stocky man repeated, still showing no greater understanding.

"M-*me?* Chiverton gasped in almost the same breath, staring in consternation at the finger pointing in his direction.

"You!" the spokesman confirmed definitely. "And, by God, if you don't lay it on *hard,* I'll take the chance of breaking the law and make you wish you *had*!"

Showing the respect he felt for his employer, the stocky man held the quirt forward without further discussion. Running the

---

Dream, From Hide and Horn, Set Texas Back on Her Feet, and *Sidewinder.* There is a more detailed description of a Goodnight operation in *Waco's Debt. J.T.E.*

tip of his tongue over his lips, Chiverton accepted it with such hesitancy he might have believed the leather would be red hot. Covered by the two Colts, whose owners showed no sign of relaxing their vigilance, Breda and Bratton were not presented with any chance of intervening.

"D-don't you use that mother-something thing on me!" Schulman shrieked, looking over his shoulder as his companion walked toward him, but bound in such a fashion he was unable to do anything more positive about avoiding his fate.

"I—I don't have any choice, Irv!" the straight man pointed out hoarsely.

"Anyway, Dummy," the father added, "when he's through, *you'll* have your chance to do it to *him*!"

Taking a warning from the comment and paying no further attention to his partner's almost hysterical protests, Chiverton swung the quirt. Its plaited leather lash landed hard on the writhing white back, eliciting a screech of pain and leaving a vicious red weal. To give him credit, the straight man looked at the leader of his captors before—being ordered to do so—he continued with the flogging. Blow after blow landed, each delivered as vigorously as the first. In the beginning, the former comic shrieked profanities and threats. These turned into blubbering sobs interspersed by cries of agony as the quirt tore repeatedly into the quivering and, soon, bloody flesh.

"That's enough!" the spokesman stated as the twenty-fourth blow was delivered and its recipient subsided into a faint. "Cut him down and revive him. Then put the Wisenheimer up in his place so he can pay back what he's been given."

"Hot damn, Paddy!" Breda remarked, watching the orders being carried out. "I bet those two bastards are cursing the day they agreed to perjure themselves for Handsome Phil."

12

I DON'T KNOW EVERYBODY *IN FALLS COUNTY*

"Poor ole Reece Mervyn's jaw 'n' nose are busted and, way they looked, them fancy falsi-ficated teeth of his'd got tromped on," Sergeant Jubal Branch reported in a voice that might have struck some people as filled with sympathy although none of his audience considered it in that light. "Then, when one of Dex Armstrong's deputies found his car in that old cottonwood grove 'bout a mile out of town, all its tires had been ripped wide open. That fancy spotted cat's hide'd been torn to doll rags. There's not so much's one piece of glass left unbusted in it and all that hell-agrant painti-fying 'n' crow-mee-nimum's scratched up something awful. Didn't make a whole heap of never-mind about the tires being flat, though. It couldn't've been driven in on account of there being iron filings in the oil sump and sugar mixed with the gasser-lane, which hadn't done the mecker-nicals too much usefulness at all. Fact being, tooken all together, I'd say the counselor won't wind up showing much of a profat-ability out of getting Handi-some Phil found not guiltery."

It was nine o'clock in the evening on the day of the conclusion of Philip "Handsome Phil" Foote's trial.

Sitting with the big bluetick coonhound sprawling apparently asleep at his feet, the elderly peace officer was delivering his information in the dining room of a hunting cabin maintained by Judge Robert J. McCrindle close to the western border of Falls County. In addition to other members of the company of Texas Rangers to which he belonged, his commanding officer and the owner of the property were present.

"Let's hope he's taken out enough insurance on the car to cover the damage," Sergeant Alexandre "Frenchie" Giradot remarked, almost sounding as if he was sincere in the sentiment he uttered—but not *quite*. "It'll be a mortal shame if he hasn't."

"Well, now, *mon hammy*," Branch drawled. "Going by what he told the sheriff when he got to hear about it, he's got his-self caught neck deep and with the water up over the willows in that said morat-ual shame."

"The car isn't insured then, Jubal?" McCrindle asked—being aware that the term "water up over the willows" had originated in the days of the great trail drives as severe flooding was one of the most dangerous hazards faced by the cowhands handling the cattle—making no attempt to conceal his satisfaction over the possibility.

"Nary so much as a teensy in-sure-you-ate, Your Honorably," Branch confirmed, still employing a tone that seemed filled with commiseration, and his leathery features gave no indication to the contrary. "Seems he's been so all-fired busy since he took up Handi-some Phil's dee-fensive that getting it done plumb slipped his memor-able."

"I wish I could feel sorry for him," the judge declared. "But I *don't*. Does he know who did it and why?"

"He allows he didn't get hintrer-ducted formallike to the jasper, Your Honorably," the peace officer answered. "Seem's it was a real mean cuss's got the wrong notion 'cause his wife had stopped to ask the time o' day. Give the sheriff a pretty fair desper-craption of both of 'em. Way he told it, the gal was right pretty, with some more meat on her than's mostly these days, but all of it stacked right curvied in the right places—whichever he meant by *that*— and'd long, platter-nerum blond hair."

"Do you know her, Bob?" Major Benson Tragg put in.

A good six feet tall, in his late forties, with brown hair turning gray at the temples, the asker of the question was as lean and wiry as Jubal Branch, although his Texas drawl was suggestive of his having had a better education. Being dressed in attire more suitable for going hunting did not detract from the commanding force of his personality and presence. Belonging to a family that had long been associated with the enforcement of law and order in the Lone Star State,* he had acquired the reputation for being one of the shrewdest and most progressive peace officers in the New World.

"I can't recall her to mind," McCrindle confessed after thinking for a few seconds. "But I don't know *everybody* in Falls County."

"You'd likely know somebody who looked like she was described," Tragg stated with a grin. "Or you've changed a whole heap since the last time we went hunting together."

"I wouldn't know what you mean by that, Ben," the judge claimed blandly, but showing he was far from offended by the

---

* As is demonstrated in the Rockabye County series, which covers the equipment, duties performed by, and operations of a present-day sheriff's office, the Tragg family is still concerned with the enforcement of law and order in Texas. Some details of the careers of two earlier members who served as peace officers in the Lone Star State are given in *Beguinage Is Dead!* and *Set A-Foot. J.T.E.*

assertion. "And I still can't bring her to mind. How about her husband, Jubal?"

"He's what you might call tolerable noticer-able," Branch supplied. "Close to *seven* foot tall, just 'bout's wide across as Main Street, and heavy bellied with it. Dressed and looked like a saddle bum. Top of which, 'cording to the counselor, he looked mean's all get-out, with a big red boozer's nose, a heap of long brown hair, and a beard bushier'n an old-time mountain man fresh come from the high country to the rander-viewers."

"Huh!" Sergeant David Swift-Eagle grunted, darting a glance at the youngest Texas Ranger present. "A feller who looks like that ought to be easy to locate, even on a crowded street. Damned if he wouldn't stand out even more than Ranse here."

"Why, sure," Sergeant Ranse Smith agreed, his deep drawl that of a Texan who had received a good education. "But there's one good thing. I don't reckon anybody could mistake *me* for him."

There was some justification for the latter part of the Kiowa peace officer's comment, and the reply it had elicited.

While Smith would certainly stand out in any crowd, other than in size and bulk he appeared to have nothing in common with the man who had assaulted Reece Mervyn. Almost three inches taller than Swift-Eagle, possessing tremendously wide shoulders, he slimmed to a flat-bellied waist and his entire physique was indicative of exceptional fitness and health. He was in his early twenties, with short ash-blond hair. His almost classically handsome features were pleasant, tanned, and clean-shaven. He had on a black leather vest, to which his badge of office—glistening with newness—was fixed, an open-necked clean tartan shirt, and spotless Levi trousers such as a cowhand might wear, but the legs were tucked into his polished brown, calf-high, and low-heeled hunting boots. A British-made Webley-Fosbery automatic revolver rode in the flower design embossed Model 30 crossdraw holster at the left side of his George Lawrence Gunslinger belt. Behind the rig was a pouch holding two Prideaux Quick Loaders, each of which would allow him to feed six .455 cartridges into the cylinder of the unusual weapon with a single movement when the need arose to reload in a hurry.*

"I don't recollect anybody around Falls County who matches that description either," McCrindle declared, paying no discernible attention to the remarks of the two peace officers. "What does Dex Armstrong say about it, Jubal?"

"He's of the same mind as you, Your Honor-ably," Branch answered. "Wasn't neither him nor any of his deputies could bring the gal nor her husband to mind, which—'specially the one's's young 'n' spry—they wouldn't be likely to have missed somebody as shapeful as she's said to be."

"I know I *wouldn't*!" Giradot inserted, rolling his eyes in a particularly Gallic fashion.

"That's 'cause you're French, *mon hammy*," the elderly peace officer pointed out. "I mind how the fellers back to your old country used to go a-chasing after the mam-swells when I was over there with Black Jack and the A.E.F."** Swinging his gaze to the major and the judge, he continued in—although there was no noticeable change in his tone—a more serious vein. "Anyways, having heard tell's how the counselor doesn't allus stick upright and true-fully to his matter-rimonious vows, I sort of pushed him a mite further about what had come off. He allowed the girl never let on *she* was married until after her husband showed up all mean 'n' ornery. Afore that, she'd reck-

* More detailed information regarding the Webley-Fosbery automatic revolver is given in Part One, "Persona Non Grata," *More Justice From Company Z. J.T.E.*
** "Black Jack": Sobriquet of John Joseph Pershing (1860–1948), commanding general of the American Expeditionary Force in Europe during World War I. *J.T.E.*

oned's she wasn't hitched and'd been staying around town with kin for a spell, but was figuring on taking a bus ride down to Austin. 'Cepting for one thing's come out later, although the counselor wouldn't speak up and admit I'm calling the play right, I'd've reckoned he'd done the misorney-able and offered to let her ride there along with him. Which same'd explain what for her husband jumped him and done such meanness to his car."

"What makes you think otherwise?" the judge asked.

"According to what one of Dex's deputies was told while asking about them around the town, the counselor's head he-hooper, Wilfri-red Plant'd, been seen and heard getting friendly and offered a ride along of him to a gal who must've been her earlier that morning," Branch explained. "Only, when he got to his car, it wouldn't start up so's they could get going and she lit out on him."

"Cars break down all the time, *mon ami*," Giradot pointed out. "And when it happens, a girl who's been offered a ride tends to get riled."

"You'll likely be talking from hex-perry-mence, I reckon, *mon hammy*," Branch conceded dryly. "Only, reason being this 'n wouldn't start was it'd had its rotor arm wideelooped while he was lally-gagging with her. Which same, tooken with him allowing it was *her*'s whomped him over his pumpkin head in the parking lot at the Palace Hotel, strikes a half-smart li'l ole country boy like me as just a *teensy* mite such-pes-cerous."

"*She* hit him?" McCrindle queried.

"That's what he said," the elderly sergeant confirmed. "Allows she did it when, seeing what was happening to his boss, he turned to go for help."

"Then she and her husband must have been in cahoots!" the Judge deduced.

"Well, yes," Branch admitted. "That's how the sheriff reads the sign, and I float my stick along of him."

"But why did they do it?" McCrindle inquired.

"The counselor's not the most like-abled jasper in Texas, way he goes on in court 'n' private-airly 'cording to rumor," Branch supplied. "Could be they was after him to settle a grudge."

"He would have recognized them in that case," McCrindle objected. "Going by their descriptions, they're neither of them the kind of folk you'd be likely to forget."

"I ain't gainsaying it, Your Honor-ably," the elderly peace officer countered. "Only they was maybe settling it for some-body else."

"Who?" the judge wanted to know.

"Well, now, Your Honor-ably," Branch replied, "that's something neither the sheriff or me's got figured out."

"How about the girl's father, Jubal?" Smith offered deferen-tially, his demeanor redolent of respect for the man he was addressing. "He'd brought along a rifle, which looks like he was thinking about doing *something* should Foote get off, and he wouldn't take any too kind to the part Mervyn played in bringing about the acquittal."

"He wouldn't," Branch acceded, but the reservations with which he regarded the possibility was made without any sug-gestion of airing superior wisdom over the younger and much less experienced peace officer. "Only, having toted that old Winchester along what he thought was secretlike, I don't reckon he'd've hired anything else done."

"He didn't strike me as the kind who would hire *anything* like that done," Tragg assessed. "If he was so minded, he'd have done it himself."

"I'll go along with you on that, Ben," the judge seconded, having made the acquaintance of Simeon Oakes during the trial and formed a favorable opinion of his character. "He might have gone after Foote and Mervyn, but it would have been in hot blood and not by hiring somebody to do it for him."

"On top of which," the major went on, nodding concurrence,

"going by the way the girl and her husband took out Mervyn and Plant, what they did was planned well in advance. So it's my opinion that they were working off some personal grudge against him."

"Or for somebody else, but *not* Mr. Oakes," Branch drawled. "That's the way Dex Armstrong sees it, Maj'."

"Does he want us to lend a hand on it, Jubal?" Tragg asked, the Texas Rangers only being supposed to participate in an investigation if—as had been the case with the trial—they were invited by the local law enforcement agencies.

"Said he'd be right obliged if we would, seeing's how he's certain sure the gal and her husband don't hail from his baili-wick and're likely long gone out of it," Branch affirmed. "Are you of a same mind on it, Your Honor-ably?"

"I am," the judge declared. "A couple of strangers who looked like them couldn't have been around Falls County, much less in Marlin, for more than a few hours without getting talked about. If either, or both, had been here for days, I'd have heard some mention of them. Do you reckon they're tied in with the try at killing Chiverton and Schulman?"

"There's nothing to prove they were, or weren't," replied Swift-Eagle, to whom the question had been posed. "But I'd be inclined to say no to it. Wouldn't you, Frenchie?"

"I would, *mon ami*," Giradot confirmed, having teamed up with the Kiowa peace officer to investigate in the absence of Sergeants Benjamin Goldberg and Hans "Dutchy" Soehnen. "And the sheriff's of the same mind."

"What do you make of it?" McCrindle inquired.

"We started out by figuring the shooting was done because Handsome Phil isn't as grateful to those two longhorns for their help as you'd conclude he should be, seeing what they'd done for him in the witness box," Swift-Eagle obliged. "Which being, whoever he had trying to make wolf bait of them are likely professionals and not even part of his gang. Should that be the case, they'd be up and running for the tall timber as soon as things started to go wrong."

"Why didn't you see them?" McCrindle asked.

"They weren't anywhere we could from your place, Judge," Swift-Eagle replied, sounding a trifle defensive, as he and Giradot had been assigned to the task of watching the rear of the judicial building. "We heard the shots and Colin Breda cutting loose, but there was nobody in sight by the time we reached the street."

"No witnesses either," the Gallic sergeant added. "Which isn't too surprising, seeing as how almost everybody in town was out front of the courthouse when it happened."

"The way it looks to us," Swift-Eagle elaborated and, as he went on, Giradot nodded in agreement, "the shooting couldn't have been tied in with what happened to Reece Mervyn. Handsome Phil wouldn't have any cause to be riled at *him,* particularly as it was likely him who set up the fake alibi. Knowing how close Mervyn is to Hogan Turtle, Foote wouldn't chance trying to do anything even if he should have doubts, particularly not using hired guns to do it."

"I suppose not," McCrindle conceded. "Could the fellers who tried to shoot Chiverton and Schulman be the same who took them and made them cut each other's backs to ribbons with a whip on the road to Groesbeck?"

"I wouldn't reckon so," replied Tragg, to whom the two peace officers had reported via the telephone that had been used to lure them into the building. "If it had been them who tried to do the killing, they wouldn't have taken the chance of holding up Colin Breda and Paddy Bratton. Or restricted themselves to just making Chiverton and Schulman whip one another. They'd have started throwing lead as soon as the car stopped outside the diner."

"Then who were they?" McCrindle wanted to know.

"Colin and Paddy have no idea," Tragg admitted.

"Couldn't either Chiverton or Schulman tell them?" the judge suggested.

"Seems not," the major replied. "From what Colin said, it puts me in mind of a joke they used to do. Schulman would say how he'd had a letter from a man saying he'd kill him if he didn't stay away from his wife. When Chiverton asked if he was going to do it, he replied, 'I would, but the feller didn't sign his name.'"

"You mean there's so many after them for the same thing, they can't guess who it can be?" McCrindle guessed, having seen the point of the joke.

"That's about the size of it, Bob," Tragg agreed. "Colin and Paddy figure it was done as a result of those two horny sons of bitches having got a couple of girls pregnant while they were still playing the burlesque houses. That would explain why the man who did most of the talking called them the Wisenheimer and the Dummy instead of by their names. Anyways, I told Paddy and Colin to see happen they can cut those fellers sign *after* they've seen the prisoners safe to Texarkana."

"I'd like to say I hope they're successful. But, after what those two lying bastards did in my court, I *can't*," McCrindle drawled, knowing that the delay in commencing the investigation would reduce the chances of its success and feeling sure the point had not escaped the major. Instead of raising the matter, he elected to change the subject. "Did Butch Cope say what he was doing at the Brendon Hotel, Jubal, or who put him down?"

"Reckons he just went there to sort of keep an eye on the gal's daddy, Your Honor-ably," Branch replied. "He allows he didn't see whoever it was whomped him over his pumpkin head, nor knows anything 'tween then and when he come round in the jailhouse."

"His pockets had been turned out when Dave and I came on him, Judge," Giradot supplemented. "We found his wallet by him, empty. All his money, even the small change he'd got in his pockets, had been taken along with his watch and jewelry."

"God damn it!" McCrindle protested indignantly. "We don't have that sort of thing happen in Marlin!"

"You've never had the town so close to bursting at the seams with strangers, or so many of the municipal and county peace officers concentrated in one small area either," Tragg reminded the judge. "Even so, what happened could have been done that way to make it look like it was no more than an ordinary robbery."

"You mean that Simeon Oakes could have figured Cope would be around and made it look that way after taking him out?" McCrindle guessed. "What do you think of that, Jubal?"

"It's mighty smart figuring, Your Honor-ably, but there's just one thing wrong with it," the elderly sergeant answered, sounding almost apologetic over having to demolish the theory of a leading light in the legal profession. "I saw Butch across the street from the hotel, just *afore* I went up to make sure Mr. Oakes didn't have the notion to stop Handi-some Phil feeling so happy over having been found hinner-cerent. Which means he's got him a pretty fair ally-bical, was I asked."

"It would certainly hold up in a court of law," the judge assessed in his most judicial fashion.

The sound of a car approaching brought the conversation to a halt. It was stopped in front of the building. As everybody in the room looked around, footsteps came from the vehicle and crossed the porch.

"*Saludos, amigos,*" greeted Sergeant Carlos Franco, coming through the front door. "Benny and Dutchy called from Jonestown, Major. They got Foote there safely and with no trouble along the way."

"*Bueno!*" Tragg exclaimed. "Did they say whether the warden had taken the precautions I suggested?"

"*Sí,*" the Chicano peace officer confirmed. "They said he went along with them all the way."

"That's the best news I've had for a spell!" the major declared. "Thank God *something* has gone right!"

13

THEY NEVER PUT A FOOT WRONG

"Hey, in there! How about one of you *gentlemen* showing some of your Southern gallantry by helping me fetch in the coffee and cookies?"

The request, which was made in a feminine voice with the accent of one who had been born and raised in the better class society of New England, came from the kitchen of the hunting cabin. It prevented anybody from commenting upon the statement made by Major Benson Tragg with regard to the information he had just received.

"Like I told you before you started, Rita," Sergeant Ranse Smith replied, standing up. "All you have to do is ask."

The young woman who entered the dining room a few seconds later was very attractive, with a graceful carriage. There was a healthy glow to her tanned face indicative of much time spent out of doors, engaged in active pursuits. While her reddish-brown hair was cut in a fashionably short, curly and tousled looking, windblown bob, she clearly paid little attention to the current trend for the feminine figure. The thick white woolen turtleneck sweater, the kind of riding breeches known as jodphurs, and suede chukka boots covered a well-developed and curvaceous body that was far from being boyish in its contours. On the arrival of Judge Robert J. McCrindle at the cabin, she had been introduced by the major as Miss Rita Yarborough, but no explanation of her presence was given or requested.

"Do you know something, Jubal, Ben?" the judge remarked as he went to his car accompanied by Tragg and Sergeant Branch after having partaken of refreshments and talked for a short while longer about the events of the day. "Although I shouldn't be saying it, I won't exactly lie awake at nights feeling sorry for Mervyn, his clerk, Cope, Chiverton, or Schulman, happen whoever rough-handled them isn't caught. But it's that son-of-a-bitch Foote who sticks deepest in my craw. There's no doubt in my mind that, despite the verdict the jury had to bring in on the evidence they were given, he's guiltier than all hell."

"Nor in mine, Bob," the major admitted, and the elderly peace officer signified concurrence with a vigorous nod. "In fact, Schulman came close to admitting they'd committed perjury before Chiverton made him stop speaking."

"Even being able to *prove* they'd lied under oath couldn't change things as far as Foote's concerned," the judge growled bitterly and regretfully. "He's had his day in court on the charges that were brought and he can't be fetched back to face them again now the verdict's been delivered. Sure, I know it'll be jail and not just a fine for the bootlegging he was supposed to be doing on the night he raped and killed that young girl, but he'll still be getting off too goddamned lightly."

"That's the law of the land, Bob," Tragg said quietly. "And, although I'd be the last to say there's any foolproof way to change it and still give a square deal to the genuinely innocent, it can be twisted so many ways to save the guiltier-than-hell as well as protecting them."

"Like you say, Ben, that's the law of the land," McCrindle conceded, going to sit behind the steering wheel of his car. "Anyways, the best of luck to you with this new company you've formed." His gaze flickered to Branch and a smile came to his lips as he continued dryly, "Not that you'll be needing too much *luck,* with the kind of men you've been given. Let me know how things go, will you, happen I don't see you again before you pull out?"

"I'll do just that, Bob," Tragg promised. "And thanks for everything."

"Just how much does His Honor-ably know, Maj'?" the elderly sergeant inquired, watching the rear lights of the judge's vehicle departing along the narrow trail that connected the cabin with the main road to Marlin.

"No more than most other people, although he's *guessed* there's something more to the company," Tragg replied. "He came out here to make sure that, should he be asked about what's been happening today, he'll have the *right* answers."

"We need more around like him," Branch praised. "Only, could be he'll start putting two and two together should we go through with it."

"Could be, but I reckon we can count on him to keep whatever he figures to himself," the major asserted with complete assurance. "Anyways, we're going ahead with it regardless. That's why Company Z's been formed. I only wish we didn't have to throw so much on young Alvin and Mark."

"You-all can count on them like you can on us old hands, Maj'," Branch declared, showing just as much confidence. "They never put a foot wrong on the chores they've handled so far, same's young Ranse 'n' Miz Rita."

"I know that," Tragg claimed, but shook his head and went on somberly, "Only this goes way beyond anything they've had to do so far. It's *that* and not whether they can do it which gets to me."

"Those boys know why it had to be them who was handed the chore," the elderly peace officer stated with conviction. "And why, no matter how much we want to, you, me, or any of the other old hands couldn't do it."

"I know that too, Jubal," the major confessed, his demeanor showing the depth of the emotions he was feeling. "But I still wish there wasn't the need for any of us to have to do it."

"If there wasn't the need, Maj'," Branch drawled, his tone and leathery visage showing he understood but did not underestimate the gravity of the situation, "there wouldn't be any need for Company Z neither."

"You've got some company for the night, *Mr. Foote*," announced the burly, if elderly and generally amiable, guard, entering the cellblock in which the gang leader was the only prisoner.

Despite the purpose for which the building was intended, Philip "Handsome Phil" Foote, having had time to settle down and do some thinking since his arrival the previous evening, now concluded he was far better situated than he had anticipated during the journey from Falls County.

Over the years, the State Prison Farm at Jonestown had become accepted as the repository for those criminals serving sentences who were known to be well behaved and nonviolent. As a result, discipline was much less severe than in the other penal establishments. Furthermore, the guards tended to be easygoing, older men who asked little other than to be allowed to spend their remaining periods of service as quietly as possible prior to retiring.

On being delivered to his revised destination, the gang leader had been given what he considered was official corroboration for the disturbing information he had received from his escort.

In answer to the protest he had commenced on learning where he was to be accommodated, the warden had explained that the state attorney general personally had sent instructions for him to be segregated from the other inmates as a security measure. While there had only very rarely been any violence showed by them, Hogan Turtle wielded such a moral ascendancy over the criminal element of Texas that some might be willing to change their pattern of behavior in order to earn his approbation. Wishing to avoid subjecting them to the temptation, which might result in orders being given for punitive measures detrimental to *everybody* on the farm, it had been decided that Foote was to be put in the execution block. As was generally the case, this was empty and its cells offered a standard of comfort equal to that supplied throughout the rest of the establishment. Nor, he had been assured, was it likely his stay there would be lengthy in duration.

At first, Foote had experienced considerable qualms over being in such close proximity to the room in which the executions were carried out. He had even tried to avoid as much as glancing at the door which gave access to the fatal chamber. However, he had gradually overcome his misgivings. The guards assigned to the block had not been friendly or sociable, but neither were they abusive and he was never overly susceptible to atmosphere.

Having slept badly, the gang leader had spent the night thinking about his future. By the time morning had come, he had concluded it might not be anywhere nearly as gloomy as he had envisioned during the conversation with the two Texas Rangers. For one thing, possibly in the hope that he would supply incriminating information about other criminals, the authorities were clearly concerned about keeping him alive and in good health.

One of the conclusions at which Foote had arrived was that, as he was reconciled to the probability of his receiving a prison sentence and not a fine for the pretended bootlegging, he should do everything in his power to try and arrange to be sent to serve it at the farm. Everything he had seen had convinced him that it was deserving of the reputation it had acquired as being a "rest home," the underworld's term for a prison where discipline was not severe nor the work given to the inmates too strenuous. All of which would suit his needs. Provided he could make his peace with the Big *Hombre,* he could take advantage of the easygoing conditions and, by exerting the full force of his ruthless personality over the more passive prisoners, would become the unofficial ruler of the establishment. He might also be able to retain control and continue running the operations of his gang from inside the farm. He was aware that such had been done in similarly lax penal institutions in other parts of the country.

"Company for the night?" the gang leader repeated in a puzzled tone, knowing there was no inmate awaiting capital punishment. He also doubted whether a man sentenced to death elsewhere would be transferred to the farm and have the punishment inflicted after only one night as the comment had implied. "How do you mean?"

"An out-of-state U.S. marshal's put the arm on a couple of owlhoots who're real bad wanted here and thereabouts," the guard replied. "Only his jalopy got a flat down the road a piece and he can't get them locked up good 'n' safe in Austin afore nightfall. So he's asked the warden could he bed them down here until morning."

"Why in *here*?" Foote asked, as much from a desire to continue the conversation after the uncommunicative way he had been treated all day as through a desire for information. "Are they a couple of hearse men?"

"They're real likely to wind up's gallows dancers, what I've heard of them, but they've not been tried and sentenced to it yet," the guard answered, aware that the term "hearse man" meant a convicted murderer awaiting the death penalty and employing a name for a person who was to receive capital punishment. "I reckon it's the same with them's with you. The warden likely figures they're such ornery sons of bitches he doesn't want 'em mixing with and giving such like notions to all the good old boys we've got rooming with us here."

"Who are they?" Foote requested, concealing his resentment over the way in which the information had been supplied.

"Name of Rapido Clint and Comanche Blood," the guard obliged. "Do you know 'em?"

"I've been hearing some about them just recently," the gang leader admitted, remembering he had given much the same answer to his escort after they had told him about the activities of the two men in question. "How'd they get taken?"

"I wouldn't know," the guard admitted, sounding as if he did not care either.

The opening of the main door brought the conversation to an end.

As Foote was turning his attention to the entrance, he gave thought to what he had heard about Rapido Clint and Comanche Blood prior to the story told to him by the two sergeants. Although comparative newcomers to the criminal scene, they had already acquired a reputation as being *pistoleros valiente*— as professional killers were known along the international border with Mexico—of the first water. Clint in particular was said to be exceptionally skilled in the use of firearms, efficient, cold-blooded, and deadly.

Studying the handcuffed pair who followed the gray-haired captain of the guards into the block, the gang leader decided he could identify them without the need to be introduced. However, in spite of the rapidity with which they had come into prominence, he was not particularly impressed by what he saw. Neither would be beyond his mid-twenties, and they had on cowhands' clothes that clearly had never been worn for work of any kind.

Despite his hair being rusty red, if the nickname he had acquired and the moccasins he wore were any guide, the taller of the newcomers was "Comanche" Blood. His handsome face, set in a surly scowl that was understandable under the circumstances, was sufficiently bronzed to indicate he had Indian as well as white antecedents. Slender in build, he had a lithe stride suggestive of fast and, when necessary, silent movement backed by a wiry, whipcord strength. There was, in fact, something latently savage about him that warned he might be a *very* bad *hombre* to cross, especially when there was a knife in the now-empty sheath on his waist belt.

At first, particularly when compared with his companion, the second prisoner gave no sign of how he had gained his reputation. Certainly it was not because he possessed an exceptional physique. Nor was there anything particularly commanding about his face. He had on a black Texas-style Stetson with a fancy leather band decorated by silver *conchas* and an unfastened new waist-length brown leather jacket. Tightly rolled, the ends of a scarlet silk bandanna trailed over the breast of a dark-blue satin shirt with a white arrow motif on its pockets. Around his waist, a wide belt with a floral patterning and a monogrammed silver buckle held up his smart brown striped trousers, which hung outside tan Justin boots.

Trying to reconcile the physical appearance of Rapido Clint with the stories being circulated about his prowess both as a gun- and fistfighter, Foote looked more closely at him. It would be unwise, the gang leader concluded after a moment, to dismiss the tales as falsehoods or exaggerations on account of his lack of size. There was a good spread to his shoulders, and he trimmed down at the waist in a manner implying he might have strength well beyond the average for his height. Nor, despite being tight-lipped and frowning, was there anything weak about his features. All in all, he too could be a man with whom it would be unwise to trifle.

The prisoners were followed by, as the badge of office pinned to his vest indicated, their captor. Black haired, tall, well built, and middle age, his rugged, leathery, and heavily mustached face might have been carved out of granite for all the expression it showed. He had on a tan Stetson with a Montana peak crown,* a dark-brown three-piece suit of good cut and material, a white shirt, black necktie, and black "old man's comfort" boots. Although he gave no sign of being armed in any other way, the sawed-off double-barreled ten-gauge shotgun cradled on the crook of his left elbow suggested how he could have managed to take the pair alive. Faced by it and its grim-visaged owner, even the most hardy and desperate wanted criminal would realize that to do other than surrender as ordered was futile and, in all probability, would be sure to prove fatal.

"Put them in next door to Foote, Joe," the captain ordered. "They'll be company for each other."

"On the side nearest the room," the marshal supplemented, his accent that of a Montanan, gesturing toward the door of the execution chamber. "It'll keep them in mind of what's coming to them *real* soon."

"Yo!" the guard replied, giving the time-honored assent of a cavalryman to a command and leading the way past the gang leader's cell.

"Hold the scatter for me, please, Captain," the marshal requested, as the prisoners were going through the door opened by the guard. "Stay put there, Clint. And you go stand with your face to the far wall, Blood."

"My, he's a real old scaredy-cat, Rapido," the taller young

---

* "Montana peak" crown: One that rises to a point in a similar fashion to the hats boy scouts used to wear. *J.T.E.*

man remarked in a tone filled with mockery, but nevertheless carrying out the instructions he had been given. "Now isn't he, though?"

"He for certain sure acts like one, Comanch'," the shorter prisoner agreed, his voice firm yet without any trace of bombast serving to hide fear. Turning and holding out his hands, he went on. "You can take them off, Uncle Long Arm.* I promise I won't jump and whup you while you're doing it."

"And I'll see that you don't get the chance, count on it," the marshal answered, handing the shotgun to the captain and taking a small bunch of keys from his coat pocket. "My name's J. B. Macauley, not Dutchy Soehnen. You won't rile me into doing something rash so you can jump me. But, happen you've a mind to try, just make a stab at it."

"So you've heard about that, huh?" Clint inquired, noticing that his captor was avoiding coming into the possible line of fire of the captain and that, having cocked the hammers of the weapon, the latter was holding it ready for use. "Only I don't aim to hand you any excuse to have us gunned down in 'self-defense' either. There's not one small chance you'll be able to get Comanch' and me found guilty on *any* charge."

"That's for the courts to decide, not me," Marshal Jason Bowen Macauley pointed out disinterestedly, unfastening and removing the handcuffs in a cautious, but not nervous, fashion. "All I do is haul in smart-assed young sons of bitches like you pair so's they can be brought to trial. What comes after that's none of my never-mind. Back off to the wall and lean with your hands against it while the breed comes to be set loose."

---

* "Uncle Long Arm": An abbreviation of "Uncle Sam's Long Arm of the Law." A derogatory name given by criminals to any peace officer serving with a federal and not a state, county, or municipal law enforcement agency, so having jurisdiction throughout the whole of the United States. The local officers are restricted to the regions from which their appointments are granted. *J.T.E.*

"How tough they get how quick, when they've got the drop," the taller prisoner commented, advancing while his companion moved away to do as ordered. "It's like to scare a body 'most to death."

"Whatever you fellers on duty in here do," the marshal counseled, his tone charged with warning as he stepped back quickly and closed the door after having liberated Blood, "don't let them rile you into taking chances with them."

"You can count on it!" promised the guard to whom the advise had been directed, impressed by the deadly serious way in which it was delivered.

"If it's all right with you, Captain," Macauley went on, "I'd sooner the door to their cell wasn't opened for *any* reason unless I'm here. Should it need to be, I'll be bedding down in the guardhouse and, no matter what time it might be, I'll come straight over as soon's I'm called."

"That's all right with me," confirmed the senior member of the farm's security force, showing no resentment over what might have been construed as a lack of faith in the abilities of his men. "Fact being, Mr. Macauley, seeing's how I'm a mite shorthanded right now, it'll save me putting any more of the boys on watch in here."

Being conscious of his position of importance among the criminal element, Foote had not wished to appear too openly interested in the new arrivals and had remained seated on his bed during their incarceration. He had, however, watched and listened to everything that happened, finding it enlightening. Taking notice of the extreme caution displayed by the marshal while dealing with them, he was more impressed than he cared to admit even to himself. Clearly, despite being inside the confines of the farm and with numerous armed guards close at hand, the peace officer had taken a warning from what had happened to Sergeant Hans "Dutchy" Soehnen and did not intend to present them with an opportunity to escape.

Studying the two prisoners as the marshal, the captain, and the guard walked away, the gang leader reached a conclusion. Young and comparative newcomers to the criminal scene in Texas though they might be—and, in the case of Rapido Clint, insignificant looking—he and Comanche Blood were clearly far more dangerous than showed on the surface. They were, in fact, the kind of men Foote would have tried to enlist if he had been at liberty.

14

I'M NOT GOING TO TRY TO ESCAPE

"Morning, Marshal Macauley," the guard on duty in the execution block greeted sleepily, having risen from the table at which he had been dozing and opened the main door in response to the sound of its bell. "Lordy, Lord! And is it half-past four already?"

"As close as damn it," the visiting peace officer replied, entering. "Have you had any trouble with them?"

"Nary so much's a peep from either of them," the guard declared, glancing along the dimly illuminated passage to the cell that housed the two temporary inmates. Then he closed the door. Swinging his gaze to the coffeepot on the stove behind the table, he continued. "If you haven't had breakfast, I can let you have a cup of java."

"I've grabbed a bite to eat at the guardhouse," the marshal answered, taking a hip flask from the left-hand pocket of his jacket. "And, anyways, this'll go down a heap better than coffee."

"Likely," the guard conceded, eyeing the flask apprecia-tively. "I reckon it would have to be knowing the kind of coffee they make there."

"Here," Macauley said, some of his grimness departing briefly as he held out his right hand. "Take a nip for looking after those two young bastards for me, 'less it's against your religious beliefs."

"Any time it gets to be," the recipient of the offer granted, showing neither surprise nor disapproval at the suggestion that he should contravene the Volstead Act, "damned if I don't right quick change religions."

Despite his cheerful concurrence with committing a misde-meanor and eager as he was to accept the flask, the guard restrained his first impulse to drink deeply. Even in the Lone Star State, where pride of place among the hierarchy of peace officers tended to be accorded to a major or captain of the Texas Rangers, a United States marshal was still a person of considerable importance. Deciding it might be impolitic to arouse the ire of one who held such an influential post, he restricted himself to a sip, which merely titillated his taste buds and produced a desire for more.

"Hell, friend, take a *good* drink," Macauley instructed amia-bly, as the flask was held toward him. "There's plenty more where I filled that from."

"*Gracias,* Marshal," the guard responded, and did as he had been authorized. Having lowered the level of the liquid consid-erably, wishing his own station in life offered such opportuni-ties to obtain so excellent a product, he wiped the neck with the palm of his hand and returned the container to its owner. "By cracky, that son of a bitch sure went down smooth."

"I'll just bet it did," the marshal replied, showing no annoy-ance at the reduction to his property that had taken place, but he made no attempt to drink. Instead, he replaced the stopper and dropped the flask into the pocket from which it had come. "Give me the keys and I'll go fetch my prisoners out."

"Sure," the guard assented instantly, without giving a thought to the other's abstinence being at odds with the reason for which the hip flask had ostensibly been produced. He turned toward the desk, but before he could pick up the keyring that lay on it, he swayed and gasped, "What the—"

"Easy now!" Macauley said, stepping forward quickly. "You'd best sit down!"

Taking the guard by the shoulders with both hands, which he was able to do as he did not have the sawed-off shotgun with him, the marshal did not rely upon his words alone to cause the man to be seated. Finding himself being guided around the desk and eased into his chair, an expression of mingled realization, alarm, and anger came to the guard's face. However, although he tried to rise and shake off the grip on his shoulder, he found he was so weak that he was held down with no difficulty in spite of his burly build. He knew such weakness was not normal and, even though his head was spinning, he could guess how it had been induced.

For a moment, as the realization that he had been drugged came, the guard tried to throw off the restraining hands and opened his mouth with the intention of raising the alarm. No sound left it, and, giving a convulsive shudder, his body went limp. Tilting him forward at the waist and lowering him gently until his head was resting on the table, the man responsible for his condition picked up the keyring and walked swiftly along the passage.

By the time Macauley reached their cell, Rapido Clint and Comanche Blood were on their feet. It was obvious that they had seen but were not in the least surprised by what had happened to the guard. Apart from the former having removed his hat, they were fully dressed and had not even taken off their footwear before going to sleep. Knowing what was expected of them, the marshal studied each one's face as he opened the door and they joined him in the passage. Reading only expressions of grim determination, he was satisfied they were both still ready, willing, and would be able to carry out their part in the far from pleasant task that lay ahead.

"That'll teach him not to drink on duty, for shame!" Blood remarked in a low yet even voice, nodding toward the table on emerging from the cell. "And I'd surely hate to have a head as sore as his will be when he wakes up. Talking of which, how's about Foote?"

"He didn't so much as stir as I came by," Macauley replied, equally quietly, leading the way to the cell of the man in question.

"I thought only the just slept well," Clint commented, speaking as quietly as his companions and looking through the bars of the door.

"The just are likely too worried over sons of bitches like him to sleep easy," Blood replied grimly, yet with a slight trace of satisfaction. "Which they're going to have one *less* to worry about real soon."

"Let's go and fetch him out!" the marshal ordered, having turned the key in the lock while his supposed prisoners were speaking.

Although Philip "Handsome Phil" Foote had been so tired he was sleeping soundly, either instinct or the slight noise made by the opening of the door disturbed him. Living the kind of life he had prior to his arrest had given him the ability to wake up swiftly and with his faculties starting to function almost immediately.

Almost, but not entirely!

Coming to his feet in an instinctive reaction, clad in a pair of garish silk pajamas that had been in the suitcase of spare clothing he had brought from Marlin, the gang leader stared at the two figures who were entering the cell side by side.

"What's u—" Foote commenced, momentarily assuming the visitors were guards. Then, recognizing Clint and Blood, he realized he was in error. A moment later the recollection of something he had been told about their recent activities came and led him to reach a most disturbing conclusion over the reason for their presence. Trying to sound amiable, he went on hurriedly. "Thanks, fellers, but I'm not going to try and escape with y—"

At that moment, seeing the man he had believed to be a United States marshal behind the two young Texans, the gang leader brought his declaration to a halt.

The reaction was caused by Foote remembering his escort had claimed that Clint and Blood had sought out and severely beaten a man who had incurred the displeasure of Hogan Turtle. Taking into consideration the peace officers' intimation that this had not produced the anticipated gratitude on the part of the Big *Hombre,* he had assumed they were now seeking to earn his approbation by offering him the opportunity of escaping with them.

The presence of Macauley—if that was his name—proved the theory to be badly, even frighteningly, incorrect!

To have gained admission to the State Prison Farm and obtained such cooperation from its staff called for some means of identification, including a badge of office that would pass as genuine.

Such items were anything except easy to come by. They could only be produced by an organization with considerable facilities available.

Hogan Turtle controlled such an organization.

Beginning to appreciate the alarming alternative to his original conclusions, Foote sucked in a gasping breath that he intended to expend on shouting for help at the top of his voice.

Clearly anticipating what was portended by the action, Clint lunged forward.

Then something took place that caused the gang leader's vocal chords to freeze instead of responding to his wishes.

Suddenly, Rapido Clint no longer seemed to be small.

By some means that Foote was at that moment too startled to comprehend, the Texan appeared to have grown until he was the largest man present.

To silence the proposed outcry, Clint did not merely rely upon the strength of his personality, which—as the gang leader would have realized in less demanding circumstances—had created the apparent physical metamorphosis.

Bending his left arm in front of his chest, the *big* Texan whipped it around and up with a rapidity that illustrated to Foote how he had acquired his nickname. However, he did not deliver a conventional punch with a clenched fist. Left open, with the fingers extended together and thumb folded across the palm, it was the heel of the hand and not the knuckles that made the contact.

Unusual as such a method might appear to one trained in normal fistfighting, it proved most effective!

Caught just below the Adam's apple and experiencing a sensation such as might have been caused by a blow from a blunt ax, Foote was unable to shout. Reeling away from his assailant, gasping hoarsely and half strangled, the back of his head struck the wall of the cell. Although the impact did not render him unconscious, he was too dazed by it to put up any resistance as the trio closed upon him. First he was twirled so his hands could be fastened behind his back. Then a bandanna was knotted about his mouth to act as a gag and a hood made from thick black cloth descended over his head, blindfolding him.

With everything accomplished very quickly, having been swung around once more, the gang leader felt his arms being grasped from each side. Even as his mind was striving to gather his scattered wits and catch up with developments, he was compelled to start walking between the two men who were holding him. However, such was the perturbed state of his reasoning powers that he had no idea of the direction in which he was turned on leaving the cell. All he knew for certain was that his captors were hustling him along the passage with an irresistible force. Then they guided him through a door that was unlocked by the man he had heard going ahead of them.

As there was no breeze, or any other indication, Foote surmised he was not being taken out of the building.

Before the still-dazed mind of the gang leader could arrive at any conclusions from the discovery, he found himself being hauled rather than steered up a short flight of wooden steps.

Alarm had been assailing Foote ever since he was bound, gagged, blindfolded, and forced to leave the cell. It increased as, having been propelled across what was clearly a floor of planks at the top of the steps, he was stopped and his ankles were swiftly fastened together. When the hood was jerked from his head, he stared around. What he saw did nothing to relieve his sense of trepidation. Rather it grew and turned to panic-stricken terror. In spite of the lights being switched off in the portion of the building to which he had been brought, the moon was sending sufficient illumination through the windows of the roof—there were none in the walls—for him to identify his surroundings.

They were similar to those in which the gang leader would have paid the ultimate penalty if his guilt of raping and murdering Eloise Charmain could have been proven at the trial!

Realizing he was standing on the trap of the gallows in the execution room of the cellblock, Foote tried to throw himself from it. His efforts were to no avail. The men on either side were holding his arms in a grasp like the closed steel jaws of a bear trap. He was unable to pull himself free, even from the surprisingly strong hands of the smaller of the pair.

Stepping forward, the third of the gang leader's abductors— whom he discovered was no longer wearing the insignia of a

United States marshal—deftly slipped the waiting noose over his head. It was adjusted with a speed and precision that implied the man had performed a similar task on more than one occasion.

Still restrained by Rapido Clint and Comanche Blood, feeling as if he was on the verge of collapsing, Foote watched their companion—who most definitely could not be considered in any other way—cross to the lever on the wall at the side of the platform. Struggling without any success at getting free and guessing what was coming, he was prevented by the gag over his mouth from even uttering the plea for mercy he wished to make.

"Philip 'Handsome Phil' Foote!" intoned the grim-visaged man who had established his identity as U.S. Marshal J. B. Macauley on his arrival at the State Prison Farm. His voice was unemotional yet as filled with inescapable menace as the crack of doom as he went on. "The jury at your trial in Marlin, Falls County, had to find you not guilty of raping and murdering Eloise Charmain. But we know and *you* know you were guilty as charged, and you're going to pay for doing it—now!"

Having uttered the last word of the menacing pronouncement in a louder tone, the obviously bogus peace officer grasped and thrust the lever downward!

Releasing their holds when they received what was clearly a prearranged signal, the two young Texans sprang away from the gang leader.

Before Foote could try to avert his fate by duplicating the prisoners' evasive action, the trap hinged away from beneath his feet. He plummeted down until the slack of the sturdy hemp rope was taken up. There was a sharp *crack* as his neck was broken. His body jerked spasmodically for a moment, then dangled limply.

The execution of the rapist and murderer of Eloise Charmain

had been carried out as efficiently as if he had been sentenced to death by the court that had tried him.

To an onlooker possessing knowledge of such matters, it would have been obvious that Macauley had either been very fortunate or was competent at the task he had performed. The length of the "drop," a matter of vital importance, had been just right. If it had been too short, Foote would have been strangled instead of killed instantly. On the other hand, should the distance have been excessive, when the downward progression of the body was suddenly brought to a halt, its weight could have torn the head from the shoulders.

As it was, the amount of slack in the rope had been calculated correctly and death was instantaneous.

"Whooee, Jason!" Blood exclaimed, staring at the gently swinging but otherwise unmoving corpse of the gang leader. "That was clean and sudden!"

"I *always* try to make it clean and sudden," replied the man whose full name—which, although he had never before carried out his specialized occupation anywhere near Texas, might have betrayed his true identity to the warden or some of the guards—was Jason Byron Macauley Farringdon. "Let's get him taken down and back to his cell, boys. Then we can be on our way."

After returning the corpse of Philip "Handsome Phil" Foote to the cell, the trio of extemporaneous executioners placed it on the bed and covered it by the blankets to give the impression it was only asleep. With that done, while Rapido Clint was collecting his Stetson, the man who had performed the hanging with such competence resumed the pose of being a United States marshal.

After donning his badge of office, Jason Byron Macauley Farringdon secured the wrists of the Texans in front of them with the handcuffs. Then, passing the unconscious guard at the table, they behaved like a peace officer and his prisoners on leaving the execution block. The bogus marshal had brought the dark-blue Apperson 8-20 four-door sedan in which they had arrived to the front entrance. Although it bore no insignia to denote official status and its license plates were not of Texas issue, there was evidence that it had been prepared carefully for its purpose. Its interior was fitted with certain additions that were frequently installed in vehicles used for law enforcement duties and had given added credence to his assumed identity.

Allowing Clint and Comanche Blood to climb into the back, giving the impression he was compelling them to do so, Farringdon took his place behind the steering wheel. Then, starting the powerful engine, he set the vehicle into unhurried motion.

An astute observer watching the preparations for departure might have been made suspicious by noticing that, unlike on his arrival, the marshal was no longer taking the kind of precautions he had then apparently considered necessary. He had left his sawed-off shotgun on the front passenger seat while going to fetch out the two men who had the reputation for being desperate criminals and against whom he had warned the farm's staff to be exceptionally wary. Furthermore, despite Macauley having spoken of Clint's escape from custody on one occasion by taking advantage of a lapse on the part of his escort, he and Blood were being allowed to sit behind their current captor. Nor had the peace officer offered to couple their handcuffs to the short chains attached to the floor of the car as an aid to increased security.

However, nobody was in the immediate vicinity to notice the omissions.

Even those "tower hacks" in the lookout posts on the walls that offered a view of the execution block were paying no attention. As was the case with all the staff, the passive nature of the State Prison Farm's usual inmates had lulled them into such a state of complacent relaxation that the watch they kept was desultory at the best.

Nor were the guards on duty at the main entrance any more alert and conscientious. Having been warned the previous evening that it was the intention of the marshal to take an early departure, they made no attempt to stop the Apperson. Seeing it approaching, they opened the gates and did no more than give a cursory glance inside as it went past. Satisfied that all was well, they did not even wait until the rear lights were out of sight before closing and locking the gates once more.

Passing the keys of the handcuffs to Clint as soon as he was informed of the guards' actions, Farringdon increased the speed of the vehicle while his "prisoners" were releasing one another. However, even after they were at liberty, neither of the young Texans nor their "captor" spoke much as he drove them swiftly toward the rising sun. After having traveled on the otherwise deserted highway for about ninety minutes, at a speed that rarely dropped below fifty miles per hour, they turned along a narrow and little used trail across the rolling range country. Covering something over another five miles, at a rate that was of necessity reduced, they passed through a fair-size area of fairly dense woodland. On emerging, they came upon the first sign of human beings they had seen since leaving the prison farm.

Despite the dilapidated state of the adobe buildings that looked to have been the headquarters of a small and not too prosperous ranch, there were clearly people in occupation. However, the quality of two of the cars in front of it—the third being an obviously hard-used 1920 Ford Model-T center door, four-seater sedan more in keeping with the surroundings—and the privately owned Curtis JN-6H "Jenny" biplane standing at the rear suggested that whoever might be inside were not the original owners of the building.

As the Apperson came to a halt alongside the Ford and the

trio climbed out, the door of the cabin opened. Followed by three men and an attractive young woman, a big bluetick coonhound appeared. Wagging its tail languidly and walking as if doing so was a great physical effort, the dog preceded the human beings across the porch and towards the car.

"Why, howdy there, Lightning, good old buddy!" Blood greeted, displaying none of the surprise and consternation that might have been expected from a badly wanted criminal who clearly recognized the animal and the people behind it. "I'm real pleasured to see you're as lively as ever."

"I'm damned if I know how a man can stand having a dog that excitable around," Clint added, his reaction to seeing who had come from the cabin much the same as that of the taller Texan. "He should be trained to slow down some."

"Howdy, Alvin, Mark," responded the foremost man of the party from the building, running his gaze in a speculative—but far from hostile or wary—fashion over the "prisoners" rather than their "captor" as he was speaking. "How did it go?"

"Without a hitch, Ben," replied the United States marshal, showing as little concern as his companions over being confronted by three members of the Texas Rangers. Knowing the leisurely way in which they had arrived would have informed the speaker that they were not being pursued, he deduced what had actually been implied by the question and went on. "These two boys of yours did *real* good. I couldn't have asked for anybody better to be siding me."

"*Bueno,* Jason!" Major Benson Tragg declared, nodding in satisfaction. Then, taking his watch out and looking at it, he continued. "They don't have reveille at the farm until six, so the guard in the execution block shouldn't have been found yet. Take that mustache off, *amigo,* and, while you're washing the dye out of your hair, Rita and Ranse will fix some breakfast for us. When we've eaten, I'll fly you over to Austin and see you safe on your way back to Montana."

"That's fine with me, Ben," Farringdon asserted, rubbing at his top lip. "I won't be sorry to get rid of this damned thing."

"Now me," Tragg drawled, "I thought it looked real fetching."

"Are the rest of the arrangements still the same, sir?" asked Rapido Clint, gently massaging the ribs of the hound that had sprawled at his feet with the toe of his boot.

Far from being a badly wanted outlaw, the small Texan's status and name was Sergeant Alvin Dustine Fog. He had adopted that particular alias in honor of his illustrious paternal grandfather who had also used it on occasion.*

"Nothing's changed," the major confirmed. "Rita and Ranse will get you to Polveroso City and Jubal will fetch Mark there."

"Jubal and *Lightning,* or maybe it should be the other way round," added Sergeant Mark Scrapton, who had also selected his sobriquet as having been one favored by his equally famous maternal grandfather,** jerking his right thumb to where the bluetick was lying on the ground to all appearances asleep. "There now, Rapido, didn't I tell you's how I always get the better class of company?"

"I'd be the *last* to be giving you any ar-grew-ment about *that,* young Comanch," Sergeant Jubal Branch drawled. "Only, when you gets to be *my* age and wisder-imum, which ain't espesh-tically like' to heaven-trate less'n you right soon change

---

* An occasion when Captain Dustine Edward Marsden Fog, C.S.A., assumed the alias Rapido Clint is recorded in *Beguinage* and *Beguinage Is Dead!* J.T.E.

** The maternal grandfather of Mark Scrapton was Loncey Dalton Ysabel, better known as the Ysabel Kid, for whom we have the honor to be biographer. Two periods when the Ysabel Kid called himself Comanche Blood are recorded in *Hell in the Palo Duro, Go Back to Hell, The South Will Rise Again,* and Part Three, the Ysabel Kid in "Comanche Blood," *The Hard Riders.* Further details of his career and special qualifications can be found in the Civil War and other volumes of the Floating Outfit series. *J.T.E.*

your sinful ways, you'll know a whole heap better'n say such *afore* you've had your breakfast cooked by the *other* company."

"Much as I hate to admit it, but I agree with Jubal," the girl put in. Knowing something of the reddish-haired Texan's culinary tastes, she continued with an almost angelic innocence. "Isn't it lucky we've remembered to bring plenty of tomatoes to mix with *every*thing, Ranse?"

"It surely is, Rita," Sergeant Ranse Smith agreed, being equally aware of Scrapton's antipathy where that particular vegetable was concerned. "But this is the first time I've seen them used with hominy grits."

"You'll notice you didn't get warned until *after* you'd been let make a fool of yourself, Comanch'," Alvin Fog remarked, just as cognizant that his companion was very partial to hominy grits. "Which's just about what you'd expect from an ornery old lawman."

Watching and listening to the conversation, Major Tragg felt relieved. Circumstances had compelled him to put the two young men through what must have been a harrowing and very traumatic experience. From all appearances, they were satisfied that what they were helping to do was necessary and unavoidable, and they were not being plagued by pangs of misguided conscience. Even if there had been any lingering doubts among those in the know, this latest and by far most difficult assignment that they had brought to a successful conclusion proved they were both worthy members of the Texas Rangers' newly formed, specialized, and secret Company Z.

15

IN EXPLANATION

Only a few people in Texas were aware of the existence of Company Z. Even fewer were informed about the special and clandestine duties it had been formed to carry out. Its men were the pick of the Texas Rangers, mostly officers with considerable experience in all branches of the duties performed by that organization and of lawbreakers throughout the Lone Star State. As they were all familiar figures to members of the underworld, however, a few younger men were enrolled whose connection with law enforcement in general and the Texas Rangers in particular was not known.*

The events leading up to the unofficial, though completely justified, hanging of Philip "Handsome Phil" Foote was the kind of assignment Company Z was created to perform.

* Unless already holding it on enrollment, every member of Company Z was given the rank of sergeant to enhance his authority when handling cases. *J.T.E.*

Having studied the evidence, on learning that the gang leader —whose life up to that point had been far from blameless, although nothing could ever be proven in a court of law—had engaged Reece Mervyn to conduct his defense, Major Benson Tragg had suspected the specialized services of Company Z might be required to ensure justice was done. Although it was certain Foote was guilty as charged, knowing the attorney had contrived to win cases for other clients of equal culpability, the major had been determined that the gang leader would pay the appropriate penalty no matter what verdict the jury could be cajoled or compelled to bring. Furthermore, he had promised himself that should Foote be found not guilty as a result of legal skullduggery, he would try to ensure that Mervyn would be made to suffer and, at the very least, lose some of the revenue acquired as a result of the miscarriage of justice.

The major had been in Forth Worth on an assignment with members of Company Z when Foote's arrest had taken place. Unfortunately, the case on which they were engaged and a certain amount of rivalry on the part of the chief of the Dallas Police Department had prevented them from intervening before the essential witnesses were killed, injured, or scared off. Accepting that other means must be found to ensure that justice prevailed, Tragg had taken advantage of the delay in deciding upon a suitable venue for the trial. By the time the choice had been made, he and his men were ready to deal with the situation that they anticipated yet hoped would not arise.

From the beginning, the major had displayed the tactical genius and ability to make the most of whatever was offered by circumstances, which explained why he had been chosen to command Company Z. Without waiting for the trial to begin, even though he had hoped the need to put them into effect would not arise, he had commenced formulating plans to cope with the contingencies he was anticipating.

The production during the trial of the hitherto unmentioned

Seth Chiverton and Irvin Schulman, to give their "evidence" on Foote's behalf, had been the deciding factor so far as Tragg was concerned. Although the attorney for the prosecution had been unable to disprove their testimony, due to the way in which Mervyn had had them coached and the apparent credibility of the story they were given to account for their participation, the major decided that—outside the witness box, at any rate—they could prove to be the weak link in the defense. Believing they could be induced to supply proof beyond any shadow of a doubt of Foote's guilt, which was vitally necessary before the intended operation could be set into motion, he had made preparations to have this obtained. Furthermore, by the kind of coincidence no writer of fiction would dare include in a novel, he had been aware of how they might be punished for their perjury if there was no way of having this done legally.

Having hunted on numerous occasions with Judge Robert J. McCrindle, the major was conversant with the geography of Marlin and Falls County. He had put this knowledge to use when laying his plans. Aided by a certain amount of good luck and considerable foresight in anticipating how the opposition would react, the various parts of the operation had gone smoothly and produced all that was required of them.

While Sergeant Jubal Branch had been watching the room at the Brendon Hotel occupied by Simeon Oakes on the last day of the trial, he had not been the real subject of the surveillance. Being aware that his specialized military service was a matter of public knowledge, Tragg had made sure that Foote learned of the Winchester 1876 model rifle he had brought with him in what he believed to have been secrecy. As was anticipated, Butch Cope had noticed his absence from the courtroom and, little realizing that a trap had been laid, had gone to carry out the instructions given by the gang leader.

The elderly peace officer and Sergeant Carlos Franco were occupying a room at the Brendon Hotel, on the opposite side of the passage to that of the bereaved father. On Cope's arrival, the knife and lock pick he was carrying had implied he was not intending to restrict himself to just verbal dissuasion.* However, before he could effect an entrance, Branch had approached silently and undetected from behind to render him unconscious with a blow from a sap. Chloroform applied by the Chicano peace officer, who had earlier played an essential role in another part of the operation, had ensured Cope remained in that condition until he could be used for the furtherance of the major's plan. The money and property taken from him to create the impression he had been the victim of a robbery, a pretense he was willing to accept rather than chance having his reasons for being at the hotel questioned, had been delivered later and anonymously to the offertory box of the local church. Leaving Franco to attend to the gangster, Branch had used the lock pick to gain admittance and, aided by his inseparable companion, Lightning, kept Oakes from committing what would have been a serious breach of the law.

After Chiverton and Schulman were led to believe that Foote had contrived to avoid traveling in their company, their suspicions had been aroused before they were taken out of the courthouse. The shots were fired to narrowly miss and frighten them by Sergeant David Swift-Eagle and Sergeant Alexandre "Frenchie" Giradot, who had been allowed to use the judge's house ostensibly to keep watch for and prevent any genuine attempts at assassination. The two peace officers had then collected Cope from the Brendon Hotel. Because most of the population was outside the courthouse, they had delivered him to

---

* At a later date, Butch Cope admitted to Alvin Dustine "Cap" Fog—who was working, under his alias, Rapido Clint, on another case—that, fearing Simon Oakes's skill as a sniper might be used to take revenge against him at some time in the future, Foote's orders were as Sergeant Jubal Branch suspected. Cope was to kill the bereaved father and give the room the appearance of a robbery having been the motive. *J.T.E.*

the parking lot unobserved and in a manner that conveyed the impression of his complicity in the shooting. Although Chiverton's intervention had saved them from being open to a charge of perjury, Schulman's almost-completed comment had been sufficient to establish Foote's guilt to the satisfaction of Major Tragg. It had also been enough for him to order the arrangements for their punishment to be implemented.

Not only had the major served during the Great War with the father of one of the girls made pregnant by "the Wisenheimer and the Dummy" in their days as burlesque entertainers, but he and the man's employer—now a prosperous rancher— had been friends for a number of years. They had, in fact, been officers in the same regiment and fought with the American Expeditionary Force in Europe. It had been Tragg, with the support of the employer,* who had prevented the father from taking violent reprisals on learning what had happened to the girls. However, knowing all his men would be fully occupied elsewhere and unavailable, he had decided to let the intended punishment take place. It would be so belated that, with there being so many other irate parents who had cause to carry it out, the chances of the victims guessing who was responsible would be minimized.

Using Franco as an "anonymous" intermediary, the major had had his friend notified that the errant pair would be taken to Texarkana in a way that offered an opportunity for the reprisals. The Chicano peace officer had made the telephone call that informed the waiting party of the kind of vehicle to watch for, so there would be no mistakes in laying the "trap." Tragg had no doubt that, being a man of honor and otherwise law-

---

* Even at this late date, beyond saying the man in question had served with distinction with the American Expeditionary Force and had three times been decorated for valor, Alvin Dustine "Cap" Fog declines to disclose his identity. *J.T.E.*

abiding, his friend would take precautions to ensure the escort would not be harmed. Furthermore, Sergeant Colin Breda and Sergeant Aloysius "Paddy" Bratton had known what to expect. On being "captured," they had contrived to let the onus for them having surrendered without fighting fall upon their prisoners. Arranging for Chiverton and Schulman to be compelled to inflict the whipping upon one another had been the sergeants' idea, but their superior had expressed his approval when informed of what they had done.

As the employer and the father—who was *segundo* on his ranch—were prominent in the cattle business, they had taken the precaution of wearing hoods to conceal their identity. Being less well known, the black man had agreed to let his face be seen as he played the part of the diner's fry-cook in case the peace officers were aware such a person existed. Not that he had had anything to fear. Breda and Bratton had been deliberately vague when describing him to the sheriff of Limestone County. Nor, on being informed of the circumstances, was that official inclined to expend too much energy and effort in trying to catch those who were involved. As the father of three young daughters, he considered whoever had committed the offense was justified, and he conducted only a token investigation before announcing they had eluded him and left the area of his jurisdiction.

While the efforts of Company Z had established that Foote was guilty and had caused the pair whose false testimony had saved him to suffer (although the law could not have touched them so long as they refused to admit they had lied under oath), the affair was far from being over. Even if they had confessed to committing perjury, the rule of "double jeopardy" would still have prevented the gang leader from being taken back to court to face for a second time the charges of which he had been acquitted.

There had been no chance involved in the decision that Foote

was not to be taken directly to Texarkana to await the trial for
the nonexistent bootlegging. It was made in advance and with
the aid of the wave of adverse publicity in the newspapers that
Mervyn had instigated. Doing as Tragg requested without asking questions,* the attorney general had brought pressure to
bear on the heads of every law enforcement agency in the state.
They in turn had passed it on, via their subordinates, to the
discomfiture of the criminal element.** By exaggerating the
amount of resentment and hostility this was creating, the major
had had his suggestion accepted that the State Prison Farm at
Jonestown would be the safest place in which to keep Foote
away from any vengeance being contemplated by disgruntled
members of the underworld.***

To give the attorney credit, he had intended to have the precautionary escort for his client on the journey to—he assumed
—Texarkana carried out by his confidential clerk. However,
knowing he had made a similar arrangement on other occasions, Tragg had not only been ready to counter the move, he
had used it to make Foote susceptible to the explanation of its
absence given by Sergeant Benjamin "Benny" Goldberg and
Sergeant Hans "Dutchy" Soehnen.

* Cap Fog has instructed us to state that neither the governor of Texas nor
the state attorney general were informed of the line of action being contemplated by Major Benson Tragg. One of the conditions he had stipulated
when asked to form and command Company Z was that he alone must be
conversant with and control its clandestine operations. As a result of the
stricture being accepted, this is the first time a full account of the Philip
"Handsome Phil" Foote case has been made public. *J.T.E.*
** Although the treatment of Eric "Side-Wheeler" Heifer was not originally intended as a part of the Philip "Handsome Phil" Foote assignment,
it was mentioned to help convince the gang leader of the threat to his life.
While we have the notes of the case that resulted in the punishment of
Heifer, we have not yet found time to examine them in full and know only
the facts recorded in this volume. *J.T.E.*
*** For obvious reasons, the location and name of the State Prison Farm at
Jonestown has been changed. *J.T.E.*

Like his employer, Wilfred Plant was not averse to dalliance
with attractive members of the opposite sex. Luring him away
from his vehicle so the rotor arm could be removed by Franco
had been easy. The bait was Rita Yarborough, wearing a long
platinum-blond wig and suitably revealing attire. Using the
name Rita Ansell, she had first become involved with Company
Z during its members' second official "unofficial" assignment.
This had been to bring a dishonest financier back to the United
States, in spite of his having acquired Mexican citizenship that
rendered him immunity from legal extradition.* He had been
responsible for the murder of her parents, and the courage and
determination she had displayed while trying to avenge them,
believing the law could not, had led to her enrollment as an
active—if honorary and not officially registered—member of
the company.

Having dealt competently with the matter of delaying Plant's
departure, Rita had helped to inflict a well-deserved punishment upon his employer. Ably supported by Sergeant Ranse
Smith, the most recent official recruit to Company Z, who was
also wearing a disguise—including a coir-padded "paunch"
that helped stave off the effects of the blow to the stomach
delivered by Mervyn—and behaved in a most convincing fashion as the outraged, if dull-witted "husband," she had set up
the situation in the parking lot of the Palace Hotel. Such was
the consummate skill with which both had played their parts
that the attorney never suspected the true state of affairs. In
addition, not only had she prevented the clerk from raising the
alarm on his inopportune arrival, but she had helped with the
exterior damage to Mervyn's Packard, which had been done in
the woodland where it was abandoned. This, added to the de-
struction of the engine resulting from the iron filings and sugar
poured respectively into the oil sump and gasoline tank by her

* The assignment is recorded in *Rapido Clint*. *J.T.E.*

companion prior to leaving the parking lot, had reduced the vehicle to little better than a wreck.

So thoroughly had Rita and the giant young Texan carried out their instructions that—as Branch had later surmised—the replacement of the Packard, added to the cost of his medical and dental treatment, left Mervyn with very little of the fee he had received for obtaining the acquittal of a man he had known from the beginning was guilty of rape and murder.

Satisfying and justified though the treatment accorded to the attorney and, inadvertently, Plant had been, it was Foote who ranked as the primary object of Company Z's attentions. They were all in complete agreement with their commanding officer's determination to ensure that the gang leader was made to pay the full penalty for his crimes, regardless of the verdict forced upon the jury due to the connivance of Mervyn. Knowing of the lax conditions prevailing in the State Prison Farm at Jonestown, Tragg had been confident that arranging for the execution to be carried out and, even more important, the escape of those involved could be accomplished.

Of Company Z, with the exception of Smith—who was required to perform other duties—only Sergeants Alvin Dustine Fog and Mark Scrapton could hope to enter the farm without running the risk of being identified as a peace officer by either a member of the staff or an inmate. All the others had served with distinction as Texas Rangers for long enough to be well known in their official capacity. However, neither had had any experience in carrying out an execution, and the major was aware of the problems that might arise if they attempted to do so.* Realizing the same objections applied as those that pre-

---

* In the chapter entitled "String 'Em Up," of *Wyoming Rugged But Right,* my good friend William F. Bragg, Jr., recounts how murderer Big Nose George Parrott was twice "strung up" by inexperienced lynch mobs and each time they failed to achieve their purpose. He was, however, subsequently hanged by men who knew what they were doing. *J.T.E.*

vented the more senior of his officers from going to the farm, where employing one of the professional executioners who were active in the Lone Star State was concerned, Tragg had brought in a friend who served in such a capacity in Montana.

Arriving after the trial had commenced, Jason Byron Macauley Farringdon had joined his two young assistants. They had waited at the dilapidated empty ranch house for the major to give them the order to commence. While they were doing so, as a precaution against him being recognized by somebody at the farm who might have made his acquaintance elsewhere, Farringdon had made changes to his appearance. On receiving the go-ahead, using a car—its license plates changed—that belonged to Company Z and supplied with the necessary means of establishing his identity, he had arrived at the farm in the guise of a United States marshal transporting two desperate and dangerous prisoners.

The rest of the case has already been recorded.

Philip "Handsome Phil" Foote had contrived to escape the meshes of the legal system, using the loopholes that were created by the rules intended to protect the innocent. Company Z had seen that justice was done and he paid the penalty for the crime!*

---

* The inquiry into the death of Philip "Handsome Phil" Foote concluded that he had been killed by the fake United States marshal and the two "prisoners" at the instigation of "a person, or persons, unknown." The participation in the affair by Rapido Clint and Comanche Blood enhanced their reputations in a way that proved beneficial to their further activities and the future operations of Company Z. *J.T.E.*

The
CHRISTMAS
JOURNEY

WINNIE GRIGGS

Steeple
Hill®

Published by Steeple Hill Books™

STEEPLE HILL BOOKS

Steeple
Hill®

Recycling programs
for this product may
not exist in your area.

ISBN-13: 978-0-373-82822-7

THE CHRISTMAS JOURNEY

Copyright © 2009 by Winnie Griggs

www.SteepleHill.com

Printed in U.S.A.

Delight yourself also in the Lord; and he shall give you the desires of your heart. Commit your way to the Lord, trust also in Him, and He shall bring it to pass.

—*Psalms* 37:4–5

To my dear friend Joanne Rock, who dropped
everything to give me a much needed "fresh eyes"
read and invaluable assistance in brainstorming
when I needed it most.

Chapter One

November 1892
Knotty Pine, Texas

"Hey!" The reedy voice coming from inside Wylie's Livery and Bridle Shop thrummed with outrage. "You can't take those horses 'til you settle up with Joe."

Ryland Lassiter halted outside the entry and swallowed an oath. Sounded as if a disagreement was brewing inside.

The last thing he needed was another delay. This trip had already taken too long. He wasn't about to sit cooling his heels, waiting for the railroad tracks to be cleared—not when he was this close.

Ry reached into his coat and fingered Belle's letter. There'd been an air of desperation in her plea to see him, a sense of urgency that gnawed at him. And the closer he drew to Foxberry, the stronger that feeling grew.

Pushing back the worry, he tugged on his shirt cuffs. Might as well wade in and do what he could to help settle matters. The quicker he could get going again, the sooner he could find out what was going on with Belle.

A burst of rough laughter from inside the stable added impetus to his decision. That first voice had been a boy's, but these sounded older and about as friendly as cornered badgers.

In the space between one heartbeat and the next, Ry stood inside the wide doorway. His jaw tightened as he spied a boy of ten or so squaring off against a pair of sneering thugs, looking for all the world like David before Goliath.

Unfortunately, this would-be giant-slayer didn't have so much as a sling to do battle with.

The larger of the two men, a barrel-chested brute with a scraggly mustache, shoved past the boy. "Outta my way, kid. Those are our horses and we aim to get 'em."

The man's heavy-handed move forced the boy back a step, but the youngster kept his balance and gamely thrust out his jaw. "You can't take them until you settle your bill," he insisted, hands fisting at his sides.

Ry silently applauded the boy's pluck.

But the pair of philistines didn't share his admiration. The second oaf, whose crooked nose and scarred cheek gave him a more villainous appearance than his partner, scowled. "Like we already said, we settled up with Joe this morning." The man's voice rasped like a dull saw on a stubborn log.

The boy crossed his arms. "Joe didn't say nothin' about it."

Mustache stopped in the act of opening a stall gate. "You calling us liars?" He swiveled toward the boy, jabbing his fist into his palm with a forceful *thwack*.

That did it. Ry couldn't abide bullies. And he was pretty sure the good Lord hadn't put him here at this particular moment just so he could stand by and watch.

Clearing his throat he strolled forward, casually nabbing a

pitchfork from a pile of straw. "Good day, gentlemen. Is there a problem?"

The pair froze, then turned to eye him suspiciously. Ry held his genial smile as he mentally gauged his options.

As he'd expected, once they got a good look at his tailored clothes and "citified" appearance, their cocky grins reappeared. Better men than these had mistakenly equated polish with softness. His years at law school had added the polish, but he was still a born and bred Texan, able to stand with the best of them.

"No problem," Scarcheek finally answered. "The boy's confused is all. You just stay out of the way, and we'll be done in a minute."

Not likely. Another three unhurried steps placed Ry between the youth and the two men. He pulled out his pocket watch and flicked it open with his thumb.

As expected, both men's gazes latched onto the gold-cased timepiece with a covetous gleam.

"I don't know." Ry glanced down, then closed the heirloom with a snap. "It appears this is taking a good deal longer than a minute, and I've already wasted more time in Knotty Pine than I cared to."

Scarcheek met Ry's relaxed opposition with a lowered brow. "Unless you want to get them fancy duds and that pretty-boy face of yours messed up, you'd best stay out of matters that don't concern you."

Ry flashed a self-deprecating smile. "Well, now, that could be difficult. You see, it's an unfortunate failing of mine that I find there are so many matters that *do* concern me."

Scarcheek drew his pistol and pointed it at Ry's chest. "Don't know where you come from, Mister, but around here that's not a very healthy attitude."

Ry's smile never wavered as he coolly calculated his next

step. Using the pitchfork to knock Scarcheek's gun out of his hand would be an easy maneuver. Handling Mustache, who was just out of reach, was a bit trickier. He'd hoped the sight of his watch would tempt the bully to step closer. Still, a few agile moves and a bit of finesse just might help him avoid a bullet while he disarmed the man.

He hoped to handle this without drawing his pocket pistol—the fewer bullets zipping around, the less chance of the boy getting caught in the crossfire.

Bracing himself, Ry shifted his weight and tightened his hold on the pitchfork. No time for doubts. But, as his mother had liked to say, there was always time for prayer.

Lord, I know I don't say it often, but Your help is always welcome, and right about now would be a good time to provide a distraction.

No sooner had Ry formed that thought than the metallic click of a cocked rifle sliced through the tense quiet of the livery. "What's going on here?"

"Joe!" The boy's shout signaled both relief and warning.

Then everything happened at once.

Scarcheek spun around, gun raised, just as the boy started toward the newcomer, putting himself directly in the line of fire.

Fueled by concern over the boy's safety, Ry swung the pitchfork with a speed and force that surprised even him. The blow connected with Scarcheek's wrist, drawing a yelp and string of curses from the man as the gun went flying.

Before the gun hit the floor, Ry dropped the pitchfork and dove for the boy, tackling him to the ground. Covering the boy's back with his own body, he left the newcomer's line of fire clear to take care of Mustache if need be.

"Hands where I can see them." The rifle-wielding local's command carried the cold hardness of a marble slab.

With the sunlight at their rescuer's back, Ry couldn't make out many of his features. All he got was the general impression that this Joe fellow was a wiry young man who radiated a give-no-ground toughness.

Deciding it was safe to let the squirming stableboy up, Ry stood, though he kept a restraining hand on the lad's shoulder. Now that everything seemed under control, he was actually feeling a bit proud of the way he'd handled himself. He still had it in him, it seemed.

Joe's gaze shifted briefly toward the two of them. "You okay, Danny?"

"I am now." The boy rubbed an elbow as he glowered at Mustache and Scarcheek. "They was fixing to take off without paying what they owe."

"Is that right?" The inquisitor turned back to the surly pair, tightening his hold on the rifle. "You two planning to leave town without settling your bill?"

"Look here, no need to get all riled up." Scarcheek cradled his wrist against his chest. "Clete and I were just pulling the kid's leg a bit." He shot Ry a hot-for-vengeance look. "Before this stranger stuck his nose in, we was about to pay up."

Danny stiffened. "Hey! That's not—"

Ry squeezed the boy's shoulder, cutting off the rest of his protest. Joe was obviously in charge of the livery and it would be best to let him control the stage for now. Ry did, however, slip his free hand into his coat, palming his pistol. Wouldn't hurt to be ready if things turned ugly again.

He felt rather than saw Joe's gaze flicker his way. Apparently his movement hadn't been as subtle as he'd thought.

Then the livery operator's focus returned to Scarcheek and Mustache. "Well, you can hand over the cash now or decide which horse you're going to leave as payment."

Scarcheek scowled, then called over his shoulder. "Pay up, Clete."

Mustache reached into his pocket and pulled out some crumpled bills. He took a step forward, but halted when Joe shifted the rifle, pointing it dead center at his chest.

"Just set it on that barrel." There was a flash of teeth as Joe gave a wolfish grin. "Being as you two are such reliable souls, I'll trust it's all there."

Confident *and* cautious. Ry's assessment of the man raised another notch.

"Now, get your horses and gear, and move on." Joe lowered the rifle, but Ry doubted anyone in the stable thought he'd lowered his guard. "And don't plan on doing business here again."

With dark looks and muttered oaths, the men complied, and in short order were leading their horses into the street. The look Mustache shot Ry as he brushed by was pure venom.

Ry released his hold on Danny and the boy bolted to Joe's side.

The livery operator dropped an arm around the lad's shoulder never taking his gaze from the unsavory pair as they rode off.

Retrieving his hat, Ry brushed at the brim. He'd give them another minute to reassure themselves, then maybe he could finally get down to the business of renting a rig. Now that the little melodrama was over, he was more anxious than ever to be on his way. While Novembers in Texas weren't nearly as cold as those in Philadelphia, the days were every bit as short. He needed to make good use of what daylight was left.

Belle had said in her letter that he was her last hope—an ominous statement coming from the down-to-earth girl he remembered. She'd been like a sister to him back when they were growing up and he still felt that old tug to look out for her.

As he watched the man and boy, something about their pose

from, but that don't mean beans around here. If you want to risk your own hide, that's your business, but your blamed fool actions put Danny in danger, too. That's either pebble-brained stupidity or grizzly-sized disregard for others, neither of which I can stomach."

"Nor can I." The man's words were controlled but she didn't miss the flash of temper in his storm-gray eyes. "I also can't abide bullies. When I arrived, Danny was already trying to face them down. I only—"

"What!" Jo's heartbeat kicked up a notch as she swung around. "Daniel Edward Atkins, is that true?"

Danny's face reddened even as he thrust out his jaw. "They owed us for a week's feed and stabling. With Thanksgiving and Christmas coming up, we need that money."

This was her fault. She shouldn't have left him alone knowing those two polecats had mounts stabled here. He could handle a lot of the work right enough, but at eleven he just wasn't old enough to understand all the consequences of his actions. If anything had happened to him while she was at the feed store…

Jo leaned forward, baring the full force of her frown on the unrepentant boy. "I've told you before, nothing's worth getting shot over. If someone gives you this kind of trouble, let it go and we'll get Sheriff Hammond to handle it afterward."

The boy kicked at a clod of dirt. "I'm big enough to hold my own."

Jo blew the stray hair off her forehead with an exasperated huff. If only that were true. Someday, Danny would be old enough to take over and she'd finally be free to go her own way. But today's actions only proved how far away that day was.

Offering up a quick prayer for patience, she placed a hand on his shoulder. "Danny, I got to know you're going to mind what I tell you when I leave you in charge."

He gave a reluctant nod, then glanced past her, reminding Jo they weren't alone.

And that she had some crow to eat.

Someday, Lord, I'm going to learn to get all the facts before flying off the handle. Your teaching about thinking twice before speaking once is a sure-enough tough one for me to learn.

Squaring her shoulders, she turned to the gent who'd introduced himself as Ryland Lassiter. "Looks like I owe you an apology, Mister. And a big thank-you to boot." She thrust out her hand, not sure if he'd take it after the way she'd lit into him.

But he seemed willing to let it go. Taking her hand, he gave a short bow before releasing it. Well, wasn't he a fancy-mannered gent.

"Apology accepted. And there's no need for thanks. It's you who actually saved the day. Miss…" He cocked his head to one side with a questioning smile.

"Wylie. Josephine Wylie. But everyone just calls me Jo."

"Well, Miss Wylie, I'm glad I could be of service."

Miss Wylie—she couldn't remember the last time someone had called her that. Certainly not since her pa died and she took over the livery.

She was suddenly very aware of just how unladylike she looked in her overalls and boots. Certainly not like any of the prim-and-proper misses a fancy gent like him must be used to.

Jo turned and hung the rifle on a set of pegs near the door, as much to hide her sudden discomfort as anything else. He probably thought she was a bumpkin who didn't know how a lady was supposed to dress or act.

Then she gave herself a mental shake. There was absolutely no reason why she should give a fig what he thought of her. He was likely just passing through Knotty Pine—she'd never see him again once he went on his way.

When she turned back around she was ready to look him in the eye again. But she glanced at Danny first. "Time you headed up to the house. Cora Beth has your lunch ready by now. And the train's been delayed, so we picked up a couple of boarders for tonight. I'm sure she's going to need your help getting everyone settled in."

With a nod, Danny turned to his rescuer. "Thanks for your help, Mister." He flashed a cocky grin. "We make a pretty good team, don't we?"

The man nodded with a smile. "I'd be happy to have you on my side anytime."

With a wave, Danny left the livery, whistling as he went.

Which left her alone with Mr. Lassiter.

Her first apology had been a bit grudging. Time to fix that. "Sorry I snapped at you. You stepped in to help Danny when you could've just stood by, and for that I'm beholden. No telling what those two snakes would've done if you hadn't come along."

He shrugged and gave her another of those let's-be-friends smiles. "I did what needed doing. Danny's more than just your stableboy I take it."

She nodded. "Foster brother."

"Well, he was brave to stand up to those thugs the way he did."

"Pigheaded, more like." She tilted her chin, irritation flaring again. "He might've gotten himself killed." Just the thought of what could have happened set her stomach churning.

"He's just a boy."

"But *you* aren't." Fool greenhorn. Didn't he realize how serious that little dust-up had been? Her hands fisted at her sides as she fought the urge to shake a finger in his face. "I know you mean well, and it might be different where you come from, but it's best you learn that in these parts there are men who'd as soon shoot you as look at you."

His jaw tightened. Probably didn't like getting lectured to, but it was for his own good.

"Where I come from," he said, each word dropping like a stone, "is Hawk's Creek Ranch, about eighty miles northwest of here."

Jo's head went up and her hands unclenched. He was a Texan? And a rancher to boot. Well, he sure as fire didn't look or dress like any rancher she'd ever met.

"And no," he continued, "as it happens, it isn't any different from Knotty Pine, at least not in the way you mean. I find bullies are pretty much the same wherever you find them."

Wherever you find them. She knew he hadn't meant anything by that, but the words still carried the bite of a scorpion sting.

"Now, if you don't mind getting down to business," he said, "I would like to rent a rig and I'm in a hurry."

Getting down to business sounded just fine to her. She leaned back against a stall and met his gaze head-on. "When do you need it, for how long and where are you headed?"

"The when is right now. The where is Foxberry and I'm not certain how long I'll be gone, but it will likely be about a week." He raised one brow. "Do you have a rig for lease or not?"

She had the feeling this gent was used to getting his way. Too bad she'd have to disappoint him. "Sorry. The buggy and buckboard are both leased out for the day. The buggy's due back by suppertime, though, if you want to wait."

He impatiently brushed a bit of straw from his sleeve. "I don't."

Jo straightened. "Look, I reckon you came in on the train. I heard there was a problem with the tracks up around Tatter's Gully. It's happened before. They ought to have it fixed by noon tomorrow."

"Like I said, I'm in a hurry." He ran a hand through his hair, mussing it just enough to take a dab of the polish off his dandified looks.

She approved of the change.

"If there are no carriages, what about renting me a horse and saddle?" He nodded toward the two animals still in the stable. His tone had been polite, but she saw the muscles in that square jaw of his tense. Impatience flashed in his see-through-you eyes.

She didn't much blame him for wanting to be on his way. She'd been dreaming of getting out of Knotty Pine for what seemed her whole life.

Jo retrieved the pitchfork and leaned on it, studying her would-be customer. He was a sure-enough puzzlement. Obviously well-heeled. And not a bad-looking man if you liked the broad-shouldered, smooth-as-worn-leather type. But he wasn't a too-good-to-get-his-hands-dirty gent either. Knew how to handle himself, too. That had been a slick move he'd made, knocking the gun from Otis's hand and then covering Danny's back.

"Let's see," she said, thinking out loud, "Foxberry is about a day's ride—assuming you're an experienced rider." She paused and he nodded stiffly. Not that she'd expect him to answer otherwise. "It's just past noon so you won't get there today. Let's say three days for the trip there and back then, and maybe five days' stay. That means you'd have the animal tied up for about eight days, give or take."

Jo rubbed her chin, ready for a bit of dickering. "That kind of time won't come cheap. You sure you wouldn't rather wait? My family runs a boardinghouse and I'm sure my sister has a comfortable room we can rent you for a fair price."

Mr. Lassiter pulled a wallet out of his coat. "I appreciate the offer, but no thanks. Name your price so I can get going."

Jo's knuckles whitened as her grip tightened on the pitchfork. He could just whip out that wallet of his and go wherever he wanted, whenever he wanted. And he didn't even seem to realize how lucky he was. Much as she hankered to get out and see something of the world, she'd never traveled more than twenty miles from Knotty Pine in her entire twenty-three years.

Lord God, it just ain't fair.

"One hundred dollars." The words were out of her mouth before she'd even realized what she was going to say.

"A hundred dollars?" His eyes narrowed. "I could practically *buy* the animal for that price."

Too late to back down now. "Not one as good as these. Besides, I don't have any guarantees you're going to return the animal, do I?" She ignored the way he'd stiffened. "Like I said, you'd be better off waiting for the train."

To her surprise, he pulled out a wad of bills. "Here. Anything to get on my way."

Realizing her jaw had dropped, Jo hurriedly closed her mouth. This fool was actually carrying that kind of money around with him? And a hundred dollars didn't even clean him out—the wallet was still plump when he stuffed it back into his jacket. "But—"

He'd grabbed her hand and the shock of that physical contact shut her up. He slapped the money into her palm, then moved to the stalls.

Guilt pinched at Jo's conscience. She'd expected him to haggle a bit—not actually agree to her outlandish price. It just wouldn't be right for her to take all this money.

She bit her lip, staring at his stiff back. How could she give some of it back without sounding like a henwit?

I know, Lord, it's my own fault for letting envy get the best of me.

Stuffing the money in her pocket, Jo followed him to the far end of the livery. "Of course," she said as casually as she could, "you'll get half of this back when you return the horse." Much as she tried, she couldn't stop the heat rising in her cheeks.

He shot her a look she couldn't read. Then he nodded and pointed to the larger of the animals. "I'll take this one."

"That's Scout." The knot in Jo's stomach eased as she settled back down to discussing business. "I'm afraid he's a bit fractious—doesn't take to strangers much. You'd be better off with Licorice."

He shrugged. "He's the better of the two horses. And I've handled more spirited animals before, both Texas-bred and foreign. I've even helped saddle-break my share. So I think I can manage Scout here just fine."

Jo clamped her lips closed. There he went, hinting about his travels again. That was the worst part about this job. Watching other people come and go, hearing about all the places they'd been or were headed to, while she just stood and watched life pass her by. Would she ever be able to act on the plans she and Aunt Pearl had made?

Without waiting for assistance, Mr. Lassiter began gathering tack. He moved with an ease and sureness she had to admire. But he also seemed in an awful hurry. Made you wonder if he was running *from* something or *to* something.

"You manage this place all on your own?" he asked, not pausing from his efforts.

"Yep. Lock, stock and barrel." Somebody had to support the family and for now she was it.

"Seems a mighty big responsibility."

She stiffened. "For a woman, you mean."

He glanced up and his expression reflected friendly curiosity, nothing more. "No offense, but I admit I find it an unorthodox arrangement."

Did he believe this was how she'd planned for her life to turn out? "It's a family business—my pa passed it on to me." She jutted her chin out. "Like you said earlier, we do what needs doing. I can handle it."

He grinned. "I don't doubt that for a minute."

For some reason that response bothered her more than anything else he'd said since they'd started this strange conversation.

She jammed her hands in her pockets. Did he think less of her because she wasn't some soft, helpless female who needed a man looking out for her?

Not that she gave a hoot for his opinion. After all, she barely knew the man.

Jo did her best to ignore the niggling voice in her head that chided her for not being completely honest with herself.

Chapter Three

$\sim\!\!\!\sim$

As he saddled the horse, Ry eyed the livery operator from the corner of his eye. Why in the world was she so prickly?

True, he *had* mistaken her for a man at first, but she didn't know that. And he'd stepped in to defend her brother at no small personal risk. Why, he hadn't even haggled over the outrageous price she'd demanded for the use of her horse.

Still, he couldn't forget he'd actually let this woman—a member of the fairer sex for all her rough edges—face down a pair of armed thugs while he'd stood by.

His gut clenched every time he thought about it. It was an unforgivable act, going against everything he'd been taught about duty and honor. So he was willing to give her more than the usual bit of leeway.

He felt her gaze studying him as he worked, could almost see the questions forming in her mind.

Finally, she broke the silence. "I suppose you're anxious to get your business taken care of so you can spend Thanksgiving at home."

Home. Ry paused, patting the horse absently. Lately he'd

been trying to figure out exactly where that was—in Philadelphia with his grandfather or Hawk's Creek with his brother and sister.

Sometimes he was torn between the two. Other times he felt as if he didn't belong in either place. And holidays hadn't felt special or festive in a very long time.

He gave himself a mental shake. Time enough to work through that problem after he saw Belle. And Miss Wylie was watching him curiously, expecting a response. "My family's not big on holiday celebrations."

That earned him a surprised frown, but no further comment. Instead, she moved across the stable and grabbed a bedroll. Retracing her steps, she hefted it onto the stall next to him. "Quinlinn is between here and Foxberry. You should reach it well before dark, but if you end up having to sleep on the trail you'll need this. Gets cold at night this time of year."

He grinned. "Believe me, this is mild compared to New England."

Far from setting her at ease, his words deepened her scowl. It had been a while since he'd found it so difficult to coax a smile from a woman. But it seemed he couldn't say anything to charm this one.

Well, so be it. The bedroll would come in handy since he wasn't planning to stop in Quinlinn. He'd push on as far as he could until darkness made traveling dangerous, then get up with the first lightening of the sky. The sooner he reached Foxberry, the sooner he could get the answers he wanted.

He had to hand it to Miss Wylie, though. He gathered she was her family's provider—a responsibility she appeared to take seriously. Even if life had set him on a different path, he could certainly respect that.

How big a family was it? He'd already met Danny and she'd mentioned a sister. Were there more?

"You got any kind of weapon with you?"

He raised a brow at her unexpected question, then reached into his coat and pulled out his pocket pistol. "I carry this when I travel."

She surprised him with an unladylike snort. "That peashooter won't be much protection on the trail." Moving with quick strides, she retrieved the rifle she'd wielded earlier. "Here, take this. Never know what kind of varmints you'll meet up with—and I don't mean just the four-legged kind."

Ry slipped his unjustly-maligned derringer back inside his coat. The double-barreled pocket pistol was more formidable than it appeared. "Don't you need that rifle yourself?" He wasn't about to compound his first blunder by riding off with her best means of protection.

But she shrugged off his concern. "I've got another one." A nod toward the far wall indicated a second rifle.

He studied her a moment, noting her earnest expression, the tightly concealed concern lurking in her eyes. It appeared she was making a peace offering and it would be rude to brush it aside.

He took the weapon. "Thanks. I'll return it when I bring the horse back."

She nodded. "Once you leave Quinlinn in the morning, it'll be an easy half day's ride to Foxberry."

"I'll be fine."

"I don't imagine you've had lunch yet." She fiddled with a straw she'd plucked from the pitchfork. "If you were of a mind to remedy that before you head out, you could head over to the boardinghouse. Just tell my sister I—"

Ry held up a hand. "Thanks, but I'll just purchase a few supplies from the mercantile and head out." The itch to be on his way had returned with a vengeance. He'd wasted too much time already.

He mounted the horse, gathered the reins and turned to say a quick goodbye. Then paused.

She'd shoved her hands in her overall pockets and stood watching him. For just a moment, despite her outspokenness, Ry sensed something wistful, something almost vulnerable about the unorthodox female. He had the strangest urge to climb back down and lift some of the weight from her shoulders.

Which was strange. She wasn't at all the sort of girl he was usually attracted to.

Then she straightened and her eyes narrowed. "You take good care of Scout, you hear. I raised him from a colt and I'd take it poorly if you let something happen to him."

So much for his instincts. There was nothing vulnerable about this woman. If he offered to help her she'd no doubt throw the offer back in his teeth. And Belle, who actually *wanted* his help, was waiting in Foxberry.

"Don't worry." He tipped his hat. "I'll treat him as if he were my own prize thoroughbred. See you in about a week or so." With that, he set the horse in motion.

Jo felt another stab of jealousy as Mr. Lassiter turned to go. What must it be like to just pick up and head out anywhere, anytime you took a notion to? Someday she'd find out.

Or so she prayed every night.

She rubbed the side of her face. *I truly am trying to be patient, Lord. But I'm twenty-three and not getting any younger.*

With a sigh, she let it go and watched Mr. Lassiter ride the short distance to Danvers' Mercantile. One thing she could say for the man, he sat a horse well. Seemed to have a knack for appearing both relaxed and in command at the same time.

Seemed he'd do all right with Scout, after all.

At least he wouldn't have the weather to worry about.

November was one of those changeable months in these parts. You could have mild weather one day and frost the next. This was one of the sunnier days.

Jo watched him step past the table of pumpkins and gourds Mr. Danvers had set up out front and enter the mercantile. With a shake of the head, she decided she'd wasted enough time worrying about the stranger, and turned back to the livery. Then frowned.

Otis's and Clete's horses were hitched in front of the saloon. Now, why in blue blazes were they still hanging around town?

She retrieved the second rifle and carefully loaded it. They probably wouldn't be back to bother her, but it wouldn't hurt to be prepared. Especially if those polecats were getting liquored up.

Jo sat at her worktable where she had a clear view of the street, and picked up a harness that needed mending. From here she could watch both the mercantile and the saloon.

A few minutes later Mr. Lassiter stepped back out on the sidewalk. Sure hadn't wasted any time. He quickly attached a bundle to Scout's saddle and gathered up the reins.

Yep, something had definitely lit a fire under that man.

As if he felt her watching, he glanced up and his gaze locked on hers. Even from two blocks away, Jo felt the impact of that look down to the tips of her toes.

Land sakes—what was it about this man that could irritate her, confuse her and make her want to squirm all at the same time? And if he thought she would look away first he could just—

A wagon passed between them and the connection was broken. When Jo's line of sight was clear again, Mr. Lassiter had already mounted up and was headed out of town. Not wanting to be caught staring again, Jo managed to watch his progress without looking directly at him.

When he passed in front of the livery, Mr. High-and-Mighty

Lassiter gave her a brief tip of the hat, but didn't bother to pause or speak. Which was just fine with her. She didn't care if he paid her any notice or not.

After he'd passed by, she slammed the bridle down with a *thunk* and stood, stretching her muscles. She suddenly felt restless, felt the urge to do something physical.

Then she stilled. Someone else was watching Mr. Lassiter leave town. Otis and Clete lounged outside the saloon, all but licking their chops, nudging each other like a pair of weasels who'd spied a way into the chicken coop.

Even after they stepped back inside the saloon, Jo couldn't shake the notion they were up to no good. And that Mr. Lassiter was their target.

She retrieved her lunch pail and absently picked at her meal, not tasting a single morsel.

Sure enough, ten minutes later Otis and Clete swaggered out of the saloon, mounted their horses and rode off in the same direction as Mr. Lassiter.

Otis glanced her way and the ugly smile he flashed sent alarm skittering up her spine like a frightened centipede.

She had to do something. But what?

Jo tugged on her earlobe. Business wasn't exactly brisk right now. She could likely afford to leave things unattended for a bit.

A few minutes later she was marching down the sidewalk, her pace just short of a trot, trying to figure out exactly what she'd say to Sheriff Hammond.

Otis and Clete had caused enough trouble in town lately that she was sure the sheriff would be inclined to believe they were up to no good. But she didn't really have any proof, other than a sick feeling in the pit of her stomach. And even if he agreed with her that Mr. Lassiter was in danger, would he be willing to take action now that they were headed away from Knotty Pine?

A few minutes later Jo marched back into the livery, as frustrated as a frisky dog on a short leash. Just her luck—Sheriff Hammond was out. No telling when he'd be back either. And she just couldn't shake the feeling that every minute counted.

She might be wrong about this whole mess, but fool or no she had to find out what Otis and Clete were up to. If those two varmints ambushed Mr. Lassiter she didn't have a whole lot of trust in his ability to hold his own.

Heavenly Father, help me figure out what to do.

She tugged on her ear again, trying to come up with a plan. A heartbeat later she spied a familiar towheaded boy on the sidewalk, and as quick as that made up her mind. "Tommy, I need you to do me a favor. Head up to the boardinghouse quick-like. Tell Danny I need him back here for a spell."

With a nod, the boy set off at a run.

Jo grabbed a saddle and headed toward Licorice's stall. She set to work, praying alternately that her suspicions were wrong and that she wouldn't be too late.

By the time Danny arrived she was ready to go.

She gave him a smile she had to force. "I need to ride out after that Lassiter gent. He forgot something." Like watching his back. "Think you can keep an eye on things while I'm gone? It might take a while to catch up with him."

Danny's chest puffed out. "You can count on me."

Jo ruffled his hair. "Especially when it means you get out of doing chores for Cora Beth, huh?"

Danny answered with a prisoner-set-free grin.

"Don't forget what I said about not getting into any dust-ups while I'm gone." She patted Licorice and casually retrieved the rifle.

Danny frowned at the firearm. "You expecting trouble?"

"Just being careful." Jo mounted up. "Mr. Lassiter's had a good head start so tell Cora Beth not to worry if I'm late for supper."

Before Danny could ask more questions she headed out.

As soon as Jo was clear of town, she nudged the mare into a trot. Otis and Clete hadn't seemed in much of a hurry to catch up with Mr. Lassiter. Even no-account slugs like those two would know better than to bushwhack the man too close to town. Sheriff Hammond would be on them like a hungry hound on a meaty bone.

No, more'n likely they were going to hold back for a while. Which meant she had a chance to—

Jo eased Licorice to a walk. To do what?

Otis and Clete were between her and Mr. Lassiter. What would she do if she caught up with them before they caught up to him? And how much time did she have?

She did some quick reckoning. They'd wait until they were well out of Knotty Pine, but would want to strike before Quinlinn. Up ahead a piece, the trail cut through a stretch of woods where there wasn't even a farmstead in hollering distance. Even though it was November, there were plenty of leaves left and the brush was thick enough to provide good cover if a body had need of it.

Past that the trees gave way to Whistler's Meadow. Just a small clearing really, but a spring cut through it, and most folks stopped to refill their canteens and water their horses.

The cowards could use the tree line for cover. Even if Mr. Lassiter didn't stop, just slowed a bit, they'd be able to pick him off, easy as shooting a penned colt.

Jo nudged Licorice into a trot again as a plan took shape in her mind. She'd hang back just a bit. But as soon as she got close to the meadow, she'd fire a few shots in the air, then hightail it for the cover of the woods. That ought to put Mr.

Lassiter on the alert, make him aware he wasn't alone. For a man as sharp as him, that ought to be enough.

Dear Lord, please let me get there in time. And give that fool Samaritan the smarts to recognize the warning shot for what it is.

By the time she neared the meadow her back and neck were stiff with tension, and her head pounded with the effort to stay alert to everything around her. So far she hadn't seen any hint of a scuffle or heard any shots.

She slowed Licorice to a walk. The meadow was about a quarter mile ahead. Time to make her move if she was going to do it.

Jo pulled the horse to a full stop and lifted her rifle. The road ran nearly straight from here to the meadow. She stared hard, trying to make out what lay ahead. Otis and Clete weren't the smartest curs in the pack—not by a long shot. Surely she'd see some sign if they were there.

Nothing seemed out of place. A crow cawed in the distance, some squirrels scurried in the nearby trees—just normal forest sounds.

Had she imagined bugaboos where none existed? Had her own yearning for adventure set her mind to creating one for her?

Or what if she'd guessed wrong about where they would spring the ambush? If she fired now, would she be tipping her hand?

A second later she spied the glint of sunshine reflecting off metal. A gun barrel!

Praying again that her plan would work, Jo quickly fired off a shot. Two other shots rang out before the echo died.

A high-pitched squeal of pain followed closely behind the blasts. Her heart in her throat, Jo abandoned her plan to duck for cover. Instead, she urged Licorice into a gallop, full tilt ahead. Sounded like the man needed reinforcements.

If her shilly-shallying had cost Mr. Lassiter serious injury she'd never forgive herself. The least she could do was race in, fire a few shots to distract the bushwhackers, and then get out before they could react.

She refused to believe she might already be too late.

Chapter Four

Ry grimly took stock of the situation from his position behind the fallen horse.

He thanked God for the hunter who'd fired that shot. If the sound hadn't caught his attention it would likely be his blood staining the ground instead of Scout's.

The horse jerked, making a feeble attempt to get up. Ry patted the animal's back. "Easy boy." Scout's muscles quivered under his hand.

Ry's jaw clenched at the animal's struggle. Those gunmen had a lot to pay for.

But he couldn't collect on that debt if he stayed belly to the ground with only the horse for cover. His pistol wouldn't do him much good unless the highwaymen got a whole lot closer, something he'd rather they not do.

If he could just get to the rifle Miss Wylie had loaned him…

The scabbard was tantalizingly close, yet too far to reach without giving the unseen enemy a clear shot. Silently apologizing to Scout, Ry pulled against the saddle with one hand, tugging at the weapon with the other. The rifle slid a few inches, then stopped.

More shots rang out and a searing pain exploded through Ry's shoulder. With an oath, he flattened himself to the ground again.

A quick check revealed that the bullet had passed through the fleshy part of his upper left arm. Lots of blood and it felt as if a hot poker were pressed against his skin, but the wound probably wasn't serious. Leastways, not nearly as serious as things were going to get if he didn't yank that rifle free.

"He ain't firing back."

That sounded like Scarcheek's voice hissing across the clearing. So this wasn't a random attack.

"You reckon he's hit, or just playing possum?"

That had to be Mustache.

"Only one way to find out."

The gunmen didn't try to hide their approach. They'd be on him in a minute and he had no doubts about what would happen next.

He had to get hold of that rifle! If he could fire before they were on him, he might have time to get off two shots.

Keeping as flat as possible, Ry ignored the pain in his arm, grasped the rifle with both hands, and yanked for all he was worth.

But it was no good, not from this angle anyway. He pulled out his derringer and prepared for the worse. He wouldn't make this easy for them. *Sorry Belle, seems I'm not going to be there for you after all.*

A moment later, two man-sized shadows blocked the sun.

"Well, looky here. Pretty Boy done got all mussed up."

Ry twisted his neck to see the two men looming over him, their ugly grins and rifles pointed at his back. He slowly raised himself to a crouch, carefully keeping his pistol hidden. He might not live to see nightfall but at least one of these cowards was going down with him.

"That's right." Scarcheek made a menacing motion with his rifle. "Up where I can see your face and hands."

Tension coiled inside Ry. His muscles bunched, ready to spring. He had to make this move count.

It would be the only one he had.

"Ayyiiieeeeee!"

The shrill war cry shattered nerves already drawn taught. Scarcheek and Mustache whirled around as a wildman swooped into the clearing, riding at breakneck speed straight toward them.

Thank you, God.

Scout made another spasmodic attempt to rise and Ry dove for the rifle. Ignoring the pain in his arm, he jerked the weapon free an eyeblink before the horse collapsed again.

The mounted banshee fired two shots that missed their marks.

Mustache returned fire and the one-man cavalry charge leaned lower in the saddle. The rider's hat went flying and a tawny braid flapped free, whipping in the wind like the tail of a kite.

Miss Wylie!

Was the woman insane? He'd wring her neck over this fool stunt.

If they lived long enough…

Seeing the men take aim at his rescuer, Ry gritted his teeth against the throbbing in his arm and tried to simultaneously fire his rifle and position himself between the gunmen and Miss Wylie. His first shot found its mark and Mustache went down with a grunt.

But a second shot echoed his own and Ry whirled in time to see Miss Wylie's horse go down.

It was getting more difficult to hold the gun steady, but Ry pushed harder, moving between her and Scarcheek, firing again.

He swore when he took a misstep and his shot missed the mark. From the corner of his eye he saw the horse get up.

But not Miss Wylie.

At least he'd turned Scarcheek's attention back toward him. If only it wasn't too late...

Ry fired again. Or at least attempted to. Either the rifle chamber was empty or it had jammed.

Tossing the useless weapon aside, he dropped to one knee, barely dodging another bullet as he jerked out his derringer and fired.

This time there was a satisfying report.

Unfortunately, Scarcheek was a split second faster.

Jo shook her head, trying to clear it, as she pushed up from the ground with both hands. The fall had knocked the wind clear out of her. Her entire left side, from shoulder to hip, felt bruised and battered. Looking up, she spotted Licorice, tail high, galloping back toward home.

Bam! Bam!

She flattened again, twisting around to see where the shots had come from. She saw Mr. Lassiter's back first and then Otis beyond him. How had the greenhorn got himself between her and that snake in the few seconds since Licorice had stumbled?

As she watched, Mr. Lassiter went down, hitting the ground with a jarring thud.

No! Her heart stopped and then stuttered painfully back to life.

Dear God, please, let him still be alive.

It took her a moment to realize Otis had turned his attention back her way.

"Well, now," he said nastily, "first I get to give Pretty Boy the comeuppance he deserves, and now you land in my lap too. Must be my lucky day."

The words cleared the last of the wool from Jo's head and she frantically looked around for her dropped rifle.

He snickered. "Don't even try to go for it or I'll shoot you where you sit."

There! The rifle was just a few feet away. "Don't know that it matters much," she said, trying to give herself time to think. "You're just going to shoot me anyway."

"Maybe. Hadn't decided yet." He moved closer, keeping the gun pointed at her. She winced when he paused to give Mr. Lassiter's leg a vicious kick. "I thought we might have a little fun first." He licked his lip in a disgusting manner. "See if there's really a woman under all those man's clothes."

His leering words made the decision for her. She'd rather chance getting shot than endure the fate he was planning.

She scrambled on all fours toward the weapon, hearing Otis laugh as if at a bawdy joke, knowing she'd never reach it in time, but driven to try anyway.

As she dove the last few feet to the rifle, Jo braced for the bullet, prayed he'd miss, or if not, that it would kill her clean.

She flinched when she heard the anticipated shot, but felt nothing, not even the bullet's impact.

Had he missed?

Her hand closed reflexively on the rifle to the sound of Otis's screams and vile oaths.

She flipped onto her back with the weapon aimed and ready, but instead of finding the brute still bearing down on her, he stood clutching his side, blood streaming through his fingers, his rifle lying useless on the ground.

She looked past him and saw Mr. Lassiter, pale and unsteady on his knees, but blessedly alive and strong enough to aim his pistol at Otis. He'd apparently managed to get a shot off, one that had saved her life.

Relief washed through her in giddy waves as she got to her knees. If Otis had been able to carry out his threat—

She fought down the sour bile rising in her throat.

Otis, still spitting out a stream of curses, reached down for his rifle.

"Don't," Mr. Lassiter rasped.

Otis froze, his hand less than a foot from the weapon.

"The way I see it," her wounded hero continued, "is that no matter how good a shot you are, between Miss Wylie and me, one of us is bound to get you before you can get both of us."

Otis looked from one to the other of them, then slowly straightened, one hand still clutching his side.

"Smart move." Mr. Lassiter made a sideways motion with his weapon. "Now step away from the gun."

Otis moved back several paces.

"Far enough." Mr. Lassiter's eyes flickered her way briefly before returning to the low-down skunk still moaning over his wound. "Are you all right, Miss Wylie?"

"I'm fine." The way he insisted on addressing her so respectful-like after all her carryings on today struck her as oddly sweet.

Now why was she thinking on things like that at a time like this? That fall must have rattled her more than she reckoned.

She stood, trying not to wince at the pain from her bruised muscles. Nothing broken at least, but she'd be moving gingerly for a few days. "Just bruised up a bit," she reassured him.

"Think you can find something to tie up our friend with?"

"Be my pleasure." She started toward Scout, but kept a watchful eye on Mr. Lassiter. He held his gun pointed at Otis, but he didn't attempt to stand. His shirt was soaked with blood, his forehead was beaded with sweat, and as she watched he swayed, then leaned heavily back on his haunches.

The man had to be keeping himself upright by sheer willpower.

She pushed herself to move faster, trying to ignore the fire that licked at her ankle with each step. But she'd only covered half the distance when she saw his aim waver.

"Mr. Lassiter!" Changing course, she made a beeline toward him, but before she could reach him, his eyes fluttered closed. He swayed, then slowly crumpled to the ground.

Jo charged across the last few yards, her pulse pounding an urgent rhythm. This was her fault. She should have done more to warn him, should have intervened sooner.

He *had* to be okay. She would *not* have his death on her conscience.

An eternity of seconds later, Jo dropped to her knees beside him, braced for the worst. A part of her registered the sound of Otis's retreat, but he'd left his rifle behind so she let him go. Right now Mr. Lassiter's well-being was more important than getting vengeance on that bucket of pond scum.

Jo gently brushed the hair from his brow. The low moan that greeted her was the sweetest sound she'd heard in quite some time.

No time to savor her relief, though. He might be alive, but he was far from okay. He hadn't opened his eyes and his breathing was thready. The red stain that drenched his shirt was getting darker by the minute. Even more worrisome was the blood that matted one side of his head.

Gorge rose in her throat but she sent up a prayer for strength. This wasn't the time to act like some prim and proper twit—Mr. Lassiter needed help and right now she was all he had.

Jo gently probed his head where the blood seemed thickest. Yep, there was the wound. Nothing lodged there—best she could tell the bullet had grazed him, gouging a furrow as it went. No way to know how serious it was until Doc Whitman got a look at it.

Trying to remain alert in case Otis circled back, she turned her attention to Mr. Lassiter's arm. Using her pocketknife, she cut open his sleeve to get a better look. The source of all that blood was quickly found—a nasty hole in his upper arm, an ugly, gaping thing that oozed a sluggish stream of blood.

Tightening her jaw, she gingerly examined the wound.

When Jo found the exit hole on the other side of his arm, she swiped her sleeve across her forehead and got her breathing back under control. At least she wouldn't have to try to dig the blamed bullet out.

Now that the initial gut-churning shock was behind her, Jo's control snapped back into place.

First order of business—stop the bleeding. Between the two wounds, and pushing himself to defend the two of them, he'd lost entirely too much blood.

Had he really thrown his already-injured-body between her and Otis? The man was either the flea-brained fool she'd called him earlier or one of the most heroic men she'd ever met.

Maybe both.

If he hadn't stopped Otis—

Her mind rebelled, refusing to finish that thought.

Setting her jaw, she cut his now useless sleeve completely off, then did the same with his other one and both of hers. Taking a few precious minutes to wet one of the strips in the stream, she used it to clean his injuries as best she could. Then she formed pads with the remaining cloths and bound them in place.

Sitting back, Jo stretched her leg to ease the throbbing. She watched her unconscious hero closely for a few minutes, then nodded in satisfaction. The blood seemed staunched, for now at least. It would be nice, though, if he'd open those gunpowder gray eyes again, even if it was just for a moment. Long enough to assure her he'd be all right.

She took a quick glance around. They seemed to be out of

any immediate danger. Otis was long gone and Clete hadn't moved from where he'd fallen.

She squared her shoulders and slowly turned to her right. Like a coward, she'd been avoiding what she knew had to be done.

Rising heavily, she headed toward the fallen horse that had served as Mr. Lassiter's living shield.

Chapter Five

Scout had quit struggling, but his muscles quivered with each labored breath. It was obvious the animal's injuries were irreparable, his time left extremely painful. Jo felt the hot tears come as she knelt to stroke the horse's neck.

The horse she'd raised from a colt gazed at her with pain-filled eyes as she gently finger combed the tangles from his mane.

Heavenly Father, help me through this 'cause I don't think I can do it on my own.

"I'm so sorry," she said, her voice breaking on the last word. With a final pat, Jo wiped her eyes, stood and aimed the rifle.

A heartbeat later, it was over. She lowered the gun, still holding it with both hands. The weight seemed almost more than she could bear.

But mourning was a luxury she couldn't afford right now—time to refocus on the needs of the living. She paused by Mr. Lassiter's side long enough to assure herself he was still breathing, then, steeling her nerve, Jo limped over to where Clete lay. Doing her best to ignore the sick feeling in the pit of her stomach, she rolled the body over. A quick look was all it took. The beefy outlaw was quite dead.

Everything had happened so fast when she charged into the meadow. She hadn't aimed, just fired, trying to draw attention from Mr. Lassiter. Could one of *her* bullets have done this?

That thought broke the last thread of her control and she found herself on all fours, heaving.

It was several minutes before she could straighten back up.

Determined to be practical, Jo averted her gaze from Clete's unseeing stare and pulled out her pocketknife again. Making quick work of it, she cut large strips from his shirt. It felt like grave robbing, but it wasn't as if Clete had any more use for the shirt, and it was a sure bet she'd need additional bandages for Mr. Lassiter before this was over. And with evening coming on she couldn't afford to sacrifice any more of their own clothing.

She wadded up the swaths of cloth, then retrieved the dead man's rifle, using it to ease herself back up with a groan. Yep, she'd be feeling the effects of that fall for several days.

Playing a hunch, she studied the wooded area where Clete and Otis had hidden earlier. Catching a glimpse of movement, she gave a satisfied smile. Sure enough, a few minutes later she found Clete's horse, tethered to a low branch just inside the wood.

Thank goodness Otis hadn't bothered to take the animal with him. With Licorice halfway back to Knotty Pine and Scout dead, this horse would give them some much needed options.

Once she had the mare tethered near the stream, Jo returned to Mr. Lassiter's side, wiping his face with a damp cloth. It wasn't much, but it was all she could think to do at the moment. His breathing seemed stronger, but he was still unconscious and pale as moonlight.

She hated feeling so all-fired useless. He needed more than puny old wet cloths. He needed a doctor, and the sooner the better. But all she could do for now was make him as comfortable as possible.

Jo rubbed her calf, trying to ease a bit of the throbbing. Too bad there wasn't anyone here to see to *her* comfort.

Oh, well, like it or not, being the one to do the looking after had become her lot in life.

With a sigh, she stood and began gathering wood to make a fire, one that would not only ward off the coming chill of evening but would also create lots of smoke.

Whenever the search party came looking—she refused to believe that wouldn't happen soon—she wanted to make finding them as easy as possible.

Ry stirred, then grimaced. His head throbbed as if a judge were pounding a gavel in his skull, and there seemed to be a branding iron pressed into his shoulder. He shifted, trying to get more comfortable, then fisted his hands against the pain that shot through his leg. Thunderation! It felt like he'd been mule kicked.

Was that *grass* under his hand? Had his horse thrown him? He couldn't think straight—his mind felt thick as sludge. He tried opening his eyes, but only managed slits.

Then the memory of what had happened came stampeding back and his heart slammed in his chest as he struggled to get up. He had to make sure Scarcheek didn't get to Miss Wylie—

"Whoa there." A hand pressed him gently but firmly down.

Relief surged through him. That had been her voice. She was okay. *Thank You, Lord!*

But where was Scarcheek? He renewed his efforts to get up. "My gun!" Was that croak really his voice? "Where—"

She cut off his words by pressing him down again, this time wiping his brow with a damp cloth.

"Easy. No need to get stirred up. We're in the clear now."

Had his last desperate shot found its mark? If only he could remember…

As if reading his mind she answered his unvoiced questions. "Clete won't be bothering anyone—not ever again. And Otis is long gone. High-tailed it out of here, bleeding like a stuck pig, as soon as he saw you fall."

Realizing he'd obviously blacked out, leaving her to deal with a hornet's nest on her own, he wanted to howl in frustration and self-disgust. How long had he been unconscious?

Whatever had happened, it was a good thing the gun-wielding outlaw was gone. He couldn't even sit up right now, much less fight off anything more threatening than a gnat.

He studied Miss Wylie, looking for signs of injury. "What about you? Your horse fell—"

"Got bruised up a mite, nothing serious."

Her tone was light but the strain in her expression told a different story. Was she hurt worse than—

The memory of Scarcheek's threat suddenly slammed back into him. He grabbed her wrist. "Did he touch you? So help me, if he did there's no place far enough—"

"Whoa there, hero." Her smile was more genuine this time. "Otis never laid a hand on me. Thanks entirely to you."

Hero—hah! Ry suppressed a groan at her attempt to make him feel better. Still, he couldn't help but admire her courage and fortitude.

This woman was unlike any he'd ever met. How could she find something to smile about after all she'd just been through? Most women he knew would be hysterical, would be looking for him to comfort *them*.

Aware that he was still squeezing her wrist, he released her and leaned back. He realized there was a bandage on his head and another on his otherwise bare arm.

A woman of many talents, it seemed, and one who didn't let squeamishness get in the way of doing what had to be done.

She reached beside her and lifted a canteen. "How about a drink of water?"

At his nod she rested the canteen on his chest then twisted around, reaching for something he couldn't quite see. "First, let's try to get you propped up a bit."

A second later he realized she was maneuvering a saddle into place behind him.

"Easy now." She slipped a hand under his neck, supporting him while she nudged the makeshift prop under his shoulders. She was surprisingly strong. No doubt due to her work at the livery. Funny how nice those callused hands felt against his skin.

He tried to keep the wince from his expression as the movements dug the branding iron deeper into his shoulder. He wasn't going to add to her already piled-high worries.

"There now," she eased him back, "how does that feel?"

"Better, thanks."

"Good." She held the canteen to his lips, once more supporting his neck. The water tasted heavenly and felt even better going down. The liquid smoothed away the sawdust lining his mouth and throat. He couldn't get enough of it, as if he were a parched bit of earth that hadn't seen rain in months.

"Easy now," she repeated, a touch of humor in her voice, "There's a whole stream of this stuff over yonder so there's no need to worry we'll run out before you're quenched."

Her teasing surprised an answering grin from him. "Are you maligning my table manners, Miss Wylie?"

She shrugged, her expression bland. "Not me. I'm used to being around animals that drink from troughs, remember?"

Ry chuckled at her unexpected dry humor. At least the day's events hadn't robbed her of her spirit.

"And there's no need to be so formal, especially considering the fix we're in. Just call me Jo."

He hesitated, not wanting to offend her, but not certain he wanted to comply. The use of Miss Wylie had been a deliberate effort to make up for his having mistaken her for a man, even if she wasn't aware of his gaffe. Calling her Jo, a man's name, just didn't sit right with him after so ungentlemanly a blunder. But she didn't seem like a Josephine either. "What if I call you Josie instead?"

A flash of surprise crossed her features. But her only response was an offhand "I reckon that'll do."

"And of course you can call me Ry."

With a nod, she raised the canteen to his lips again. He took care to drink more slowly this time, taking the opportunity to look around. She'd built a fire while he was out, one that was emitting enough smoke to cure a side of bacon. A second saddle lay on the ground next to him and what looked to be the rest of the tack and gear from two horses was placed in neat piles nearby.

A whicker drew his gaze toward the stream. A horse stood tethered there. Not the horse she'd charged in on and certainly not Scout. How in the world had she managed to find another mount out here?

Then he spied what was unmistakably a body covered by a couple of horse blankets.

His gaze shot back to her.

Her smile was gone and her jaw tightened. "It's Clete," she said. "I thought covering him up was the decent thing to do."

Ry leaned back against the saddle, glad for its support.

Her fingers fiddled with the cap of the now empty canteen. "I didn't see him go down. I don't know which one of us—"

"It was my shot," he said quickly, realizing what she feared.

"Oh." She searched his face for a moment, then the tension in her eased. She stood and waggled the canteen. "Better refill this."

Ry shifted again, chafing at his weakened condition as he

watched her limp toward the stream. She was hurt, yet she hadn't spoken a word of complaint. How long had she been sitting there, wondering if she'd been responsible for taking a man's life?

His opinion of her character rose another notch.

"How long was I out?"

"About thirty minutes or so," she called back over her shoulder. "Had me worried for a while."

Again, her light tone didn't quite cover the underlying strain. He knew it wasn't all due to the physical pain and exhaustion she must be feeling. The emotional turmoil she'd been through had taken its toll as well.

She paused to check on the horse before stooping with some difficulty at the stream to refill the canteen. Her action reminded him of what had happened to Scout. Had the animal died of its wounds, or had she been forced to deal with that, as well?

Either way, he had a lot to make up for. Starting now.

"Only thirty minutes, huh?" he said as she returned. "It appears you made good use of the time."

She shrugged. "I'm used to keeping busy."

That he could believe. "Well, you've set up a tight little camp here." Pulling on every ounce of strength he had, Ry propped himself up on one elbow. "I ought to be comfortable enough while you head back to town."

Her eyes widened. "What?"

"Take that horse and ride to town. You can send a wagon back for me. There's no point in us both just sitting here hoping someone will come along."

"Uh-uh. Whether we like it or not, we're in this together. I'm not leaving here without you, not after all the trouble I went through to save your hide."

"And you can finish the job by sending a wagon back for me."

"What if Otis comes back?"

Exactly. He had to make certain she was well out of harm's way. "Look, Josie, you said yourself Otis was long gone. Besides, I'm not hurt so bad that I can't hold my own for the time it'll take you to get to town and send help back. Just leave me one of those rifles and I'll be fine."

She snorted. "Fine my left foot." Thrusting a rifle at him, she walked off, positioning herself several yards behind him. "Okay, hero, I'm Otis. Defend yourself."

Ry struggled to sit up and at the same time swivel his body to face her. He failed miserably. On both counts.

"Might as well quit trying." The edge of irritation in her voice exacerbated the ache in his head. "If I was Otis you'd already be dead. And that's with lots of warning to boot."

She stood over him, glaring. "Hang it all, Mister, there's no shame in admitting you're hurt. It's just plain selfish, too— making more work for me. Look at you. All that tomfool twisting and turning set your arm to bleeding again. At this rate we're going to run out of bandages before we can get you to the doc."

Even if he'd had the energy to take offense, Ry knew she was right. For a moment he didn't even have the breath to speak.

He flopped back with a thud that amplified the pounding in his head. It was getting colder too. He couldn't suppress the shiver that wracked his body.

Josie removed the rifle from his grasp, her brow furrowing. "How are you feeling?"

"Thoroughly useless."

She patted his hand, as if he were some wet-behind-the-ears kid who needed comforting. "Sorry I lit into you that way— ain't your fault you don't like being stove up. My ma used to say that trying times were God's way of keeping us humble and reminding us to look to Him for our strength."

She leaned back. "Just think of it as taking a bit of time off from all that rushing around you've been doing."

Belle! Hang it all, with everything that had happened he'd forgotten all about her cry for help. If only she hadn't been so cryptic about what she needed from him.

"Can't afford to take time off right now." He shivered again. So cold. So tired. "Belle needs me."

He closed his eyes to keep the spinning sky from drawing him into the maelstrom.

Belle. Josie. Different as night and day. In fact, the only thing they had in common was that they were facing big troubles.

And he was powerless to lift a finger to help either of them.

Chapter Six

W ho was Belle?

Jo tried to ignore her curiosity and concentrate instead on keeping Mr. Lassiter from passing out.

His eyes drifted closed again and she chewed on her lip. How serious *were* his injuries?

"Come on, Mister—Ry—try to stay awake. Just until help comes. It shouldn't be much longer."

His eyes fluttered open. "Sorry. Feeling drowsy."

"Talk to me. Where you traveling from?"

"Philadelphia."

"Hah! I knew you weren't a rancher."

That got a reaction from him. "Not calling me a liar, are you? I said I was *raised* on a ranch. My family's still there."

"But not you."

"My grandfather lives in Philadelphia. I stayed with him while I went to law school."

"So which do you call home, the ranch or Philadelphia?"

His face creased in annoyance. "Too many questions."

She tried another tack. "So why were you in such an all-fired hurry to reach Foxberry?"

"Still am. Supposed to meet someone there, someone who asked for help."

"You came all the way from Philadelphia to answer a call for help? Must be an awfully good friend."

"She is."

She? Was it this Belle woman he'd mentioned?

He lifted a hand, then let it drop. "Sounded urgent. Hadn't heard from her in years. She must be desperate."

He shifted again and winced. "What makes you so sure help is coming?"

Jo threw another stick on the fire. "Whenever Licorice gets spooked she heads straight for home. As soon as she shows up without me, Danny'll put out the alarm."

"And if she doesn't get there this time?"

"My sister's the worrying type. By now she's started hounding the sheriff and won't let up until he sends someone out to look." If only she hadn't told Danny she might be late. No point worrying him with that little bit of information though. "Don't you worry, we'll get you to a doctor soon enough."

"Not worried. Just thinking we should make use of that horse."

"We already talked about that. I'm not leaving you here alone." She tugged on her ear. "I could try making a litter I guess. We have most of the materials—the bedroll, rope, leather from the bridle." She glanced toward the shrouded body and shivered. "I could even use the horse blankets if we needed 'em. Just have to try to cut a few saplings for the poles—"

"Or we could ride double."

She studied him. "Do you think you could mount up?"

His mouth tightened. "I might need a hand, but I could do it."

"I don't know if we should put you to the test until we have to. There's still time for help to get here before dark."

His jaw clinched and she could tell he wasn't happy with what he was about to say. "Look, I'll be honest. Right now I believe I have the strength to do this, with your help. But I'm not sure how long that'll last." He stared at her with fiercely determined eyes. "So if we're going to mount up, it had better be soon."

Jo glanced toward the trail from town. No sign of help. The temperature had already started dropping and it'd be dusk soon.

She also didn't care much for the flushed look of his face. If he developed a fever things could go from bad to worse in a hurry. He was right. Time to fish or cut bait.

The thing was, she wasn't just worried about getting him up on the horse, though that was going to take more than a bit of effort. Was he really up to the long ride back to Knotty Pine? He'd admitted his strength was fading. His wound could start bleeding again, or worse, he could fall off. If that happened they'd be worse off than before.

What a pickle!

Jo drew her shoulders back. Better to leave the hand wringing to Cora Beth. It wasn't a great choice but it was the only one they had. The last thing she needed was to be caught out here after dark, with Otis roaming around somewhere.

"Okay, let's give it a shot. You conserve what strength you have while I put out the fire and get the horse ready."

He nodded.

"Just try to stay awake." Grabbing the fallen branch she'd been using as a makeshift cane, Jo levered herself up. She'd probably be sore for the next few days but she'd put up with worse aches before. And it wasn't anything like what Mr. Lassiter was dealing with.

She still had trouble thinking of him as just Ry. Funny thing how he'd insisted on addressing her as Josie instead of Jo. No one had called her that before. Ma had always used her given name of Josephine, and her nieces called her Aunt JoJo. But to everyone else she was just plain Jo.

Josie. Kind of had a nice ring to it. Not too frilly or fancy sounding, but definitely recognizable as a girl's name.

The thought struck her then that she would finally have a story of her own to add to her journal. Not that this was the way she'd wanted it to happen, but it was an adventure just the same.

Heavenly Father, I know I've been praying for an adventure and now that I've found myself smack-dab in the middle of a humdinger of one it don't seem quite right for me to be asking You to end it so soon. But I guess that's what I'm doing.

Mr. Lassiter don't deserve to suffer just 'cause I want some excitement. Especially since he pushed himself so hard to save me. So please, whatever it takes, keep him safe.

Ry roused to the feel of a damp cloth on his forehead.

He opened his eyes to see Josie staring down at him, her face creased in worry.

"You sure you want to try this? We can always wait a little longer for help to come."

"I'm all right. Just resting."

Doubt flashed in her eyes at his obvious fib.

"Let's see if you can sit up first," she temporized.

Determined to reassure her, Ry steeled himself and pushed up with his good arm, doing his best to ignore the spinning sensation. He gritted his teeth, chafing at this unaccustomed feebleness. If he hadn't had her hand at his back he might not have made it.

After a moment he felt steady again and took his bearings. He must have been out for more than the few seconds he'd thought. She'd managed to douse the fire without him even noticing.

"First we're going to put that arm of yours in a sling and

secure it against your chest so we can keep from jarring it as much as possible. Won't do to have you bleeding to death on me."

Where had she found those strips of cloth? His eyes flashed to the blanket-covered body in sudden understanding. The woman not only had gumption but she was cannily resourceful.

"That was a mighty vicious kick Otis gave you," she said, bringing his gaze back around. "You sure you can stand okay?"

That explained why his thigh hurt so bad. "I'll manage."

"Have you ever ridden bareback before?" she asked.

"Yes, of course."

"Good. 'Cause I figure that's our best chance of getting the two of us on that animal.

Made sense. Riding double with a saddle was not a comfortable proposition.

"Problem is, without stirrups we need a mounting block. There's a fallen tree over where I've tethered the horse. If you use me as a crutch, can you make it?"

He eyed the distance separating him from the horse. About ten yards. Might as well have been a mile. "I'll make it."

"Good." She studied her handiwork with the sling. "How does that feel? Not too tight is it?"

"It's fine." Enough talk, time for action.

"Okay then. Whenever you're ready, put your good arm around my neck and I'll help you up, nice and steady."

Bracing himself, Ry nodded and did as he was told.

By the time he finally stood upright, he was as winded as a racehorse after a gallop and drenched in sweat.

Josie supported him, not saying a word or clucking over him in useless sympathy. He appreciated her patience and restraint.

He was also determined not to lean on her one jot more than necessary. He just needed her to provide an anchor when the waves of dizziness hit.

He'd be hanged if he'd let any of his injuries stop him. It was imperative that he get her away from here, and it seemed the only way to budge her was to go with her.

Lord, let me make it to that horse without giving this woman more troubles than she's already had.

He let her lead him across the short patch of ground, focusing on placing one foot in front of the other. And on not falling.

When they reached the makeshift mounting block he paused, gathering every bit of energy he still possessed for the effort ahead.

Before he could move, she spoke up. "Now this is going to be the tricky part. I'll need to ride up front so I can guide the horse. That means I should mount first. Can you support yourself while I do that?"

Ry nodded. It had to be done, so he would do it. He'd always prided himself on his horsemanship—time to give it a *real* test. Mounting with no stirrups and only one good arm would be tricky under the best of circumstances. Doing it while he was weak as a babe and she was already taking up a good chunk of available space would ratchet it up to a whole new level of difficulty.

He moved his arm from her shoulders to the horse's back, aware that she kept her hand on him, ready to assist if he should fall.

"Steady now. Once you're ready I'm going to let go so I can mount up. I'll help you up after me as much as I can."

He took a deep breath. "Let's get this over with." Almost before he had time to draw a second breath she was up on the horse. She scooted forward then reached down. "I'll hold the horse as steady as I can. Take my hand so I can help pull you up.

The next few minutes were fragmented splinters of motion. He grabbed hold of her hand, then found himself chest first over the back of the horse, pain clawing through his injured arm and shoulder. The next thing he knew he had somehow gotten his leg over the horse without any memory of doing so, and was maneuvering himself into an upright position.

Which brought him face-to-face with his next dilemma.

"This isn't the time to worry about niceties," she said, obviously reading his mind again. "Ain't no way you're going to be able to stay on this horse without holding on to me. We're not budging from here until that arm of yours is around my waist."

She was right of course. Still, it felt like taking liberties he wasn't entitled to. "Yes, ma'am." He eased his right hand around her surprisingly trim waist, but managed to hold himself erect, keeping several inches between his chest and her back.

She set the horse in motion. "I'm going to try to keep a slow, steady pace. This probably won't be the most comfortable ride you ever took, but it'll be best if we go straight through without stopping."

"I agree." He swallowed an oath as the horse tossed its head before settling into a steady rhythm. "The sooner we get back to town, the better." He wasn't certain he could climb back up on this animal if he ever got off of it.

He'd just have to live with the fact that they were headed back to Knotty Pine and not toward Foxberry. For now, Josie's needs would come before his, and even before Belle's.

Jo wasn't ready to celebrate just yet. Getting him up on the horse had only been half the battle. The other half would be keeping him there until they reached town.

The man had a lot of grit, she'd give him that. Not many would have managed to come through that ambush and lived to tell the tale.

She'd been well aware of his efforts to spare her during their walk across the clearing, and again when he'd mounted up.

Even now, with his hand around her waist, she could feel his effort not to lean against her. If she'd had reason to question whether he was an honorable man before, she could set her mind at ease now.

Probably be best to keep him talking so she could gauge how alert he was. Besides, she liked the sound of his voice. "Tell me about that family of yours back on the ranch."

"I have a brother and a sister, Griff and Sadie." His voice had slowed and deepened, his Texas drawl coming out. And she could feel the warmth of his breath stir the hair at her nape.

She told herself the shiver that fluttered her shoulders was due to the dropping temperature. "I said tell me about them, not name them."

"What do you want to know?"

"The usual stuff. Are they older or younger than you? Are they married? What are they like?"

"Both younger—Griff by two years, Sadie by five. Neither is married."

He paused and she wondered if he would give her any more information.

"Griff takes after Pa—a rancher through and through. Hawk's Creek is in his blood and you couldn't pry him away with a crowbar."

So, was he implying that he himself wasn't so tied to the land? She could sure relate to that. God had made this world way too big to limit yourself to one little patch of it.

"Sadie's what you'd call impetuous. She's a bit on the clumsy side, but she doesn't let that stop her. She's as comfortable at a barn raising as she is at a ladies auxiliary tea."

Sounded like someone she'd get along fine with. "How often do you see them?"

"Two, three times a year."

It was like wresting a bone from a dog to get any information out of him. Did he hurt too bad to talk? Or did he just not like the questions she was asking? "Tell me about the ranch."

"Hawk's Creek? It's just north of Tyler. Covers about six hundred acres all told. My family raises some of the finest Hereford stock around. Not to mention cutting horses."

There was an unmistakable touch of pride in his voice. Sounded like he still had a fondness for the place. "So how did you end up going to law school?"

"Long story."

His voice was getting deeper, his words dragging. She had to keep him alert. "Seems we've got nothing but time. Talk to me."

"My grandfather's a lawyer and prominent member of Philadelphia society. Mother was his only child."

He paused and she leaned against him briefly. She could almost see him pull himself back together.

"She was the apple of his eye," he continued. "He didn't like it much when she up and married my pa and moved to Texas. Took it even harder when she died without ever moving back."

"And?" she prodded, placing her hand on top of his at her waist.

"Grandfather always wanted a son to follow in his footsteps. The year I turned sixteen, he asked my father to send one of us boys up to Philadelphia to spend a few months with him. Truth be told, I think Pa felt guilty over having deprived Grandfather of his daughter. Whatever the reason, he agreed."

"And you volunteered."

"It was only supposed to be for the summer."

That sounded almost defensive.

He shifted but his hand never moved from her waist. "When summer was over, Grandfather wanted me to accompany him on a trip to Boston. When we returned he needed help researching a major case. Then he wanted to show me his lodge up in the Adirondacks. The entire fall stretched out that way, one 'one more thing' after another, and it was Christmas before I made it home."

The offhand, almost resentful way he cataloged his travels, as if he'd just taken a not-too-enjoyable walk around the block, flabbergasted her. She'd give her eyeteeth to have such an experience. "Sounds like he went all out to give you a taste of what your mother's world had been like."

"I never thought of it that way." He seemed to ponder on that a moment before he went on. "Anyway, before I left Philadelphia, he asked me to consider returning to attend the university and perhaps enter law school. It was hard to leave because I knew he was lonely and that in a way I was a tie to his daughter."

"Is that the only reason you went back?" Surely life in a big city like Philadelphia would have spoiled him for something as simple as life on a ranch.

"Things had changed while I was away. Pa relied more on Griff to help run the ranch. Sadie was growing into the lady of the house. Pa spent more time with his work than with the family. Everything appeared to be running smoothly without me." He shifted slightly. "I just seemed like more of an outsider there than I had at Grandfather's."

Much as Jo wanted to get away from Knotty Pine and see the world, there was something sad about his story. Family was so important. No wonder he hadn't answered when she asked which place he called home.

"Don't know why I just told you all that," he said gruffly. "Must be woozier than I thought."

"Is your pa still around?"

"No. He died two years ago. Griff runs the ranch now."

Did he resent his younger brother for stepping in to the oldest son's role? Or was he relieved not to have that burden?

They rode in silence for a while. Jo figured as long as his grip on her waist was firm enough he wasn't in any danger of drifting off.

And it definitely was firm, though not uncomfortably so. At least not in the usual sense. His hold wasn't the least bit inappropriate. He merely used her to steady himself. He'd have held onto a sack of flour the same way. Even so, something about the near-embrace made her feel safe, secure, protected in an almost intimate kind of way. She'd never experienced such feelings before.

She'd always done her best to discourage any thoughts the men in Knotty Pine might have of walking out with her. After all, she had big plans to travel some day, and marriage would only get in the way. She needed wings, not roots.

Not that the menfolk had lined up to come courting. She wasn't exactly the kind of woman men looked for in a wife. Too outspoken and independent, she supposed.

Funny, though, how that didn't seem to bother Mr. Lassiter...

She gave her head a shake, not comfortable with where that line of thought might lead. Time for more talk and less thinking. "So nowadays you spend most of your time in Philadelphia? Do you get to travel to other places?"

"Sometimes."

"Like where?"

"There's that hunting lodge in the Adirondacks my grandfather owns—we spend several weeks a year there. And I've been to most parts of New England at one time or another."

"Ever been to another country?"

"Once."

His one word answers were less than informative. "Where to?"

"Greece." He seemed to be speaking with an effort. "A client hired me to check on some legal aspects of an estate he'd inherited there."

Greece! She had a world map in her room, one of her dearest treasures. On it were pins marking all the interesting-sounding places various travelers had told her about. This was the first one from Greece. "The good Lord willing, I aim to do my own share of traveling some day."

"Is that so?"

She hadn't realized she'd voiced that thought aloud. No shame in it though. "Yep. Just as soon as Danny's old enough to take care of the livery on his own I plan to set out and see as much of the world as I can."

"By yourself?"

"Sure. Other women have done it. Look at Ida Pfeiffer and Nellie Bly and Isabella Bird. And my own Aunt Pearl."

"If any woman can, you…"

The slurred words drifted into something incoherent as his grip on her waist slackened.

"Mister!" She grabbed his hand. She had to keep him on this horse.

If he slid off there'd be no getting him back up.

Chapter Seven

The sharp command jerked Ry back to consciousness. There had been more than a warning in her voice, there'd been worry edged with outright desperation. And it was his fault.

On top of everything else on her plate right now she had to worry about keeping him on the horse as if he were some toddler astride his first pony.

"Sorry. I'm okay now." He hoped he sounded more confident than he felt.

"Lean against me if you need to. Just don't you dare fall off this animal."

"Yes, ma'am." Despite the seriousness of the situation, Ry found himself amused by her military general attitude. And also touched by her courage.

But he refused to let himself take advantage of her generosity any more than absolutely necessary. He'd keep himself upright under his own steam as long as possible. And he offered up a prayer that his "steam" would last long enough to get them where they were going.

"Tell me about this Aunt Pearl of yours."

"She was a really colorful woman. Spent most of her life as the personal companion to an opera singer. The two of them traveled all over the world and met lots of exciting people."

"Sounds like an interesting life." He tried to focus on her words, anything to keep the blackness at bay.

"Oh, it was. Aunt Pearl was fifty-one when Madame Liddy passed on, and she came to live with us. I was six at the time and used to spend hours listening to her stories."

She gave a selfconscious laugh, a surprisingly feminine sound that brought a smile to his lips.

"Aunt Pearl used to say she saw herself in me. Made me promise to not let myself get locked away in Knotty Pine, at least not until I'd tasted what the rest of the world had to offer."

"How old were you when you made the promise?"

"Eight. But I never forgot it. And I'm going to do it someday, too, even if it takes me another fifteen years to work out the hows and wherefores."

"I believe you." And he did.

They rode in silence for a while. Or maybe she did some talking. But his efforts were now wholly focused on staying upright and he didn't have room to pay attention to anything else.

Twice more he caught himself as he slumped forward. The third time she halted the horse and stared at him over her shoulder. The worry in her eyes cut as deep into him as any blade.

"I hope you're a praying man, Mister, 'cause we need some help from the Almighty to get us the rest of the way home."

She chewed on her lower lip a moment then seemed to come to a decision. "I have to climb down to take care of something. If you can hold steady for just a bit, you can lean over the horse's neck as soon as I'm out of the way. Think you can manage?"

He nodded, then wished he hadn't. The world spun dizzily.

"Okay, we'll do this nice and easy." She moved his hand

from her waist and he suddenly felt set adrift. But before he could flounder, her voice came to him from somewhere in the vicinity of his knee.

"Just lean forward. That's right, all the way. Take hold of the mane with your good hand."

Her tone was soothing, her words mesmerizing. Before he knew it, his chest rested against the horse's neck. It was a relief to let the tension ebb away, to not worry about burdening her with his weight or inadvertently taking ungentlemanly liberties. If he could just rest here for a few minutes, he should be able to hold himself together for another go at this when she mounted up again.

Ry tried to pry his eyes open, but they weren't cooperating. He couldn't seem to get his bearings, and was having trouble telling up from down.

How long had he been out this time? Couldn't have been too long—he could still feel the heat of the sun beating down on him, scorching him all the way to his core. Where was that cool breeze when he wanted it?

He could feel the movement of the horse, hear the plodding of its hooves. At least he'd managed to stay astride.

It was so hot! This felt like a Texas summer, not fall. "Water." The word came out as a raspy croak. Right now he'd give every bit of cash in his wallet for a sip of cool liquid.

"Try to hold out a little longer. I promise you can have all the water you want as soon as we reach town."

Startled, he realized the voice hadn't come from in front of him. Why hadn't he realized before now that he was still slumped over the horse's neck?

He managed to open his eyes enough to see Josie walking beside the horse, one hand on his thigh to steady him.

How long had she been walking? Had she ever intended to remount in the first place? He tried to sit up. "What are you—"

"Settle back down. You'll get that arm to bleeding again and I've run out of bandages."

Ry fought the returning blackness, tried to protest, but the words came out as garbled nonsense. He shut his eyes, pushing back the molten darkness swirling about him, trying to gather both his strength and his wits, focusing on the feel of her hand on his knee. The heat was sapping what little energy he had left.

He wanted—needed—to convince her to get back on the horse, but his mind couldn't form the right words.

"That's it," she said. "Just concentrate on staying up there. Don't worry, I won't let you fall. Why, we'll be back to town before you know it."

Her words turned into a pleasant buzzing, then nothing. For a time—he couldn't say if it was minutes or hours—he battled the boiling current, surfacing into a sort of smoke-filled awareness before being ruthlessly tugged back under.

He was so hot! He felt like the rich man of the parable, locked in torment, pleading for Abraham to send Lazarus to slake his thirst. Was that it? Was this punishment for his failings?

No, he wasn't totally lost. Mercy had been granted. Someone was there, someone with calloused but curiously gentle hands, trickling liquid through his parched lips, wiping his brow with a cool cloth, providing relief until the next wave of searing darkness swallowed him again.

At one point Belle drifted in through the haze. He tried to reach for her, tried to apologize for not getting to her sooner. But no matter how hard he fought to reach her, the current tugged at him, held him back, and she stared at him with pleading eyes until the haze swallowed her again.

Through it all, those calloused hands and the sound of Josie's voice became his lifelines. Not that he understood much of what she said, but he knew when she was there and clutched at those moments of sanity. Sometimes her tone was soothing and gentle, other times it was coaxing or scolding. He even thought he heard her exhorting the Almighty on his behalf.

Finally the boiling eased, the current cooled and he floated aimlessly for a while. When the darkness came again, it approached as a friend, ready to wrap him in a blanket of peaceful sleep.

Ry roused reluctantly, trying to burrow back into the blessed painlessness of sleep. But his parched throat protested, urging him to full wakefulness.

He wasn't on the horse any longer. Instead he was lying on a nice comfortable bed. Where was Josie? Had she made it back okay?

He missed the nearness of her that had been his lifeline on that long nightmarish ride—the warmth of her hand on his at her waist, the earthy scent of her that had invaded his senses, the feel of her hair as strands fluttered back to tickle his face. And finally the comforting hand at his knee, connecting him to her, assuring him he was in good hands.

A rustling sound drew him back from his drowsy state. He couldn't see anyone, but it had to be his dictatorial rescuer.

"Water." Had that croak really been his voice?

"Goodness, you gave me quite a start."

Though definitely female, it wasn't the voice he'd expected. Ry pried his eyes open to find an apron-clad woman standing over him with a soft smile on her face.

Nope, definitely not Josie.

"It's so good to see you finally awake. And calm."

What did that mean? Vague images returned to him, images that he hoped were merely dreams. "Miss Wylie. Is she—"

"Don't you go getting all stirred up. Jo's just fine."

"I must have passed out again. I'm afraid I don't remember much about how I got here."

"I'm not at all surprised. Why, by the time the search party found the two of you, you were burning up with fever. You certainly gave us quite a scare."

Where exactly was "here?" Had he been dropped off at a farmhouse along the road back to town? "I'm sorry, Miss…"

"Collins. Cora Beth Collins. And it's Mrs." She reached for the pitcher on the bedside table and poured a glass of water. "I'm Jo's sister."

This was Josie's *sister?* He'd gotten the impression the livery owner was the provider for her household, that her sister would be younger, like Danny. But this woman appeared to be the older of the two by several years.

Mrs. Collins propped some pillows behind his head and then put the glass to his lips, cutting off any further questions. She, on the other hand, seemed quite happy to chatter on.

"I can't tell you how thankful we all are for the way you saved our Jo. You're a true hero."

Ry choked, sputtering precious drops of water. *Hero.* Didn't the woman know he was the one who'd actually put her sister in harm's way? And what all she'd endured to get him back to town?

Mrs. Collins dabbed his chin with a napkin. "I apologize if I was giving it to you too fast. Let's try that again, but slower this time." She held the glass to his lips again.

"After all that thrashing about," she continued, "I imagine you're hungry as a bear in springtime. But don't you worry none. I've got a nice pot of broth simmering on the stove and I'll fetch you a bowl just as soon as I leave here." She lowered the now empty glass, finally giving him a chance to speak.

"Your sister—" A fit of coughing sent a bolt of fire through his arm, making it impossible to finish his question.

His nurse-hostess made soothing noises and patted his hand until the coughing subsided. "There now," she said when he finally got his breath under control, "don't push yourself too much just yet." She set the glass down and straightened. "As for Jo, she's all right—thanks to you. Bruised up a bit, but she's not letting that slow her down."

Mrs. Collins smoothed the coverlet. "Speaking of Jo, I'd best send word you're awake. She's been worrying over you no end."

Disjointed memories surfaced again. Vague impressions of someone demanding he not be such a "pigheaded fool" and quit trying to get up because he'd fall flat on his face and how it would just serve him right if he did. He could venture a guess as to who'd delivered that acerbic advice.

His hostess stepped back. "You rest up for a bit while I fetch that broth."

"Thank you, Mrs. Collins. I certainly appreciate all you've done for me."

"Glad to do it. After all, you were there for Jo when she needed you."

Her words brought back another memory. How could he have forgotten? "I need to send a telegram."

"Of course. After I fetch your broth—"

"No, this is important." Her expression told him his words had come out too harsh, too abrupt. He fought to moderate his tone. "I'm sorry, but I must send word right away so the person I was traveling to see will know what happened."

Her expression changed into one of concern. "Of course. Your friend must be very worried. I'll fetch a pencil and paper right away."

"Thank you." Ry settled against the pillows and closed his

eyes, but not to sleep. His racing thoughts wouldn't allow it. Had Belle given up on him, decided he'd let her down?

"Well, now, don't you look all comfy."

He opened his eyes to see Josie standing in his doorway, shoulder propped against the jamb. How long had she been there?

Wondering how much of his vague memories were real and how much a mere dream, he shifted uncomfortably. "Your sister's a good nurse. Hope I haven't been too much trouble."

A flash of emotion flickered in her eyes then disappeared. "Don't worry about Cora Beth. She's happiest when she has someone to fuss over. And I'm afraid I don't play the part of patient near well enough to satisfy her." She pushed away from the jamb. "Won't find a better mother hen anywhere in the county."

She crossed the room, holding up the paper and pencil she'd brought with her. "I just came in from the livery to check on things and Cora Beth said you were in an all-fired hurry to get a telegram sent off."

"Yes, I—" He frowned as he noticed the way she favored her right leg. "Should you be up and about?"

Her glare was fierce enough to stop a charging bull. "Don't you start in on that. I have enough with Cora Beth nagging at me until I'm about ready to move out and set up camp in the livery."

He sympathized with her sister if this was an indication of the kind of patient Miss Wylie made. "At least it appears your temper hasn't suffered any ill effects."

She grinned. "Sounds like yours is recovering too."

Another allusion to the fact that he might have been less than docile while he was out. "What time is it?"

"Almost one o'clock."

He grimaced. "So, I was out for nearly a day."

"Two. It's Monday."

Two days! And he wasn't likely to be fit for travel today

either. He certainly hoped whatever was plaguing Belle would hold off another few days.

Miss Wylie pulled up a chair next to his bed. "So, I suppose the telegram is for your friend in Foxberry. Guess she's probably worrying over what happened to you. 'Specially since the train started running again this morning."

There was likely an "I told you so" lurking in her words, but Ry decided to ignore it. "Which is why I need to send the telegram off as soon as possible."

She held the pencil over the paper. "Ready whenever you are."

"Send it to Belle Anderson—no, make that Belle Hadley—in Foxberry, Texas." He'd almost forgotten her married name.

Which brought up a question that had nagged at him since he first received her telegram. Where was her husband?

Chapter Eight

Jo scribbled the name and destination. She'd figured it would be this Belle person—he'd kept going on and on about needing to get to her the whole time he'd been locked in that fever. He'd even mistaken her for Belle once and tried to reach out to her.

She pushed that thought aside, feeling uncharitably annoyed by this woman she'd never even met. "What do you want it to say?"

"The text should read *Unavoidably delayed in Knotty Pine. Will resume travel earliest possible or send funds for you to travel here if you prefer. Please advise if there is anything I can do to assist in the interim. Yours, Ry*"

Jo kept her head down as she wrote down his message. Had he been carrying a torch for this woman all these years? Sure sounded like it was someone he was sweet on. And someone who needed a man to look out for her.

Well, *she* didn't need a man to look out for *her*. After all, she'd been taking care of this household for going on six years now without anybody's help.

And once she could ease out from under that yoke, she was

fully prepared to set off to see the world, just like Aunt Pearl, all on her own. No siree, she didn't need a man or anyone else looking out for her.

"Here we go." Cora Beth sailed into the room, carefully balancing a tray holding a steaming bowl of broth. Jo noticed there were also the fancy details her sister was so good at—like a crisply folded napkin and a pair of pansies arranged next to the bowl. A man like Mr. Lassiter probably appreciated such niceties.

Sure enough, he gave her sister a welcoming smile. "Mmm. That smells good."

"Cora Beth's broth is better than Doc Whitman's medicine for what ails you." Jo stood. "I'll stop by the telegraph office on my way to the livery and make sure Amos sends this right away."

Cora Beth set the tray down. "Actually, Jo, I was hoping you'd help Mr. Lassiter with his lunch. I'm doing some baking and can't leave things unattended for long. Besides, Mr. Lassiter has some questions about how he ended up here."

Jo held up the piece of paper. "But the telegram—"

"Don't worry about that." Cora Beth plucked the note from her fingers. "Uncle Grover'll take care of it. And he can let Freddie know you'll be a little late getting back to the livery." With that she breezed out of the room as if the matter were settled.

"Who's Freddie?"

Jo shifted her focus back to the man lying in the bed. "Freddie Boggs. He's the son of one of the local farmers. He helps out at the livery when I can't be there." A telltale rumbling lifted one corner of her mouth. "From the sounds your innards are making I'd say you're ready for this broth."

"It's that loud, is it?"

"Uncle Grover probably heard it clear down the hall."

He winced as he tried to sit up.

She put out a restraining hand. "Hold on. Let me help you."

"I'm not helpless," he grumbled.

"Wasn't saying you were, but no point overdoing it first thing out the chute." She grabbed a quilt from the foot of the bed and folded it into a large, plump rectangle. Then she slipped a hand under his back and provided some support and a little extra push as he sat up.

Once she had the blanket in place, she stood back. "How's that?"

"Comfortable. Thanks." His gaze scanned the room, pausing to study the large pin-covered maps decorating the far wall, before moving on to the mismatched furniture and the wooden train on the top of the chest of drawers.

Finally he turned back to her. "So just where am I?"

"I told you, you're at our place. The boardinghouse."

"But whose room is this?"

She could tell by the way he looked at her that he'd already guessed. There was really no reason for her to feel so selfconscious, but her cheeks warmed anyway. "Mine."

He frowned. "And where are you staying?"

"One of the extra guest rooms upstairs."

"So not only do you come to my rescue *twice* against those thugs, but you give me your room as well. Seems my debt to you keeps mounting."

If only he would stop staring at her so…well, so fiercely.

"Don't get to feeling you're getting special treatment. The only reason we put you here is because it's on the first floor and saved us having to cart your delirious carcass up the stairs."

She pulled her chair closer and picked up the bowl and spoon. "And it's not like I haven't done this before. Whenever any of the family takes sick they end up in here. It's easier for Cora Beth to keep an eye on the patient when they're close to where she spends most of her days."

"And at night?"

How did he know just what questions to ask to get her all flustered? "We took turns sitting with you." Better not to dwell on how difficult the past two nights had been, how worried she'd been—they'd all been—over his condition.

Jo ladled up a spoonful of broth and gave him her cheeriest smile. "If you think this smells good, just wait until you taste it. Cora Beth is one of the best cooks in these parts."

He swallowed and smiled in agreement. "You're right. It's delicious."

"Like I said, Cora Beth has a real knack for cooking. Come Thanksgiving week, the whole house is going to fill up with some of the most toothsome smells you can imagine. Plumb makes my mouth water just thinking on it."

"Your sister introduced herself as Mrs. Collins. Where's her husband?"

"Philip died just on four years ago."

"And so you moved in with her to help out."

"You have that backward." Jo wasn't quite sure why his misguided assumption bothered her. "This is the home my grandfather built and where we grew up. My sister moved back in here with us." She ladled up another spoonful. "When Philip died, Cora Beth had a two-year-old kid, another on the way and not much in the way of funds."

"So you took her in."

She shrugged. "She's my sister and family takes care of each other. Besides, Ma needed help running the place, not to mention that she liked having her grandchildren close by."

"Liked?"

He sure didn't miss much. "Ma passed away a year after Philip."

"I'm sorry."

"Nothing for you to apologize for—it wasn't your fault. Besides, she got to see her youngest grandkids born and spend time with them. And her passing was easy. She simply went to bed one night and never woke up." Josie stirred the broth before offering him another sip. "Ma never was one to fear dying. Always said she was just passing through this world to get to the next."

He eyed her over the spoon, his expression like Uncle Grover's when he was studying a new kind of bug he'd stumbled on. "So," he said after he'd swallowed, "in addition to running the livery, you take care of a household that includes Danny, and your sister and her two kids."

"Three kids. Cora Beth's youngest turned out to be twins. Then there's Uncle Grover." She could feel the walls closing in on her just listing them all. She loved her family, but sometimes she wished they were a bit more able to fend for themselves.

"Uncle Grover?"

"He's actually Philip's great-uncle. A good man but kind of forgetful-like. Once Philip passed on, Uncle Grover didn't have anyone else to watch out for him, so he just sort of tagged along with Cora Beth when she moved back here."

"And now he's part of the family too."

"Family's important. And it's not just made up of blood kin. It's like with Danny. When he was just a toddler, his family was passing through town and his pa got bad sick. They stayed here at the boardinghouse 'til he could get his strength back, but he never did. His ma passed two days after his pa."

"And your folks took him in."

"He didn't have anyone else. And he's as much my brother today as makes no never mind."

She thought she saw a shift in her patient's expression, but it was there and gone so quickly she couldn't be sure.

"Mind if I ask a question?"

She rolled her eyes. "Seems like you've done nothing but since you woke up."

He ignored her gibe. "Why did you come after me?"

She ladled up another spoonful. "I saw Clete and Otis ride out after you and something about the way they were acting just didn't smell right. I tried to get the sheriff to handle it but he wasn't around."

"So you decided to come yourself."

"Two against one just didn't seem fair." She lifted her chin. "Sorta like when you came to Danny's rescue."

He gave her a lopsided grin. "Not exactly the same thing. Even the Good Samaritan didn't go chasing after trouble."

"But he didn't shirk his duty, either."

"Even so, it was a brave, selfless act. You could have gotten yourself killed—very nearly did."

She shifted, uncomfortable with the direction this had taken. "But I didn't, thanks mostly to you."

He brushed her words aside. Then he crooked his head. "That first shot, just before the ambush, that wasn't a hunter, was it?"

"It was supposed to be a warning, but I was too late."

"Not too late to save me."

His voice had taken on that deep timbre again—the one that seemed to set an echoing vibration inside her. And he was staring at her as if trying to see deep into her mind. Whatever it was he saw there, his expression made her all fidgety feeling.

Time to change the subject. "So, with Thanksgiving and Christmas coming up, I suppose you'll be spending time at Hawk's Creek with your own family."

His expression closed off. "It depends on how long Belle needs me for."

She nodded sympathetically. "Nice of you to be willing to

sacrifice your holiday to help a friend. But maybe it'll work out so you can do both."

He waved a hand, dismissing her concern. "It's not as if they're expecting me. My family doesn't do much to mark the holidays."

She fed him another spoonful of soup while she absorbed that surprising bit of information. "I guess every household has its own set of traditions. But holidays just seem sort of a natural time for gathering close to family."

His expression turned thoughtful. "Actually, it wasn't that way when I was growing up. My mother loved the holidays and started decorating the house in late November. She always gathered family and friends around on Thanksgiving and Christmas, especially those who were alone. She made the day as festive as she could." He paused a fraction of a second. "The year I turned thirteen, though, she passed away two days before Christmas."

Josie's heart went out to him and his family. "That must have been hard on all of you."

He seemed to give himself a mental shake. "Naturally none of us felt like celebrating that year," he said matter-of-factly. "The next year, Pa didn't want us to bring out any of the decorations mother was so fond of, or host any of the festivities. So we had a quiet day that, except for the elaborate meal Inez insisted on cooking, was barely distinguishable from any other."

For goodness sake! "Your pa should be ashamed of himself."

"What?" His wrinkled brow told her it wasn't the reaction he'd been expecting.

"I don't like to speak ill of someone I never met, but the way he acted seems mighty selfish, to my way of thinking. He robbed his children of the joy that comes with celebrating the holidays. And what about the happier memories of your mother? Do y'all ever talk about her?"

"I don't know how we got off on this subject." There was a bit of a huff to his tone.

"We were asking each other nosy questions is how."

His brows lifted at that but then he grinned. "So we were."

He leaned against the pillows as she set aside the now empty bowl. "Thank your sister for the meal. I'm feeling stronger already."

"Glad to hear it."

"When's the next train to Foxberry?"

"Tomorrow."

He nodded. "I might need some assistance, but I should be well enough to travel by then."

"Hold on there. I don't care if you have the Queen of Sheba waiting for you in Foxberry, you aren't in any shape to be getting on a train, not until Doc says you are. There'll be another southbound come through in three days. Your friend's waited this long, a few more days won't hurt."

His glare would have stopped a rearing stallion. "I think I'm the best judge of what I can and can't do."

"Oh, yeah. Like you were back at the meadow when you wanted me to head back to town without you?"

His jaw clinched. "That was different."

"Not by my reckoning. Don't think I don't notice the way you flinch every time you move that arm of yours. It's still paining you, and more than just a bit."

"I'll manage."

"Huh! You'll manage. What kind of tomfool statement is that? Doc says you lost a lot of blood and that fever didn't help much. You're weak as a day-old pup and have just about as much sense."

"I'm getting stronger by the minute and I have a whole day to rest. Besides, I don't need a functioning arm to ride a train."

She fisted her hands on her hips. "I didn't follow you all the way out to Whistler's Meadow, play nursemaid over you, and then haul your wounded carcass back here just so you could pass out on some train between here and Foxberry."

"Miss Wylie, I sincerely appreciate all you've done, but I have to get to Foxberry. And no offense, but I don't see as you've much say in the matter."

As if she didn't have enough responsibilities already, now she had a pigheaded patient to deal with. Fool man. He might have come to her rescue, but his shining armor was starting to tarnish.

How could a man who'd so bravely defended first Danny and then her not have enough sense to understand he needed to take it easy until he healed proper? Was it because he was so eager to play the hero for his precious Belle?

She glared down at him. "Oh, don't I? Let's see you get out of this room without your boots or pants."

That caught his attention. He glanced around the room, then back at her with narrowed eyes. "Where are they?"

"In the washroom. Cora Beth takes her duty as lady of the house very serious."

She grabbed the tray with enough force to rattle the dishes and headed for the door. The man ought to realize just how lucky he was. At least he *could* look forward to the day when he could leave. If she were in his place that alone would be enough to sweeten her temper a bit.

Of course, he was in a hurry to see this Belle of his. Jo paused at the doorway and gave him a narrow-eyed look of her own. "Your lady friend will just have to wait a bit longer. If she's worth her salt, she'd want you to take care of yourself first."

From the tightening of his jaw she saw she'd riled him. Well, sometimes that happened when you were looking out for folks. Being in charge of everyone else's welfare didn't always make you the most popular gal around.

And if someone else wanted the job, then by George she was more than willing to let them take over. But so far, no one had come forward to claim it.

Chapter Nine

Ry watched Josie exit the room, his irritation at her high-handedness tempered by a reluctant admiration, and maybe something else. The woman's concern for his well-being was misguided but genuine. She was such an intriguing mix—full of spit and vinegar, but with a generous heart that drove her to try to take care of anyone she thought needed her.

Like him.

He still marveled at the way she'd disregarded her own welfare to come to his rescue, then put herself through the grueling ordeal of getting him back to town. He hadn't felt that kind of focused, genuine concern in a long time, and he wasn't quite certain how to react. It was tempting to stay awhile and try to learn more about her.

But right now his priority had to be Belle. They'd been good friends during those four years she'd spent at Hawk's Creek before he moved to Philadelphia. In fact, she'd been like a sister to him. They'd lost touch after she married—the life of an itinerant preacher's wife wasn't conducive to regular communication. But he still felt that same sense of kinship and responsibility for her he had all those years ago.

What had driven Belle to send that dire-sounding telegram? He shifted restlessly, itching to climb out of bed and head for Foxberry despite Josie's admonitions to the contrary. Those three stark lines from her telegram had played relentlessly through his mind ever since he'd first read it.

SITUATION DESPERATE. MUST SEE YOU WITHOUT DELAY. PLEASE COME.

Why hadn't he thought to send Griff on ahead to see to her? Perhaps he should still—

"My, my, young man, whatever did you do to set Jo off like that?"

Ry turned to find a balding gentleman peering at him over horn rimmed glasses from the doorway. "Sir?"

"Jo. I just passed her stomping down the hall muttering something about 'stubborn, pigheaded fools' under her breath."

Stubborn, huh? Now there was a case of the pot calling the kettle black. "We had a slight disagreement over how soon I'd be well enough to be on my way."

"Oh-ho, I see." Ry's visitor chuckled and stepped into the room. "Jo's not ready to turn loose of her hero just yet."

There was that word again. What had that mind-of-her-own woman been saying while he was unconscious? "I'm no hero, sir. Far from it in fact."

"Jo seems to think otherwise, and she doesn't give praise lightly. I'm Grover Collins by the way."

So this was Josie's Uncle Grover. "Glad to meet you, sir. But you have the story backward. It's Miss Wylie who did the rescuing."

"Please, call me Uncle Grover. And no need to be modest, my boy. Between Danny's account of the fracas in the livery and Josie's telling of the shoot-out in Whistler's Meadow, we're all quite determined to declare you a bona fide hero."

Ry swallowed a groan. "Let's just say, then, that Miss Wylie and I rescued each other."

The older gentleman chuckled. "A man who understands when to dig in his heels and when to compromise. Yes, you'll do."

Do for what?

Uncle Grover, however, seemed ready to change the subject. "Do you like bugs?" he asked.

"Bugs?" Josie had said the man was forgetful, but was he addled as well?

The older man waved a hand. "You know, insects."

"I can't say as I've thought about it much."

"Fascinating creatures. Remarkable, really. Most are highly organized and amazingly efficient." He leaned back on his heels and hooked his thumbs in his suspenders. "People could learn a lot from the way bugs conduct themselves."

Ry relaxed as understanding dawned. "I take it you're an entomologist?"

The man beamed at him. "You're familiar with the science."

"Only in passing."

"Ah, well, we'll remedy that. Once you're feeling better you can accompany me on an entomological expedition. I dare say you'll be surprised at what exciting specimens can be found right here in the woods around Knotty Pine."

"That sounds fascinating, sir, but I'm afraid I'll have to be on my way as soon as I'm able to travel."

"Ah, pity. Well, perhaps you can stop by for another visit on your way back through here."

"Perhaps." Ry kept his response deliberately noncommittal.

"Excellent. In the meantime, I'll let you rest. Jo left strict orders not to tire you out with a lot of talk. I'm sure we'll have a chance to chat again before you leave."

So, even though she thought him a "pigheaded fool," she was still worried enough to try to mollycoddle him.

Women sure were a tough lot to understand. Especially this particular, very hard-headed, very intriguing woman.

"Shh, Pippa, you'll wake him up."

Ry roused from a half sleep. Had that been a child's voice? Or was he hallucinating again?

"Is this what a hero looks like, Audrey?" The whisperer sounded doubtful.

Josie's nieces? He was starting to feel like the main attraction at a circus exhibition.

"Of course, silly." There was a definite note of authority in the response. Audrey was undoubtedly the ringleader.

"But he's just laying there."

"I'm glad. I didn't like it when he was carrying on. I thought he was gonna hurt Aunt JoJo."

Ry mentally winced. What had he done while feverish?

"He wouldn't hurt her, Lottie. He's a true enough hero. He got shot up saving her from the bad men, remember?"

Ry opened his eyes to find three little girls standing beside his bed. The two youngest, as alike as a pair of pennies, took an involuntary step back.

The oldest, however, who must be all of six or seven, graced him with a never-met-a-stranger smile. "Hello," she said brightly. "I'm Audrey."

Yep, definitely the ringleader. "Hello, Audrey. And who are your friends?"

"My sisters, Pippa and Lottie. Actually their names are Philippa and Charlotte, because they were named after our pa, Philip Charles Collins. But I wasn't named after anyone so I'm just Audrey."

A chatterbox in addition to being a ringleader. "Well, Just Audrey," he said, "to what do I owe the honor of this visit?"

Audrey giggled. "You even talk like a hero."

Ry resisted the urge to roll his eyes. Was he ever going to live down that appellation? "Why don't you just call me Mr. Lassiter? So, you were around when they brought me in?"

"Yes, sir. You sure were carrying on something awful, arms flying and mumbling about fire and rivers and bells. Momma said you were de-lir-us."

Ry winced at the reminder. And just what had he said about Belle? "My apologies, ladies, if I upset you."

"Oh, you didn't scare us or anything." The self-appointed spokeswoman glanced toward her sisters. "Well, maybe Pippa and Lottie, but only a little. We were just worried 'cause I heard Doc Whitman say you might die from the fever, and that upset Aunt JoJo a lot."

"What are you girls doing in here?" Cora Beth stood in the doorway, a fresh pitcher of water in her hands. "Scat now. Mr. Lassiter's supposed to be resting. And Audrey, didn't Mr. Saddler assign you some lessons to go over?"

"Yes, ma'am." The three girls scooted past their mother, but not before Audrey gave him a friendly goodbye wave.

"I'm sorry if they disturbed you," Cora Beth said. "I should have known Audrey would head straight here as soon as she got home from school. And of course the twins take their lead from her."

"No need to apologize. They weren't bothering me."

"That's kind of you to say, but we don't want to tax your strength. You're still on the mend, after all."

"Actually, I'm feeling much stronger. Must be that wonderful broth of yours."

She beamed at his compliment. "Why, thank you. I do pride

myself on being a passable cook. If you're still here next week for Thanksgiving, I'm planning quite a feast." She set the pitcher on the bedside table. "Still, you mustn't try to do too much too soon. I have enough of that with Jo."

He frowned. "Is something ailing your sister?"

"She got bruised up pretty bad when her horse threw her, not that she'd admit as much. I tried to talk her into taking it easy for a few days, but that sister of mine has a head harder than a brick. That's the only reason Danny hasn't been in to bother you, too—I sent him to relieve her as soon as he got home from school."

Cora Beth shook her head, a look of exasperation on her face. "Not only won't she take it easy, if anything, between watching over you the past two nights and spending all day at the livery, Jo's been working harder than before."

Ry frowned. He'd assumed it was Mrs. Collins who'd sat up with him, not Josie.

His hostess paused in the act of pouring a glass of water and gave him a guilty look. "Oh, dear. I didn't mean to imply—"

"That's all right, ma'am. I should be the one apologizing for the trouble I've caused. And I'm truly grateful to your whole family for all you've done. But you can rest easy—I promise I won't need any watching over tonight."

She gave him a generous smile. "You're a good man. I can see why Jo is so taken with you."

Taken with him? He certainly hadn't seen any signs of that in their last encounter. Other than that whole hero thing. Still, the thought made him smile.

Before she could try to lift the glass to his lips, Ry took it from her with his good hand.

She nodded approvingly. "I can see by the way you were talking to my girls that you're good with children, too. You're going to make a great father someday."

Ry barely avoided choking on his water. Was it mere coincidence that she'd conversationally tied him to both Josie and fatherhood in the matter of seconds? Surely she wasn't trying to play matchmaker between him and her sister.

Not that he had anything against Josie. Sure, she was more gruff than most ladies of his acquaintance, but she was also a bold, spirited woman with lots to offer some lucky man.

Just not him. The two of them would make about as good a match as a cougar and a wolf.

The muffled sound of a hail interrupted his thoughts.

"Oh, there's Dr. Whitmore," Cora Beth said. "He promised to check in on you this afternoon."

The doctor—good. Ry should be able to help convince these nice but overly cautious folks that he was strong enough to travel. It was a train ride after all—not a headlong gallop over rocky terrain.

It was high time he was on his way.

Jo marched down the sidewalk rolling her shoulders and neck to ease the stiffness. Her bruises were mostly healed now, though she still had a tender spot here and there. Not that she'd admit as much to Cora Beth. There was nothing her sister liked better than mollycoddling folks, and nothing Jo liked less than having someone think they knew better than she did what was best for her.

She'd be hanged if she'd pay someone her hard-earned money to watch the livery when she was capable of doing so herself.

"Hey, Jo." Amos stepped out of the telegraph office, waving a piece of paper. "That Lassiter fella's got a response already."

Well, that was fast. "Thanks, I'm just heading up to the house now."

Jo continued down the sidewalk, fighting the urge to unfold

the note and read it herself. He'd said he hadn't seen the woman in over twelve years. Why the long separation? Had they had a falling out of some sort? Who'd done what to who?

Was Belle the sort of woman to play on a man's honorable nature to get her way? What if the message made him more anxious than ever to get to Foxberry? What if Belle had awful things to say about him being delayed?

Jo fingered the telegram as she paused on the front porch. The last thing Mr. Lassiter needed was more guilt heaped on his plate right now.

Her finger was actually between the folds when she got hold of herself. No matter her reasons, it was wrong to pry in someone else's personal business.

But so help her, if this Belle tried to make him feel the least bit guilty...

She found Mr. Lassiter's door open a crack, but knocked anyway. "Hello, it's me, Jo."

The bed creaked and then he said something she couldn't quite make out. Deciding it was an invitation to enter, she pushed the door wider. Then frowned as she saw him swaying on the edge of the bed.

"Just what in blue blazes do you think you're doing?"

"Sitting up," he said through gritted teeth.

"And a fine job you're doing of it, too." She marched across the room and set the telegram on the bedside table. "Here, let me help you back down."

It was an indication of how much the effort had cost him that he didn't protest. "Let me guess," she said as she straightened the coverlet over him once more, "you were planning to sneak out and walk to Foxberry."

The sideways look he cut her was a mix of exasperation and exhaustion. She suddenly felt sorry she'd fussed at him.

"Just testing my limits." His voice sounded forced.

"Is that what the doc told you to do?"

"He gave me the usual doctor talk about getting plenty to eat and lots of rest. He also said that, so long as I didn't overtax myself, I should regain most of my strength in short order."

"Looks to me like you're doing a bit of that overtaxing now."

He set his jaw. "Regardless of any ideas you have to the contrary, I plan to get on that train tomorrow."

They'd see about that. Rather than challenge him, though, she changed the subject. "Speaking of Foxberry, you got an answer to your telegram already."

His expression shifted, and the tension in his jaw was back. "Read it to me."

Jo lifted the telegram, hating herself for her eagerness to learn what it had to say. Then she hesitated. "You sure?"

He nodded.

She glanced down and read the first line.

REGRET TO INFORM YOU BELLE HADLEY PASSED AWAY YESTERDAY

Jo's hand went to her throat as the words sunk in. Dead!

She'd been so callous about his concern, had dismissed his impatience to get to his friend as mere eagerness to see her again. She should have been more supportive, should have believed in his instincts about the urgency of the matter.

The look on his face almost did her in. There was such self-recrimination, such loss reflected there.

"What else does it say?" The strain in his voice was painful to hear.

Her hands shook slightly as she read the rest of the message.

WILL ARRIVE ON NEXT TRAIN TO DELIVER VIOLA AND OTHER BELONGINGS LEFT TO YOU. REV EDMOND FIELDS

* * *

He'd been too late. And now Belle was dead.

How had she died? Was there something he could have done to prevent this? Is that why she'd wanted so desperately for him to come to her?

Why hadn't he left Philadelphia as soon as he received her telegram? That one afternoon he'd spent wrapping up his current case might have made all the difference.

"Mr. Lassiter, I'm so sorry. I had no idea…"

He gave himself a mental shake, trying to focus on the present. Josie had such a stricken look on her face. "It's not your fault."

"It's not yours, either."

The firmness of her tone surprised him. But he wasn't so certain his delay hadn't been at least partially responsible. He wouldn't know until he spoke to this Reverend Fields. At least he hoped the clergyman would have answers for him.

Why hadn't he done more to keep in touch with Belle?

"She was a musician?"

"What? Oh, the viola. Yes, Belle loved music. I suppose she must have acquired an instrument along the way."

"Want me to have someone meet the train for you on Wednesday?"

He shook off the memories. "I'd appreciate that." No point in pushing himself now. He'd have a two day wait to get his answers. Assuming this Reverend Fields *had* the answers he sought.

Ry felt her troubled gaze on him, sensed her uncertainty as the silence drew out. But he had nothing in him to say, no reassurance to offer right now.

Finally she set the telegram on the table and shoved her hands in her pockets. "I'll see if Cora Beth has another bowl of broth ready."

He nodded. With one final searching look, she left the room.

The fact that Belle had left him her belongings tore at Ry's already shredded conscience. It spoke to the fact that she'd had no one else she felt close to there at the end.

And she hadn't even had him with her to ease her final hours.

Chapter Ten

Ry spent what was left of the day being the perfect patient. He ate every bit of food sent his way. He played three rounds of checkers with Danny. When Uncle Grover brought in a collection of moths he'd acquired, not only did Ry admire them but he asked all the right questions to give the gentleman an opportunity to expound on their individual characteristics. He even got out of bed long enough to walk across his room and back.

In short, he tried to keep himself too occupied to dwell on the news about Belle. But that night he lay awake long after the last lamp was trimmed. All he could think about was that he'd failed Belle, without having any idea what she'd needed from him.

The next morning, Josie brought in his breakfast tray right after sunrise. "Figured you'd be up early. I thought I'd save Cora Beth the trouble and bring this in before I head over to the livery."

"Thanks." He managed to sit up without her assistance.

"How you feeling today?"

"Better." He was pleased to see the tray contained a second dish. He'd had enough of his own company for a while. Josie pulled a chair up beside the bed, took a seat and lifted the extra dish. "Hope you don't mind if I join you." She wanted to gauge his mood this morning, to see how he was coping with what had happened.

"Company's always welcome."

She situated his plate in comfortable reach, then speared a bit of egg from her own dish. She decided there was no point beating around the bush. "What are you planning to do now that you don't need to go to Foxberry?"

He gave her a surprised look, then shrugged. "Wait for Reverend Fields to arrive and find out what happened to Belle."

"Then what? You going back to Philadelphia, or to Hawk's Creek?"

"I'll probably stop in at the ranch and visit with Griff and Sadie for a week or so."

Being around family would likely be good for him. "I'm sure they'll be right glad to have you home for Thanksgiving."

"I'm not certain I'll stay that long." He must have read the surprise in her face. "As I've said before, the Lassiter family doesn't expend much effort celebrating holidays."

That still didn't seem right, but she had something more pressing to discuss. "Do you want to talk about her?"

He paused, as if seriously considering her question. At least he hadn't taken offense.

"She was the niece of our ranch foreman," he said slowly. "The summer I turned twelve, her folks died and she came to live with him. Harvey was a good man and a great foreman, but he didn't know anything about raising kids, especially girls. And Belle was a city girl—she'd never lived on a ranch before."

"So you took her under your wing?" Seems he'd had that hero streak even then.

"It wasn't my idea." His voice sounded defensive. Then he gave a sheepish smile. "I was a twelve-year-old boy, after all."

He pushed around the last bit of egg on his plate. "Belle spent a lot of time in the kitchen with Inez at first, but Mother thought it would be good for her to have someone her own age to spend time with. So she suggested I give Belle riding lessons."

"And y'all became friends." Jo tried to imagine what twelve-year-old Ry had been like and felt a little stab of jealousy toward Belle.

He nodded. "Before long she was like a sister to me."

A sister, huh? Jo perked up a bit. "Thought you already had a sister."

"Sadie's five years younger than me." He pointed his fork at her. "When you're twelve, that's a big difference. Belle was my age."

He leaned back, his expression turning inward. "Once Belle was comfortable in the saddle, whenever I wasn't busy with chores, we took long rides all around the ranch. I showed her all of my favorite places. Taught her how to do birdcalls and how to fish. And I listened to her talk about what her life had been like before her folks died."

Yep, definitely a hero in the making. "I'm sure that meant a lot to her."

"It wasn't all one-sided. Her father had been a whip maker and had taught her how to use one. And she taught me." His expression turned sober. "It was about a year after she arrived that my mother died. Belle…well, Belle had been through that before. It was good to have her to talk to."

Jo placed a hand on his arm before she'd consciously formed the thought to do so.

He stared at her hand for a long moment, an unreadable expression on his face. Just as she started to pull away, he met her gaze, his eyes filled with something that looked suspiciously like gratitude.

A second later the expression was gone and he reached for his glass as she pulled her arm back. "So, is this Freddie you mentioned yesterday the only help you have at the livery?"

Ready to change the subject, was he? "He watches the place at night. Actually, he sleeps mostly. But it means someone is there to keep an eye on things."

"What about someone to help during the day?"

"Not necessary. I can handle most of the business that comes my way, and Danny helps out after school if I need him to." She gave him a dry smile. "And there's always Uncle Grover to help out in a pinch."

"Did I hear my name?" Uncle Grover stood in the doorway, smiling jovially at the two of them. He set his focus on Josie. "Cora Beth wanted me to remind you to stop at Mrs. Potter's and see how many pumpkin pies she wants for the Thanksgiving baskets this year."

"Will do. And you're just in time to keep Mr. Lassiter company. I need to head off to the livery."

Jo left the room, her mind rolling the conversation over in her thoughts like a river stone between her fingers. She'd learned a lot about the kind of man Ry was just by reading between the lines of what he'd said. And she'd give a pretty penny to know just what it was that had shone in his eyes when he stared into hers a few minutes ago.

Remembering that look, something warm and soft seemed to unfurl inside her.

For once, Ry didn't mind seeing Josie go. It was high time he got out of bed, and accomplishing that would be a lot easier without her around to admonish him for trying to do too much.

Uncle Grover, on the other hand, was easily recruited to help him clean up a bit and shave.

With that taken care of Ry felt almost civilized again.

Uncle Grover stayed around afterward, apparently taking Josie's words to entertain him to heart. Ry was treated to a surprisingly interesting discussion on the various species of grasshoppers in the area and their feeding and migratory habits. At one point, the older gentleman left, only to return shortly with a board, affixed to which was a grouping of grasshoppers, carefully labeled and arranged by size.

In the course of their visit, Ry managed to slip in a few questions of his own about the Wylie household. He found the answers enlightening.

The older man left no doubt that Cora Beth was the domestic center of this household, fussing over everyone like a mother hen, keeping them well fed, clothed and healthy. But there was another thread running through the conversation, offhand references to Josie, that strengthened Ry's perception that she was the glue holding them together, the one they looked to for direction. A very capable woman with a lot of heart.

Like the way she'd listened to him talk about Belle this morning. There'd been a moment of connection then, as if...

No, he was imagining things. It was just that they'd been through something intense together, that was all.

Which reminded him...

Ry penciled a note and had Uncle Grover promise to take it to the telegraph office. Assuming Griff followed his instructions, that would take care of one of the debts he owed Josie, whether she wanted repayment or not.

Shortly after Uncle Grover left, Cora Beth brought Ry his lunch. To his relief, instead of another serving of broth, it was a hearty bowl of rabbit stew. She offered to stay and help him eat, but Ry assured her he was capable of feeding himself.

"I'm glad to hear you're feeling stronger today. Call me if you need anything else." She flashed a teasing smile. "After lunch you'd better rest up while you can. When Danny and Audrey get home from school they'll be wanting to pester you some more."

"I don't mind their company," Ry assured her. And he meant it. The last thing he wanted right now was to be alone with his own thoughts.

But the early afternoon hours drew out interminably.

He pushed aside thoughts of Belle and his failure to reach her. What's done was done, and all the guilt in the world wouldn't change it. There were still questions to be answered, but those would have to wait until tomorrow.

It would be more productive to focus on resolving issues he still had control over. Like figuring out the answer to the question Josie had asked him.

Where *did* he call home?

It was a question that had begun to niggle at him with increasing frequency since his father's death two years ago. He'd never intended to spend his life in Philadelphia, had always figured he'd return to Texas someday to open a law practice of his own. Somehow, though, the time had never seemed quite right.

Perhaps now it was.

Ry moved his injured arm, trying to ease into a more comfortable position. And realized he was no longer alone.

Two identical pairs of eyes stared up at him from the foot of his bed. "Hello."

"Hello," they answered in unison.

"Is there something I can do for you?"

Two pigtail-adorned heads nodded.

"And what might that be?"

One of the girls moved to the side of the bed where he could get a better look at her. She was closely followed by her sister, who kept both hands behind her back.

"Lottie needs a hero," the first child, obviously Pippa, proclaimed solemnly.

Uh-oh. This did not sound good. Why were they coming to him for help instead of their mother? He had absolutely no experience with children—especially ones in crisis. "And just why does Lottie need a hero?" he asked cautiously.

Lottie moved her hands forward, revealing one fist stuck inside a preserve jar. "It won't come off," she said, her voice ending on a sniffle.

Please, Lord, don't let her start crying, at least not before I can get her mother in here. "Does it hurt?" He kept his voice calm, hoping it would help soothe the child.

She shook her head, another sniffle escaping.

No pain—that was good. "Well, then, there's no reason to fret. We'll just get your mother to—"

"Oh, no!" Pippa shook her head violently. "We can't tell Ma. That's why we need a hero."

Ry eyed her suspiciously. "And just why can't you tell your mother?"

"Because we weren't supposed to be playing with Danny's things," she said in a rush of words. "But we didn't go in his room, honest. He left two of his marbles on the floor in the kitchen. We just wanted to play with them for a little while, then we were going to put them right back."

Ry hid a smile at her rationalizations. "What do Danny's marbles have to do with getting Lottie's hand stuck in the jar?"

"We put them there so they wouldn't get losted. But when Lottie tried to get them out, she got stuck."

"I see. Come closer so I can have a look at your problem."

Lottie dutifully moved forward and set her hand, jar and all, on the bed next to him.

"Did you try opening your fist?" he asked.

Lottie nodded.

"We pulled and pulled but it just won't come out," Pippa said, joining her sister. "Can you help us?"

He studied the small hand. It appeared swollen, but not injured. "I think so." He looked at Pippa. "Can you fetch me some lard from the kitchen?"

The child nodded.

"I need a great big spoonful."

With another nod, Pippa turned and raced out of the room, leaving Ry alone with the still sniffling Lottie. He sent a silent "hurry up" plea Pippa's way. "Don't worry," he said awkwardly. "We'll have your hand out of there in just a few minutes." Hurry Pippa.

Lottie gave him a wide-eyed, trusting look, and nodded solemnly. At least the sniffles had stopped.

Pippa returned, a spoonful of lard bobbing precariously in her hand. "Here it is."

"Good. Now, take some and smear it all around the part of Lottie's wrist you can reach and around the inside lip of the jar."

"This feels icky," Pippa complained. But she did as he'd instructed.

"All right, Pippa, that looks good. Lottie, I'm going to hold the jar and I want you to ease your hand out, nice and slow. Okay?"

Holding the base of the jar with one hand, Ry watched with satisfaction as the small, well-greased hand did indeed slide right out of the jar.

Both girls looked at him with bright, relieved smiles. "See,

Lottie," Pippa said, "I told you heroes help people who are in trouble."

Ry handed the jar back to Lottie. "You girls put this back where it belongs, and I suggest you wash your hands as best you can if you don't want your ma to ask what you've been up to."

With a chorus of thank yous, they skipped out of the room.

Ry chuckled, relieved that their problem had been so easy to resolve.

Would that his own could be handled so easily.

Chapter Eleven

As predicted, Danny and Audrey both stopped by to visit once school was out. Neither visit was quite as dramatic as the one with the twins, though.

Audrey sat on the chair next to his bed, swinging her legs and telling him about her day, from the time she stepped into the classroom to the moment she came home. The highlight, apparently, had been when she received her assigned part for the upcoming Thanksgiving program. Thanksgiving, it appeared, was a major event in Knotty Pine.

"I'm going to be a gardener," she said. "I can tell everyone why I'm thankful for the sun and the rain and the seeds and the fruit and everything."

And for Audrey, "everything" would undoubtedly be taken literally.

Danny came by next and challenged him to another game of checkers. They played two, winning one apiece.

Once he left, Ry tried to sleep, and to his surprise, did drift off for a short nap.

When he woke up, he decided he'd been confined long

enough. It was time he tested his legs on something more ambitious than crossing the room.

Moving with care, Ry got dressed. He appreciated the use of Uncle Grover's sleep shirts but it would feel good to be in his own clothes again. Maneuvering his injured arm into the shirt sleeve caused more then one wince, but getting his boots on was even trickier.

Once he was fully dressed he had to sit again to get his second wind. He contemplated leaving off the sling, but then decided it was best not to ignore the doctor's advice just for the sake of his pride.

At last he stood and crossed the room, determined to prove to himself and the Wylie household that he was no longer an invalid.

Once in the hallway, Ry paused to get his bearings. His room—or rather Josie's—was situated on the far end of a long corridor. Based on the enticing smells emanating from the room across the hall, he'd guess that would be the kitchen. Which was probably a good place to start.

When he pushed open the door, Cora Beth looked up from the stove. "Why, Mr. Lassiter, whatever are you doing up and about? If you're hungry, all you had to do—"

He held up a hand. "No need to fret, ma'am. That is, I *am* hungry but that's not why I'm here. I figured it was past time I started doing for myself again. I've imposed on your hospitality long enough."

"Don't be silly." She wiped her hands on her apron. "While I'm glad you're feeling well enough to be up and about, you were a very undemanding patient." She turned to her oldest. "Audrey, please set another place at the table for Mr. Lassiter."

"Yes, ma'am."

Josie pushed through the door, brushing past her niece.

"Cora Beth, if you have Mr. Las—" She stopped short when she saw him standing there.

"What in blue blazes are you doing up?" She fisted her hands on her hip. "You should—"

"I'm fine," he said firmly. He rather liked the way her eyes flashed when she was irritated.

Cora Beth intervened before Josie could continue to argue. "Jo, why don't you take him in and introduce him to everyone while I dish up the peas."

Seeing the stubborn thrust of Josie's chin, he thought she might refuse. But she finally gave a curt nod and headed back into the hallway.

Without saying a word or slowing her step, she escorted him past what appeared to be a large dining room and to a door near the front entryway. Ry followed her into a comfortably appointed parlor containing three unfamiliar persons.

"Mr. Lassiter," Josie said with uncharacteristic formality, "allow me to introduce you to Mrs. Beulah Plunkett, her daughter Honoria, and the town's schoolteacher, Mr. Odell Saddler."

Ry nodded a greeting to each in turn.

"Folks, this is Mr. Ryland Lassiter, the gent I told you about."

Mrs. Plunkett, an elderly woman whose figure and hook-shaped nose put him in mind of a plump parrot, spoke first. "So you're the young man who fought off those hooligans."

He bowed, hiding a grimace. "With Miss Wylie's help."

"Modest as well as dashing—an admirable combination. Don't you agree, Honoria?"

The younger woman, as slight and shy as her mother was broad and outspoken, flushed. "Yes, indeed, Mama," she responded, without ever quite meeting his gaze.

Mr. Saddler intervened, mercifully taking the spotlight from the younger woman. "Tell us, sir, where did you travel from?"

"Philadelphia."

"Really." The schoolteacher leaned forward. "How fascinating. Philadelphia is such a rich cornucopia of our nation's history." The man's face all but glowed with enthusiasm. "Have you advantaged yourself of the museums and exhibitions?"

"On a number of occasions."

"Ah, I envy you." He gave a self-deprecating smile. "I'm a bit of a history enthusiast."

Danny stepped in the doorway with a quick "Dinner's ready" announcement before disappearing again.

As they trooped into the dining room, Ry was surprised to discover everyone ate together, borders and family, from Uncle Grover right down to Pippa and Lottie. But the double-sized room with the proportionally long table easily accommodated all of them, with room to spare.

Uncle Grover took a place at the head of the table and Mrs. Collins took hers at the foot. Ry had every intention of sitting next to Josie, but somehow found himself holding a chair out for Mrs. Plunkett instead.

The next forty minutes was an interesting experience for Ry. Conversations were lively and the subject matters wide-ranging. Everyone contributed, including the children, joining in or not as the mood struck them. Discussions ranged from how everyone's day had gone, to next week's Thanksgiving festivities, to the relative merits of this year's crop of pears versus last year's. Audrey chattered on about her role in the upcoming school program and Danny bragged about how he could have won the schoolyard game of mumblety-peg if the tip of his knife hadn't broken off in the last round.

It was chaos, but a comfortable sort of chaos, wrapping itself around Ry like a brightly-colored patchwork quilt on a chilly evening. This was what a family should be, he thought, what his *had* been before his mother died.

Ry found his gaze drifting to Josie time and again throughout the meal. He was glimpsing a side of her he hadn't seen before. Gone was the guarded, overly-responsible, got-to-fix-everyone's-problems personality she normally wore with him. Instead he saw a relaxed woman who laughed and teased and chatted comfortably with those around her, a woman who had the confidence that came with knowing she belonged.

He envied her that.

Jo kept a surreptitious eye on Mr. Lassiter throughout the meal. He seemed to be holding up well, considering all he'd been through. He was doing more observing than joining in, but that might have more to do with his being seated next to Mrs. Plunkett than with his recovery. The woman tended to dominate any conversation she took part in.

Still, he didn't show any signs he was ailing. In fact, he looked mighty good. She straightened, giving her head a mental shake. She'd meant from a health perspective, of course.

She glanced toward Pippa and Lottie, and felt herself soften again. When she'd arrived home this evening she'd caught them whispering, and in no time had gotten the story of the hand in the jar incident out of them. It seemed Ry was a hero in more than one sense of the word.

He glanced across the table just then and his gaze met hers. A slow, appreciative smile warmed his face and Jo's breath caught in her throat. Then his attention was captured by a comment from Mr. Saddler and his gaze released her, allowing her to breathe again.

She glanced down at her plate, confused. How could one fleeting smile from him leave her feeling so tingly and on edge?

She must still be tuckered out from those nights spent watching over him, waiting for his fever to break. A good night's rest would put things back in proper perspective.

She was relieved when the meal finally came to an end. As usual, Mrs. Plunkett and Honoria retired to their rooms while Mr. Saddler stepped out for his evening constitutional.

Mr. Lassiter stood, looking uncertain about what to do with himself.

He had a big day tomorrow, one that was likely to be difficult for him. And regardless of how he looked, he'd already been up and about long enough for the first time out of his sickbed.

"Mr. Lassiter," she said, claiming his attention, "would you like Uncle Grover to help you back to your room?"

He frowned. "No, thank you, I can manage on my own."

There was no need for him to sound so prickly. She was only thinking of his health. "Well, then, please don't let us keep you from your rest."

That annoyed frown made another appearance. Then he turned to Cora Beth. "That was a wonderful meal, ma'am."

"Why, thank you. I'm glad you enjoyed it."

"I wonder if you have any reading material I might borrow?"

"Sure do," Jo answered before Cora Beth could say anything. Did he think they were illiterate? "There's a bookcase plumb full of books in the family parlor."

"Why don't you show him where that is," Cora Beth suggested. "We'll get started with the evening chores."

Mr. Lassiter paused. "If there's anything I can do to help—"

"Don't be silly." Cora Beth waved him off. "You're our guest. Go on with Jo and find yourself something to read."

Now why did he take Cora Beth's concern with a smile while he frowned at hers?

Jo mulled that over as she dutifully led him to the family

parlor, the one room their boarders never entered. She opened the door and waved him inside. "The bookcase is there on your left."

Leaning against the jamb, she crossed her arms while he looked over the titles. It might not be much compared to what he was used to, but she was certain there was enough there to satisfy his needs for today. There were Uncle Grover's insect books, Aunt Pearl's books about far-off places, Cora Beth's poetry books, some morality tales and lighter fiction, books about gardening and some of her father's books about carriages and harnesses.

He finally selected two volumes. "These should do for now. Thanks for the loan."

She straightened, shoving her hands in her pockets. "Feel free to come in here and fetch a book whenever you want."

They stared at each other awkwardly for a moment. Then he gave her a crooked smile. "Guess I'll head back to my room and put these to good use."

"Yes, of course." She stepped aside to let him pass.

But not quite far enough. His arm brushed against hers and she was startled by the way her pulse jumped in response. Had he felt it too?

She watched him walk away, absently rubbing the place on her arm he'd touched. There was no sign that his injuries were bothering him.

Or anything else, for that matter.

Chapter Twelve

Ry closed the book with a resounding *thunk*. He'd read the same page three times and still had no idea what it contained. Not that it was the book's fault. The part of the travelogue he'd managed to absorb proved both entertaining and informative.

Trouble was, he found himself unable to concentrate. Too many of his own thoughts crowded out the words on the page. He eyed the bed from his vantage across the room with a jaundiced eye. No doubt the same restlessness that kept him from enjoying the book would prevent him from sliding into an easy slumber.

Muted sounds of conversation and laughter floated in under the door. So, the Wylie household hadn't turned in for the night yet.

The sound was seductive, enticing.

It had been quite some time since he'd been in a true family setting. Life at his grandfather's was comprised of a string of formal interactions. On the few occasions each year when he returned to the ranch, he and his siblings interacted with each other like near-strangers.

And at supper he'd felt like one of the borders. Allowed into the Wylie family circle for a time, but still an outsider. Sort of the way it was when he tried to pin down his own family life. Part of both worlds, belonging in neither. Was it something about him? Had he forgotten how to get close to people?

What would it feel like to be a member of a large, demonstrative family like the Wylies?

He shook his head, pushing away that thought. There was no point getting too close to these folks. Once he met with Reverend Fields tomorrow and found out what he could about Belle's last days, he planned to head over to Hawk's Creek. Probably never pass this way again.

For some reason, that thought didn't sit well with him either.

He dropped the book on a side table and stood. On the other hand, it wasn't as if he'd form any long-term attachments just from joining them for an evening.

Before he could change his mind, Ry headed for the door.

When he stepped into the kitchen he had a few moments to look around before anyone noticed him.

The Wylie family—blood kin and otherwise—were gathered around the table. Cora Beth sat at one end with some sewing, an oil lamp at her elbow.

Audrey stood on a chair nearby, reciting what sounded like lines for the Thanksgiving program with all the verve and passion of a seasoned thespian. Pippa and Lottie sat cross-legged at her feet, playing the part of rapt audience.

Halfway down the table, Uncle Grover and Danny were shelling pecans and having a lively discussion that had the older man gesticulating enthusiastically.

It was Josie, though, who caught and held his attention. Was she carving a pumpkin?

Then Danny said something Ry didn't quite catch and Josie, laughing, reached across the table, snagged a bit of pecan shell and tossed it at him.

The cozy family scene, complete with the scent of a pie in the oven and a warmth that came as much from the people as from the cook stove, sent an unexpected pang through Ry, one he refused to analyze too closely.

A moment later Josie looked up, and, predictably, greeted him with a frown. "Shouldn't you be resting?"

He ignored both her question and tone, turning instead to Cora Beth. "I hope I'm not intruding. It's too early for sleep and I'm afraid the book I chose didn't hold my interest as I'd hoped."

"Please, come on in," she answered with a warm smile. "You're more than welcome to join us."

Josie set her knife down and pulled a chair out. "Here, have a seat." It was more command than suggestion.

"Thanks." As he eased into the chair, the others resumed their activities.

"What's that you're working on?" he asked, nodding toward the pumpkin.

She shrugged, her face reddening slightly. "Cora Beth cleaned out this pumpkin yesterday to make some pies. I'm just tinkering around with the shell."

"Jo's being far too modest," Cora Beth interrupted. "She's a real artist with a carving knife."

Ry studied Josie's handiwork and found he agreed with Cora Beth. The top third had been artfully removed from the pumpkin, leaving a bowl shape with a fluted rim. But it was the design on the bowl itself that was truly remarkable. A dragonfly hovered above an almost-completed flower. The detail was amazing.

"Just trying out a new design I might use for the Thanksgiving Celebration." Josie sounded uncharacteristically hesitant. "Not sure yet if I like it."

"Well, I do." Ry's words earned him a pleased smile from Josie. "So what's this Thanksgiving Celebration?"

"It's like a big party," Danny answered. "The whole town gathers together. There's lots of food and games and contests. And the grown-ups dance."

Ry smiled at the sour face the boy made over that last bit.

"Don't forget the pageant," Audrey chimed in.

"Jo's pumpkins and gourds are used as decorations," Cora Beth paused mid-stitch to explain. "They hold fruit and flowers, and once evening sets in, they're used to hold candles."

"Does that mean you're going to be making a lot of pumpkin pies?"

Josie laughed. Ry decided he liked the sound of it.

"Most of the ladies around here donate the empty shells from their own cooking," she said. "By next week we'll be tripping over pumpkin shells and gourds around here."

"I'm sure that'll be a sight." Not that he'd be here to see it.

"Is this enough?" Danny held up the bowl of pecans for Cora Beth's inspection.

She put a finger to her chin as she studied his offering. Finally she nodded. "I suppose you've earned yourself an extra piece of fruitcake when we cut it."

Danny let out a whoop that echoed through the room.

"Must be some fruitcake," Ry said dryly.

"Yes, sir. Best you're ever gonna taste."

"It's a holiday tradition around here," Josie added. "Both for Thanksgiving and Christmas. Lot's of folks want one for their own table, and they fetch a handsome price. In fact she has two in the oven right now."

Ry noticed the pride in Josie's tone. "Sounds like quite a delicacy."

"That they are," she said. "Cora Beth takes a blue ribbon at the county fair every year."

"Now you all hush before you give me a big head. I'm

certain Mr. Lassiter has been to any number of fancy restaurants that serve finer desserts than my fruitcake."

"Well, ma'am, there's been many a time when I would've traded those so-called fancy restaurants for good home cooking."

Cora Beth set her needlework aside and stood. "Then we'll cut one right now."

Ry held up a hand in protest. "Please, I wasn't angling for a taste. Especially if you have customers waiting in line." He didn't want to steal from their livelihood.

"Nonsense," she waved a hand dismissively, already taking saucers from the cupboard. "The family usually samples a few of them, anyway."

"Just to make certain she hasn't lost her touch." The crinkles at Uncle Grover's eyes belied his serious tone.

"In that case, I confess to being both curious and eager to try a bite."

"Hey, girls!" Danny set down his bowl of pecans. "We're going to slice into one of the fruitcakes."

Ry accepted the dessert-laden saucer and forked up a bite, aware that every eye in the room was on him. He mentally prepared himself to give them the reaction they expected, no matter what.

Because, as Cora Beth had said, he'd eaten at some of the finest restaurants in New England. And he'd dined at the homes of socially prominent hostesses who prided themselves on hiring only the best chefs for their kitchens. He'd be very surprised if this dessert could compete with their signature creations.

But as soon as the first bite entered his mouth, Ry found he didn't have to pretend. This was unlike any cake he'd ever tasted. It had a robust, burst-in-your-mouth flavor, both ambrosially sweet and slightly tart at the same time, without any of the heaviness usually associated with fruitcakes. And there was an underlying flavor he couldn't quite identify that added a tantalizing zest to the whole.

"Mmm. I understand why these are so popular."

"It's Cora Beth's own recipe," Josie bragged. "She uses a honey syrup and spiced apple cider and some other special ingredients. Ladies around these parts have been trying to pry the recipe from her for ages."

Ry eyed Josie thoughtfully. Even though he knew Cora Beth could drive her crazy, she hadn't stopped bragging on her sister since he'd entered the room. There was a deep bond between the members of this family that he found oddly touching.

He cleared his throat and refocused on the rest of the room. "So, are these only available to locals, or can anyone order one?" Purchasing some of the fruitcakes would be a way to repay part of the debt he owed the Wylies.

But Cora Beth shook her head. "If you're wanting one for yourself, we'll just consider it an early Christmas present."

"No, no. I was actually thinking of purchasing several as gifts. One for my brother and sister, one for the hands at the ranch, one for my grandfather, one for his law partner…"

Cora Beth laughed. "My goodness, if you keep adding on orders you're going to become my biggest customer ever."

"Absolutely." He pointed his fork at her. "Honestly, this will be a huge help to me. I never know what sort of gifts to get for my family and friends at Christmas, but each and every one of them will love this."

Cora Beth relented at once. "Well, of course, if you're certain you want them, just let me know how many and I'll add your order to my list."

"A dozen ought to cover it."

Cora Beth blinked, her eyes growing rounder. "My goodness, a dozen?"

"If that's not too much trouble."

He caught the speculative look Josie shot his way. Was she on to him? Had he overdone it?

"No, no, not at all," Cora Beth said. "I've just never had such a large order from one person before."

"In Philadelphia you'd have folks banging down your door, begging for the chance to order these."

"Hey, why don't we play the 'where in the world' game?" Danny had obviously grown tired of this talk of food.

"I don't know, Danny." Josie carried her own saucer to the sink. "Mr. Lassiter probably—"

"But we always play it when we have someone new at the boardinghouse," Danny protested.

"Mr. Lassiter isn't exactly a boarder."

Ry wondered if her reluctance had anything to do with him. He leaned back. "What is this 'where in the world' game?"

"Jo made it up," Danny explained. "When someone new comes around, we ask them to name the most interesting place they've ever visited. Then they have to say what makes that place so interesting to them."

Ry gave Josie a considering look, remembering the maps covering the walls of her room, as well as the things she'd told him about her Aunt Pearl. "I see. Sure, I'll be glad to play."

Everyone took a seat and stared at him expectantly.

"Let me think—the most interesting place. Hmm. I'd say that would be New York Harbor."

Josie still leaned back against the sink, but even from this distance he could sense the keenness of her interest, almost feel the thirst she seemed to have for his words. And he suddenly wanted to paint the most vivid picture he could.

"Why there?" Danny asked.

"It's an energetic place," he answered, keeping his eyes

focused on Josie. "I've never seen anything like it. It's busier than a stirred-up ant hill. People coming and going, speaking more languages than you would have heard at the Tower of Babel, goods from the most commonplace to the unimaginably exotic being loaded and unloaded on the docks, the smells of spices and smoke mingling with that of fish and brine. And everything moving at a pace that makes you dizzy just remembering it all." He looked around at each of them in turn, then returned his gaze to Josie. "But none of that is what makes it the most memorable place I've been to."

He paused, deliberately taking another bite, inexplicably wishing he could actually show her the sight that had so captured his own imagination.

"Then what is it?" Audrey finally asked.

Ry smiled and pointed his fork at the child. "The most amazing thing of all is the Statue of Liberty, standing tall and beautiful, guarding the harbor." His gaze slid back to Josie. "It's a sight that, once seen, can never be forgotten. She stands a little over three hundred feet tall and is majestic in a way that has to be seen to be appreciated. She's an especially stirring sight when one is returning home after a trip abroad."

The faces around him showed varying levels of interest, but in Josie's he saw a longing, an almost painful yearning that made him want to scoop her up and take her there straightaway.

"Three hundred feet." Danny whistled, breaking the spell. "Why, that's even taller than the church steeple."

Ry nodded. "Probably about ten times taller."

"Amazing." Cora Beth stood. "But we don't want to tire Mr. Lassiter out with all our questions. Girls, it's time for the three of you to get ready for bed. I'll be up to tuck you in and hear your prayers as soon as I clear these dishes."

"You go on," Josie offered. "I'll finish up for you."

Ry caught Cora Beth's look of surprise, quickly followed by a flash of understanding. "Thanks," she said. "Danny, please check the lamps on the landing. Uncle Grover, would you please lock the front door for me before you head upstairs?"

The older man stood. "Come along, Danny, my boy, it seems we have our marching orders."

In a surprisingly short time, Ry and Josie were alone in the kitchen. He should head back to his room, but he was strangely reluctant to leave. Instead, he stared at her back, watching her wash and rinse the dishes with the same efficiency she tackled everything she set her mind to.

He studied the carved pumpkin, noticing the delicate detail, the fine craftsmanship, so at odds with the impulsive, heavy-handed image she projected. The contradictions in this woman continued to intrigue him.

"I've seen pictures of the Statue of Liberty," she said, breaking into his thoughts. "I bet it's really something to see in real life."

"That it is."

"I plan to see it for myself someday, you know. That and lots of other places."

Something in her tone caught his attention, made him remember the yearning expression of a few moments ago. "Do you now?" he replied softly.

"As soon as Danny's old enough to take over the livery. I want to see the world, or at least as big a piece of it as I can."

"Because of the promise you made your aunt?"

She glanced over her shoulder with an annoyed frown. "I made that promise because it's what *I* want, not just to please her."

"You know," he said slowly, "I've done a fair share of traveling in my day, and after a while it loses a bit of its luster.

There's plenty of folks who'd give anything to have what you have right here with your family."

He saw her shoulders stiffen. "How old were you when you set off from that ranch your family runs?"

"Sixteen. But I only did it to appease my grandfather. And I only intended it to be for a short time."

"You never really went back, though, did you? Not to stay."

Ry swallowed a wince as her words brought back his frustration over his current arrangement.

"Do you regret it?" she asked, not waiting for an answer to her previous question. "Going off to spend time with your grandfather, I mean?"

Did he? If he'd stayed at Hawk's Creek he'd never have gotten the first-rate education he'd received, never become a lawyer, never been able to appreciate all his mother gave up to marry his father. But he'd also never have found himself so alienated from his siblings.

"There's no simple answer to that question," he finally said.

That earned him an inelegant snort. "I think that's an answer in itself."

Ouch! Seemed her sympathy only extended to his physical injuries. One thing about Josie, she didn't have any problem speaking her mind. The proverbial thorn on the rose.

But he was beginning to believe the bloom was worth risking a few scratches for.

He stood abruptly. Better not to go any further down that path. "If you're certain you don't need my help, I believe I'll turn in."

"See you in the morning." She threw the response over her shoulder without bothering to turn around.

Jo resisted the urge to stomp her foot.

It wasn't fair that he had everything *she* wanted and seemed so discontented. Yet *he* judged *her* for daring to set her sights beyond Knotty Pine. He wouldn't think her life was so rosy if he were the one living it. Too bad they couldn't up and change places. If he had all her family responsibilities...

She stilled. What if he *did* have her responsibilities? It was obvious the family already liked him. And he seemed equally taken with them. If she could somehow make him an actual part of the family, he was the sort of man who'd do everything he could to provide for and protect those in his care.

Cora Beth admired him. She could see he liked her too. As for the rest of the family, after that ruckus in the livery Danny practically hero-worshipped him. Ry had shown he could deal with her nieces—why, he even got along with Uncle Grover. They'd all be in good hands.

As for Ry's part, what man wouldn't be attracted to Cora Beth? She had that sweet domestic air about her that drew men looking for a wife like bees to honey.

If Ry and Cora Beth were to get hitched, she would be free to leave Knotty Pine knowing the family was well cared for.

So what if she'd been doing a bit of daydreaming over him herself? It was just because he'd been so all-fired heroic the other day and, to be honest, handsome as all get out. But, even if the thought stung a bit, she was realistic enough to know a man like Ryland Lassiter wouldn't fall for a girl like her.

Besides, she didn't need a man to tie her down. Just the opposite—she wanted to cut her tightly knotted bonds to this place so she could fly free.

In that respect, Ry *was* the answer to her prayers. God's hand had been in the timing of his trip through Knotty Pine, she was certain of it.

Jo lifted her chin. If this tug of attraction she felt for him was a way of testing her resolve, she was more than up to the challenge. All she needed for her plan to work would be for someone to give Ry and Cora Beth a little push.

And no matter how much her silly heart protested, she was just the person to do it.

Chapter Thirteen

Ry watched the world outside his window shift from black, to gray, to the rosy shades of dawn. He probably hadn't slept more than three hours last night, and that only in fits and starts.

Today he'd get some answers about Belle—or whatever answers were available. Then what?

Last night with the Wylies—experiencing firsthand their closeness and shared sense of purpose—had strengthened the feeling that had gradually grown in him the past few months, that he was merely drifting through life.

He had family, of course. Sadie and Griff and Grandfather Wallace—his Texas family and his Philadelphia family.

The problem was, he didn't have strong roots in either place. He mattered to his siblings, but if he passed away tomorrow it wouldn't leave any big gap in their lives. And he mattered to his grandfather, but only as someone to carry on the Wallace family legacy. Griff would have done just as well if he'd been the one to go to Philadelphia that fateful summer.

But the fault lay with him as much as with his family—maybe more so. He'd never truly committed to either world.

It was time that changed. He was twenty-nine years old. Time he made some decisions, set down some deeper roots. Perhaps time he started a family of his own.

Family. Home. A sense of belonging and mattering to folks in a real way. Those were things that gave a man a sense of purpose.

For some reason, Josie's face popped into his mind on the heels of that thought.

The sound of someone stirring around brought a welcome interruption to his musings. Ready for something to occupy him besides his own thoughts, Ry quickly got dressed.

He found Josie in the kitchen, frying up some eggs.

"Good morning," she called over her shoulder. "I'll be out of your way in a minute."

"Take your time," he drawled.

She jerked her head around. "Oh, sorry. I thought you were Cora Beth." Her surprised expression changed to one of curiosity. "What are you doing up so early?"

He shrugged. "No point staying in bed once you're awake."

Without asking if he was hungry, she cracked a couple more eggs and mixed them up with hers in the skillet. "Worried about meeting with Reverend Fields?"

Ry smiled as he watched her quick, efficient movements. He was surprised but pleased that she assumed he would share a meal with her, and that she would go through the trouble of cooking it. "Not worried," he replied. "Just ready to get some answers."

She nodded. "Plates are in the cupboard above the sink."

No false platitudes from this one. He took down two of the plates and set them on the counter next to the stove. "Anything else I can do to help?"

"Coffee cups are in the next cabinet over. I take mine with just a dab of cream."

As he poured up the two cups of coffee he thought how comfortable this was, sharing the start of day in this relaxed, un-hurried way with someone who didn't chatter on just to fill the silences and who seemed so attuned to his thoughts and mood.

Jo finished scrambling the eggs, never looking up but very conscious of his movements. Not that she could help it. He was such an imposing man—tall and broad shouldered, moving with a wholly masculine, wolf-like grace despite his injuries, and just out-and-out filling a room with his presence.

Her matchmaking job should be easy. How could Cora Beth *not* fall for him?

And of course, given time to get to know her better, he would fall for Cora Beth too. After all, her sister wasn't still single for lack of offers.

Jo dished up the eggs just as he set the cups of coffee on the table. She set the plates next to the cups, noting from its color that her coffee was prepared just the way she liked it.

They sat across from each other and ate in comfortable silence for a while. Finally, he wrapped his hands around his cup and looked up. "When does the next northbound train pass through?"

She paused with the fork halfway to her mouth. "Friday." Uh-oh, she hadn't thought about this part. Once he talked with Reverend Fields there'd be nothing to keep him here. And two days wasn't nearly enough time for her plan to take hold.

He nodded. "Well, I won't make you wait to get your room back. I'll move into one of the guest chambers this morning. Just let me know which one."

"Talk to Cora Beth about that. She's the one in charge here. I'm good at the livery business but not running a household. No sir, not like Cora Beth. That sister of mine sure knows how to keep this big ole place running as smooth as kitten's fur."

Seeing his puzzled frown, Jo realized she'd been babbling.

Good heavens, best get out of here while she could, and think this thing through when she was alone. There had to be a way to keep him in Knotty Pine a bit longer.

Pushing quickly back from the table, she carried her dishes to the sink.

"Josie, are you all—"

"Gotta head over to the livery," she said, cutting him off. "Don't you worry, though, I still plan to meet Reverend Fields at the train station this morning. Uncle Grover's already agreed to watch the livery while I'm gone."

"That's not necessary. I can—"

"No problem at all. Glad to do it." She edged toward the door, ignoring his puzzled expression.

Cora Beth walked in, tying an apron around her waist. She paused when she realized she wasn't alone. "Oh, hello. Looks like I'm the slugabed this morning."

Jo felt a tiny pang as Ry smiled at her sister. Which was plumb foolish, being as that was exactly what she wanted. She was just rattled by being caught off guard by his question was all.

"Morning, Cora Beth," she said quickly. "Mr. Lassiter wants to move into one of the guest rooms. You don't mind helping him with that, do you?"

"Of course not."

"Good. Well, I better get going. Freddie'll be wondering what's keeping me." And with that she was out the door. She sucked in a deep breath, clearing her head.

With luck, Mr. Lassiter would keep Cora Beth company while getting breakfast ready for everyone else. That would give him a taste for how well her sister handled things and how comfortable she was to be around. And Cora Beth would certainly help him move upstairs. Another chance for them to be thrown together.

If only she had a few more days she was sure she could get them to see how right they were for each other.

And then, with such an honorable, hard-working man around, she would finally be free to keep her promise to Aunt Pearl.

She wasn't sure why that thought didn't put more of a bounce in her step.

Ry paced across the bare wooden floor in the Wylies' family parlor as he waited for Reverend Fields to arrive.

The guest room Cora Beth had assigned him was larger and better furnished than Josie's, and the extra window made it brighter as well. And Cora Beth had done everything possible to make him comfortable, fluttering about, adding a pillow here, a vase of flowers there, an extra lamp near the bed.

Still, he missed the other room. There had been something homey and warm about it that his new one, for all its cheeriness, lacked.

Ry shoved that irrelevant thought aside as he plopped down in one of the wingback chairs. He wasn't ready to run a race yet, but he'd be fit for travel by the time the train came through on Friday.

His fingers drummed against the arm of the chair. How well had Reverend Fields known Belle? Would the man be able to answer his questions? What had happened to her husband? How long had she been on her own?

Josie and the reverend should be here any moment now. How had the minister reacted to being met by a female livery owner? He hoped her unorthodox dress and manner hadn't caused any awkwardness. Surely a man of the cloth would be slow to judge, would take the time to see beyond the overalls and work-shirt to the strong, selfless woman inside.

Not that Josie couldn't fend for herself. Still, he sensed a hidden vulnerability in her. And he felt a tug to defend her from any snubs or slights that might be directed her way.

Which was only natural, he told himself, considering all he owed her.

The house seemed quiet, as if it too was holding its breath, waiting. The only discernable sound was the rhythmic beat of the parlor clock's pendulum.

After what seemed an interminable delay, the front door opened, letting in a gust of air strong enough to chill him where he sat. The tension inside him coiled a notch tighter and a muscle in his jaw pulsed.

The muted sounds of conversation slid down the hall as he stood. Was that another woman's voice?

A moment later, Josie ushered in not only the man he assumed to be Reverend Fields but a woman and a child holding tight to a cat. He hadn't counted on the reverend bringing his family with him. This might make it difficult to have a frank conversation.

Josie motioned his direction. "This is Mr. Lassiter." She seemed to be trying to convey a message with her eyes. A warning perhaps? But of what?

"Mr. Lassiter, you didn't need to stand on our account." Reverend Fields, a tall, spare man with a horse-like face, approached Ry with an outstretched hand. "Miss Wylie told us of your unfortunate accident." Ry managed not to wince as the reverend vigorously pumped his hand.

"Thank you, sir, but I'm better now." Ry remained standing. "And thank you for making this trip on my behalf."

"Under the circumstances, we thought it best not to waste any time in carrying out Mrs. Hadley's wishes."

What did he mean, "under the circumstances?"

"Mrs. Hadley insisted right until the very end that you would have come sooner if you could have," the reverend continued. "I'm pleased to see her faith in your friendship was not misplaced."

"Thank you, sir. I just wish—"

The reverend cut him off, drawing the woman and child forward. "Please, before we continue, allow me to introduce my wife, Mrs. Fields."

Ry made a slight bow, wondering how to signal Josie to take Mrs. Fields and her daughter into another part of the house. "Ma'am."

"And this, of course," the gentleman put a hand on the child's shoulder, drawing her forward, "is Viola."

Chapter Fourteen

Ry froze. Viola? Had he heard right? Surely this wasn't—

Trying to ignore the unease tickling the back of his neck, he studied the child, looking for an indication he'd read this wrong.

Instead, what he saw—the familiar mahogany-colored ringlets, toffee brown eyes and tip-tilted nose—proved just the opposite.

There was no mistaking that this was Belle's daughter.

What was going on? Why had Belle sent the child to him?

The little girl moved closer to Mrs. Fields and drew the cat to her chin. A trembling in her lower lip brought Ry back to his senses. Whatever Belle's intent, the child needed reassurance.

"Viola," he said, keeping his voice soft, "do you know who I am?"

She nodded. "You're Mr. Lassiter, my momma's best friend in the whole world. Except for me and my daddy."

Had Belle still thought of him that way? "That's right. Your mother and I were very good friends. I knew her back when she was a little girl."

Viola nodded. "She told me."

At a loss as to what to say next, he glanced toward Josie.

HOW TO VALIDATE YOUR
EDITOR'S FREE GIFTS!
"THANK YOU"

1 Peel off the FREE GIFTS SEAL from front cover. Place it in the space provided at right. This automatically entitles you to receive two free books and two exciting surprise gifts.

2 Send back this card and you'll get 2 Love Inspired® Historical books. These books are worth over $10, but are yours absolutely FREE!

3 There's no catch. You're under no obligation to buy anything. We charge nothing — ZERO — for your first shipment. And you don't have to make any minimum number of purchases — not even one!

4 We call this line Love Inspired Historical because every other month you'll receive books that are filled with inspirational historical romance. This series is filled with engaging stories of romance, adventure and faith set in historical periods from biblical times to World War II. You'll like the convenience of getting them delivered to your home well before they are in stores. And you'll love our discount prices, too!

5 We hope that after receiving your free books you'll want to remain a subscriber. But the choice is yours — to continue or cancel, anytime at all! So why not take us up on our invitation, with no risk of any kind. You'll be glad you did!

6 And remember . . . just for validating your Editor's Free Gifts Offer, we'll send you 2 books and 2 gifts, *ABSOLUTELY FREE!*

YOURS FREE!
We'll send you two fabulous surprise gifts (worth about $10) absolutely FREE, simply for accepting our no-risk offer!

Steep
Hill®

▼ DETACH AND MAIL CARD TODAY! ▼

YES!

PLACE
FREE GIFTS
SEAL
HERE

I have placed my Editor's "thank you" Free Gifts seal in the space provided above. Please send me the 2 FREE books and 2 FREE gifts for which I qualify. I understand that I am under no obligation to purchase anything further, as explained on the opposite page.

We want to make sure we offer you the best service suited to your needs. Please answer the following question:
About how many NEW paperback fiction books have you purchased in the past 3 months?
❑ 0-2   ❑ 3-6   ❑ 7 or more

102 IDL EZND   302 IDL EZPZ

FIRST NAME   LAST NAME

ADDRESS

APT.#   CITY

STATE/PROV.   ZIP/POSTAL CODE

FOR SHIPPING CONFIRMATION

EMAIL

PRINTED IN THE U.S.A.

(LIH-EC-09R2) © 2009 STEEPLE HILL BOOKS

The Reader Service — Here's How It Works:

And, as if waiting for his signal, she stepped forward and smiled. "Viola, I'll have you know my sister bakes the best honey pecan tarts in all of Texas. What do you say we head to the kitchen and find us a few to sample? And I can introduce you to my nieces, Pippa and Lottie. They're twins you know, alike as two blades of grass, and I know they'd love to meet your cat."

Ry was both surprised and grateful at the easy way she interacted with the child.

Viola hesitated a moment, glancing first at Ry and then at Mrs. Fields. Finally she took Josie's outstretched hand and the two exited the room.

As the door closed behind them, Ry scrubbed a hand across his face. "I'm sorry, Reverend, Ma'am, please have a seat."

Reverend Fields seated his wife on the sofa and then took a chair next to Ry. Ry finally sank into a chair himself.

The reverend leaned forward, studying Ry with a solemn expression. "I pride myself on being able to read people, and unless I'm mistaken, you were surprised by Viola's presence."

"Yes sir, extremely so. It's been over twelve years since I last saw Mrs. Hadley and I had no idea she had children."

"But surely you received my telegram?"

"I'm afraid I misunderstood. I assumed you were referring to a musical instrument."

"I see."

Ry took a deep breath and asked the question that had haunted him these past few days. "What happened to Belle?"

Reverend Fields steepled his hands. "Mrs. Hadley was passing through Foxberry when she had an accident. Broke her leg. It was bad, but for a while, she seemed to be recovering. Then an infection set in."

Ry's stomach tightened as he thought about the pain she

must have suffered. Was there something he could have done if he'd gotten there in time?

"Dr. Holcomb counted it a miracle she survived as long as she did," the reverend continued. "I believe it was her desire to speak to you before she passed that kept her going."

And he'd failed her in that. "Did she indicate why she wanted to see me?"

"I assume it was to discuss Viola's future."

"Of course." Ry raked a hand through his hair, then winced as his fingers brushed against his injury.

He still hadn't quite absorbed what the child's appearance meant. "Do you know what happened to Viola's father?"

"Mrs. Hadley indicated he died of a snakebite. Happened a month or so before they arrived in Foxberry."

So Viola had lost both parents in a short time. "Did Belle leave instructions as to what she expected me to do for Viola?"

Perhaps she needed him to act as escort, to deliver the child safely to her new guardian, whoever that might be. Or maybe she wanted to have Ry provide for the child's future. It was the least he could do. He would see that Belle's daughter received a top-notch education, that she never wanted for anything—

"Mr. Lassiter." This time it was Mrs. Fields who spoke, her voice gentle but firm. "I don't think you quite understand. Belle named you as Viola's guardian."

Ry's mind rebelled at that thought. It was too big a responsibility. He was a bachelor. What did he know about raising a child, much less a daughter? What had Belle been thinking? *Surely* there was someone else—

"She gave this to me the day before she died." Reverend Fields held out an envelope. "She asked me to deliver it if you didn't arrive in time for her to speak to you. Perhaps it provides some of the answers you seek."

Ry took the envelope but didn't open it. He wanted to be alone when he read whatever Belle had written.

"Mr. Lassiter, please consider this carefully." Reverend Fields leaned forward, hands clasped between his knees. "This was obviously what Viola's mother wanted, but your wishes are important as well. Viola is a dear child who's experienced a great tragedy. She deserves the comfort and security of being raised by someone who truly wants her. If that person isn't you, there's no shame in admitting as much. And I assure you Viola would be well cared for. There are several families in Foxberry who would be glad to give her a loving, God-fearing home."

Ry was very tempted. Surely the girl would be better off with one of those families the reverend referred to? What if he failed the child the way he'd failed her mother?

"I only want what's best for Viola," he said slowly.

Reverend Fields nodded. "Of course, as do we all. Mrs. Fields and I plan to spend the night here in Knotty Pine and return to Foxberry on tomorrow's train. It's not much time, I grant you, but I encourage you to use it to get to know the child a bit and for her to get to know you. And most of all to spend time in prayer, seeking the Lord's guidance, before you make such a momentous decision."

He motioned toward his wife. "We will pray for you, as well."

The woman nodded, her smile gentle, empathetic. "I have confidence this will work out according to God's plan."

Ry only hoped her confidence hadn't been misplaced.

Feeling like an intruder, Jo balanced one end of the tray Cora Beth had saddled her with on the hall table and rapped on the parlor door before opening it.

"Sorry for the interruption," she said as she entered, "but my sister thought you might like a glass of lemonade."

Ry's expression was that of a prisoner who'd just received a reprieve. "No need to apologize," he said quickly. "That was quite thoughtful of your sister."

As Jo set the tray down, he added, "Reverend and Mrs. Fields plan to stay the night in Knotty Pine. I suggested they take a room here rather than the hotel."

"Of course." Jo wondered if Ry was trying to toss a bit of business their way, or wanted to have the Fields close by to make it easier for Viola.

Either way, he was still living up to his hero image. "We have a very comfortable room available and I can promise you my sister sets a much finer table than any you'll find at the hotel."

Reverend Fields turned to his wife. "What say you, my dear?"

She nodded. "It sounds lovely."

Jo moved to the door. "That's settled then. Let me just step over to the kitchen and talk to my sister about getting the room prepared while you enjoy your lemonade."

She didn't miss the dazed look on Ry's face, and couldn't say she blamed him much. The poor man had been blindsided by Viola's arrival.

A few moments later Cora Beth bustled into the room. "Reverend and Mrs. Fields, I'm so pleased to have you as our guests for the night. Allow me to show you to your room so you can rest and freshen up a bit after your trip. We'll be serving lunch soon. I hope you like black bean and ham soup."

"That sounds delicious. We appreciate you taking us in on such short notice."

"Not at all." Cora Beth motioned for them to precede her. "And I've already sent over to the depot for your bags."

Reverend Fields turned to Ry. "The large trunk with our bags contains Mrs. Hadley's and Viola's things."

Ry nodded. "Thank you. I'll see to it."

After the others left the room, Jo studied Ry. "You okay? Want me to help you back to your room?"

"I'm fine." He shook his head as if to clear it. "Belle appointed me Viola's guardian." He rubbed his temple. "Heaven help that child."

"So you're going to take the job?"

"How can I not? I have to believe Belle had her reasons for doing this. Besides, it's not the kind of responsibility one can just walk away from. You of all people should know that."

"That's different. This is my family." Did he truly realize what he was taking on?

"And now it seems, Viola is mine."

She saw the determination reflected in his eyes. Well, it was his choice. She had to hand it to him, though. As much as he seemed bumfuzzled and downright scared spitless, he also appeared ready to step up and do what was required.

"Raising a kid is not an easy thing," she warned. "Especially for a man on his own. Even Cora Beth, as good as she is with young'uns, moved back in here when Philip died. It was just too much for her to handle by herself."

He raised a brow as one corner of his mouth kicked up. "You trying to change my mind?"

"Just want to make sure you know what you're taking on."

"Believe me, I know it won't be all sunshine and daisies. I suppose I'll wind up hiring a nanny."

That's right, he had money. Well, it was going to take more than money to raise that little girl. Leastways if he wanted to do it right. Which she was pretty sure he did.

But that's something he'd figure out for himself soon enough. One thing for sure, whether he knew it or not, his traveling

days were about over. If he went through with this, he was going
to get a taste of what *her* life had been like the past six years.

Actually, this would work right into her matchmaking
plan. With a kid of his own to care for, he'd be more likely
now than before to be looking for a wife. And who better
than Cora Beth?

Sure, Cora Beth had said she didn't intend to marry again.
But Ry was the kind of man who could melt any woman's heart.
In fact, if she wasn't careful, she could fall for him herself.

Jo straightened. That was not going to happen. Ry might
be a good man—charming, handsome, heroic even—but
marriage didn't fit into her plans for her future, at least not
short term.

Time to put some distance between them. "If you don't
need my help, I'd better head back to the livery. Don't want
to leave Uncle Grover on his own for too long." She gave him
a pointed look. "Viola's in the kitchen with Cora Beth and
the twins."

After she'd gone Ry fingered Belle's letter. This was it—his
best chance to find the answers he'd been looking for ever
since he received her telegram.

Mentally bracing himself, Ry opened the letter.

My dearest Ry,
If you are reading this it means I did not survive to see you.
And, knowing you, you are riddled with guilt for not getting here
in time, but there is no need. I believe God is in control of all
things and whatever comes to pass, all will be well in the end.
There is so much I wanted to say to you. But mostly I want
to thank you for taking me under your wing at a time when I
had no one else. You'll never know what your friendship meant

to me—still means to me. You brought back joy and light into my life when both had been all but extinguished.

I took those memories with me when I left Hawk's Creek, and my life was the richer for it. Horace and I had a good life, truly blessed, and it was made even better when Viola came along. It was only after Horace was taken from us so unexpectedly that I realized what our child missed because of our nomadic way of life.

Viola has never had a permanent home, has no aunts or cousins, no close friends except for her cat. And now she will not even have parents.

She will be very much alone once I am gone—just as I was all those years ago when I arrived at Hawk's Creek. Which brings me to why I wrote this letter. I had hoped to take the little bit of money Horace and I had put aside and use it to give Viola a real home. It seems, though, that the Good Lord has other plans for me. So now I am asking you to do for my daughter what I cannot. I know this seems a heavy burden to hand you, but I would not ask it if I did not know firsthand how well suited you are to the task. And I feel in my heart that it will bring you an equal measure of joy.

Please do for her what you did for me. Bring joy and light into her life. Show her she's not alone, that someone cares for her. Give her a home. Teach her to see the beauty in the world around her. Allow yourself to take joy in her as well.

And above all, raise her in the Word.

Yours in our Lord,

Belle

Ry slowly folded the letter, his mind churning, spinning from one random thought to another.

Belle didn't blame him for not making it to Foxberry in time.

She saw God's hand in all that had happened. She had entrusted her daughter to his care.

There was no way he could turn his back on her dying request.

Ry squeezed his hands at his sides, praying fervently that he could live up to her trust.

Chapter Fifteen

When Ry pushed open the kitchen door, his gaze went straight to Viola. She and the twins sat cross-legged on the floor dangling a bit of yarn for the cat to play with. Pippa and Lottie were giggling but it was the smile on Viola's face that held his attention. It transformed her, turned her into the carefree child she should have been.

As soon as she saw him, however, the smile was replaced by a look of worry. She reached for the cat and hugged him tightly against her. Ry wasn't certain if she drew comfort from her pet or if she thought she was protecting the animal from him.

Cora Beth set her cooking spoon down. "Come along, Pippa, Lottie. I have something upstairs I need your help with."

When Viola started to rise, Cora Beth motioned her to stay put. "Not you, dear. You're our guest. You and Mr. Lassiter can visit while we're gone." She gave the girl an encouraging smile. "Why don't you pass him one of the pecan tarts?"

"Yes, ma'am."

Ry took a seat at the table, waiting for her to serve him. What in the world would they find to talk about?

Lord, please give me the words. Don't let me make her world scarier than it already is.

She handed him the tart and he took a bite. "Mmm-mmm. These sure are good."

Viola merely nodded, her gaze remaining fixed on her cat.

"I'm sure Mrs. Collins wouldn't mind if you had another one."

This time she shook her head. She certainly wasn't much for talking. Time for a question that couldn't be answered with a yes or no. "That's a mighty fine looking cat. What's his name?"

"Daffy."

"Daffy? Is that because he acts silly?"

Her eyes got rounder. "Oh, no. Daffy's a very proper cat, I promise."

Okay, no teasing about the cat. "So how did he get his name?"

"It's really Daffodil, because of his color. But Ma and I—" her voice wavered slightly then recovered "—Ma and I decided Daffodil wasn't really a good name for a boy cat so we decided to call him Daffy instead."

He nodded approvingly. "That makes sense. And how long have you had Daffy?"

"A long time. Ma said Pa gave him to me for my third birthday. But I don't remember that far back."

She finally looked up and met his gaze. To his dismay, he saw unshed tears in her eyes. Had he said something wrong already?

"Please don't make me give him away." Her voice wavered alarmingly.

Stunned, Ry sat up straighter. "Of course I won't make you give Daffy away. Whatever gave you that idea?"

She sniffed. "Annie Orr told me lots of men don't like cats, not for pets. She said all three of her uncles *and* her grandpa won't let them in their houses 'cause cats make them sneeze."

"Well, cats don't make me sneeze." He held out his hands. "Mind if I hold Daffy for a minute?"

She hesitated and he wondered if she'd trust him enough to comply.

"After all," he said, keeping his tone conversational, "if Daffy and I are going to be friends we should start getting acquainted, don't you think?"

She still looked apprehensive, but gave a slow nod and handed her pet over. He lifted the cat so they were at eye level. "Well, Daffy, what do you think? Will we get along?"

The feline's answer to that was an inelegant sneeze.

"Uh-oh." Ry wrinkled his brow. "Do you suppose he's trying to tell me something?" Then he gave her a mock-worried look. "I sure hope *he* doesn't try to keep *me* out of the house."

To his relief she gave him a you're-so-silly smile.

"Here," he handed her the cat, "you better take him back before he sneezes again."

Viola gave the cat another hug, then set him down where he commenced washing himself.

"I've been thinking," Ry chose his words carefully, "if we're going to become a family like your ma wanted, maybe we ought to get to know each other better."

"How do we do that?"

"Well, I could ask you some questions, and then you could ask me questions."

She nodded. "All right."

"You start. Go ahead, ask me anything you want to know."

"What should I call you?"

Her question set Ry back for a moment. "Father" or "Pa" didn't feel right and "Mr. Lassiter" was much too formal. "How does Uncle Ry sound?"

"Uncle Ry." Her nose wrinkled as if she were tasting some unfamiliar food. Then she nodded. "Okay." She rubbed her arms. "Your turn."

"So what should I call you?"

"My name."

"Ah, but which name? You have so many. Miss Hadley, Viola, Button."

Her nose wrinkled in surprise. "Button?"

"With that cute little button nose of yours," he said, tapping it lightly, "surely someone calls you Button?"

She shook her head, rubbing her nose. "That's silly."

"But it suits you. Now, your turn again."

She smiled at his teasing, but moved on to her next question. "Do you live here with all these people?"

"No. I'm just staying here until my arm heals."

"Then where's your home?"

That question seemed to come up a lot lately. "Actually, I have two homes. There's Hawk's Creek ranch, the place where I met your mother and where my brother and sister live. But I spend most of my time in a city back east called Philadelphia where my grandfather lives." What would his family think of his taking on the role of guardian?

"Oh." She seemed to think about that for a minute. "Then which place would we live at?"

"Hmm, I haven't thought about that yet. Maybe I could take you to visit both places and then we could decide together."

She nodded solemnly. "That would be nice. And I'll ask God about it in my prayers tonight, too."

"That's a fine idea. Now it's my turn again." He searched his mind for another innocuous topic. "How old are you?"

"Seven."

So young to have been through so much.

She chewed on her lip a moment. "How did you hurt your arm?" she asked at last.

How much should he say? No way he was going to lie to her, but he didn't want to frighten or worry her either. "I'm afraid I got in the way of a bullet. But don't you worry, it's healing nicely and should be good as new in a day or two."

He quickly moved on to another subject. "What's your favorite food?"

She didn't hesitate. "Strawberries with sweet cream."

"Ah, I admire a girl who knows what she likes. Your turn again."

Jo quietly moved away from the back door. She'd passed through the kitchen to snag a pecan tart on her way out earlier, and truth be known, to make sure Viola was settling in okay with the twins. Not that she needed to concern herself. She should have known Cora Beth would have it under control.

She'd paused on the back porch to pull on her work boots. A problem with the laces had held her there a few moments longer.

When she heard Ry come in, her curiosity had gotten the better of her and she hadn't been able to resist the urge to eavesdrop.

She was glad she had. Despite his own doubts, she'd heard enough to decide Belle had made the right choice in naming him Viola's guardian. Ry would make a fine father to the little girl.

And wouldn't Cora Beth, who already had such great experience in the parent department, make the perfect mother...

When Danny and Audrey returned from school, Audrey latched on to Viola as if they were long lost friends. At supper, Viola was introduced to the other boarders, and Audrey promptly asked Mr. Saddler if Viola could accompany her to school in the morning.

"Of course," he answered. "Miss Viola is welcome to attend while she's here. That is, if Mr. Lassiter is agreeable."

Viola immediately looked to him for permission, an act Ry found unnerving. With blinding clarity, he realized this is what his life would become—making decisions, large and small, for another person who would trust those decisions unquestioningly.

Lord, please give me the wisdom to make the right ones.

He nodded agreement, guiltily relieved she would have something to occupy her for most of the day tomorrow.

Once supper was cleared, Ry and Viola joined the Wylies as they gathered in the kitchen.

He helped Josie shell pecans while Cora Beth mixed the ingredients for another of her fruitcakes.

Uncle Grover and Danny pulled out a chessboard. The twins sat on the floor, absorbed in a game of make-believe with a pair of rag dolls. Audrey and Viola played with a set of tiddly winks nearby.

Ry was encouraged to see Viola and Audrey were becoming fast friends. But he still worried that the child was too quiet and reserved for a seven-year-old. Had she always been this way? Or was it her current situation? Was there something he should be doing to make this easier for her?

"She'll come around," Josie said softly.

His head swung around, his gaze meeting hers. "What's that?"

"I said, she'll come around." Josie expertly separated the meat from the shell on the pecan she'd just cracked, and reached for another. "Give her time. She's just lost her parents, and now she's been plopped smack-dab in the middle of a group of strangers, in a place she's never seen before. That would be hard on anyone, but especially a youngster."

"I know." Her comment was reassuring. In the short time he'd known Josie he'd come to trust her judgment. "I only wish I was sure Belle made the right choice in naming me Viola's guardian."

"Seems to me she knew exactly what she was doing." Josie cracked another pecan. "In fact, I can't think of anyone who'd take the responsibility more seriously."

"Thanks. But it's my ability rather than my intent I'm worried about."

Josie tossed a pecan shell, startling him when it bounced against his chest. "Have faith" was her only response to his questioning frown.

Ry stared at the ceiling, resigned to the fact that he'd spend another restless night.

This morning he'd lain in bed feeling guilty for failing Belle, and hoping to get a few answers. The only real problem in front of him at that point, though, had been deciding whether he wanted to call Texas or Philadelphia home.

Tonight he'd found himself the guardian of a much-too-somber seven-year-old and her cat. Sort of put things in perspective.

A sound from the hallway caught his attention. Was someone else having trouble sleeping?

Curious, he crossed the room and cracked open his door. It was dark on this end of the hall, but the stairway was gilded with moonlight from the window over the landing.

A child-sized form, a cat clutched in her arms, tiptoed toward the stairs.

Ry grabbed his pants and stepped into them. What was Viola up to? Surely she wasn't planning to run away? Alarmed, he grabbed a shirt and followed her, still working the buttons. He got as far as the bend in the staircase before he realized she'd sat down on the bottom tread.

He paused. Now what? Did he give her some privacy to work out whatever was on her mind? Or did he try to comfort her?

Before he could decide, Josie stepped from the kitchen and paused. "And just what are you doing sitting here in the dark, young lady?"

"Me and Daffy couldn't sleep."

Should he make his presence known?

"I see. Mind if I join you?" The tread creaked as Josie sat beside her.

Ry decided it would be less intimidating for Viola to have just one adult to deal with. And he trusted Josie to find the right words.

"So," Josie asked in a stage whisper, "do my nieces snore?"

Viola giggled. "No. Well, maybe just a little," she temporized.

"But that's not why you can't sleep, is it?"

The child raised the cat to her cheek as she shook her head.

"You know," Josie's tone was that of someone sharing a secret, "I lost my ma, too. It was three years ago but I still remember like it was yesterday. It left a big old hole right in the middle of my heart that hurt awful bad."

"Did you cry?"

"Sure did."

There was a bit of a pause, then she looked up at Josie. "Do you still cry sometimes?"

"No, not about my ma's passing. But it took awhile. I had to get over being mad at God first."

Even from where he stood, Ry could feel the shocked surprise pouring out of Viola. It was pretty much a reflection of his own.

"You were mad at *God?*" The child's words were hushed, as if she were almost afraid to voice the question.

"Yep." Josie spoke as if such an admission was normal. "I mean, He already had my pa, why'd He need to take my ma too?

"But God is good." Viola appeared to be trying to reason with Josie. "You're not supposed to get mad at Him."

Josie leaned back against the banister. "Let me ask you this. Did you ever get a little bit mad at your ma when she wouldn't let you have your way?" She scratched the cat behind the ears. "That doesn't mean they're not good or that we don't love them anymore, just that we're angry with them. It's the same with God. Being angry with Him doesn't mean we don't love Him anymore, it just means we're hurting. And because He loves us, He understands. As long as we don't let our anger push us away from Him, as long as we keep talking to Him and letting Him know how we feel, we'll eventually get to a place of peace about whatever has happened."

"What do you mean?"

"For instance, my being angry about my ma's passing. After a while, I stopped fussing and fuming quite so much and started listening to what God had to say."

"What did He say?"

"Well, whenever I'd read my Bible I'd come across passages about the freedom from pain and sorrow to be found in heaven, and the unbounded joys of being with the Father, and about there being a season for living and for dying. Then I got to re-membering how my ma always talked about dying as a home-coming. Of course, I'd known all along she was in heaven. Just like you know your ma and pa are too."

Viola nodded.

Josie placed a hand on Viola's knee. "I realized it was selfish of me to be wishing she'd have to live one more minute down here when she could be enjoying all that glory has to offer."

"But don't you still miss her?"

"Of course I do. I think about her most every day. But I keep all my good memories close to my heart and I know that some day, when God figures the time is right, I'm going to join her up there in heaven and we'll be together again."

Ry closed his eyes, thanking God for putting Josie here to talk to Viola.

How had she done it? Opened her heart to Viola in such a simple, sensitive manner. He wasn't certain he could have handled the child's hurt nearly so well.

But he'd been hiding in the dark long enough. Ry started down the stairs, making certain his footsteps would be heard. "Well, hello, ladies. Are you two looking for a late night snack, too?"

Josie stood, studying him as he descended. He could tell she was trying to figure out how much he'd overheard.

She glanced at Viola. "That sounds like a good idea. I think there's a few pieces of Cora Beth's apple cobbler left from supper. What do you say we raid the pie safe?"

"Mmm." Ry patted his stomach. "Sounds like just what I need. How about you, Viola?"

The child nodded, stroking Daffy's back.

Ry helped Viola to her feet. He met Josie's glance over Viola's head and mouthed a heartfelt "Thank you."

She reddened slightly, but nodded as she took Viola's other hand and returned a silent "You're welcome."

They strolled into the kitchen, Viola between them, and Ry suddenly felt like things might just work out after all.

Chapter Sixteen

Ry strolled along the sidewalk, fighting the urge to whistle. It felt great to be outdoors again. He passed several people as he made his way to the livery, all of them strangers, all of them seeming to know his name and offering friendly greetings.

The sound of the train whistle carried to him from the depot, signaling the arrival of the southbound train. The Fieldses would be boarding soon, severing Viola's last link to her past, tying her irrevocably to him.

But that thought wasn't as daunting this morning as it had been yesterday. Seeing Josie with Viola last night had planted a seed in his mind, one that had taken root during the night.

Viola didn't need a nanny. She needed a mother.

A woman who was strong, caring, God-fearing. A woman who could help him love and guide Viola on the path to becoming a woman herself. A woman he'd be comfortable sharing his own life with.

A woman like Josie.

On that thought, he found himself once more at Wylie's Livery and Bridle Shop.

As soon as Josie spied him, she frowned. "What are you doing out here? And where's your sling?"

Was her concern a sign that she cared about him, even if just a little? "I'm fine without the sling. I thought it was time I took in some fresh air and saw what Knotty Pine has to offer."

"Well, now that you proved you're on the mend, set yourself down on that crate and give yourself a rest."

"Yes, ma'am." He was actually beginning to enjoy her tendency to fuss over him.

She studied him suspiciously but he maintained a bland expression and she finally went back to work, carving on another pumpkin. "Viola get off to school okay this morning?"

"Yep. Audrey had her by the hand, chattering away about all the fun they were going to have."

Josie shook her head. "I'm afraid Audrey inherited the bossier side of the Wylie family traits."

Ry suppressed a grin. He'd been thinking the girl was a lot like her Aunt Josie. "It'll be good for Viola. Being with other children will give her something to think about besides her loss."

Josie nodded. "Are there any kids running around that ranch of yours?"

Ry shook his head. "No. Even Inez's kids—she's our cook— are grown now."

"How about at your grandfather's place?"

"I'm afraid I'm the youngest one there."

"Then maybe you ought to think about staying around here for a spell." She kept her eyes focused on her work and her voice seemed a bit too casual. "Through Thanksgiving, anyway. Like you said, it'll be good for Viola to be around other kids. And you said your family isn't much for celebrating and such."

Ry's mood improved yet another notch. Without any prodding, she'd unwittingly helped him set his plan in motion.

Now he'd have a legitimate reason to hang around, giving him time to do a bit of wooing and to convince her they'd be a good match. "Thanks for the invitation," he answered. "And you may be right. Spending Thanksgiving here, with all of you, will be a real comfort to her." And he was rather looking forward to an old-fashioned family Thanksgiving himself.

Josie gave him a pleased smile. "Good. That's settled then."

She glanced toward the sidewalk. "Hello, Sheriff. Something I can help you with?"

"Hi, Jo."

Ry sized up the tall man with the slow Texas drawl who was staring straight at him. He decided the seemingly lazy exterior hid something decidedly more formidable.

"I heard your new boarder was out and about today and I thought I'd come around and introduce myself."

Ry stood. "Hello, Sheriff. I'm Ryland Lassiter."

"Glad to make your acquaintance. Name's Mitchell Hammond."

They shook hands and then the sheriff stepped back, crossing his arms. "I put the word out on Otis. If he shows up at any town within sixty miles of here he'll be dealt with as he deserves."

"That's good to hear. If you need anyone to testify against him, let me know."

The sheriff nodded. "I've heard Jo's version of what happened. When you have a few minutes, why don't you drop by my office and fill me in on yours."

Ry decided there was more command than suggestion in the invitation. "I'll stop in on my way back to the boardinghouse."

"Good, I'll be looking for you." He tipped his hat Josie's way. "Guess I'd better let you folks get on with your business."

Once they were alone, Ry rubbed the back of his neck, trying to decide what it was about the man that seemed so intimidating.

"Sheriff Hammond's a good man," Josie said as if reading his thoughts. "Easygoing most of the time. But he takes his job seriously and doesn't let anything stand in the way of his duty."

"I can see that." A movement in one of the far stalls caught his attention. "What do we have here?" Ry moved to the back of the livery where a horse and foal were penned. "You purchase some new stock?" Had she already taken steps to replace Scout?

"Those aren't mine. Miz Parsons left for Shreveport yesterday to visit her daughter and new grandbaby. I'm taking care of her horses while she's gone."

Ry leaned on the stall gate, studying the pair. The foal, a filly he could see now, couldn't be more than a week old. The mare was in good shape—not up to the bloodlines Hawk's Creek stables produced, but obviously well fed and cared for.

"Excuse me, ma'am. Is the owner around?"

Ry swung around at the sound of the familiar voice. It couldn't be—

But it was. His brother stood just inside the livery with their sister at his side. Both were staring at Josie with uncertain expressions, as if not sure what to make of a woman working in a livery, and one dressed the way she was.

Griff held the lead to a roan horse. So they'd delivered Kestrel in person—he hadn't figured on that. Watching them, he realized they hadn't noticed him standing back in the shadows.

"I'm the owner," Josie stated as she stood. He watched her size his siblings up.

They returned the favor, reacting to her announcement with barely concealed surprise. Sadie, especially, had her lips compressed in a disapproving line.

Josie crossed her arms. "Jo Wylie at your service. Something I can do for you?"

Ry had heard that tone before. He quickly stepped forward to help smooth things over. "Hello, Griff, Sadie. Nice to see you."

"Ry!" His sister raced forward and threw her arms around his neck. "Are you all right? I've been so worried."

"Hi, Sadie." Ry winced at the near collision, but gave his impetuous sister a one-armed hug. For someone whose head barely reached his chin, she sure packed a powerful wallop. "I'm fine. Or at least I was until you tackled me."

She released him immediately and stepped back. "Oh no. Did I hurt you? Are you injured?"

"Like I said, I'm fine. Nothing to worry that pretty head of yours over." He looked past his sister to his brother, who'd made no move to step forward. "Hello, Griff. I wasn't expecting you two to deliver the horse personally. Figured you'd send Red or one of the other hands."

His brother shrugged. "Coming wasn't my idea. When Sadie saw your telegram, though, there was no holding her back. And I certainly couldn't let her come out here on her own."

Ry frowned. "All I said was that I'd be here in Knotty Pine for a while and requested you send Kestrel."

"That phrase you slipped in about dropping by the ranch when you were 'able to travel' set our sister's alarm bells ringing. She was convinced you were at death's door."

"Nothing quite so dramatic." Was that Josie's snort behind him or one of the horses?

Sadie didn't seem the least convinced by his reassurances. "I was right to be worried. I told you, Griff. Look how pale he is." She shook a finger in Ry's direction. "Ryland Jeremiah Lassiter, don't lie to me. You're hurt, I can tell."

Ry raised his hand in mock surrender. "Okay, I ran into a bit of trouble, but I'm healing quite well, as you can see."

"More like he's too ornery to stay down."

Ry stepped aside, widening the circle to include Josie. "Speaking of which, I believe you've already met Miss Josephine Wylie. She's the one who saved my life."

"Saved your life!" Sadie plopped her fists on her hips. "I knew there was more to this than you were letting on. Will you *please* tell me what happened?"

Ry ignored her demand. "Josie, this overly-dramatic chit is my sister, Sadie, and the gentleman with her is my brother, Griffith."

Griff gave a short bow. "Miss Wylie."

Sadie didn't waste time with the amenities. "Josephine, did you truly save my brother's life?"

"Call me Jo. And your brother is exaggerating just a tad."

"Not at all." Ry enjoyed turning the tables and putting *her* heroics center stage for a change. "I stumbled into an ambush and she came charging to my rescue, guns blazing, in true hero form."

Sadie stepped forward and enveloped Josie in a bear hug, all her previous reservations forgotten. "Thank you so much for helping my brother. I'll be forever in your debt—we all will."

Josie blinked, a what-just-happened expression on her face.

Sadie stepped back with an arch smile. "Now, I know it must be a fascinating story and you're going to have to tell me all about it, because Ry will skip over the interesting parts."

Ry, deciding to leave Josie to deal with Sadie for the time being, turned to his brother. "How'd Kestrel make the trip?"

Griff led the horse forward. "No problems. You'd never know it was his first train ride."

Ry took the reins and gave the animal a careful once-over. "You've done a good job caring for him. He's turned into a fine animal."

His brother shrugged. "It was part of our agreement."

There was a time when he and Griff had been the best of

friends. But somewhere along the way they'd lost the ability to speak to each other with anything but resentment.

Feeling a sense of regret, Ry turned to the ladies. "Josie, this is Kestrel. He's a three-year-old out of one of Hawk's Creek's finest stallions."

"He's a beauty." Josie stepped close enough to rub the animal's nose. "If this is the kind of stock you're breeding I can see why you'd be proud of the program."

"Kestrel is Ry's prize," Sadie said. "He has big plans—"

Ry gave his sister a quelling look. "Actually, he's just one of Monarch's many offspring."

Sadie blinked, staring at him as if he'd said the animal had two heads, and even Griff wore a puzzled frown. Better barrel on through before they bungled this any further. He thrust the lead at Josie. "Glad you like him. He's yours."

Ry ignored the startled expressions from his siblings. He hadn't told Griff why he'd wanted the best three-year-old in his stable brought here. "I know Scout was special to you," he continued, focusing on Josie, "and it won't be easy to replace him, but Kestrel's a fine animal out of a strong line. He'll make a good work horse as well as a mount."

"But I can't—"

"Nonsense. I won't take no for an answer."

Her jaw set in a firm line. "This animal is obviously valuable and I don't accept charity."

"This isn't charity. It's repayment of a debt." He gave her his sternest courtroom look. "You of all people should know about repaying one's debts."

Josie stuffed her hands in her pockets and worried at her bottom lip. Finally she nodded. "All right. But only if you let me return the money you paid for the use of Scout."

"It's a deal." Ry's quick agreement seemed to surprise her.

But he knew Kestrel was worth a great deal more than the hundred dollars he'd paid for the use of her horse. And he'd find other ways to provide cash to the Wylie family, ways that wouldn't infringe on Josie's pride.

Besides, if things worked out as he hoped, it would be all in the family before long.

Ry turned to his siblings. "You'll need a place to stay while you're here. Josie's family runs a boardinghouse and her sister's cooking rivals Inez's."

"Sounds perfect," Sadie said, her manners smoothing over her surprise. "That'll give us a chance to corner you for a nice long chat. In fact, why don't we all go over there now and Jo can tell us about this amazing adventure the two of you had."

Josie shook her head. "I need to keep an eye on the livery. But y'all go on. I'm sure you want to freshen up and rest after your trip."

"Nonsense." Sadie waved away Josie's objections. "We'd much rather pump you for information about what Ry's been up to. There must be someone who can take over for you for a bit."

"There's someone who watches the place at night. But he won't be by until nearly suppertime."

"Well then, we'll just find someone else. I insist that you join us. I know I won't get the full story out of Ry unless you're there to keep him from leaving out the exciting bits."

"You might as well give in." Ry gave Josie a mock-defeated look. "Sadie may appear demure, but once she gets the bit between her teeth there's no stopping her."

Josie looked from him to his sister. "I suppose I could check with Edgar from the boot shop across the street," she said uncertainly. "He might be willing to watch the place for a bit."

"Splendid." Sadie nodded as if the matter were settled. "Y'all just go on up to the house and freshen up. Your brother can show you the way. I'll join you as soon as I have Kestrel here settled in and talk to Edgar."

Ry hesitated, then caught the speculative look in his sister's eye. No point tipping his hand just yet. "All right. We'll see you back at the house." Sheriff Hammond would just have to wait for that chat a bit longer.

Josie watched Ry leave with his brother and sister, then began settling in the horse.

There was definitely something going on with those three that she couldn't figure out. Like his obvious surprise that they'd come instead of sending one of the ranch hands. And the fact that he and his brother barely exchanged a handful of words even though it had been months since they'd seen each other.

That sister of his was quite the lady, though. She looked small and delicate as a honeysuckle bloom, even if she was a bit excitable. Her clothes were every bit as fine as those in the fashion magazines Cora Beth liked to pour over. And she had a bit of a pampered look about her.

Was that the kind of female Ry was used to keeping company with? Would his sister's visit have him making comparisons that weren't flattering?

Good thing she didn't care what he thought about her, not in that area at any rate.

As for Cora Beth, she could hold her own. What she lacked in polish, she more than made up for in her sweet temper and domestic skills. A man could do a lot worse selecting a wife than casting his eye toward Cora Beth. She only hoped Ry was smart enough to realize that. Because the sooner she could make this match happen, the sooner she could shake off her family obligations and follow her dream.

She'd already decided the first place she'd go, too. Ever

since Ry had described New York harbor in such lively detail she'd had a hankering to see it for herself.

The thing was, every time she imagined the scene, she pictured Ry standing beside her.

Chapter Seventeen

"If you ask me, it sounds like you two saved each other."

Jo shot an exasperated frown at Ry's sister. Not that Sadie seemed to notice.

She and Ry had spent the last thirty minutes telling what had happened the day of the ambush in Whistler's Meadow. At least they'd tried to.

Seemed like every time Jo tried to paint a true picture of Ry's heroics, he interrupted, making light of his part and trying to paint her as the hero of the story.

And Sadie seemed inclined to accept Ry's version.

Griff, on the other hand, hadn't said much at all. He'd leaned back in his chair the whole time, listening to their story as if it had happened to some stranger rather than his brother.

But now that there was a pause in the conversation, he rubbed his jaw. "So, did you ever find out why Belle sent for you?"

That was the part of the story Griff wanted to focus on? Did anyone but her see the painful emotion flash across Ry's face?

"Because she was dying." Ry's voice betrayed nothing of his feelings. "Unfortunately, I didn't make it in time to see her one last time."

Sadie reached for her brother's hand. "Oh, Ry, I'm so sorry."

Griff's only reaction was a tightening of his jaw.

"Which brings us to another interesting twist to this story," Ry continued.

Sadie's hand went to her chest. "You mean there's more?"

Ry nodded. "Belle's husband also passed on, about a month before she did. And they had a daughter, Viola."

"That poor child. What's to become of her?"

Ry's lips twisted into a sort of half grin. "Belle named me as guardian."

"Oh, Ry, no." Was Sadie dismayed on Ry's behalf or on the child's? Either way, it wasn't the reaction Josie had expected.

"You can't be seriously thinking about raising a child on your own." Griff's reaction was even less flattering.

That did it. "I'll have you know your brother has done quite well with Viola so far." Jo glared at both of his siblings. "From where I'm sitting, a kid couldn't ask for a better pa."

She ignored Ry's startled look. Besides, she wasn't finished. "Viola's ma handed your brother this responsibility slap-dab out of the blue and he never so much as flinched. I'd think his family would be a mite more supportive of his efforts."

Three pairs of eyes stared at her with varying degrees of surprise. The silence in the room was deafening, surpassed only by the growing tension.

When Cora Beth and Uncle Grover entered the parlor, each carrying a tray loaded with goodies, it was like opening a steam valve and letting off the pressure. Everyone was suddenly keenly interested in the new arrivals and what they'd brought in.

"I'm sorry I took so long." Cora Beth set her tray on the low table in front of the sofa. "I had to take care of something in the kitchen." She turned to take Uncle Grover's tray. "I hope you don't mind that I invited Uncle Grover to join us."

"Not at all," Ry answered. "In fact, I'm pleased to be able to introduce him to my brother and sister."

After introductions were made and refreshments passed around, Cora Beth took on her make-everyone-feel-at-home hostess role, one she excelled at, and the conversation turned to tamer topics.

Jo let the discussion flow around her as she continued to mull over the strained relationship that seemed to exist between the Lassiter siblings.

Ry stepped into the hall as soon as he heard the front door open. Danny, Audrey and Viola spilled inside the house, cheeks pinkened from the blustery day, the two girls laughing at something Danny had said.

Daffy, who'd remained out of sight most of the day, trotted down the stairs right on cue, stropping himself insistently against Viola's legs.

"Hello," Ry included them all in his greeting. "Viola, how was your first day at Knotty Pine's school?"

"I like Mr. Saddler, and everyone was very nice."

"Except for Mary Alice Johnson," Audrey corrected. "But she doesn't count because she's not nice to anyone."

"Audrey Elizabeth Collins, what an unkind thing to say." Cora Beth stood at the kitchen door, a large cook spoon in one hand.

"Sorry, Ma." Audrey looked suitably abashed, but Ry noticed her contrite expression didn't quite extend to her eyes. He decided to rescue her by turning the subject.

"Viola, I have some people I'd like you to meet."

"We have company?" Audrey tried peering past him into the parlor.

But her mother was quicker. "I need you and Danny in the kitchen. You can meet Mr. Lassiter's guests later."

Viola studied Ry as if scenting a trap. She picked up Daffy then straightened, seeming to brace herself for the worst.

"There's nothing to be alarmed about," Ry said, trying to reassure her. "You're going to like these folks." At least he sincerely hoped so.

He placed a hand on her shoulder as they stepped into the parlor. "Viola, this is my sister and brother, the ones I told you about yesterday."

"Hello, Viola." Sadie's voice held all the delight of a child who'd found a new toy. "I've been looking forward to meeting you all afternoon."

Viola stepped closer to Ry, as if for support. He rested a hand on her shoulder, feeling curiously touched by her gesture.

"Hello," she replied softly. Then she cocked her head to one side. "Does that mean you're my aunt?"

Sadie gave her a radiant smile. "Why yes, I suppose I am." She flashed a quick, delighted grin Ry's way, then turned back to the girl. "I'm your Aunt Sadie. And this," she said pointing to her other brother, "would be your Uncle Griff."

Griff gave a short bow, his stiff stance relaxing as he too smiled. "Hello, Viola. You're just as pretty as your mother."

Ry was surprised at the change in his brother's demeanor. This was the Griff he remembered from his childhood. Was he only surly when it came to the interactions between the two of them?

"Did you know my mother too?" Viola asked.

Griff nodded. "I sure did."

"Oh." Viola smiled. "I've never had an aunt and an uncle before. Except for Uncle Ry, and I just met him yesterday."

"Well, you have us all now," Sadie said.

"Uncle Ry said you live on a ranch." Viola was obviously warming up to his sister.

"That's right. Would you like to come live there, too?"

Viola glanced up at Ry. "We haven't decided yet."

Sadie seemed put out at that. Before she could say anything, Ry stepped in. "I'll take Viola to Hawk's Creek for a nice visit. Then we'll go to Philadelphia so she can meet Grandfather. It'll be soon enough to decide where we'll call home once that's done."

"Seems like an easy enough choice." Griff's tone had regained that hard edge. "Especially since Belle lived at Hawk's Creek once. Of course you and I never saw eye to eye on that subject."

"Not all of us have as clear a vision of what we want out of life as you, Griff." Ry regretted the words as soon as they left his mouth. But there was no calling them back.

So instead, he smiled down at Viola. "Why don't you and Daffy see if Mrs. Collins needs help in the kitchen?"

With a nod, and a last uncertain smile at Sadie and Griff, Viola exited the room.

"Oh, Ry, she's adorable." Sadie clasped her hands together. "I can see how you formed such a quick attachment. And Josie was right—you *are* good with her."

That reminder of how Josie had defended him brought back an echo of that warm feeling deep in his chest. It was good to know she was on his side.

"Thanks," he told his sister. "I only hope you're right."

Griff's frown indicated he didn't wholly agree. "Just don't drag your feet deciding where to settle down." His glare carried something more than its usual fierceness. "Kids need roots, need to feel like they have a solid foundation that's going to be there no matter what." Griff's jaw tightened further. "Without that, they might just make a wrong turn and never find the way back."

Ry stared at his younger brother, wondering how much of what he'd said was prompted by concern for Viola, and how much was an indictment of the decisions Ry had made.

Sadie, never comfortable with the tension between her

brothers, turned to Ry with one of her charm-your-socks-off smiles. "I'm certain you'll make the right decision when the time comes." She tugged him over to the nearby sofa. "Now, let's talk about your upcoming visit to Hawk's Creek. It's been a while since there were children in the house and I know Inez is going to be beside herself when she learns about Viola."

Ry let his sister chatter on, but it didn't quite drown out the memory of Griff's pointed comment. What he'd said about a kid needing roots made sense.

Right then and there Ry decided he'd select a permanent home for him and Viola—and hopefully Josie—by Christmas.

At supper that evening Ry was pleased to see that Sadie and Griff appeared to enjoy the boisterous, informal atmosphere.

Sadie sat next to Cora Beth and, as the ladies of their respective households, they found a number of things to discuss. Griff, who sat next to Danny, was drawn into a detailed discussion on the art of roping cattle. Danny hung on to every word with rapt attention, peppering Griff with questions whenever he paused.

Ry watched the way Griff not only tolerated but encouraged Danny's questions and remembered his earlier interactions with Viola. Was that the key—having children around? Would introducing Viola into the mix at Hawk's Creek lead to a more relaxed atmosphere there—not just at mealtime, but overall?

As for himself, tonight he'd managed to wrangle a seat next to Josie and had engaged her in a spirited conversation on the relative merits of quarter horses and Morgans. He found himself admiring the way her eyes lit up and her expression became animated when she discussed something she was passionate about. He could watch her like this all evening.

When it was time for dessert, Cora Beth carried in one of her fruitcakes and Ry rubbed his hands together, giving his brother and sister a grin. "Get ready, you two are in for a rare treat."

Sadie took one bite and her eyes widened in surprise. "This is absolutely delicious. I've never tasted a fruitcake so decadently rich and so delightfully light at the same time. I absolutely must have your recipe."

Cora Beth shifted uncomfortably. "Why, thank you. I—"

Ry tapped his sister's saucer with his fork. "You and every other woman in town." He saw Cora Beth relax. "I'm afraid you're out of luck. The recipe is a closely guarded secret."

"But surely—"

"None of your pestering or cajoling, Sadie. Mrs. Collins has a small business selling the cakes to folks in these parts."

"Brothers!" Sadie made an unflattering face at him. Then she turned to Cora Beth. "I must say, that's very enterprising of you." She leaned in conspiratorially. "But if I can't have the recipe then I will content myself with purchasing several so I can serve them to anyone who visits for the holidays."

Ry shook his head, pointing his fork her way. "You mean have something new and different to lord over your neighbors. Rest easy, little sister. I've already commissioned Mrs. Collins to make a pair of them for you."

Sadie ignored his dig and clapped in delight. "Oh, Ry, you're so thoughtful. And Mrs. Collins, your cakes will be the centerpiece of our Thanksgiving meal."

Ry accompanied Sadie and Griff to the train station the next morning.

"I wish you were coming with us," Sadie said with a pout. "You certainly seem to have recovered well enough to travel."

He gave his sister's hand a squeeze. "Like I told you yesterday, Viola and I need to get more comfortable with each other before we go gallivanting across the country together."

Griff raised a brow. "Leaving will be harder on her once she's begun to form attachments to this place."

Ry was afraid it was already too late to worry about that. Besides, he was counting on the attachments going both ways when it came to the Wylie family. "Perhaps. But she announced after school yesterday that she'd been assigned a role in the Thanksgiving program. I don't want to squash her excitement by saying she won't be here to participate."

"I'd hoped you'd be at the ranch for Thanksgiving." Sadie's pout grew more pronounced.

"Sorry. But I promise we'll be there soon after."

To Ry's relief, the train whistle signaled its imminent departure. He wrapped his sister in a hug. "Give Inez my love."

He turned to his brother and offered his hand. After a quick handshake, Griff picked up their bags. "Come on, Sadie," he said, "time to head home."

As Ry watched them go, it struck him that they called Hawk's Creek home when speaking to each other, but "the ranch" when speaking to him.

It seemed, for all their tugging at him to make a choice, they weren't quite certain where he belonged, either.

Chapter Eighteen

Ry straightened his shirt cuff and slipped on his jacket. There was only a slight twinge in his arm to remind him of his injury. Before long he'd be good as new.

He glanced out the window and smiled. It was a beautiful, clear Sunday morning and he and Viola were going to attend church services with the Wylie family.

Josie took Sundays off, which meant she'd be free all day. It was time to move on to the next stage of his plan. Her quick defense of him yesterday, coupled with her obvious affection for Viola, gave him hope that she would at least be open to his proposal. He just needed to lay a bit more groundwork.

Because she was a sensible sort of woman, he figured she wouldn't be swayed by fanciful, romantic notions. Which was fine by him. Keep it businesslike, that was the ticket, perhaps stress how much Viola needed her, and how she had all the qualities he wanted in a partner. He could even offer to take her on a trip from time to time to satisfy that itch she had to see the world.

Once downstairs, he found most of the family assembled in the dining room. Viola sat swinging her legs as she and Audrey exchanged whispers.

A quick head to toe glance confirmed she was neatly dressed and ready for church, for which he had Mrs. Collins to thank. Getting her ready would be his job soon, just one of the many responsibilities that made him break out in cold sweats at night.

He had to convince Josie to accept his offer. If not—

He glanced up as a door down the hall opened, and all other thoughts fled before the vision that greeted him.

Josie was wearing a dress.

What a difference it made in her appearance—one he definitely approved of. Gone were the baggy overalls and work boots. Instead she wore a soft blue dress that fit just as a dress ought to, and showed off her surprisingly trim waist. Sensible but feminine shoes peeked beneath the hem of her skirt and her normally ragged braid had been tamed into a soft coronet, with a few loose tendrils framing her face. He wanted to protest when she placed a bonnet on her head, hiding most of her hair.

"What's the matter?" Josie stopped in front of him, tying the ribbon under her chin with a bit more force than seemed necessary. "You didn't think I wore overalls *all* the time, did you?"

Ry blinked, trying to clear his suddenly jumbled thoughts. "No. Of course not. I just…I mean, you look very nice today."

His compliment—or was it the stammering delivery—earned him an irritated sniff as she moved toward the dining room.

"Sorry to keep everyone waiting. We'd best get going if we don't want to be late." With that pronouncement, Josie turned and headed for the entryway. Ry barely had time to step ahead of her and open the door.

She walked past him with a swish of skirts, and he was left standing there while the others trooped out after her. And he still didn't know what he'd done to earn him that reaction.

Uncle Grover brought up the rear and he gave Ry a sympathetic smile. "I fear the workings of a woman's mind will forever be a mystery to us menfolk, son. Don't try to understand it. Better men than you have made the attempt and failed."

Ry smiled at the sage advice. As they joined the others, he remembered Mrs. Plunkett's attempts to flirt with his would-be mentor. Was Uncle Grover as oblivious to her advances as he appeared?

"Look, Cora Beth," Danny called out, "the sun is shining and it's not cold at all." He gave her a hopeful look. "Doesn't it feel like picnic weather?"

Before she could answer, Audrey took up the plea. "Oh please? Can we? I want to show Viola our special place."

Cora Beth turned to Josie. "What do you think?"

"I think we ought to take advantage of this weather while we can." Josie's gaze remained focused straight ahead. "December's almost here."

"Very well." Cora Beth smiled at the waiting children. "A picnic it is."

Danny let out a *whoop* as Pippa and Lottie clapped.

Audrey nudged shoulders with Viola. "Just you wait," she said. "Our picnics are the bestest ever."

Ry had planned to lend an arm to Josie on the short walk to church, but somehow he found himself beside Cora Beth, as Josie linked arms with Uncle Grover and walked ahead.

He had no choice but to offer his arm to Cora Beth. "I want to thank you, ma'am, for all you're doing to make Viola feel comfortable here."

"No need for thanks." Cora Beth's smile was warm and sincere. "She's a sweet girl and she's good company for Audrey."

"For such different children, they do seem to get along well."

Cora Beth gave him a sideways look. "Don't you know it's the differences that add just the right glue to bind a friendship?"

Ry found his gaze wondering to Josie. "Guess I never thought of it quite that way."

"It's true. Take me and my Philip. I'm a fussbudget, pure and simple. Like to have things nice and tidy and I like taking care of folks. Philip, on the other hand, was a relaxed, take things as they come person. Not lazy, mind you, not by a long shot, just not too concerned about having things just so. Still, we suited well together." She sighed. "I did love that man."

Something caught her eye and she shifted immediately into mother-hen mode. "Philippa Louise, however did you get dirt on your sleeve? Come here and let me see if I can brush it off."

The little group paused while Cora Beth attacked the offending smudge. As they waited, Ry noticed a large building sitting off in a nearby field. Not a house, not a barn. It looked more like a warehouse.

"What's that over there?" He directed his question to Josie. She followed his glance. "That's Knotty Pine's Town Hall."

"Town Hall? It's mighty big for a town this size."

"There's a reason for that."

He was relieved to hear she no longer sounded testy. Whatever had set her off this morning seemed forgotten.

"That land it's sitting on was owned by Mrs. Nora Stansberry," she continued. "Her husband died when she was quite young. Then her only child died in a swimming accident a few years later."

"Must have been terrible for her." Ry glanced at Viola, feeling the weight of that tragedy with new insight.

"Yes, it was. But Mrs. Stansberry didn't let it sour her. She was one of the most pleasant, generous women I ever knew. Anyway, when she passed away six years ago, she didn't have any family to leave her estate to. So she willed her land to the town, to be used for some purpose that would benefit the whole community."

"So y'all built a town hall."

"Yep. Took us a half dozen town meetings spread out over a couple of months to decide. But once we decided, everyone pitched in. We had a barn raising to construct it and the ladies went to work decorating it while the men built the furniture."

"So what do you use it for?"

She shrugged. "We hold town meetings there, of course, but it's also used for dances, holiday celebrations, school plays. Seems like there's something going on here all the time. It's been a real blessing to this town. That's where we'll have our Thanksgiving Celebration." She waved a hand in an inclusive gesture. "We use it for other things too. Last year, when the Helmon's home was struck by lightning, the family lived here until they could rebuild."

"Impressive."

Cora Beth signaled they were ready to move on and this time Ry was able to secure a spot beside Josie.

They reached the church just as the service was about to start and had to move quickly to take their seats. Once again, Ry found himself outmaneuvered without quite knowing how it happened. One minute he was ready to slide into the pew beside Josie and the next he had four little girls between the two of them and Cora Beth on his right.

Josie had orchestrated this, he was certain of it.

The question was, why? Had he read her wrong after all?

Jo pulled out the picnic blanket and gave it a shake. It felt good to be in her everyday clothes again. Though she had to admit, it hadn't been altogether unpleasant to see Ry's reaction to her being all gussied up.

It would have been a mite nicer, though, if he hadn't acted so all-fired surprised about it. Not that she should give a fig for his reaction when she was supposed to be doing her ever-loving best to get him to notice her sister.

But there had been a moment when his eyes lingered on her, a moment that set moths to dancing in her stomach…

Lost in that thought, she was startled when Ry grabbed the other end of the blanket. "Thanks, but I can take care of this," she announced. "Why don't you help Cora Beth with the basket?"

He held on to the cloth. "Danny's taking care of that."

Continuing to refuse his help would be silly, so she nodded and let him help her spread the square of cloth out on the ground.

"So, this is a family tradition, is it?" he asked.

"Yep. Goes all the way back to when my parents were courting." Jo anchored her two corners with fist-sized rocks while Ry did the same. "Pa proposed to Ma in this very meadow, under that tree over yonder. After they got hitched, they started coming here regular for picnics every Sunday, weather permitting."

"Sounds as if your parents were romantics."

Was he poking fun at them? A quick look at his expression satisfied her that it had been a simple observation. "My parents were very much in love."

"Well, that's one thing we have in common."

Her head shot up and her pulse kicked up a notch. What did he mean?

He stared straight into her eyes. "My parents were very much in love, too."

Of course. Jo stooped down, smoothing the blanket and hiding her face, which felt uncomfortably warm at the moment.

Uncle Grover wandered over just then and she could have hugged him for providing a distraction.

"Come along, my boy, you must see the millipedes I found near that fallen log. One of them is nearly five inches long."

Ry raised a brow. "Five inches, you say? That's something worth seeing."

They headed toward the site of the momentous find. "Of course," she heard Uncle Grover explain, "millipedes are not really insects, but I still find them fascinating creatures."

She saw Ry's nod and heard him ask a question about what millipedes fed on before they moved out of range.

With Ry gone, she sat back on her heels and took herself in hand. She had to push harder to get him and Cora Beth together if she ever wanted to see New York harbor and all those other places on her map. For Viola's sake too—that sweet little girl needed mothering.

By the time Ry and Uncle Grover returned, the meal was spread out and ready to enjoy, and Jo had herself back under control. Cora Beth asked Ry to say the blessing, and he did so after only the slightest hesitation.

Once the meal was over, Jo popped up and volunteered to keep an eye on the girls. "I thought we'd check out those persimmon trees over at the edge of the tree line. Mr. Lassiter, you don't mind helping Cora Beth clean up, do you?"

Cora Beth immediately protested. "That's not necessary. I can handle this on my own."

Ry, predictably, did the gentlemanly thing. "But you prepared this feast, Mrs. Collins," he argued. "It wouldn't be right for you to have to clean up after it, as well."

Jo strolled away with the girls, confident that having the two of them working side by side would set them on the road to a deeper attraction.

She returned forty minutes later to find Cora Beth knitting, Uncle Grover napping and Ry and Danny nowhere to be seen.

Her sister looked up with a smile. "Hello, girls. Any luck?"

"There's lots of fruit," Jo answered, "but none ripe enough

to pick." She took another look around. "Where's Danny and Mr. Lassiter?"

"Oh, they wandered off about twenty minutes ago. Danny wanted to show him Fist Rock."

Jo plopped down next to her sister and hugged her knees in exasperation. All her planning seemed to have been in vain. But at least they'd had twenty minutes or so together. Maybe that had been enough to sow a few seeds of interest.

And it was hard to be angry with Ry. He was a good man, in the truest sense of that word. He allowed Uncle Grover his dignity. He got along well with the children. He was scrupulous in repaying even the smallest of debts. And he obviously had the means to support a large family.

He'd make a great husband for Cora Beth, no doubt about it. Her sister would easily adapt to life in his world, in fact would flourish in such a setting.

But Viola was the real key. Cora Beth had a soft spot for children and would be both willing and happy to add Viola to her brood. And of course Mr. Lassiter would welcome having someone as loving and capable as Cora Beth to help him raise his ward.

The plan was perfect.

So why didn't she feel as enthusiastic as she had earlier?

Jo gave herself a mental shake. She had to remember the prize she was aiming toward—her freedom. This was still her best shot.

Jo clicked her tongue as she gave the reins a flick. Somehow, despite her best efforts to arrange things otherwise, Ry sat on the front seat of the buckboard beside her.

She'd expected him to argue when she insisted on taking the reins. But to her surprise he'd merely nodded.

As they moved down the road, she was vaguely aware of

Cora Beth and Uncle Grover chatting together behind them, but Ry's presence seemed to crowd everything else out. Not that he was doing much of anything. In fact he was leaned back all comfy-like, with his legs stretched out at an angle that brought his boots up close to hers. And he hadn't said a word since she'd set the horse in motion.

But there was something about his nearness, about the way he watched her with that little half smile, that made her all fidgety inside. Finally, she couldn't take it any longer. "What's the matter?" she groused. "I got dirt on my face or something?"

His smile widened. "Not at all." He tilted his head. "I was just trying to decide if the green in your eyes is closer to the color of spring clover or that of the hummingbirds that used to flit around my mother's flower garden."

His voice was pitched low enough that the others couldn't hear him without trying. The deep rumble of it spread through her like a cup of warm cocoa on a chilly day. Jo felt as if he'd trapped her gaze with his own. For the life of her she couldn't look away. No one had ever said such things to her, had ever looked at her the way he was now.

An endless heartbeat later she got hold of herself and abruptly faced forward. She was reading too much into his words. Besides, those were the kinds of things he should be saying to Cora Beth, not her.

The slight hitch in her breathing was merely surprise and frustration, nothing more.

Before she could figure out how to respond, he changed the subject. "Thanks for including me and Viola in your outing today. I think she really enjoyed herself." His voice had returned to normal, his expression nothing more than friendly. It was as if the past few moments hadn't happened. For some reason that didn't improve her mood any.

"Glad to hear it." Thank goodness her voice was steady.

"It was a good day for me as well." Something about his tone made her glance up but his expression gave nothing away.

"I've been thinking about your invitation to stay through Thanksgiving," he continued. "I think we ought to set a few conditions."

Uh-oh. The man and his conditions—what was he up to now? "And those are?"

"First, you let me pay for our board, just like any of your other customers."

She thought about that a minute. It didn't sit right with her, being as he'd saved her life and all, but if it was the only way to get him to stay…

She nodded. "That sounds fair. But since Viola's sharing a room with Cora Beth's girls, you only pay half price for her."

Had his lips twitched? What did he find so all-fired funny?

"Agreed." His tone made her wonder if she'd imagined that grin.

Better move on. "What else?"

"You agree to let me help out around the livery and the boardinghouse. I get bored just sitting around doing nothing."

She could understand that. "All right, but only if you promise not to do anything to set your healing back."

It was his turn to look surprised at her agreeable response. Thing was, she figured having him do a few chores around the house would give Cora Beth something else to admire about him.

"Then it looks like Viola and I will be availing ourselves of your hospitality through Thanksgiving."

And if her plans worked as well as she hoped, for quite some time after as well.

Fifteen minutes later, Jo stopped the buckboard in front of the boardinghouse. "Everybody out," she ordered. "Danny, make sure you grab the hamper and blanket." She rested an arm on her knee while the kids scrambled out of the back and Uncle Grover helped Cora Beth step down. "I'll take care of the wagon and horse. Just make sure you save me some supper."

Ry made no move to step down. "I'll lend you a hand." He turned to Cora Beth. "That is, if Mrs. Collins would be so good as to watch Viola for a bit."

Before Jo could protest, Cora Beth nodded. "It would be my pleasure."

"Thanks but I can handle this just fine." Ry was supposed to be spending time with Cora Beth, not her.

He raised a brow. "Remember our bargain. Not backing out on me already, are you?"

Feeling outmaneuvered, she grimaced and set the wagon in motion.

He thought he was so clever but he hadn't seen clever yet. She was already making a mental list of chores that would keep him way too busy around the boardinghouse for him to even think about working at the livery.

She didn't need him messing with her mind the way he'd been doing lately. She was so close to achieving her dream, nothing, or nobody, was going to change her mind now.

The wheel hit a bump, causing his shoulder to brush against hers, and her pulse jumped in response.

So much for her self-control.

Heavenly Father, this man sure does present a powerful temptation. Please give me the strength to see this through to its proper outcome.

Chapter Nineteen

Ry wiped his brow with the back of his wrist, then leaned against the handle of the pitchfork. "So, tell me about this Thanksgiving festival. I take it it's a big to-do."

Josie examined a piece of leather she'd just trimmed. "Just about the biggest doings in these parts," she answered without looking up. "The whole town takes part, or them that can, and the celebrating goes on all day."

Ry tossed a forkful of hay in the middle stall. He'd spent the morning mucking them out and now he was spreading fresh straw. Seemed Josie had taken him at his word when he said to put him to work.

"So exactly what does this celebrating entail?" It was like pulling teeth today to get her to talk to him. Had he been too forward on the ride home from the picnic yesterday?

"It pretty much follows the same pattern every year." She leaned back in her seat and finally faced him. "Folks start arriving around eight o'clock. Reverend Ludlow preaches a short service to kick things off on the right note. Then there's games and competitions, like horseshoes, wheelbarrow races and pie eating contests. 'Round about eleven o'clock everyone troops inside and the kids put on their program."

She stretched out her legs and tipped her chair back. "Afterward, everybody sits down for the best-tasting, button-popping, belt-loosening meal you ever did eat."

"And that's it?" Of course he knew it wasn't, but he liked listening to her unique way of describing things.

Josie gave an unladylike snort. "That's just the morning. The early afternoon is more games for those who have energy to burn, and visiting or table games for those who prefer something quieter. At some point the men's quartet will serenade us. Later in the day, someone will pull out a fiddle, the center of the floor will get cleared and we'll have us a foot-stomping dance."

She gave him a wickedly amused smile. "I have to warn you, you'll be in high demand once the dancing starts."

His alarm was only partially feigned. "Surely you're joking."

"Not a bit. You're new in town, you're eligible, and you can be passably charming if you put your mind to it." She flashed a teasing grin. "All highly desirable qualities when it comes to claiming a dance partner."

Did *she* think they were "highly desirable qualities?" "So it has nothing to do with me personally? Just that I'm a fresh face and my ma raised me to be polite?"

"That's about the size of it."

"Sounds like a fun time will be had by all."

She laughed at his dour expression, just as he'd intended her to. Actually the thought of dancing, as long as it was with her, was rather appealing. What would it feel like to hold her and twirl her around the dance floor? Could he tease one of those beautiful, light-up-her-eyes smiles from her?

* * *

The family gathered in the kitchen after supper again that evening. Funny how in such a short time he'd come to consider himself and Viola almost a part of the family.

He glanced toward his ward and smiled. She was practicing her lines for the Thanksgiving program alongside Audrey. It was the most animated he'd seen her since she'd arrived five days ago.

"Mr. Lassiter, I want to thank you for fixing that loose baseboard." Cora Beth spoke without looking up from the pie crust she was making. "I've been meaning to tend to it for ages."

"Seems the least I could do after all you folks have done for Viola and me." Ry cast a surreptitious glance Josie's way. Had she taken note of how much use he could be to her and her family?

So, Ry had helped Cora Beth around the place after he left the livery this afternoon, had he? Was her sister starting to notice how nice it would be to have him in her life permanently? She'd be a fool not to. Any woman would be lucky to have a man like Ry.

"What are you doing?" Ry was watching her with a puzzled frown.

She raised a brow. Wasn't it obvious? "I'm peeling apples."

"But why are you taking such care?"

"Just practicing." She grinned at his puzzled look.

"Jo wins the apple peeling contest every year," Danny added.

"Apple peeling contest? If you're trying to be the fastest—"

"Not the fastest." Josie picked up the peel from the last apple she'd worked on. "It's to see who can get the longest unbroken piece."

"Ah, I see." Then his expression took on a challenging glint. "And can anybody enter this contest?"

Thought he could take her, did he? "Yep. But I'm warning you, it's not as easy as it looks."

Ry reached for an apple and a knife. "We'll see about that."

* * *

Josie stood at the back of the buckboard Thursday morning, carefully loading her carved pumpkins and gourds as Audrey and Viola carried them from the house. It was a beautiful day for the Thanksgiving festival, clear and crisp without being too cold. The trees all around, the ones that still had leaves at any rate, were sporting bursts of yellow, orange and red. And the air fairly crackled with excitement. Groups of townsfolk were moving toward the town hall, children skipping ahead of the adults.

Ry interrupted her thoughts as he lifted his fifth hamper into the buggy. She frowned, worried he might be putting too much strain on his arm.

"You'd think your sister was feeding an army," he groused.

"She is." Josie studied him carefully but saw no sign of discomfort.

"Didn't you say *everyone* brings food?"

"They do." She smiled at his raised brow. "All the food is set up together on long tables across one side of the room, and folks try to sample a little of everything. It's a matter of pride amongst the women to bring the most popular dish." She took the pair of gourds Audrey and Viola handed her, the last of the lot. "Besides, most folks will eat both lunch and supper there."

Ry lifted first Pippa and then Lottie into the back of the buckboard, easing them gently in amongst her pumpkins. "You girls are in charge of guarding your Aunt Josie's masterpieces," he said with a solemn expression. "Do you think you can handle the job?"

Two heads bobbed in unison, while their hands made cross-my-heart motions.

His lips turned up in that heart-stopping smile. "I knew I could count on you."

Honestly, she didn't know why the man worried so much

about how he would get on with Viola. He was obviously fine father material. Cora Beth would be lucky to have him.

For some reason her mind skittered away from that thought as she dusted her hands on her skirt.

Cora Beth, Audrey and Viola stepped out of the house, shaking Josie out of her jumbled thoughts.

"I do hope I haven't forgotten anything," Cora Beth said, snuggling one more jar of relish into the largest hamper.

"Doesn't matter." Josie rolled her eyes. "We couldn't fit another thing in the buggy."

Danny scrambled into the front seat beside Uncle Grover and gathered the reins. The rest of them would walk.

Ry turned his collar up. "Shall we, ladies," he said, with a bow and a flourish of the hand.

Always so gentlemanly. Made a woman feel special.

Pushing that thought away, Josie quickly took hold of Audrey and Viola's hands, leaving Cora Beth to walk with Ry before she forgot she was trying to push the two of them together.

As they strolled down the sidewalk, Ry did his best to pay attention to Cora Beth's chatter while surreptitiously watching Josie walk ahead with the girls. He hadn't missed the deliberate way she distanced herself from him. Again. What was she up to?

A moment later, Cora Beth halted in her tracks. "Audrey Elizabeth, come here a minute please."

The little girl obediently trotted back to her mother's side. Cora Beth spun her around and fiddled with the tie at the back of her pinafore.

When they resumed walking, Ry made certain he was by Josie's side this time while Cora Beth and the girls took the lead.

They walked in silence for a few minutes, then Josie finally gave him a sideways look. "This'll probably be a letdown from the fancy parties you're used to."

"Actually, I'm looking forward to this shindig. Most of those so-called fancy parties are rather stuffy." He was certain there'd be nothing stuffy about this gathering.

She didn't appear convinced. "I've seen pictures of fine ball-rooms filled with orchestras and crowds of people gussied up all fancy-like. Must be something to see."

"It's a sight to see, all right."

"I knew it." Apparently she'd missed the sarcasm in his tone. He could see her imagining some exotic, fairytale-like scene.

Once they arrived at the town hall, the morning passed much the way Josie had described it, and Ry enthusiastically joined in. He and Viola took third place in the wheelbarrow race and the child proudly wore her yellow ribbon the rest of the day.

Ry was also stood shoulder to shoulder with Josie as they cheered Danny on in the pie-eating contest. The boy didn't take a ribbon but he seemed pleased with his showing, anyway.

And Ry gave Josie a run for her money in the apple peeling contest. She ultimately won, but her winning apple peel was less than an inch longer than his.

After the ribbons were awarded, Viola touched his arm and studied him with concerned eyes. "Don't worry, Uncle Ry, you did your best and I'm proud of you."

Ry was touched by her words, even though he knew she was likely parroting something overheard from the adults. He stooped down so their faces were level. "Thank you, Viola. It means a lot to me that you were in my corner."

She gave him a sheepish grin. "Actually, I was rooting for both you and Miss Josie. That's okay, isn't it?"

He laughed and gave her a squeeze. "Absolutely." So she

was forming an attachment to Josie. Things were definitely looking up.

After Viola ran off with Audrey and some of the other girls, Ry discovered Josie had disappeared. After several minutes of searching he finally found her inside the building, selecting tidbits from the vast array of food set on tables around the room.

"Trying to sneak in a few bites early," he accused.

She started, twisting around with an affronted frown. "Nope." Then she grinned. "Though it's mighty tempting."

Ry agreed. The tables were laden with dishes sumptuous enough to please even the most finicky hostess. The meats included platters of the traditional turkey, chicken, ham and roast, along with game such as venison, rabbit and fowl. Large pans of dressing sat alongside bowls containing sauces and gravies. Next came a dizzying array of vegetables—beans, potatoes, corn, carrots, onions and mixtures of the same. They were cooked in every imaginable way—baked, stewed, roasted, creamed. Farther along were colorful relishes, pickles, fresh baked breads, cheeses and fruit spreads.

But the real eye-catcher was the row upon row of elaborate desserts. Pies, cakes, cobblers, cookies, tarts—the women had truly outdone themselves.

Her laughter brought his gaze back around. "I declare, you look like a hungry dog who's spied a soup bone."

He grinned back, unabashed. "Said the woman pilfering from the food table."

"I'll have you know," she said, her tone haughty, "that I'm actually performing my good deed for the day."

"Is that a fact?"

"Yes sir, it is. I'm in charge of packing the shut-in baskets this year." She lifted the hamper looped over her left arm.

"Shut-in baskets?"

"If someone's not able to join us, we fix up a basket of goodies and bring it to 'em so they don't feel left out. This year Cora Beth and I get to handle the delivery."

"I see." That caretaker streak ran deep in her. "Here, let me help." He reached for the basket.

"No need. I—"

But he'd already snagged it. "Now you have both hands free." He tried for a guileless smile.

She frowned suspiciously, then nodded. "We have two families this year. Mr. Clawson owns a small farm just outside of town. His mare's about ready to foal and he didn't want to leave her."

She added another thick slice of ham to the basket before moving on to the vegetables. "Then there's Mrs. Willows and her daughter, Myra. Mrs. Willows has been doing poorly the past few years. I hear tell she barely gets out of bed these days. And Myra, bless her heart, looks out for her ma and younger sister now that her older sisters have moved on." She nodded toward a group of younger folk. "The girl over yonder in the blue and yellow dress, the one flirting with Cecil Jones, is her sister, Dolly."

The girl looked all of fifteen and seemed not to have a care in the world. "So, why isn't she taking care of her mother and sister's basket?"

Josie shrugged, but Ry didn't miss the disapproving purse of her lips. Family was important to Josie, and she obviously didn't approve of those who shirked their duty in that area.

At the dessert tables, Josie slipped two pies and a dish of cookies in the hamper, then gave a satisfied nod. "That ought to do it."

She didn't move to take the basket from him as he'd expected. Instead she cupped her chin. "You know," she said slowly, "being as you want to be so helpful, why don't *you* deliver these with Cora Beth? That way I can help get the stage ready for the children's program."

She was up to something. But before he could form a response Cora Beth bustled up, closely followed by Sheriff Hammond.

"Thanks for packing the basket while I helped Iris," she said, then indicated her companion. "And Sheriff Hammond has volunteered to go in your place. Wasn't that kind of him?"

"Actually, I need to speak to Stan Clawson anyway," the sheriff added. "Thought this would be as good a time as any."

Ry hid a grin at Josie's thwarted-plans expression. "How fortunate you should offer. Josie here was just saying she had some other matters to attend to."

"Well, that's that then." Sheriff Hammond took the basket from Ry and turned to Cora Beth. "Shall we?"

As the two made their way out of the building, Ry turned to Josie. "Now, what is it we need to do to get the stage ready?"

Chapter Twenty

As the children made their way to the makeshift stage, Josie was acutely aware of Ry sitting shoulder to shoulder beside her in the crowded hall. In fact, the man had barely left her side since mid-morning. Not that she hadn't enjoyed his company. But how was she supposed to get him and Cora Beth to see how perfect they were for each other if they didn't spend some time together?

It should be Cora Beth sitting here beside him, watching how he smiled encouragingly when Viola cast an anxious glance at the audience, inhaling his unique, spicy scent, experiencing how very safe and comforting it felt to be at his side.

Josie caught herself on that last thought. She'd had way too many thoughts like that recently. It was Cora Beth who was a match for Ry, not her. What she wanted was freedom to travel, just like Aunt Pearl. There'd be time enough to think about settling down once she had a few adventures.

The children's program went off with only the normal snags—five-year-old Amy Dobbs took one look at the audience, burst into tears, and ran off the stage. A couple of the other kids forgot or stumbled over part of their lines. Joey

Lofton stubbed his toe. But they were all given enthusiastic rounds of applause.

Audrey, of course, said her lines with a great deal of melodrama. When Viola's turn came up, Ry straightened in his seat. Josie was oddly touched as she felt equal parts pride and concern vibrating from him. When the little girl got through without a misstep he clapped louder than anyone in the audience. Just like a proud father.

How could her sister not fall head over heels for a guy like this? Why, if she wasn't so dead set against putting down roots, she might even find herself falling for him.

"Looks like you're quite the strategist, son." Uncle Grover rubbed his chin as he studied Ry's latest move on the chessboard.

Ry leaned back in his chair, keeping his gaze peripherally focused on the entry, just as it had been for the past few hours. He'd looked around for Josie after lunch without success and he was beginning to wonder if something had happened to her.

Uncle Grover made a triumphant sound in the back of his throat as he moved his bishop. "Let's see what you can do with that."

Ry shifted his gaze to the chessboard, then paused and turned back to the doorway. Sure enough, there was Josie, strolling in as if she hadn't a care in the world. She spared only a quick glance his way before heading across the room to join a small group that included her sister and several neighbors.

Trapped by the chess game, it was fifteen minutes before Ry could extricate himself.

As he stood, she threw back her head and laughed at something Sheriff Hammond had said. Ry wondered irritably why he couldn't draw that same kind of relaxed, unguarded reaction from Josie.

Surely she wasn't sweet on the lawman? Ry frowned at Sheriff Hammond's back. Any fool could see the man was all wrong for her. She needed someone who understood her spirited nature, who would encourage her rather than try to rein her in.

His jaw muscles tightened as he tried to navigate his way through the room in long, quick strides.

But the sound of someone tuning a fiddle ricocheted through the building before he could reach his goal. Suddenly everyone was in motion and Ry was drawn into the mix. Game boards and sewing baskets were put away. Tables and benches were dismantled and moved from the center of the room. Napping children roused and looked for ways to demonstrate their renewed energy.

More fiddlers took their places on the platform and in short order the room was filled with lively music. A moment later, couples began pairing off and making their way to the make-shift dance floor. Even those who preferred to sit on the side-lines joined in by clapping to the music.

Ry smiled as he saw Audrey drag Viola to the edge of the crowd and begin an enthusiastic if not graceful bit of whirling. And they weren't the only youngsters on the floor.

This was like the barn dances from his youth. He'd forgotten how family oriented they'd been.

"Do you dance, Mr. Lassiter?"

He smiled in pleased surprise as he turned to find Josie at his elbow, Sheriff Hammond nowhere in sight. Was that an invitation? "I do when I find the right partner."

She pulled her sister forward. "Then you should ask Cora Beth. She loves to dance."

Having little choice in the matter, Ry gave Josie's sister a bow. "I'd be delighted." He offered his arm. "Shall we?"

With a smile, Cora Beth allowed him to lead her onto the floor.

They'd barely taken their first turn when she met his glance with an amused twinkle in her eye. "I do believe my sister is trying to do a bit of matchmaking," she said demurely.

Ry almost missed a step. He hadn't realized she'd caught on to Josie's scheme, too. And how in blue blazes was he supposed to respond without insulting her or her sister or both of them?

She laughed. "Don't look so worried. You're not in any danger from me."

Good grief, had his trepidation been that obvious? "My apologies, ma'am, I—"

Her smile broadened. "No offense, Mr. Lassiter, but while I do enjoy your company, I'm not looking for another husband just yet." She tossed her head, for all the world like a saucy schoolgirl. "And if I ever do start looking, I'm afraid you and I just would not suit."

Ry wasn't quite certain how to take that. So he veered away from a direct response. "Shall we tell her that we're on to her?"

"Oh, heavens, no. I wouldn't want to spoil her fun. Besides, this fits nicely with some plans of my own."

"Ma'am?"

"Oh, nothing for you to concern yourself with."

Ry was beginning to believe there was the merest touch of lunacy running through the Wylie family, at least in the female members. "Whatever you say."

The song ended and he escorted her from the floor.

"Now, see if you can convince my sister not to spend all night playing the wallflower." Cora Beth leaned in conspiratorially. "She'll try to convince you she doesn't dance but I know better."

Ry spotted Josie talking to Sheriff Hammond again. He started toward her but was hailed by Dr. Whitman who inquired about his arm. The good doctor in turn introduced Ry to his daughter, Lucy. Good manners dictated that Ry invite her to dance.

Afterward he was twice more put in the position of escorting virtual strangers onto the dance floor. Josie hadn't been far off the mark when she said he'd be in demand. Once, in an effort to forestall yet another attempt, he asked Audrey and Viola to stand together as his partners. Delighted, the girls each took one of his hands and giggled their way through the entire song.

With some expert maneuvering and a good sense of timing, he managed to land beside Josie when the music stopped. "Ladies," he said with a formal bow to both girls, "I thank you for a most enjoyable dance."

The comment earned him another set of giggles.

"Did you see us, Aunt JoJo?" Audrey asked.

"I certainly did." Josie's eyes strayed to his as she answered, and he saw approval mixed with some softer emotion. "And a fine group of dancers you made."

"Come on, Viola." Audrey latched onto the other girl's hand. "Let's see if there's any lemonade left."

Josie smoothed her skirt. "Looks like you're popular with the ladies this evening."

"As you said, I'm just a novelty." He studied her, trying to figure out what was going on in that scheming mind of hers.

"You and Cora Beth looked pretty good out there. From the way y'all were smiling at each other it appeared you were enjoying yourselves."

Did he detect a touch of jealousy? That thought cheered him up. "Your sister is both a fine dancer and good company."

She gave him a sideways glance. "But you only danced with her that one time."

He shrugged. "She hasn't lacked for partners tonight. I didn't want to monopolize her time."

"She's popular because she's such a good catch. A fellow would be mighty lucky to be able to claim her for his own."

"I agree." But he was tired of discussing Cora Beth's virtues. "I noticed you haven't been out on the floor yet."

Her expression closed off. "I don't dance."

"Don't? Or won't?"

This time she crossed her arms and didn't quite meet his gaze. "Doesn't matter. I'm not getting out on that floor."

"That's where you're wrong." Ry took her hand and tugged her toward the area where couples were forming for the next dance.

Josie dug in her heels. "I said I don't dance."

He turned to face her. "I have it on good authority you're actually a very good dancer. I think it's high time you gave it another go."

He saw the mutinous look in her eye. "I'd count it a personal favor," he said quickly, "if you'd allow me to take the woman who saved my life for a spin around the dance floor."

He felt her hesitation, sensed the weakening of her resolve and decided that was as good as an agreement.

Placing a hand at her waist, he took her other hand in his and stepped forward as the music started. He smiled when he realized they were playing a waltz.

For a moment or two they simply danced, each adjusting to the other's movements. And they moved surprisingly well together.

She wasn't soft like other women he'd danced with. Years of hard work in the livery, doing the job her father had done before her, had given her firm muscles and rough, callused hands. But there was also a well-honed grace, a sureness of movement that he found much more appealing.

The dress she wore was plain, with none of the fripperies most girls seemed to enjoy—no bows in her hair, no lace on her bodice, no ribbons at her waist. Strangely, none of that detracted from her femininity, not tonight.

Holding her in his arms as they moved around the dance floor stirred all manner of unfamiliar, protective, tender feelings. And when one of the movements of the dance brought them unexpectedly close, the catch in her breath set his heart pounding with a beat he was certain she could hear.

This moment—holding her, inhaling her unique scent, trying to fathom the secrets locked in her eyes—was one of the sweetest things he'd ever experienced.

This felt oh, so right.

This was all wrong! Jo's heart hammered in her chest. Her breath caught in her throat every time she met Ry's glance. She felt plumb light-headed, and it wasn't just from spinning around the dance floor. That moment when they'd come so close together, she'd felt an unaccountable urge to kiss him, which was just plain chuckleheaded. What in the world had gotten into her?

She should never have allowed Ry talk her into this dance. How could she let herself get all besotted over him? He and Cora Beth were supposed to end up together, she had it all planned out.

She had to pull herself together. She was just letting her imagination get the best of her. Besides, he couldn't possibly be sweet on her. No man had shown the least bit of interest, at least not in that way, since she'd taken over the livery when her pa got so bad sick.

No, someone like Cora Beth was much better suited to a man like Ry.

She looked up and found herself staring into his smoky gray eyes, and her step faltered. The way he was looking at her was so…"tender" was the only word that came to mind.

Father, help me please, I think I'm in trouble here.

The song finally ended but they didn't move apart immediately. It was only when they were jostled by another couple leaving the floor that the spell was finally broken.

Josie took a deep breath, feeling as if she'd forgotten to inhale for the past few minutes. She sure didn't remember a simple dance getting a person so all-fired flustered.

Not that she would call what had just happened a "simple dance."

Ry took her elbow and moved toward the door. "You look flushed. Let's step outside for some fresh air."

Not trusting herself to speak, Josie nodded. They wended their way through the crowd, pausing to speak to others along the way.

What was he thinking? Had she given away any of her thoughts? That would be too mortifying to even consider. When they stepped outside, she took a deep breath of the cool evening air and let her jangly nerves settle a bit.

Ry motioned toward a bench set against the outer wall of the building and with a nod, she took a seat. He settled beside her, leaving a respectful distance between them. She refused to look at him, but was keenly aware of his presence, of his gaze on her.

Better to concentrate on the other things around them.

Murmurings of conversations mingled with the music of the fiddles from inside, making a pleasant backdrop of sound.

It wasn't quite evening yet but the overcast sky had made it necessary to light the lamps around the building, including the one directly over the bench she and Ry shared. A few other folks milled around outside, braving the cold to escape the crowded dance floor. Even so, situated in their own pool of light, Josie felt as if they were somehow enclosed in one of those water globes Mr. Miller had on display over at the mercantile, visible yet separate from everyone and everything around them.

She leaned against the building and stared up at the lamp, watching as the glass-enclosed flame flickered in a solo dance of its own.

Was he going to say anything? Or just sit there and stare at her? Time to turn his thoughts in a different direction.

"You know," she said, staring out at the road to town, "Knotty Pine might look like a backwater, but it's growing."

"Is that so?"

She wished he'd quit staring at her so intently. "Yep. Why, just last year Mr. Danvers added three new rooms to the hotel and Mrs. Jefferson opened a dress shop. And two new families have moved into the area since spring."

"Impressive." He picked up a penny-sized rock, rolling it between his thumb and forefinger as he continued to watch her.

She wasn't comfortable with the loud silence hanging between them. "You ever thought of doing something besides lawyering?"

"I always liked working with horses." He smiled as if he'd just admitted wanting to fly. "Once upon a time I thought I'd like to start a horse ranch. Wanted to raise and train the best cutting horses in the country."

Interest piqued, she finally turned to face him. "So why didn't you?"

"Because horse ranching and being a lawyer don't exactly mix."

Was there a hint of regret in his words? "So I guess you like lawyering better than raising horses."

He was silent for a time, seeming to ponder her words. Finally he looked up. "I honestly don't know."

He reached for her hand, and she felt her heartbeat kick up a notch as they connected. "Josie, if you've been trying to convince me that Knotty Pine has a lot to offer a man, there's no need. I'm already convinced. In fact—"

"No!" She saw the confusion in his eyes, the pulling back, and it hurt. But she couldn't let him finish what she sensed he'd been about to say.

"Pardon?" His expression was guarded now and he'd released her hand.

She missed the warmth of his touch. But this was no time to mince words. "I like you, you know that. But you have a kid to take care of now and you're looking to settle down. Don't get me wrong, I admire you for doing it, but that's not what I want from life right now."

"You still want to see the world."

At least he'd been paying attention. "Yes."

His expression was solemn. "I'm afraid the world may disappoint you."

"That's a chance I'll take." She swiveled around to face him fully. "You need to understand, this is something I have to do."

"But there's nothing that says you have to do it alone."

How could she make him see how she felt without having it sound like she resented her family? "I've been looking out for other folks for most of my life. I want to have some time where the only person I have to worry about is me. I know that sounds selfish, but for once I want to experience what it feels like not to be weighed down by other folks' wants or needs."

She took a deep breath, forcing herself to say what needed to be said. "If you want someone to settle down with, if you want to find a good mother for Viola, you'll have to look elsewhere."

He crossed his arms. "Is that why you keep pushing me at your sister?"

She winced. Had she been so obvious? "I'm not pushing." Her conscience wouldn't let her stop at that. "Well, not exactly."

His only response was a raised brow.

"Besides—" she hated that defensive note that had crept into her voice "—would marrying Cora Beth be such a bad choice?"

"Only in the sense that it wouldn't be the *right choice* for me. Or your sister, for that matter."

She stood abruptly, hating that he couldn't understand, hating that things couldn't be different.

She stared down at him with clenched fists. "You are the most stubborn, selfish man I have ever met. Can't you see what a choice like this could mean to Cora Beth and to Viola and to—" She halted, realizing she'd almost said too much.

But judging by the way his expression hardened, it was already too late.

"To who, Josie? To you?" He matched her stance. "Is that what this is all about? Marrying your sister off so you can feel free to go your merry way with a clear conscience? Even if marriage isn't what she wants?" His eyes narrowed. "Now who's being stubborn and selfish?"

His words were a slap in the face. How could he say such ugly things? She only wanted what was best for everyone. He didn't know how much she'd already sacrificed, how much she'd given up.

But she would *not* let him see how much his words had hurt.

She thrust out her chin. "I've had enough partying for one day. Please let Cora Beth know I've headed to the livery to check on a few things. I'll see y'all back at the house later tonight."

He raked a hand through his hair, a look of frustration on his face. "Look, I'm sorry. Sometimes I don't think before—"

She held up a hand. "No apology needed. I said some things I shouldn't have, too."

He moved back a half step, as if he knew she needed room. "You don't have to leave. I won't broach the subject again tonight—you have my word."

Josie shook her head. "I really should check the livery. The buggy's already been loaded up so I'll drop off the supplies at the house first. You'll probably need to help Cora Beth carry the twins home." That last comment would ensure he stayed put.

As Josie moved away, she found herself trying to stuff her hands in pockets that weren't there. Was he right in what he'd said? Was she being stubborn and selfish?

No! She was just being true to her dream.

Father, help me to be strong. I know this is the answer to my prayer if I'll but stand firm.

Ry watched her leave, giving himself a mental kick for his clumsy handling of the whole situation. Why had he pressed so hard? Her dream of escaping the confines of Knotty Pine was deeply felt and a driving force with her, probably all the more so since she'd had to put it on hold for so long. He'd known that.

She was a wild pony, yearning to trade the lush grasslands and security of the herd for a pair of wings. If only she could see those wings came with a price—a view of the world from a lonely distance, being at the mercy of the wind to chart your course, and sometimes, living life in a cage—gilded or otherwise.

Well, if her dream was that important to her, then he'd find a way to give her a taste. A journey of some sort—it would be his Christmas gift to her. But he'd do it in such a way that she would have a safety net. And in the process, maybe help her see how wonderful her life here was by comparison.

He'd just have to figure out a way to do it so she wouldn't feel as if she were taking charity from him.

Chapter Twenty-One

"I want to hire you."

Jo looked up from her workbench to see Ry standing just inside the livery, his expression unreadable.

Had he said *hire* her? "What's that?"

"Viola and I will be leaving day after tomorrow."

She fought back the jolt of denial. It would be so strange not to have him here, not to see him sitting across the table from her at supper or look forward to him wandering in here every morning to lend a hand with whatever chores were on her list.

More importantly, she told herself, was that this spelled the end to her matchmaking scheme.

"We'll stop at Hawk's Creek first to visit Sadie and Griff for a few days, then move on to Philadelphia to see my grandfather."

She had herself back under control. "So what do you want to hire me for?"

"The thing is, I'm not ready to take on sole responsibility for Viola's care, especially on a long trip. It would be better if I had someone to help watch over her." His gaze drilled into hers. "Preferably someone Viola's already comfortable with."

Jo's heart thumped painfully against her chest. Was he really offering to take her with them?

"Since I know how much you want to travel, and since Viola is comfortable with you, I thought your joining us might be a good solution for everyone."

Did he know what a prize he was offering her?

Of course he did. He was doing this as part of his misguided effort to apologize for the words they'd exchanged last night. Not that his reason mattered. This was the opportunity—

Reality crashed back in. "I can't."

"Why not?"

Because I'm already half in love with you. Because my resolve is not as strong as I thought. Because I'm already close to throwing away my dream to be with you.

"Because I need to run this place, that's why. There's no way I could shut it down for that length of time."

"I'm not suggesting you do. I said I wanted to hire you. I plan to pay enough to cover the cost of hiring someone to watch the place while you're gone." He shrugged. "You wouldn't make much profit off the deal itself, but you'd get a chance to see other parts of the country. And I promise to get you back here in plenty of time to spend Christmas with your family."

He eyed her thoughtfully. "Unless you don't care for the idea of playing nanny-companion to Viola."

"You know I've taken a liking to her. She's like one of my nieces." Closer in some ways. There was something about the way Viola held part of herself back, the way she didn't quite fit in with the other kids, that Jo identified with on a gut level.

It was so tempting, but was it the right thing to do? Would having just this little taste make her even more discontent with her lot when she returned to Knotty Pine? Or would it make her work even harder to make it a permanent way of life?

Besides, if Ry escorted her back here for Christmas, it would give her a last chance to throw him and Cora Beth together.

Ry gave her a crooked smile. "Funny, I thought you'd jump at the offer." Something flickered in his eyes. "If it's me you're uncomfortable traveling with, I assure you—"

"No, of course not." The heat rose in her cheeks. "I mean, Viola will be with us, so of course there's nothing improper about it. It's just…"

She rubbed the back of her neck, trying to sort out her thoughts. Surely she could keep her feelings for him in check. After all, with new places to see she'd have other things to occupy her mind. "It's not just the livery," she said slowly. "I have responsibilities to my family. I need to talk this over with Cora Beth, make sure she's okay with taking charge while I'm gone."

"Perhaps this will let her test the waters a bit. After all, if you do eventually set out on your own, it would be good for both of you to know how everyone will fare."

Josie mulled that over. "I guess that makes sense."

"Then you're willing to take the job?"

Was she? A finger of excitement traced its way up Josie's spine. She grinned. "Yes, I suppose I am."

As familiar landmarks came into view, Ry felt the stirring of eagerness and dread he always felt when returning to Hawk's Creek. It was home. But a home where he felt more guest than resident.

"The house is around this bend and over the next hill," he said to his companions.

Viola and Josie straightened. They'd arrived at the Tyler depot almost an hour ago. He'd enjoyed pointing out some of the town's features to Josie, both the commendable and the notorious, as they'd passed through. She'd latched on to every novelty, every new sight or sound as if she could capture and pin them to a board to re-examine later, like Uncle Grover with his bugs.

Of course, once they'd left Tyler, the scenery hadn't offered anything different from the countryside around Knotty Pine.

For the past ten minutes, they'd been cutting through Hawk's Creek property, land that had been painstakingly cleared by his grandfather and further expanded by his father.

As they topped the rise, the main buildings came into view. The arched ironwork sign at the head of the drive informed the traveler that this was indeed Hawk's Creek Ranch. Beyond that, the sprawling two-story house shone a gleaming white, and proudly welcomed visitors with a well-maintained front drive and an expansive porch. The bunkhouse, barn and stable were just beyond.

Josie's reaction was just as he'd expected. Her eyes widened and she leaned forward to get a better look. Viola, however, clutched Daffy and wore a worried expression.

Was something bothering her?

"Do you think they'll mind if Daffy comes inside?"

Puzzle solved. "Not a bit," he reassured her. "When I was a kid we had dogs running in and out of the place all the time. What's one little cat compared to that?"

His answer seemed to appease her.

They'd barely turned into the drive when Sadie rushed out the front door, waving excitedly.

"I thought you'd never get here," she exclaimed as soon as the buggy stopped. "I was just thinking I'd saddle Dusty and ride out to meet you."

Ry shook his head as he stepped down from the buggy. "Impatient as always." He grabbed Viola around the waist and swung her down before offering a hand to Josie.

"Manny will get your bags," Sadie said. "You just come on inside and make yourselves at home."

Was that a slip of the tongue? Did his sister truly think of him as a guest or was that more for Josie and Viola's benefit?

"We have refreshments ready." Sadie chattered on, taking Viola's hand. "I hope you like strawberry tarts, because Inez cooked up a fresh batch this morning."

Viola nodded. "Strawberries are my favorite."

"Mine, too!" Sadie said that as if it were the most wonderful of coincidences. "That's another thing we have in common."

Ry and Josie followed, apparently left to their own devices.

"Your sister is quite…enthusiastic," Josie commented.

He grinned. "A regular Texas whirlwind."

Inside, Sadie paused at the foot of the staircase. "I imagine you'll want to freshen up." She nodded Ry's way. "Your room is ready, as always. And since your letter stated that Josie and Viola would share a room, I had the large guest suite prepared."

She gave them a broad smile. "Ry, if you'll show them the way, I'll help Inez with the refreshments."

He swept an arm toward the staircase. "Ladies, after you."

He watched Josie eye the elaborately carved banister and the elegant stained glass window at the top of the landing. Then there was the chandelier hanging high above them. Not your usual furnishings for a ranch house. They were all touches his genteelly raised mother had added after she'd moved here.

"So, this is where you grew up," Josie said thoughtfully.

"In all its glory." They reached the second floor and he motioned to the right. "Your room is this way."

It was his turn to play host, to have her sleep under his roof, and it felt good. "This will be your room." He stood aside to let them enter the guest chamber, noting with approval that a small bed had been brought in from somewhere. It was placed near the roomy bed that anchored the center of the room.

He wanted Josie and Viola to feel comfortable and at home

here. Because, if things went well on this trip, Josie would help
him decide whether to call Hawk's Creek or Philadelphia home.

"Here comes Manny with your bags now." He took a step
back. "My room is three doors down on the opposite side of
the hall. Let me know if you need anything."

Josie wanted to hug herself and twirl around the room. The
train ride, her very first, had been exciting. She'd stared out the
window, drinking up the quickly passing countryside the way
a thirsty horse lapped water. With each passing mile her dream
drew closer to reality. At long last she was putting into motion
all the plans she and Aunt Pearl had concocted, was fulfilling
the promises she'd made to her aunt before she passed.

The town of Tyler had been an eye-opener, as unlike Knotty
Pine as a woodshed was from a barn. It was a large, bustling
city with lots of buildings and people milling about.

Ry had instructed the driver to take the long route through
town and she knew it had been for her benefit. He'd been the
perfect tour guide, pointing out people and landmarks, telling
her and Viola interesting tidbits, bringing the place vividly alive.

And now this place. She'd visited ranches before but nothing
to match Hawk's Creek. It operated on a scale far grander than
anything she'd ever seen.

Even the house was deceptively simple-looking. Everywhere
she looked were quiet signs of elegance. This huge room, with
its fancy furnishings, its roomy padded window seat and large
framed mirror, spoke of a level of comfort she wasn't used to.

Josie tried to picture Ry growing up here, to see the little boy
he'd been—racing down the stairs, climbing that tree outside
her window, roaming free across the wide expanse of this place.

The sound of Viola talking to Daffy brought Jo's attention
back to the present. She checked her appearance in the vanity

mirror one last time. No overalls for her on this trip. Cora Beth had outdone herself, producing several new dresses in the two days she had to plan her trip. Jo was more grateful to her sister than she would ever know. Now Ry wouldn't have to feel embarrassed by her appearance in front of his family and friends.

She held out her hand to Viola. "Ready for some of those strawberry tarts?"

As soon as they stepped into the hall, Ry's door opened. Was it coincidence or had he been listening for them?

He met them at the head of the stairs. "I hope the accommodations were acceptable, ladies."

Josie walked by him with a head-high nod. "They'll do."

She heard his chuckle as they descended the stairs and the deep bass thrummed inside her with a tingling sensation that was becoming all too familiar.

Chapter Twenty-Two

Ry followed Josie and Viola downstairs, smiling at Josie's unexpected quip. At least she hadn't left her down-to-earth humor behind in Knotty Pine.

When they reached the first floor, he swept an arm to his left. "This way."

Sadie waited for them in the parlor. The low table in front of her was covered with trays of pastries and preserves and his mother's china teapot. His sister played hostess with much fanfare, making certain everyone's tea was prepared just as they liked and heaping their saucers with a generous variety of treats.

"Now tell me," Sadie said as they settled down to enjoy their refreshments, "did you have a pleasant journey? Trains can be so stuffy and uncomfortable. Did you get to see much of Tyler when you passed through?"

Ry let Sadie's babble wash over him. Most of it was directed at Josie anyway. Instead he sat back and really studied his sister for the first time in years. She was twenty-four now, and still unmarried. Why? Surely there were plenty of good men around here who'd be happy to have a wife as personable and outgoing as Sadie, even if she did seem a bit flighty at times.

Was she too particular? Was she too tied to this place to want to leave it? Had someone already stolen her heart and failed to return her affection? Would his brother know the answer?

There was a short pause in the conversation and he set his now empty cup on the table. "Where's Griff?"

"Out in the east pasture." Sadie fiddled with the handle of her teacup. "He and the men are constructing a new barn out that way. But he should be home soon."

"That's a lovely upright you have," Josie interjected.

"Why, thank you." Sadie pounced on the change of subject. "It belonged to Grandma Iris. It was one of the first pieces she bought when Grandpa Jack finished the house. Do you play?"

"Afraid not. But I do admire a nice tune."

"I can play," Viola offered.

Ry straightened, surprised she would volunteer such information. "Can you now, Button?"

"Yes, sir. Momma taught me. She could play real nice."

Ry saw the way her eyes studied the instrument hungrily. "I remember. She could sing well too."

Viola's face lit up. "Pa said she had the voice of an angel."

Her smile surprised him. He'd assumed discussing her mother would only sadden her. Had he been wrong? Did she want someone to talk to, to remember with? "Would you like to play for us?"

The child immediately slipped from her seat and headed for the instrument, Daffy at her heels. In short order she was playing a simple melody. And doing it quite well.

Ry made a mental note to install a piano wherever they eventually landed. If Viola was like her mother, music was an important part of her life.

A heartbeat later he noticed Josie studying Viola as well, a soft smile on her lips. Was she finally coming to realize that the people she surrounded herself with were just as important as where she was? If so, his battle was half won.

When Viola finished, she stood and offered a curtsy to the sound of their applause, then let out a yawn.

Josie gave her a caught-you grin. "Looks like somebody's ready for a nap." She stood and held out a hand. "Why don't we go upstairs and lie down for a bit."

Sadie popped up from her seat. "Oh, please, let me take her. I have a beautiful picture book we can read together. And I'm sure Ry would be happy to give you a tour of the ranch." She drew her lips together in an uncertain line. "Unless, of course, you'd like to take a nap as well."

Josie shrugged. "I've never been one for sleeping when the sun's up."

"That's settled then." Sadie held out her hand. "Come along, Viola. Time for our beauty sleep."

Once they were gone, Josie turned to Ry. "Your sister seems to like kids. I'm surprised she hasn't started her own family."

He smiled at the way she'd echoed his own thoughts. "I guess she just hasn't met a man who's a match for her yet." He moved to the door. "Would you rather see the rest of the house or look around outside?"

"Is there any reason we can't do both?"

Direct as always. "None whatsoever."

He led her to the room next to the parlor and opened the door, moving back to allow her to precede him. "This was Mother's favorite room."

Josie stepped inside, halting after only two steps. Two of the walls were lined floor to ceiling with books. In one corner stood a piano, much larger than the one in the parlor. A flute and harpsichord were displayed on a nearby wall shelf. Across the room a desk, proportioned for a woman, sat next to a large window.

"I can see why she liked it. I don't think you'd find this many books in the whole of Knotty Pine."

"I thought you might find this of particular interest." He waved a hand to his right and Josie spied a large, colorful globe on a floor stand.

She stepped closer, studying it in awe. She'd seen such a thing in a catalog once, but it was so much more impressive in person. She reached out a hand then caught herself.

"Go ahead." There was an amused undertone in his voice. "Touch it all you like."

He stepped beside her, so close his shoulder brushed against hers, sending warmth radiating down to her fingertips.

"Here's where we are." He traced a course eastward. "And here is Philadelphia."

She forced her focus back to the globe. "It's a shame we can't stop at any of the places between here and there." Then she caught herself. "I'm sorry. I didn't mean to sound ungrateful. This trip is wonderful, just the way you have it set up."

He grinned. "That's all right. I doubt this is the last time you'll travel this route. Perhaps next time." He moved toward the door. "Ready to see more?"

Still feeling slightly rattled, she nodded and followed him into the hall.

He pushed open another door. "And this was my father's domain."

This room was very different from the other. Not only was it more masculine with its heavy desk and leather chairs, but it had a more rugged, less polished feel. No attempt to soften anything here.

"This has actually been Griff's domain since Father passed," Ry said.

Josie wondered again what had happened to alienate the two

brothers. Something in his tone, in the very lack of emotion, whenever he mentioned Griff, indicated he was clamping down on some deeper feeling. Was he even aware he did it?

"How did your pa die?" she asked.

Ry rested a hand on the leather chair behind the desk. "He and Griff were climbing into a gully where a calf had gotten tangled up. Pa lost his footing and fell, hitting his head on a rock. As quick as that he was gone."

"I'm sorry."

"It was how he would've wanted to go. One minute he was doing the work he loved, the next he was together with my mother again."

Ry straightened and moved to the door. "Come on. I want you to meet someone." He led her to the back of the house, past several other closed doors. "You've seen the heart of the house and its muscle. Now I'll show you the pulse point." With a flourish, he pushed open the kitchen door.

"Mr. Ry! Welcome home!" A short woman with a salt-and-pepper bun on top of her head bustled around the table, wiping her hands on her apron. "I wondered if you were going to pay me a visit."

Ry wrapped her in a bear hug that lifted her feet clear off the floor. "Inez, Inez, how could you doubt me? Didn't I always say you're the love of my life?"

She laughed and swatted at him to let her down. "Ah, that's what you say, but then you stay away for months at a time."

"Yes, but the thought of your cooking always draws me back."

Josie smiled at their affectionate teasing.

The older woman patted her hair. "Now, use those manners your mama taught you and introduce me to your lady friend."

"Inez, this is Josephine Wylie, the woman who saved my

life. Josie, this is Inez Garner, the world's best cook and the person who keeps this entire household running smoothly."

"Mrs. Garner." Josie extended her hand. "It's so nice to finally meet you. Mr. Lassiter always has such wonderful things to say about both you and your cooking." She smiled. "And after tasting those teacakes this afternoon I can see why."

The cook took her hand. "Now, I'll have none of this Mrs. Garner nonsense. You just call me Inez like everyone else." She gave Josie's hand a squeeze. "Sadie told me what you did to save our Ry from those awful men. As far as I'm concerned, you're one of the family now."

Josie was taken aback and could only stammer out a "thank you."

Inez brushed aside her thanks and crossed her arms over her ample bosom. "So you're the sister of the woman who made that wonderful fruitcake Sadie brought home."

"Yes, ma'am. It's Cora Beth's specialty."

"I can't say as I don't covet that recipe a bit more than the Almighty would smile upon, but I understand how a cook wants to keep her secrets. You tell her, from one cook to another, that I think her cake is one of the best desserts I've ever tasted."

"Thanks. She'll appreciate that."

Inez turned back to Ry, placing a hand on top of his where it rested on the counter. "I was sorry to hear about Belle's passing. It doesn't seem all that long ago that you and her and Griff sat here in my kitchen, begging cookies off of me."

Ry nodded, accepting her sympathy.

Inez gave him a thoughtful look. "So she left you her daughter to look out for?"

"Her name's Viola. Spitting image of her momma."

"I always thought Belle was a smart girl."

Ry gave her a crooked smile. "You think putting Viola in my care was a *smart* thing?"

"Of course I do." She waved her apron at them. "Now, you two get out of my kitchen. I have a meal to prepare and I'm sure you can find something more interesting to do than watch me cook."

Jo followed Ry out onto the back porch. "I like her."

"Inez is a special lady. She's more than a cook, though she insists on keeping the line drawn between family and hired help." He moved toward the steps. "She's been at Hawk's Creek since before Pa brought my mother home from Philadelphia. I couldn't imagine this place without her."

He waved her forward. "Come on, I'll show you the stables."

Most of the ranch hands they passed greeted Ry with a quick wave, some asked him how long he was staying. All of them greeted her with a polite tip of the hat and a friendly smile.

As they stepped inside the stables, Jo paused. Her livery and bridle shop could fit inside here four times over.

But Ry didn't give her much time to look closer. He led her straight to a large stall near the middle of the building. "This is Monarch, Kestrel's sire and the pride of my stable."

"Oh, Ry, he's magnificent. I can see where Kestrel gets his size and lines from."

Ry opened the stall gate and ran a hand along the stallion's back, whispering soothing words as man and animal got reacquainted. Amazing to watch the way the two interacted, almost as if they understood each other. How could she have ever doubted his ability to handle Scout?

He glanced up as if just remembering her presence. Giving Monarch a last pat, he stepped out of the stall. "Ought to head back. I want to be there when Viola wakes from her nap."

As they left the stable, a group of men rode toward them across the field. Josie recognized the lead rider as Griff. She immediately sensed a change in Ry. Some of the relaxed air evaporated, replaced by a sense of caution, withdrawal.

They waited there until the men arrived and dismounted.

"Hello, Miss Wylie." Griff removed his hat and tugged at his work gloves. "Sorry I wasn't here to greet you when you arrived but I'm sure Sadie made you feel welcome."

"She's been very hospitable. And what I've seen of Hawk's Creek has been nigh on perfect."

He smiled and the expression transformed him. "Nigh on perfect, is it? I can see you're a woman of keen insight."

When he turned to Ry, the smile disappeared. "Looks like you found your way back okay."

Ry's expression matched his brother's. "Monarch is looking in top shape. Thanks for seeing that he's taken care of."

Griff nodded. "If you two will excuse me, I need to see to my horse and get cleaned up."

Supper that evening was an interesting experience—starting with their seating arrangements. The two brothers did a masculine dance around who would sit at the head of the table, both insisting it was the other's place.

"For goodness sake, Griff." Ry's exasperation made his deep voice harsh. "That's where you sit when I'm not here. There's no reason to change things up when I come around."

"You're the oldest." Griff sounded just as determined. "It's yours by right."

Josie felt Viola's hand tighten on hers as they listened to the brothers argue. After a few minutes more of the bickering, she decided enough was enough. Chin jutted out in a don't-mess-with-me attitude, she marched forward and pulled the head chair out herself. "Being as neither of you gentlemen care to sit here, I'm certain you won't mind if I do."

Ignoring the identical frowns flashed her way, she sat and indicated Viola should take the seat to her left. She glanced across the table to find Sadie staring dumbfounded at her.

However Inez, who'd brought in a platter of food, gave her an approving wink. Josie's confidence bounced back and her shoulders straightened.

The brothers, with nothing left to argue over, took seats across from each other.

When it came time to say the blessing, it looked as if the same argument would erupt, but Josie gave Ry a pointed frown, nodding toward Viola. This time, thankfully, he took the hint. Bowing his head, he asked the blessing over the food.

Once the meal started, things turned civil, but Josie noticed that the brothers never spoke directly to each other.

Since Griff sat to her right, he did his part to make polite conversation. He became quite animated when she asked questions about the livestock and the workings of the ranch. When he wasn't talking to or about his brother he could be downright charming.

During a lull in the conversation, Sadie turned to Viola. "I'm afraid we don't have a pony on the ranch, but we do have a horse who's gentle as a lamb. Her name's Poppy and she'd be perfect for you if you care to ride while you're here."

Viola shifted in her chair. "I don't know how to ride."

"You don't?" Ry sounded shocked.

She shook her head.

Recovering, he gave her a reassuring smile. "Well, we'll just have to remedy that. What do you say we have a riding lesson tomorrow morning?"

Chapter Twenty-Three

Josie leaned against the paddock rail, elbow to elbow with Sadie, watching as Ry gave Viola a riding lesson. It had rained during the night, making the ground slick and muddy, but Ry seemed perfectly at ease, ignoring the dirt caking his boots and splattering his pants, standing with a sure-footedness that conquered the slippery ground.

"I remember when Ry gave me riding lessons." Sadie's voice was soft and dreamy. "I was not quite six and he was eleven. You'd think a boy that age would resent having to take care of his baby sister. But not Ry. He was the most patient teacher, just the way he is with Viola right now."

"Why didn't your pa teach you?"

"Pa was much too busy that summer clearing the west pasture, and I was too impatient to wait. Besides, Ry was more than capable, even at that age."

"He mentioned once that he enjoyed working with horses."

Sadie laughed. "An understatement. He has a way with horses, an affinity for them. It's almost like he can understand what they're thinking. Pa said he was a natural."

"And he still keeps horses here."

Sadie nodded. "Monarch is his prize. Ry painstakingly bred several bloodlines through four generations until he was satisfied that he had just the right animal to sire superior bloodstock. And he's carefully chosen a number of quality brood mares from all around the country."

"Sounds impressive."

Sadie nodded. "The foals coming out of his stable now are highly coveted. Whenever word goes out that he's ready to sell one there's a line a mile long waiting to snatch it up."

She turned back to study what was happening in the paddock. "A pure pleasure to watch, isn't it? And he obviously loves doing it. Makes you wonder why he'd want to work in some stuffy office back east when he could be here, doing this."

Josie could think of a few reasons. "They have horses in Philadelphia."

"Yes, of course. But this is where he's set up his stable. Kind of telling, don't you think?"

Josie wasn't sure how to answer that, so she didn't. "How does Griff feel about that?"

"He appreciates a good horse, but he's a cattleman. To him, horses are tools, a means to get his job done."

Josie worded her next statement carefully. "I might be out of line for saying this, but I couldn't help noticing your brothers don't get along very well."

Sadie grimaced. "It wasn't always like that. There's only two years separating them age-wise you know, and they were really close growing up—sort of like those twin nieces of yours. If you saw one, you knew the other was close by."

"What happened?"

"Grandfather." There was a wealth of distaste in that word.

"How so?"

"One summer he came for a visit. Stayed for a very long two weeks." She cast Josie a sideways look. "Pa and Grandfather didn't get along well, though they both tried to put a good face on it when we were around."

She turned back to the paddock. "Anyway, the day before he was supposed to leave, he announced he wanted to take one of his grandsons with him to Philadelphia."

"Grandsons? Not grandchildren?"

Sadie laughed. "Grandfather wasn't looking to replace my mother, he was looking for someone to follow in his footsteps."

"Oh."

"Pa didn't like it, but he sent Ry along. After all, Griff would have been like a squirrel in a rabbit hutch if he'd gone to the city—completely out of place." She rested her chin on her fists. "And it was only supposed to be for a couple of months."

She cut her eyes Josie's way. "That was the sticking point, that Ry chose to stay rather than return to Hawk's Creek once the summer ended. It seemed such a betrayal."

"Is that how you feel?"

Sadie looked away. "After Pa died, Griff asked Ry to decide if he wanted to come back and take his rightful place on the ranch or if he'd rather have the kind of life Grandfather offered him. Ry keeps saying he has to weigh all the options and consequences." She dropped her hands. "I don't understand why he has so much trouble choosing. I just want my brother back."

"Aunt Josie! Aunt Sadie!" Viola's excited cry saved Josie from having to answer. "Look, I'm riding."

"Wonderful!" Josie said, while Sadie clapped in admiration.

Sadie obviously loved her brother, Josie decided. But it was just as obvious she didn't understand him.

Then it struck her that Inez, who wasn't related to Ry by blood, was the only person who'd truly acted as if he belonged here, rather than as if he were merely a guest.

Ry lifted Viola from the saddle, pleased with the progress they'd made. She was a quick learner and hadn't let her fears get in her way. With a bit more practice Viola would make a good rider. He'd get her a steady, well-mannered pony when they found a place to settle. Maybe by Christmas?

He carried her across the muddy ground, handing her over to Josie when he reached the fence. The action had such a natural feel to it. Did Josie sense that as well?

"Did you see me, Aunt Josie?"

Josie gave her a hug before setting her down. "I sure did, sweetie. Are you certain you haven't ridden before?"

"No, never."

"Well, you sure took to it mighty fast." She glanced at Ry. "Must have been the good teacher you had."

Viola nodded. "Uncle Ry told me just what to do. And after I got used to being up so high, it wasn't scary at all."

"I think we should celebrate your achievement." Sadie offered Viola her hand. "Let's go inside and clean up, then see what Inez has in the kitchen." She paused to glance back his way. "You're going to join us, aren't you?"

"You ladies go on while I take care of Poppy. Just tell Inez to save me some of whatever she's cooked up."

"As if I have to tell her." Sadie turned to Josie with a mock-pout. "Ry always was her favorite."

Josie grinned as she took Viola's other hand, then looked back over her shoulder. "You might want to hurry with your chores," she warned. "Those clouds look ready to burst anytime now."

He touched the brim of his hat. "Yes, ma'am."

Ry watched the three of them head back toward the house. Sadie was laughing, probably at something she herself had said. There were times when she seemed as playful as a child. And she'd certainly taken to Viola. Yet it was Josie's hand Viola clung the tighter to, her skirts the child drew closest to.

The bond between those two was growing stronger. Had Josie noticed? If so, would that bond mean enough to her that she would reshape her dreams to embrace it?

Chapter Twenty-Four

"We're pulling into the station." Ry had pitched his voice to a whisper. No point waking Viola just yet. The child was curled up on the seat beside him, her head snuggled against his side.

The trip from Tyler to Philadelphia had taken four and a half days and even Josie had grown tired of the experience.

She blinked, then focused on his face. He saw her chagrin when she realized she'd dozed off. "Sorry."

"No need to be." In fact he'd enjoyed watching her nap, had admired the soft, relaxed look of her, had wondered what it would be like to kiss those generous, full lips.

What would she think if she knew of his highly inappropriate thoughts? Would she be affronted? Or pleased?

With an effort, he pulled his thoughts back to the present. "Grandfather should have a carriage waiting so we won't have to stand around for long."

Josie nodded and folded her lap blanket. He saw her gaze stray to the window, saw the eagerness creep into her expression.

He couldn't blame her. She was about to take a giant step toward realizing her dream. And he aimed to see that he did everything he could to give her her fill over the next week or so.

Only then could he bring up the subject of settling down again. He just hoped he'd guessed right about knowing where her heart truly lay. And that she figured it out for herself—soon.

He roused Viola and once he'd found a porter to take care of their bags, he picked her up, carrying her off the train. He didn't want to take a chance of her getting lost in the crowd on the windy platform. From her height, the mob of travelers rushing to get in from the cold was no doubt a daunting sight.

Josie, however, was another matter entirely. Her eyes gleamed with excitement as she drank in all the sights and sounds. Was it living up to her expectations?

He led them into the modern, bustling station building. A minute later, he spied a familiar face and lifted a hand in greeting. "Nichols, I trust you've been well."

"Yes, thank you, Mr. Lassiter."

"This is Miss Wylie and Miss Viola."

Nichols bowed to Josie, then turned back to Ry. "All is ready for you and your guests. You'll find the carriage right outside the main door and there are hot bricks inside to ward off the chill. Let me see to your bags and we'll be on our way."

Hefting Viola a bit higher on his hip, Ry placed his free hand at Josie's back and moved toward the exit.

Please, Lord, don't let me lose her to the tug and drama of the city. You know how much Viola needs her.

How much I need her.

"Ladies, this is my grandfather, Mr. Roland Wallace. Grandfather, this is Miss Josephine Wylie and my ward, Miss Viola Hadley."

His grandfather gave Josie a slight bow. "Miss Wylie, welcome to Philadelphia."

"Thank you, sir." She looked around, her eyes seeming to

drink everything in. "Your home is beautiful. And with all the greenery and ribbon draped about, it looks so festive."

"Ah, yes. Getting ready for the Christmas season and all that. Glad you like it." Then he turned to Viola. "And what is that you're holding on to so tightly, young lady?"

"This is Daffy, my cat. He won't be any trouble, honest."

"I'm certain he won't. You must keep him in the nursery wing with you and Miss Wylie, though. He might get lost in this big house if you let him roam around." He gave her cheek a pat. "I'll make certain he has a bowl of cream every morning and evening. He'll like that, won't he?"

"Yes, sir."

"I thought so. Now, I know you ladies want to freshen up. Brigit, escort Miss Wylie and Miss Viola to their rooms, please."

The maid curtsied and indicated they were to follow her. Ry gave Viola an encouraging wink, before turning to his grandfather.

"Glad to have you back, my boy. With so little warning before you left, the office has been in a bit of turmoil, but we'll set things to rights in no time now that you've returned."

Ry resisted the urge to apologize, and after a moment his grandfather continued. "After you take a few minutes to settle in, why don't you come down to the study. I want to hear more about your trip, and there are a few things I want to catch you up on regarding our cases."

Ry straightened at that. "Anything in particular?"

"The Bergmon case, for starters. It took an unexpected turn and I thought some fresh eyes might see something we're missing."

Ry nodded. He'd put a lot of hours in on that case before he left, so he was familiar with the particulars. "I'll be down in fifteen minutes."

Ry climbed the stairs, hesitating at the second floor landing.

Should he check on Josie and Viola? Deciding they were probably resting, he turned to the east wing, where his set of apartments were situated.

Fifteen minutes later, he was seated in one of the brown leather chairs that faced his grandfather's desk.

His grandfather poured a glass of port, then offered Ry one. Ry held up a hand in refusal.

"So," his grandfather said as he replaced the stopper, "will Miss Wylie be Viola's permanent governess or will she return to Texas once you and the child are settled in?"

Ry stiffened. "You mistake the situation, sir. Miss Wylie is not Viola's governess, nor is she a servant of any kind. I would consider it a personal favor if you would refrain from making her feel in any way inferior."

His grandfather held up a hand. "My mistake. But, if I may ask, in what capacity *is* she here?"

Ry considered that for a moment. He wasn't ready to let his grandfather realize how truly important Josie was to him just yet. Time for that when matters were more settled between them. "She's a friend," he finally said. "One I'm deeply indebted to. She helped me fight my way out of an ambush, her family took me in and nursed me when I was too weak to take care of myself, and she very kindly agreed to accompany Viola and myself on this trip so I'd have someone to help care for the child's needs."

His grandfather raised a brow. "Sounds like a remarkable woman."

"She is that."

The older man took his seat behind the desk. "Naturally she will be treated as an honored guest while she's here." He took a sip from his glass. "Just how long might that be, by the way?"

"I promised to have her home in time to spend Christmas with her family."

"Ah. It's good to have one's family around at Christmas." He leaned back in his chair. "Now, tell me about this misadventure of yours. How's the arm doing?"

Ry raised his arm and rotated his shoulder. "No lingering effects." He spread his hands. "As to the story, I was waylaid by a pair of hooligans. Fortunately, with Miss Wylie's help, we were able to gain the upper hand."

"Sounds like quite a dust-up. But I suppose that sort of thing is to be expected when you travel in the less civilized parts of the country."

Ry set his jaw. "You can encounter unsavory types in any locale."

His grandfather made a noncommittal sound, then moved on to another topic. "Too bad things didn't work out the way you wanted with that Hadley woman. My condolences."

Ry nodded.

"It must have been unsettling to discover she named you to be her daughter's guardian."

"At first. But the longer I'm in Viola's company the more certain I am this is the right thing to do. I've grown quite attached to her." An understatement. "Which reminds me. I would like for Viola to take her meals with us."

"Is that wise?" His grandfather's brow furrowed. "Surely the child will be more comfortable in the nursery."

"Viola is accustomed to mingling with adults in small family gatherings." Ry spread his hands. "But if you're concerned, Miss Wylie and I can take our meals with her in the playroom."

"No, no, that won't be necessary." His grandfather waved a hand. "I only thought to spare her some tedium." Then he gave Ry an approving smile. "I'm glad to see you're taking your responsibilities to the child seriously. It's time you considered settling down and starting a family." He raised a brow. "This isn't exactly how I envisioned it, but what's done is done."

Ry didn't bother to hide his annoyance. "Pardon my bluntness, sir, but when and how I start a family is my concern, not yours."

"Yes, of course. I'm only anxious for you to find the same happiness I found with your grandmother." He set his glass aside. "And speaking of family, it's fortuitous you were able to combine this bit of business with a trip to Hawk's Creek. How are your brother and sister faring?"

"They're both well."

"Good, good. By the way, the Havershams have invited us to their home for Christmas dinner. I hope you don't mind, but I've told them we'd be there. I didn't think you'd want to travel back to Texas that quickly since you've only just returned."

Ry shook his head. "I'm afraid you'll have to send my regrets."

"What do you mean?"

Was that a touch of annoyance in his voice? "As I mentioned, I promised Miss Wylie I would make certain she got home before Christmas. I certainly can't expect her to make the trip alone."

Grandfather waved a hand dismissively. "We can always send one of the servants with her."

Not a chance. "I consider Miss Wylie's welfare my personal responsibility."

"I see." The older man drummed his finger on his desk, then sighed. "Well, I suppose it can't be helped. We'll put the Havershams off until New Year's."

"Perhaps you should hold off making any plans that include me for the time being."

"Oh?" There was a definite chill in Grandfather's tone.

"I've been thinking for some time that I need to decide just what course I want my life to take." Ry steepled his fingers, meeting his grandfather's stern gaze without blinking. "That includes whether I should remain in Philadelphia or return to Texas—full time." He interlaced his fingers. "Acquiring a ward has made that decision all the more pressing."

"After your recent, near-fatal misadventures I would think the answer would be obvious." If anything the chill had deepened. Grandfather leaned back in his chair.

Griff had also said he thought the answer was obvious. Of course, he'd been referring to a completely different conclusion.

Grandfather tugged at his vest. "Here she will have access to fine educational institutions, museums, theaters, symphonies. There are modern medical facilities and electricity to light our homes safely. Can Hawk's Creek offer her anything comparable?"

"Perhaps not. But there are other things to consider."

"Such as?"

"Such as being among people and settings one feels comfortable in. Such as being allowed to act rambunctious the way a child should without worry about being disciplined. Such as having a backyard comprised of acres rather than feet and a whole forest to explore as your playground."

"I take it you don't believe those things can be found here."

"I didn't say that." Ry wasn't going to be browbeaten into making the wrong choice. "What I said was that I need to consider both options before I decide."

His grandfather nodded. "Deliberate, as always. That's why you're a superb lawyer. Which reminds me, there are a few case files I'd like you to take a look at. I hope you don't mind going into the office tomorrow."

"Actually, I thought I'd spend tomorrow showing Viola and Miss Wylie some of the sights around town."

"The Bergmon case *is* rather urgent—we go to trial in two days. But I'll be glad to keep the ladies company—Sanderson can fill you in on all of the particulars of the case."

Ry nodded reluctantly, knowing his grandfather was right, on this point at least. He'd been gone for almost a month—time to get back to work. There'd be other opportunities to show Josie around in the days to come.

Besides, it would give him an opportunity to review his client files and assess what would need wrapping up if he left the firm.

Viola slipped her hand into Josie's as they descended the staircase to the first floor. Josie didn't blame her, she felt a bit intimidated by all the opulence herself.

She smoothed her skirt. It was one of the new dresses Cora Beth had made, but she still worried it wasn't good enough. She didn't want to embarrass Ry in front of his grandfather. Maybe she and Viola should have taken their meal in the playroom.

Just as they reached the foot of the staircase, Ry and his grandfather stepped out of a nearby room.

"My, my," the older man said, "don't you ladies look lovely?" He stepped forward and offered Josie his arm. "Allow me to escort you into supper."

His admiring smile eased her fears. She lifted her head and placed her hand on his arm. "Thank you."

Ry offered his arm to Viola, and Josie hid a grin as she saw the little girl follow her example.

As they settled into the meal, Ry's grandfather turned to Josie. "I understand this is your first trip outside of Texas."

"Yes, sir. I'm looking forward to exploring everything your city has to offer."

He laughed. "My dear, it would take a lifetime to explore the entire city. But we'll see if we can show you the best parts."

"That would be wonderful." Josie couldn't suppress the flutter of excitement. Aunt Pearl would be so proud of her.

"Since my grandson will be busy at the office tomorrow," Mr. Wallace continued, "I would consider it an honor if you would allow an old gentleman like myself to show you around."

Josie's enthusiasm dimmed a bit. She'd expected Ry to be the one to show her around, to share in her discoveries. It wouldn't be nearly as much fun without him.

"That's mighty kind of you, sir." She turned to Ry. "But do you really need to get to work so soon? Couldn't you join us for our first excursion?"

He shook his head regretfully. "Sorry, but I was away longer than expected. There's work on my desk that's already waited too long."

Josie sat back. "If you'd like us to postpone—"

"Nonsense. No point wasting any of your time here." Ry nodded toward the head of the table. "Besides, Grandfather knows more about Philadelphia than I do. I'll join you another time."

"That's settled then." Mr. Wallace cut into his steak. "There are some wonderful shops on Market Street. And there are museums and libraries we can visit, if you prefer. We can plan trips to Independence Hall and Washington Square for later in the week."

Just listening to him name the places they would visit set Josie's pulse racing again. It was too bad Ry wouldn't be there to share it all.

Then she had another thought. Was he deliberately distancing himself? After all, it was one thing for him to spend time with her in Knotty Pine. But he was back in his world now. Did he see her as too countrified in these surroundings?

Maybe that was just as well. Didn't she keep telling herself that she didn't *want* his affections?

"How about you, young lady?" Mr. Wallace had turned to Viola. "Would you care to tour the city with Miss Wylie and me? I know a candy shop we can visit."

Viola's eyes widened. "Oh, yes, sir, that would be very nice." Then she turned to Ry. "Won't you be able to have any fun at all, Uncle Ry?"

Josie saw the concern on the child's face. Amazing how close she and Ry had become in the short time they'd been together.

Before Ry could respond, his grandfather spoke up. "Of course he will. In fact, why don't I purchase a pair of tickets to the theater for your Uncle Ry and Miss Wylie?" He glanced at Josie. "There's a comedy playing at the Walnut Street Theater that I hear has been well received."

"What about me?" Viola asked.

"Oh, I'm afraid it'll be way past your bedtime." Ry's grandfather pointed with his fork. "But don't worry. Brigit will keep you company."

Viola turned to Ry. "Will you tuck me in when you get back?"

"I wouldn't be able to sleep if I didn't, Button."

She nodded solemnly. "Me neither."

That seemed to satisfy Viola, and the conversation moved on to small talk. Later, when the dessert course was brought out, Mr. Wallace studied it with a frown. "What's this? I thought I requested a burnt custard for tonight."

"It was my doing," Ry explained. "Miss Wylie's sister bakes fruitcakes that are absolutely superb."

Mr. Wallace looked prepared to object, then seemed to think better of it. "Well then, let's have a go at it." With a smile, he took a large bite and his eyes widened in appreciation. "You weren't exaggerating. I don't think I've ever tasted a fruitcake quite this delectable." He raised a glass to Josie in salute. "My compliments to your sister."

"Thank you. I'll be certain to pass your compliment on to her."

"You know, I'll be hosting a small holiday gathering for the law firm's staff. Do you think I could convince your sister to ship a few of these here? I'd pay her for them, of course."

Josie waved a hand, dismissing his offer of payment. "I'm sure Cora Beth would be glad to oblige. But I can't accept your money. Think of it as repayment for your hospitality." It was a little thing, but it felt good to be on the giving rather than receiving end for a change.

The next afternoon, Ry headed straight to the nursery wing when he returned from the office. It had felt good to dive back into his work, but part of him had been distracted, wondering what Josie and Viola were doing.

"Uncle Ry!" Viola ran to greet him as soon as he entered the playroom. "We visited the most wonderful shops today."

He stooped down to give her a quick hug. "Is that right?"

"Uh-huh. There was one that had nothing but candies. Shelves and shelves filled with chocolates and taffies and rock candies and, oh my goodness, everything!"

"Amazing." He felt a little pang that he hadn't been there to experience it with her.

"And the store next door had dolls and mechanical toys and music boxes."

"I wish Danny and the girls had been with us," Josie added. "They would have loved it."

Ry smiled. Was Josie missing her family? "And did Aunt Josie find anything to catch her interest?" His question was directed at Viola, but he kept his gaze on Josie.

"Oh, she looked at some clothes and hats." Apparently fashion did not rate as high on Viola's list as did sweets and toys.

Josie laughed selfconsciously. "Your grandfather was kind

enough to introduce me to a lady at a very fancy dress shop." She smoothed her skirt. "Mrs. Richoux was very polite, but I got the impression this dress doesn't quite match what ladies here consider stylish."

Ry fought back a frown. Was his grandfather trying to be helpful or make her feel out of place?

Viola crossed the room and took her hand. "I think your dress is real pretty, Aunt Josie."

"As do I," he chimed in.

"Well, thank you both." Josie curtsied. "But I decided to splurge and get one nice new gown." She gave Ry a self-conscious look. "I didn't want to embarrass you when we went to the theater tonight."

He took both her hands in his. "I would never be embarrassed to have you on my arm, no matter what you wore." To his surprise, her cheeks pinkened, and a smile teased at her lips.

Perhaps he should offer her compliments more often.

That evening Ry decided Josie had made excellent use of her shopping time. When she came down the stairs in her new gown she looked absolutely radiant. The dark green fabric matched her eyes perfectly, and the elegant lines lent her a sophisticated air. But her most flattering accessory was the sparkle in her eyes and the flush of excitement in her cheeks.

There'd be more than one man tonight who would cast envious glances his way.

Josie rested her hand on Ry's as he helped her into the carriage outside the theater. Truth be told, she could have floated in without any asstance whatsoever. The play had been wonderful, the elegantly dressed ladies and gents impressive, and the theater marvelous. And Ry had been flatteringly attentive, introducing her to his acquaintances with a touch of pride in his voice.

There was nothing to match this in Knotty Pine.

Ry settled into the seat across from her, an indulgent smile on his face. "Did you enjoy yourself tonight?"

Josie nodded. "It was the perfect ending to a wonderful day." She lightly touched his knee. "Thank you so much for bringing me here. I know this is old hat to you but to me it was magical."

"There's no one I'd rather have with me."

She felt the light wool of his trousers under her hand and her cheeks heated with awareness. She removed her hand quickly, but the warmth of him remained on her fingertips. She shivered slightly, as much from some too-uncomfortable-to-explore emotion as from the temperature, but his smile immediately changed to a look of concern.

"You're cold. Here, allow me." He moved across the space to sit beside her, unfolding a lap blanket and settling it over her skirt. "How's that?"

"Just right. Thank you."

The carriage hit a rut in the road, throwing her against him. His arm reached out, encircling her protectively. For a moment they were so close their noses nearly touched. Their breath mingled, weaving an invisible cord that bound them together. Her breath caught in her throat as she saw his eyes darken. He stared into her eyes as if she knew some secret he was driven to learn…as if he couldn't look away. As if she truly mattered to him.

The cord tightened and his face drew closer. He was going to kiss her.

And she was going to let him.

Chapter Twenty-Five

The kiss was warm, surprisingly gentle and absolutely unlike anything Josie had ever experienced. Everything else melted away. For this one moment in time she knew she was cherished and safe and part of something truly wonderful. She felt his strength as well as his restraint, his willingness to keep her safe against all harm, and most of all a tenderness that in no way equaled weakness, all channeled through that one marvelous kiss. It was a heady sensation that turned her whole world topsy-turvy.

When he drew back she wanted to cry out in protest. But his gaze captured hers again, intense, searching.

Was he looking for signs of outrage or regret? If so, he wouldn't find any. Instead, she stroked his cheek with the back of her hand. The firm, rugged feel of it brought an appreciative smile to her lips.

With a strangled sound that was part growl, part her name, he captured her hand with his own and brought it to his lips. Then he smiled like a man who'd just conquered the world, and pulled her to him, tucking her head against his shoulder.

It felt like coming home.

* * *

Later, Josie lay in bed, too fidgety to sleep.

After that turn-my-world-upside-down kiss, the rest of the carriage ride had passed in pleasantly charged silence, as if both of them were afraid that speaking would shatter the perfection of the moment.

He'd accompanied her to the nursery wing just long enough to check on Viola, then parted with a squeeze of her hand, a chaste kiss on her cheek and a softly uttered good-night.

Now she stared at the shadowy ceiling, reliving that carriage ride, trying to figure out what it meant, how it affected her dreams and her future.

Because it *had* changed things. She could no longer deny her attraction to Ry, could no longer pretend she wanted him to marry Cora Beth.

But was she really ready to settle down, to give him the kind of wife he wanted, the kind of mother Viola needed? If not, if she needed more time, would he give it to her? Could she ask him to? He already had so much turmoil in his life—torn between Hawk's Creek and Philadelphia, at odds with his brother, trying to be a father to a five-year-old who still grieved the loss of her parents—how could she add to that?

Her hand stole to her lips, feeling again the sweetness of his kiss. Who would have guessed that the mere joining of lips could stir such a hornet's nest of emotions?

He had put so much tenderness, so much of himself into the gesture. Perhaps there really was a chance for them to be happy together, a way to combine their needs and dreams and build something altogether beautiful.

Philadelphia was a wondrous place. And there were other amazing places to see within a day's ride. A person could live here for a very long time and find something new to do or see nearly every day. Ry must see that, as well. Surely, when it came down to it, he would choose Philadelphia over Hawk's Creek.

Maybe she could reshape her dream. Maybe she didn't need to be in a rush to see the whole world. Maybe she should take time to really savor this one exciting piece of it for now.

Josie snuggled down under the covers, thinking that she could be quite happy with that.

As long as she had the right person to share it with.

Ry shrugged out of his coat and sat down to remove his boots.

Heaven help him, holding her had felt so good, so *right*. He could have held her like that forever. When she looked at him with those shining, trusting eyes he would have happily slain a dozen dragons for her. When she'd smiled with wonder in her eyes and stroked his cheek, he'd wanted to howl at the moon in sheer exuberance.

If nothing else, tonight had proven—to both of them—that she felt the strong tug of attraction between them, too. Because he was ready to admit that this was no longer about finding the right mother for Viola. He loved Josie, had for quite some time.

He wouldn't fool himself that the battle was won. She'd held on to her dream too long to let it go overnight. But it was a start. And a solid one at that.

He was determined that by the time they returned to Knotty Pine for Christmas, she'd realize she needed something deeper, something richer, than experience for its own sake.

Josie woke the next morning to a cold dose of reality. What had she been thinking last night?

She groaned and buried her face in her pillow. That was the problem—she hadn't been thinking, she'd been feeling.

If the two of them stayed here in Philadelphia, who would see to the livery? If he'd married her sister, he would have taken responsibility for her kids as well. And Danny and Uncle Grover were an extension of that. But it wasn't the same thing at all if she and Ry got hitched. She couldn't expect him to take on the whole clan just because he married her.

Oh, she had no doubt he'd send money to her family if she asked him to, but that wasn't the kind of arrangement she wanted. And without her there to keep the livery running, her family wouldn't have the means to support themselves.

She sat up and hugged her knees. There was no getting around it. She'd have to go back. Alone.

Ry belonged here. She'd seen how much his lawyering meant to him, how eager he'd been to get back to work almost as soon as they'd arrived.

Heavenly Father, I truly do appreciate You giving me this little taste of what the world outside Knotty Pine holds for me. It's all I dreamed of and more. And I know it's plumb selfish of me to want this and a life with Ry and Viola, too. But I just got to believe You put them in my life for a reason. Please, if it be Your will, help me find a way to make things work out for us.

Feeling only slightly better, Josie threw off the covers and got dressed.

How was she going to face Ry this morning? What was he thinking after that kiss? Had it affected him as much as it had her? On top of everything else, what if she'd read too much into it? Here she was, wondering how to answer a proposal that might not even come her way. After all, he was a man of the world. He'd likely kissed lots of girls. It didn't mean he was ready to ask her to marry him.

When Brigit informed her Ry had already eaten and headed

out, Josie didn't know whether to be relieved or insulted. Was he avoiding her? Did he have second thoughts about last night?

Then the young maid handed her a note, accompanied by a red rose, and Josie's emotions took another swing.

She opened the note and couldn't stop a smile. The handwriting was as bold and firm as the man himself.

Sorry I won't be joining you for breakfast, but I wanted to get to the office early so I'd be able to spend time with you and Viola this afternoon. I'll be back by two o'clock to take you out for a carriage ride.

Ry.

So she had a reprieve until this afternoon. Josie inhaled the scent of the rose and slowly walked toward Viola's bedchamber.

Chapter Twenty-Six

Ry strode down the sidewalk to his grandfather's house, ignoring the cold wind that tried to snatch at his hat. He'd been looking forward to this outing ever since he awakened this morning. He'd finally have the chance to show Josie and Viola some of *his* favorite places in the city.

The memory of how sweet, how wistful she'd looked last night had kept a smile on his face most of the day. She was coming 'round, he could feel it. His patience was finally beginning to bear fruit.

He took the steps up to the front door two at a time and tossed his hat on the hall table, shrugged out of his coat and headed for the nursery wing.

When he pushed open the door to the playroom, Viola bounced up and ran to greet him. Her greetings were becoming less reserved, more enthusiastic as each day passed. Something squeezed at his heart when he thought of the reliance and affection she'd entrusted to him.

"Hello, Uncle Ry." She gave him a hug as he stooped to greet her. "Aunt Josie told me all about the play you went to last night. It sounded wonderful."

"That it was." Ry met Josie's gaze over the child's head. "I especially liked the ending."

Josie blushed and broke eye contact as she stood. "Come along, Viola. Let's get you bundled up for our outing. We'll meet Uncle Ry downstairs."

Ry rubbed his chin as he watched the two of them hurry off to Viola's bedchamber. Was it his imagination or was Josie a bit stiff, evasive? Was it just embarrassment over last night's kiss? Or something else?

As he made his way to his own rooms to change clothes, some of the optimism he'd felt earlier slipped away.

The outing that afternoon only slightly lessened his sense of unease. He took them ice skating at Eastwick Park, a novel activity for the Texas-born-and-raised pair. Viola took to it with the quickness of a child, ready to try it on her own after only a few turns around the ice. Within a short time, Ry was ready to hand her over to Nichols while he turned his attentions to Josie.

It took Josie a bit more time to get the hang of it. Not that Ry minded. Having the opportunity to hold her while they glided across the ice was pure enjoyment. Helping her up when she lost her footing, hearing her laughter and seeing the elation on her face when she gained enough confidence for him to take her flying across the ice, his arm at her waist, was exhilarating.

And the cups of hot cocoa afterward were a definite hit.

Viola chattered excitedly about their excursion during the carriage ride back. Josie smiled and nodded and added her own enthusiastic observations, remarking how much her family would have enjoyed the outing, too. But Ry sensed a returning tension in her, a brittleness, that while subtle, was threaded through every glance, every overly bright smile she cast his way.

He bided his time, planning to take her aside for a quiet talk after supper, but she pled a headache and excused herself early.

The next day was no different—Josie was pleasant but distant and deftly avoided every attempt he made to get her alone for a few moments.

By the next morning, Ry rose determined to get to the bottom of whatever had made Josie so skittish. He wasn't going to let her put him off any longer. He'd leave the office early today and be back in time to have lunch with his two girls. Then, once Viola settled down for her nap, he'd corner the evasive Miss Wylie, and find out just what was going on.

Dear Lord, whatever problem Josie's conjured up in that wonderfully fertile mind of hers, please let me find the words to help her see that, with Your help, the two of us can handle anything together.

Ry marched into the nursery wing at noon to find Brigit setting out Viola's lunch. Josie was nowhere in sight.

"Uncle Ry!"

The way Viola's face lit up at the sight of him gave Ry's mood a boost. He couldn't imagine life without her now. "Hello, Button." He stooped down to accept and return her hug. "I thought I'd have lunch with you and Josie today."

"Aunt Josie went out with Grandfather Wallace this morning."

Ry tried to hide his disappointment. "Well, then, I'll have lunch with you, if that's okay."

"I'll fetch another plate right away." And with a quick bob, Brigit hurried from the room.

Ry let Viola chatter about her morning while the meal was brought in and set up. He tried to give her his full attention, but his mind kept turning impatiently to thoughts of how soon Josie would return.

Once Brigit left them to their meal, Viola quieted down. It took Ry a few minutes to notice the pensive edge to her expression.

"Something the matter, Button?"

She pushed the peas around on her plate. "I was just wondering if you decided where we would live yet?"

Now she had his undivided attention. "If I recall correctly, I promised you we'd make that decision together." And lately he'd hoped that Josie would have a part in making that decision as well. "I take it you've been giving this some thought."

She nodded, looking at him with large, somber eyes.

He reached over, placing his hand on hers. "Well, let's hear what you're thinking. And keep in mind, whether it's Philadelphia or Hawk's Creek, I want us to have our own house."

Her face brightened. "I've never had my own house before."

Ry leaned back, struck by the poignancy of her words. "Well, you're going to have one now." He cleared his throat, pushing the gruffness away.

She smiled, then cocked her head to one side. "But can we still go back to Knotty Pine for Christmas?"

He smiled, and made a cross-my-heart sign. "Yes, ma'am." Then he leaned forward. "I promised we would, remember? And if I give you my word about something, I will always, *always* do my very best to keep it, no matter what. Do you believe me?"

That earned him a solemn nod. "And I promise to do my very best, too."

Her earnestness touched something deep inside him. Then he straightened, returning to the matter at hand. "Let's talk about Philadelphia first, since that's where we are. You've had a good time here, meeting Grandfather Wallace and seeing some of the sights and shops of the city, haven't you?"

She nodded.

"And there are plenty of other things to see and do. Like museums and markets and parks. Then there's a fine school where you could be with lots of children your own age. And of course, if we stayed here we would get to see Grandfather on a regular basis."

He watched her carefully for some sign of what she was thinking, but for once he couldn't read her expression.

Time to discuss the other option. "As for Hawk's Creek, if we lived there we wouldn't be so crowded, there's lots of room to spread out and do whatever we want, a place to keep a horse of your very own, and Sadie and Griff would be close by so we'd get to see them whenever we wanted." It was the choice he was leaning toward. But again, there was no obvious reaction from Viola. What was she thinking?

She finally looked up and met his gaze. "Are those our only two choices?"

Her question caught him off guard. Didn't she like either place? "The thing is," he said slowly, "Philadelphia and Hawk's Creek is where my, *our*, family is. And I think it's important to be close to family." The Wylies had taught him that. He wanted that kind of closeness, that sense of acceptance and nurturing and belonging, for Viola. And for himself too.

Viola traced a circle on the table with her fingertip, not looking up at him. "Once, when I was sad about not having any family left, Audrey told me that family isn't just the folks who are blood kin to you. It can include others, too. Like the way Danny and Uncle Grover are part of her family."

Ry covered her hand with his, hurting for the sense of aloneness she'd felt. "Audrey was absolutely right. You are part of my family now, just as sure as if you were my own daughter. And that makes all of my family—Sadie and Griff and Grandfather Wallace—yours as well."

She nodded, still not looking up. "The other thing Audrey told me is that, if we wanted to, she and I could call ourselves sisters. Or at least cousins."

Yep, Audrey was very much like her Aunt Josie. "I think that's wonderful."

This time she did look up. "Then, aren't they part of our family, too? Couldn't we move to Knotty Pine?" She spoke all in a rush now. "I like it there, Uncle Ry, a whole lot. I miss Audrey and Mrs. Collins. And I liked going to school there and the Thanksgiving Celebration. There's going to be a Christmas program too." Her eyes pleaded with him. "Couldn't we at least think about living *there*?"

Ry leaned back as her words sunk in. Move to Knotty Pine? A place where he could set his own path without constantly bumping into reminders of his grandfather's and siblings' expectations? And they'd still have "family" around to give Viola the support and sense of belonging she needed.

Setting up a law practice in Knotty Pine wouldn't be much more challenging than doing so at Hawk's Creek. And as Josie had pointed out once before, Knotty Pine was growing. If they didn't already need a lawyer, they would someday. In the interim, he'd have time to focus on building a home for Viola and perhaps establishing a horse ranch.

The one fly in the ointment would be Josie's reaction. He knew she wanted to travel, but surely she'd had enough to hold her for a while. And he'd seen some signs that she missed her family. Perhaps she was finally coming around to realizing what a great life she'd left behind in Knotty Pine. And it wasn't as if they couldn't travel from time to time.

The more he thought about the idea, the more he wondered why he hadn't seen it himself. "Viola," he said, tapping her nose, "you're a genius."

Her face brightened immediately. "Does that mean we can live in Knotty Pine?"

"I'll need to work out some things, but I do believe you've hit on the perfect plan."

"Oh, Uncle Ry, thank you." She ran around the table and hugged his neck for all he was worth.

Thank you, Lord, for bringing this child into my life.

Josie could hardly contain her excitement. With the help of Ry's grandfather, she'd found the answer she'd been praying for. Having both her dream and a life with Ry and Viola actually seemed possible now.

Ry crossed the room and took her hands in each of his, smiling softly into her eyes. "Looks like someone had a fine time this morning."

"Oh, you have no idea."

"So tell me."

She laughed and pulled her hands away, savoring his attention yet too excited to hold still. She set her gloves down and twirled around to face him, eager to share her news. "Your grandfather had the most wonderful idea."

"And what was that?"

She heard the caution in his tone but brushed it aside. "We were talking about our favorite foods, and he mentioned how much he'd enjoyed Cora Beth's fruitcake. Then he suggested Cora Beth and I start our own business, *selling* her fruitcakes. Isn't that the most wonderful thing you ever heard?" The words burst from her like a spark from a flint.

Ry's reaction, however, was more puzzled than enthusiastic. "Sell fruitcakes? But you both already have businesses—the livery and the boardinghouse. Why start another?"

Didn't he understand what this meant? "This is different—it's something she and I can do together. She'll make them and I'll handle the business end. Your grandfather knows the right people to help us get started. He says folks will pay good money to buy them."

She paused, giving in to the one nagging worry she had about the scheme. "Do you really think that's true? He wasn't just being nice, was he?"

"Your sister's cakes are fabulous. I think people will line up to buy as many as she can produce."

It was going to work! Impulsively Josie threw herself at him, wrapping her arms around his neck in an enthusiastic hug. "Oh Ry, this is so exciting. Everything is finally coming together."

He held her, his warm breath tickling her neck, his arms a safe harbor. A moment later Josie pulled away, her cheeks warming. "I'm sorry, I—"

He touched her face with the back of his hand, smiling that crooked smile she found so endearing. "Don't you dare spoil a perfectly good hug with an apology. I've been wanting to do that myself for some time now."

He took her hand and drew her to the sofa. "And there's something else I've wanted to do for a while—something I need to ask you."

Josie's heart fluttered. There was a banked intensity in his gaze, a promise shining there that sent an anticipatory shiver through her.

He angled his body toward her, their knees nearly touching. "I realize we haven't known each other very long, but it's been more than enough time for me to know my heart. And lately I've had reason to hope you return some portion of my affection."

More than "some portion." Much more.

"I know you've always had your heart set on traveling the world, but—"

She touched a finger to his lips. "I don't need to see it all right away." The past few days, contemplating her life without

Ry in it, had taught her that dreams could change, evolve. It wouldn't be such a sacrifice to make Philadelphia her world, at least for now. She could take time to explore it in detail, to truly savor each experience, experiences made all the sweeter by having Ry and Viola at her side.

And unlike Knotty Pine, Philadelphia was close to other, interesting, exciting places. They could take the occasional trek along the coast from here.

Even Aunt Pearl couldn't find much to fault with that.

She saw the flare of relief—and something deeper—in Ry's expression, and knew she'd made the right choice.

Then he went down on one knee and her heart threatened to pound its way clear out of her chest.

"Josephine Wylie," his deep, strong voice sent a thrumming deep inside of her, "would you do me the very great honor of agreeing to be my wife?"

The joy surging through her was almost overwhelming. "Oh, Ry, yes."

Between one heartbeat and the next he was beside her again, pulling her to him in a fierce hug. Then he took her face between his hands and leaned in to kiss her.

This kiss was different from the first—this one spoke of claiming and being claimed, of a future together, and of the rightness of this moment.

When at last they parted, Josie rested against the crook of his arm with a contented sigh. "I never thought I could be so happy."

He squeezed her shoulder. "I promise to do everything I can to make certain you stay this happy."

She glanced up, meeting his gaze. "Everything has come together so well. You can't help but see God's hand in all of it."

"Amen."

Josie gave a contented sigh. "We're going to be so happy

here. You can continue to work in your grandfather's law practice, and I can sell Cora Beth's fruitcakes so the family won't miss the income from the livery."

She felt Ry stiffen, felt his subtle withdrawal. Had she said something wrong?

He pushed away from her just enough to stare into her eyes. "You don't understand," he said slowly. "I'm not planning to stay in Philadelphia."

Josie blinked, feeling her brow furrow. Surely she hadn't heard right. "What?"

"I don't want to make our home here." His tone was firmer, as if he could convince her he was making sense just by sounding more assured.

She shrugged out of his embrace. "You decided on Hawk's Creek?"

"No."

Hope mingled with the confusion in her mind. Somewhere else then. A new place. "Where—"

He took her hand. "Josie, I want to settle in Knotty Pine."

No! She hadn't heard right. He had to be pulling her leg. But he looked so serious... "Knotty Pine?"

His earnest expression seemed to beg her to understand. "All this time I've been trying to decide between Philadelphia and Hawk's Creek. It was like trying to choose between Grandfather, and Griff and Sadie, between being a lawyer and being a horse breeder." He spread his hands. "It never occurred to me, until I talked to Viola this morning, that there were other options, that there was a way to live a fuller life."

"But Knotty Pine?" She pulled her hand away from his and stood. "You have the whole world to choose from."

He stood, watching her pace. "Viola likes it there. She misses Audrey and the rest of your family. And I think she's more comfortable in a small town than in a city like this. As for me," he paused, as if gathering his thoughts, "well, I like the idea of a fresh start. And I like Knotty Pine and the people there just fine."

Easy for him to say, he'd already seen something of the world.

"Most importantly, though, is that I want Viola to have family close by while she's growing up."

She stilled. "You don't have family in Knotty Pine."

He smiled. "Oh, but I do. Someone once said family isn't restricted to the folks you're kin to. Viola reminded me of that again today. That wonderful, eccentric, generous household who resides at the Knotty Pine Boardinghouse is very much family. They—you—took me in and made me feel welcome. You all cared for first me and then Viola, accepting us for who we are, and generously welcoming us into your midst. That's the kind of people I want in my life and in Viola's life."

He stepped closer. "But it won't be complete unless you're one of those people."

She raised her hands, palms out. "Stop! I finally have a chance to taste what I've been dreaming of my whole life. I was even willing to compromise, to set down roots *here*. It's not fair of you to ask me to go back to the life I had before."

"But—"

"No!" She wouldn't take the chance that he would talk her into this ridiculous scheme. "Starting this business means I won't be chained to the livery any more." It was her turn to reach for his hands. "Don't you understand? I'm willing to give up my desire to travel, to settle down *here* with you and Viola."

His jaw worked. "But not in Knotty Pine."

She squeezed his hands, trying to let her determination flow through to him. "Have you really thought this through? Are you ready to give up lawyering? There's not enough business in all of Knotty Pine to keep even one lawyer busy full time."

"I don't plan to be a full-time lawyer. Sure, I'll open an office and be available to anyone who needs my services. But I intend to find a suitable piece of land and move my stable from Hawk's Creek."

She dropped his hands, feeling suddenly brittle as glass. "So, you have it all figured out so you can have everything you ever wanted."

"I was hoping it would be what we both wanted."

She turned away. "You were wrong."

There was a long moment of silence.

"Yes, I suppose I was," he finally said.

The heaviness in his voice tore at her and she turned back around. Surely they could get through this, could still find a way to make it work.

But his expression was closed, remote. "Will you at least be returning with us for Christmas?"

He was still leaving? "Does what I want mean so little to you? Can't we take some time, see if we can make it work *here*?"

His jaw tightened. "If it was just me, I would say yes. But I have Viola to think about now, and while she'd adjust, I don't think she'd be truly happy here. I won't compromise her happiness for my own." His gaze intensified. "Don't ever doubt, not even for one minute, that your happiness is important to me. That's why I'm not going to press you any further to come with us."

Her stomach churned. "When are you leaving?"

"The day after tomorrow. You didn't answer me—will you come with us?"

Just like that, he and Viola would be out of her life. "Your grandfather thinks I should spend Christmas here." She traced the scrollwork on the mantle with her finger. "The holidays will be the best time to get folks interested in buying the fruitcakes." She jutted out her chin. "Of course, I plan to go back for a visit after the new year."

A muscle in his jaw jumped. "I see." He gave her a short bow. "If you'll excuse me, I have some business to attend to."

Josie stared at the door after Ry left, wondering for a moment if she'd made the right choice.

He'd proposed, for goodness sake. This wonderful, generous, God-fearing, more-stubborn-than-a-balky-mule man had gotten down on one knee and asked for her hand. He'd looked at her with such love in his eyes that just remembering it was almost her undoing.

She did love him, more than she'd ever believed possible. And Viola too. So much so that the thought of being separated for a long period from them was like being kicked in the gut.

But he'd asked too much of her. Why couldn't he have met her halfway? She'd spent her whole life putting the needs of other folks first. It was finally time to think of herself.

So why did it feel so awful?

Josie sank down onto the sofa, crossing her arms over her chest, trying to hold the hurt inside. *Dear Father, give me the strength to get through this. You've taken me so far on the road to achieving my dream, opened so many doors to me that I never even imagined existed. Help me to see the good in this too and not focus on the things I can't have.*

She buried her face in her arms and let the tears flow.

Ry went straight from the parlor to his grandfather's study.

"Well, hello, my boy. I didn't realize you were home."

"I've come to let you know Viola and I are leaving for Knotty Pine in two days."

His grandfather raised a brow. "Not Miss Wylie?"

"Miss Wylie has decided, based on your advice, I believe, that it would be best for her new business venture to remain here for now in order to establish herself."

Grandfather nodded. "She has a fine head on her shoulders, that one. I can see why you're so taken with her." He leaned back. "But if she's decided to stay here through the holidays, surely there's no need for you and Viola to leave."

"You misunderstood. We're not returning to Knotty Pine merely to spend Christmas. I plan to establish a permanent residence there."

His grandfather stiffened. "You can't be serious."

"I assure you, sir, I've never been more serious in my life."

"Ry, think about what you're doing. How can you throw away your career, the connections you've established, to bury yourself in some backwater town that won't appreciate your talents?" He narrowed his eyes. "You're making the same mistake your mother made, and look what happened to her."

Ry was done tiptoeing around that particular issue. "What happened to her, sir, is that she lived fully and joyously, at the side of a man she loved and who loved her deeply. She bore three children and did her best to instill in each of them a spirit of self-confidence, integrity and grace."

Remembering he was talking about his grandfather's only child, Ry tempered his tone. "The fact that she died young is something that grieves me as much as it does you. But I truly believe she wouldn't have traded the life she had for even one extra day on this earth."

His grandfather's face reddened alarmingly. "Are you saying she preferred that uncivilized, heathen outpost to life with me?"

"I'm saying she wasn't afraid to leave the comforts of home to embrace the life she wanted. And that I aim to follow her example."

With that, Ry turned on his heel and left the room.

And then the irony struck him. Josie, in her own way, was attempting to do the very same thing. He rubbed his jaw as some of the anger drained from him. She had a right to pursue the life she believed would bring her the most joy, even if he didn't agree with her choice.

Still, he couldn't help but mourn the loss of the life they could have built together.

Josie shifted in her chair as the second course was served. She'd thought about pleading a headache and having dinner in her room, but she'd never taken the coward's way out, and she didn't aim to start now.

For Viola's sake she tried to pretend all was well, as did Ry. But the girl sensed something was wrong and it didn't take her long to figure out just what was at the heart of the matter.

"Aunt Josie, aren't you coming back to Knotty Pine with us?"

She gave Viola a regretful smile, doing her best to avoid direct eye contact with Ry. "Not right away, sweetie. I have some business to take care of here in Philadelphia."

"She's going to keep me company," Mr. Wallace added. "I'll get mighty lonely with you and your Uncle Ry gone."

"Oh." Viola chewed on her lip, then nodded.

Ry speared a piece of potato with his fork. "So what are your plans for the livery? Sell it?"

It was the first comment he'd directed her way all evening. "I couldn't do that," she responded. "I always planned for Danny to take it over when he got old enough."

Ry raised a brow. "Are you sure that's what *he* wants?"

Josie was taken aback by the question. "Of course. I mean, it's what we planned, even before Pa passed on." But had Danny ever said it was what he wanted? She couldn't remember.

Ry let that question go and returned to his original one. "If you're not planning to sell it, and you're not coming back to run it, then what *are* you planning? Surely you don't think Danny's ready to take it on by himself yet."

Was he baiting her? "Of course not. He needs to stay in school."

"Actually," Mr. Wallace intervened, "I suggested she take on a partner, someone who's willing to run the place and split the profits with her."

"I see." Ry nodded. "So the family continues to receive a stream of income, even if somewhat reduced."

"Yes." She felt a need to explain, to make him see that she knew what she was doing. "But there'll be one less mouth to feed, and there'll soon be an additional source of income from the new business."

"Have you got someone in mind?"

"I have some ideas. I—"

"Let me make this easy for you. *I'll* be your partner."

She dropped her wrists to the table. "You don't have to do that." Was he offering her charity?

"I know I don't have to. I want to. And this has nothing to do with you."

Josie hoped her flinch didn't show.

"Once I have my stable established, I'll want to make certain the bridle shop is well run."

"You're planning to work there yourself?"

"You doubt I could do it?"

He was twisting her words. "Of course not. I just thought—"

"At any rate, that'll be my worry, not yours. Do we have a deal?"

"If you're sure that's what you want."

He nodded. "I'll draw up the papers tonight and establish

an account at a bank here in town. The initial funds will be transferred before I leave."

Josie didn't know how to respond so she merely nodded. The sound of Mr. Wallace clearing his throat reminded her they weren't alone. She pasted on a smile and turned to Viola. "Aren't the carrots flavorful tonight?"

Viola nodded, but Josie didn't miss the troubled look she gave both her and Ry.

Ry pulled off his boot and tossed it across the room, mentally berating himself. How could he have let his temper get the best of him at dinner tonight? Especially in front of Viola. It was unforgivable.

He pulled off the other boot and set it aside. At least he'd partially redeemed himself. By getting Josie to agree to his becoming her partner in the livery, he now had a legitimate reason to keep an eye on the Wylie household and a way to know Josie had enough money to see her through the next few months.

He scrubbed a hand across his face. Why couldn't Josie see what she was giving up? Didn't she realize what a treasure she had in her family, how much he envied her their closeness? Her decision was not only short-sighted, but hurtful to the family she was leaving behind.

His grandfather was using her own dreams, and her sympathy toward his alone-in-the-world state, to manipulate her. Maybe the man wasn't doing it consciously or maliciously, but it was happening nonetheless.

The thing was, the man had no one to blame for that aloneness but himself. He'd never once invited Griff or Sadie to visit, had never made an effort, with that one eventful exception, to travel to Texas to visit them.

The man wanted family around him, but on his own terms. But he could never explain that to Josie—it was something she'd have to learn for herself. He just didn't understand why such a normally sharp woman hadn't figured it out already.

Ry paused in the act of unbuttoning his shirt.

Hadn't he allowed himself to be manipulated in the same way?

Is this how Griff had felt? Betrayed and disappointed? Had his father gone to his grave believing Ry preferred what his grandfather had to offer over the legacy he'd built with his own hands?

Ry moved to the window, leaning one arm against the frame, staring unseeing at the night sky.

He owed Josie an apology. She wasn't making the choice he'd wanted her to, she wasn't even making the choice he believed would make her happy. But she was staying true to her dream, standing up for herself, the same way he'd stood up to his grandfather this afternoon.

And, if he *really* loved her, he should trust her and not try to make her feel miserable for doing it.

Still, he couldn't help but mourn the loss of the life they could have built together.

While he was being so honest with himself, he might as well admit that Josie wasn't the only one he owed an apology to. In fact, he owed Griff much more than an apology. He hoped Viola wouldn't mind a slight delay in their return to Knotty Pine, because a stopover at Hawk's Creek was definitely in order.

Father, forgive my arrogance and the hurts I've inflicted on others, both the deliberate and the negligent. Help me exhibit the patience and humility I'll need in order to mend fences with Griff. And most of all, look after Josie, help her find the happiness and fulfillment she seeks, wherever that may be.

Josie's pulse jumped as the train whistle sounded. The bitter cold she felt came as much from inside her as from the weather.

Ry set down his bag and took her hand, staring deep into her eyes. "I want you to know, while I don't agree with your decision, I understand about needing to follow your dreams. I wish you nothing but the best and will be praying every day that you find what you're looking for."

"Ry, I'm so sor—"

He touched a finger to her lips. "I know. It's okay. And don't worry about Cora Beth and the others—I'll keep an eye on them."

She nodded, doing her best to swallow the lump in her throat. "Thank you."

He squeezed her hand. "Just please, if you ever change your mind, don't let your pride, or anything else for that matter," he glanced toward his grandfather, "get in your way."

The whistle sounded again and Josie bent down to give Viola one last fierce hug while Ry shook his grandfather's hand. "Take care of your Uncle Ry for me, okay?" she whispered in the child's ear.

Viola nodded. "I wish you were coming with us."

"Don't worry, sweetie, I'll be back for a visit real soon. And I'll write lots of letters."

"Time to go." Ry lifted Viola with one hand and within seconds the two of them had disappeared inside the train.

Josie pulled her cloak tighter across her chest, shivering as she watched the train pull out of the station. Up until this very moment she'd thought—hoped—Ry would change his mind and decide to stay.

"Don't worry, my dear." Grandfather Wallace patted her arm. "That boy loves you—it's obvious to anyone with eyes in his head. He'll see the light and come back to you."

Josie smiled, but her heart wasn't in it. Somehow, she didn't feel as confident as he did.

Chapter Twenty-Seven

❧

"You did a marvelous job selecting a tree." Cora Beth held the door open while Ry and Danny dragged in the large fir.

"Thank you, ma'am." Ry let down his end and rolled his shoulders. "But I just did the chopping. The kids picked it out." And with each of them eyeing a different specimen it took quite a bit of finesse to steer them to one everyone could agree on.

"Well, then, good job everyone." She clapped her hands the way a schoolmarm would. "Girls, while Mr. Lassiter and Danny set the tree up in the parlor, you can help me get down the box of decorations." She gave Ry and Danny a stern look. "And see that you mind my carpets."

Ry turned to Danny, flexing his muscles with exaggerated display. "You heard the lady. We have work to do."

While working together at the livery and sharing some of the heavier chores around the boardinghouse, he and the boy had developed a close relationship. Ry found himself teaching Danny some of the things his own father had taught him.

Like how to handle an ax properly and how to fix loose shingles on the roof. Like how to select the best rocks for skimming across a pond and how to tell a dog's tracks from a fox's. Like how a man looked out for those in his care and how important a man's word was.

But for today, they were merely two menfolk exchanging indulgent expressions while following orders from their womenfolk.

Twenty minutes later the tree was standing tall and proud in the parlor and the box of ornaments had been ceremoniously opened. Sitting on the very top was a stack of paper snowflakes, some looking fairly new, others yellowed with age.

"It's a family tradition," Cora Beth explained. "Each of us has our own special snowflake that we hang on the tree every year."

Audrey lifted the elaborately cut paper decorations out of the box. "We each get one of these our very first Christmas," she explained. "It has our name and the day we were born written right on it."

She lifted one from the stack. "See, this one's mine."

Cora Beth fetched two similar decorations from the mantle. "I hope you don't mind," she told Ry, "but I made one for you and Viola last night. I thought, since this is your first Christmas here and you're like part of the family now, it was only fitting."

Ry saw Viola's face light up and offered Cora Beth his heartfelt thanks.

"Think nothing of it. The tree will look the nicer for the addition." She handed them the lacy bits of paper. "Now, let me get you something to write with."

As Ry added his name and birth date to the center of the snowflake, he noted that five of the ones taken from the box remained on the table, unclaimed. One of them would be Josie's.

Was she missing this or any of the other holiday traditions her family celebrated? The tree at his grandfather's was more grand but the trimming of it much less personal than this little ceremony.

Still, spending Christmas with Josie would have made even

the most sterile of decorations shine. He couldn't believe how much he missed her, how many times he had a thought he wanted to share, a decision he wanted her opinion on. Would the hole she'd left in his life ever heal?

Cora Beth brought his thoughts back to the present as she gathered up the leftovers. "All right now. Pippa, I believe this is your year to hang the star on the top, so we'll let Lottie hang your father's snowflake. Audrey, you can take Grandma Emma's and Danny, you take Grandpa Bert's. I'll take Aunt Pearl's." She held up the last one and her smile drooped for a second. Then she turned to Viola. "Would you like to hang Jo's for her?"

Viola nodded, accepting the somewhat rumpled decoration with the care one would afford a fragile piece of crystal.

"All right then, let's get the snowflakes up and then we'll tackle the rest of these."

Once the snowflakes were duly hung, the rest of the tree trimming took place with a great deal of playful teasing. Danny and Audrey argued over whose snowflake showed to the best advantage. Pippa and Lottie tended to place any ornaments they hung at the very bottom of the tree and called foul whenever anyone tried to rearrange them. Viola placed her ornaments with a precision that earned her her own share of teasing.

And the adults were encouraged to admire the youngsters' handiwork, and listen to them as they shared bits of stories that had become part of the history of each ornament—the lacy dragonfly that Cora Beth had made for Uncle Grover, the silver rattle that had been found in Danny's belongings, a clay angel that had gotten chipped when Audrey dropped it four years ago, a small wooden train engine Josie had purchased from a tinker when she was twelve.

That last sent Ry's thoughts in a direction he had to force himself to turn back from.

When it came time for Pippa to place the star at the top, Ry was enlisted to lift her up.

"Isn't it beautiful?" Audrey asked.

"I have something I'd like to add, if it's okay," Viola offered tentatively.

"Why of course, dear." Cora Beth gave her an encouraging smile. "It's your tree too."

Viola took Ry's hand. "I need to get something from Ma's trunk."

"All right." Ry led her upstairs and into his room. She went immediately to the trunk and, after a few minutes of rummaging around, pulled out a battered hatbox. "Here it is."

Curious, Ry followed her back to the parlor.

"What's that?" Audrey asked.

Viola opened the box, to reveal a rough-hewn wooden nativity set. She lifted out the figure of Joseph. "My pa made these before I was born. Every year at Christmas, we would set them out under our tree."

"How lovely." Cora Beth fingered one of the pieces. "Your pa was very talented."

"Can I help set it up?" Audrey asked.

Ry watched the two girls with heads bent together, adjusting the pieces until they thought each one was placed just right.

How could Josie possibly want to trade this away for some other life?

Josie walked downstairs, feeling out of sorts this morning and not quite sure why.

The business was going well—almost too well. She'd already had requests for more cakes than Cora Beth could possibly produce. Ry's grandfather had counseled her not to be afraid to turn down orders. It gave the product a feeling of rarity, he'd said, of exclusivity, that would only add to the demand for it.

But he also advised her to write to Cora Beth and work out how they might increase production in the future. Once their reputation was set, it would be good business to take advantage of at least a portion of that increased demand.

And she'd had another new experience this week—snow. Not the dusting of flakes they sometimes got back home, but a true, piled high, sink your feet into, perfect for making snowballs, snowfall. Her first thought had been how much Danny and the girls would enjoy playing in it. Grandfather Wallace had listened to her chatter excitedly about it with a sort of amused tolerance for the first few minutes, but then returned to reading his paper.

So she'd gone out by herself, finding a few of the neighbor's children outside to share her enjoyment. Which was fine, really. She'd always known, once she was able to travel, that she'd look to the locals for company.

So why wasn't she happier about how things were going? She was just at loose ends, she supposed.

Josie stepped into the parlor, then halted on the threshold. A large tree was set up by the window, decorated with beautiful glass ornaments. Cora Beth would love their fragile beauty and the gaily colored ribbons all tied in perfect bows. The girls would "ooh" and "ahh" over the gilded angels. And wouldn't Danny just love the tin soldiers?

There was no popcorn garland hung on this tree. Instead it was draped in strings of pearl-like beads.

Who had set it up? And when?

The housekeeper appeared in the doorway. "Good morning, Miss. Mr. Wallace asked me to inform you that he would be down shortly to join you for breakfast."

"Thank you, Mrs. Hopkins." She halted the woman's exit with a raised hand. "By the way, I was just admiring the tree."

"Yes, Miss. Quite lovely, isn't it?"

"Very pretty. Who decorated it?"

"Why, me and the rest of the staff, just like always. We did it early this morning."

"And who picked out the tree?"

"Mr. Nichols, same as usual."

"Well, you all did a wonderful job."

The woman gave her a bright smile. "Thank you. I'll be sure to tell Agnes and Nichols you said so."

Josie studied the tree again, feeling deflated. She supposed every family had their own traditions. But this seemed so impersonal, so…empty. There was no searching until you found the perfect tree. No teasing as you hung the ornaments. No reminiscing over Christmases past. *No sharing.*

She supposed they'd put up the tree at home—after all, it was only six days until Christmas. Had Danny cut it this year? He was certainly old enough to handle the job. She'd probably have turned it over to him soon enough anyway.

This would be Ry and Viola's first Christmas together. How were they doing? She felt a soul-deep longing to be there to share it with them.

Cora Beth had said in her letter that they were staying at the boardinghouse for now, but that Ry had started laying the groundwork for his own place. Things seemed to be moving along nicely without her.

"There you are, my dear. Sorry to keep you waiting." Mr. Wallace looked past her. "Ah, I see the tree is up. What do you think of it?"

"It's quite impressive."

He seemed pleased with her answer. "Glad you like it.

"I hear you had a busy day yesterday," he commented as he escorted her in to breakfast.

"Yes, sir. I've actually turned away several orders."

"What did I tell you? The cake practically sells itself."

"I'll admit, the price you advised me to set seemed mighty steep for a cake. I wasn't sure anyone would order it for that sum."

"You must put a high value on your product if you expect others to do likewise."

She pushed the food around on her plate, feeling at loose ends. "I find myself free today."

"I'll tell Nichols to put the carriage at your disposal. Perhaps you can visit some of the shops on State Street."

Not the answer she'd hoped for. She tried a different topic. "How do you usually spend Christmas day?"

"Well, we'll attend church services first. Then afterward the Havershams have invited us to join them for their Christmas dinner and the Caldecotts have asked us to stop by for a small evening gathering."

"Don't you have your own holiday traditions?"

He gave her an indulgent smile. "Sentimentality is not my strong suit, I'm afraid. But if you'd like to host a holiday gathering, I can get Mrs. Hopkins to help with the preparations."

That wasn't at all what she'd been thinking. Besides, she didn't really know anyone here. "No, no, it was just idle talk."

"As you wish. But speaking of Christmas, the Havershams are a bit stuffy I'm afraid, but Joseph Haversham has been a faithful client for thirty years, so I wouldn't dream of offending him. And as for Charles Caldecott…"

Josie listened with half an ear as he talked about the two households they would spend Christmas with. After breakfast, he headed directly to his office. Not wanting to face that too-perfect tree again, she bypassed the parlor and returned to her room.

She stood at the window, staring at the snow-covered street. Perhaps she would visit Independence Square today, or maybe the market. She felt the urge to be outdoors, to see trees and breathe fresh air, even cold and damp as it was.

A passerby stepped onto a patch of ice and waved his arms, barely avoiding a fall. It put her in mind of the afternoon in Eastwick Park. Closing her eyes she recalled the invigorating feel of skimming across the ice with Ry holding her safe at his side.

Maybe she'd go back there today, practice up so that the next time Ry—

She stared at her reflection in the glass, studying the unhappy-looking stranger staring back at her. There wouldn't be a next time with Ry. And skating alone held no appeal for her.

Josie plopped down on her bed as she had a sudden, sickening moment of clarity. What had she done?

Heavenly Father, I'm an ungrateful wretch. Here You've given me all I asked for, and I'm still unhappy. I just never realized how lonely I would be. Maybe I'm not as much like Aunt Pearl as I thought. Because I finally figured out what Ry meant when he said it's not where you are so much as who you're with.

Your word says You have plans for us, plans to give us hope and a future. So I'm figuring that maybe Your plans included me learning this lesson. Trouble is, now that I've figured it out, I don't know what to do about it. I already threw Ry's proposal back in his face so I'm the last person he wants back in his life. And Cora Beth and the others are probably not real happy with me, either. My showing up in Knotty Pine right now would be plumb awkward for everyone.

So You see my puzzlement. Please help me figure out the right thing to do.

Chapter Twenty-Eight

Ry watched as Cora Beth settled everyone around the tree. They'd just returned from the church service and the children were eyeing the stack of presents with more than mild anticipation. He smiled at the glow in Viola's face. She was thriving here, in the middle of this warm, loving family. Thriving in a way she never would have in his grandfather's home or at the ranch.

This was how Christmas had been celebrated when his mother was still alive—everyone gathered in the parlor, laughing, exchanging gifts, bursting with anticipation and excitement. He didn't realize how much he'd missed this kind of interaction, how big a hole it had left in his life, until now.

At least he and Griff had started the healing process. He and Viola had stopped off and spent a day at Hawk's Creek on their way back to Knotty Pine.

He'd ridden out alone with Griff and they'd talked about a lot of things—about cattle and horses and the weather.

Then Ry had talked about that first year with his grandfather, how he'd come to make the decisions he had, how that had affected everything he touched from then on. He hadn't tried to gloss over any of it, hadn't made excuses or tried to place blame. And he'd apologized to Griff.

Afterward, when they were all together again, Ry had started talking about the good memories he had of their mother. Before long, Griff and Sadie had joined in with memories of their own. And they'd found themselves laughing in a way they hadn't in years.

The breach hadn't been completely healed when he and Viola left—it had been there too long for that. But they'd made a start and Ry was confident that he and his brother would become friends again.

Pippa handed him a package, bringing Ry's attention back to the here and now.

According to Wylie family tradition, each person in turn, starting with the youngest, handed out the presents they were giving the others. Once Pippa sat, everyone tore into their gifts.

The youngest of the clan had drawn pictures for everyone— his was of a stick man chopping down a large, oddly shaped tree.

Lottie handed hers out next—cutouts of paper butterflies for the female family members and paper snails for the males.

Audrey gave each person penny candy. She'd selected licorice whips for him.

Viola, whom he'd helped shop for everyone else in the room, gave him a wooden carving of a horse. Had Josie helped her select this?

Danny gave him a belt he'd made himself from strips of leather at the bridle shop.

As he added Danny's gift to the pile at his side, Ry heard the distant wail of the train whistle. He glanced at the little red engine hanging on the tree.

How was Josie faring with her first big-city Christmas? Was she enjoying the parties? The elegant decorations and sumptuous foods? Was she exploring Philadelphia, planning excursions to nearby cities?

Had she found the happiness she'd sought?

"She'll come around."

Ry looked up to find Cora Beth standing in front of him, holding out a package.

"What do you mean?"

"Just what I said, she'll come around. Josie can be mighty stubborn sometimes, but she's a smart girl."

He smiled, touched by her attempt to reassure him. "I'm sure things will turn out just as they ought." What he wasn't certain of was if he'd be happy with that outcome.

She handed him the package. "Here, this is for you."

Ry opened the gift to find an intricately stitched sampler, the center of which read Home Sweet Home.

She smiled. "I thought you could hang it in your new home, once you move in."

How many hours had she spent stitching this? Did she blame him at all for taking her sister away? "Thank you. This was mighty thoughtful." He stood. "Now, it's my turn."

He reached under the tree and pulled out a stack of packages. He'd purchased some of the gifts in Philadelphia—a steel-handled magnifying glass for Uncle Grover, a new pocketknife for Danny, and multicolored hair ribbons for Audrey. But the others he'd made himself. For Cora Beth he'd made a bookstand suitable for holding her husband's family Bible, and for each of the twins he'd made building blocks in various sizes and shapes.

It had felt good to do it. When he was growing up they'd always made gifts for each other at Christmas. Somehow, though, as he'd gotten older, it had just become easier to purchase something.

For Viola he'd done both. He'd bought her a brass flute from a music shop in Philadelphia and he'd made a carved wooden box to put it in. Cora Beth had helped him, taking care of the satin lining inside. And because he knew it would mean something to Viola, he even made a new collar for Daffy, complete with a small silver bell at the throat.

He looked down at the last parcel, the one that contained Josie's gift. He should've shipped it to Philadelphia, but somehow he'd hoped—

"Looks like I missed most of the fun." Ry's head snapped up at that sound of that oh-so-familiar voice.

"Josie!"

He wasn't certain which of the girls squealed her name the loudest.

Suddenly there was bedlam as everyone scrambled to their feet.

Everyone but him. He couldn't move, couldn't take his eyes off her. She looked beautiful. Cheeks red from the cold, a slight breathlessness emphasizing the rise and fall of her chest, the green and gold of her traveling suit enhancing the sparkle of her eyes. And it was those eyes that held him captive, those eyes that seemed to be saying something only to him.

Then she dropped her parcels as she was mobbed, everyone eager to welcome her home, everyone full of questions about what had changed her mind.

He'd like to know the answer to that one himself.

Josie attempted to answer them over the din, but her gaze remained fixed on his.

Ry slowly stood but didn't approach her, afraid to move in case he'd just conjured her image from his wayward thoughts.

Finally, Cora Beth got everyone's attention. "I know we're all excited to see Jo, but let's give her a chance to catch her breath."

Josie gave a nervous laugh, still not looking away from him.

"Sorry I didn't give y'all more warning. It was a sudden decision and I was so anxious to get the earliest train out of Philadelphia, there was barely time to think everything through."

Why had she come? How long did she plan to stay? The questions tumbled through his mind but still he held his peace.

"We're just glad you're here to spend Christmas with us." Cora Beth gave her sister a hug. Then she stepped aside and looked from Josie to Ry and back again. "Children, let's go check on that goose I have in the oven. Uncle Grover, I could use your help as well."

Her maneuvering was a bit heavy-handed, but at this point Ry didn't care. He tried to keep his expectations in check, to simply enjoy the moment. She'd probably just come home for the holidays.

Stop just staring at her and say something. "So, you decided to spend Christmas with your family after all."

She nodded, then wet her lips. "I hear you bought the old Rodgers place and are building a house."

His turn to nod. "I hope to have everything ready by the first of the year. Though Viola is going to miss living here."

"Sounds like you're serious about sticking around here."

"The town has a lot to recommend it." But not nearly as much as when she'd been a part of it. When were they going to get past these inanities? "I even bought the Boggins Building to use as my law office."

"Any clients yet?"

He shook his head. "No, but I only put out my sign two days ago." *Enough of this. Ask her.* "So, how long do you plan to stay around?"

"That depends."

He fisted his hands at his sides in an effort to keep them from reaching for her. "On what?"

Josie's insides fluttered. This was it. Time to make herself vulnerable. She'd never been so scared in her life. "On how long you want me to stay."

Ry stared at her for a long minute, not saying a word. Her senses were suddenly so acute it hurt. She heard the dishes rattling in the kitchen, heard the wind whooshing in rhythmic puffs that rattled the window panes, heard the sound of her own heartbeat. The smell of pine and roast goose and silver polish assailed her nostrils, making her want to sneeze. But mostly it was her vision that threatened to overwhelm her as she stared straight into his eyes, his pewter-gray, honest, beautiful eyes.

Why wasn't he saying anything?

Then suddenly he was across the room, taking her in his arms. "If that's the case," he whispered huskily in her ear, "then you're never leaving."

She threw her arms round his neck, wanting to laugh and cry at the same time. "Oh, Ry, I'm so sorry, I should have listened to you, should never have—"

"Shh. No more of that. You figured things out a lot quicker than I ever did." Then he disengaged her arms from his neck and led her to the sofa. He seated her but remained standing himself. "Are you absolutely certain this is what you want? No regrets?"

"Absolutely." She took his hand and pulled him down beside her. "Oh, Ry, you were so right—the finest place in the world is empty and lonely without the people you love to share it with. When it snowed, I wanted Danny and the girls to play in it with me. When I tasted something new and exotic, I wanted Cora Beth to have a bite as well. When I visited the Academy of Natural Sciences, I wanted Uncle Grover to show me around and explain what I was looking at."

She touched his cheek, savoring again the rough, masculine

feel of it. "And there wasn't a place I visited that I didn't wish you and Viola were there beside me to share it."

He pulled her to him again. "Your wish is my command."

Several minutes later, he popped up and marched to the tree, returning with a large package.

"What's this?" she asked.

"Your Christmas present. Open it."

She gave him a curious look, then unwrapped the package. When she lifted the lid her lips formed an *O* of surprise.

With his help, she lifted out the desk globe. "Oh, Ry it's beautiful."

"There's something else."

She peered inside the box and pulled out another, smaller box that rattled when she shook it. What in the world…

Opening it, she found several dozen colorful tacks. Her gaze flew to his.

"I don't want you to give up your dreams completely, Josie," he said solemnly. "This is my real gift to you. Every year, you get to stick one tack in the globe—wherever you want—and we'll plan a trip there."

Tears welled up in her eyes. "Oh, Ry, I don't deserve this."

"Probably not."

His words caught her off guard, until she saw his grin. A relieved chuckle bubbled out of her.

"But it's the only thing I have," he continued, "so you'll just have to take it."

She threw her arms around him again, and this time refused to let go.

"Merry Christmas, Josie," he whispered. "And welcome home."

* * * * *

Dear Reader,

Thank you so much for taking the time to read Ry and Josie's story. I always enjoy the challenge of starting with two people who seem very different and taking them on a journey that shows ultimately how perfect they are for each other.

As always, this story started with a few "what if" questions. What if a man crossed the county to come to the aid a childhood friend and was somehow delayed until it was too late? And then what if he found he had been named guardian to the child of this now deceased friend, a child he never knew existed? Once I had the hero identified, I needed to find a heroine who would challenge him on all levels.

Where Ry was well-to-do and polished, Josie was not only working class, but worked at a job normally held by men. Where Ry was disconnected from his family, Josie's world revolved around her family. And where Ry had reached a point in his life where he was ready to set down roots, Josie was looking forward to the day when she could fly free.

Bringing these two to their happily-ever-after offered a number of challenges, but I hope you enjoyed following their often bumpy journey as much as I enjoyed writing it.

Wishing you love and blessings,

Winnie Griggs

QUESTIONS FOR DISCUSSION

1. In the opening scene Ry mistakes Josie for a man. Did this seem believable to you? Did you feel his subsequent discomfort over this, given Josie didn't realize he'd made the mistake, overdone or in character for the kind of man he was?

2. Did you feel Josie's decision to follow Ry and the two bushwhackers was wholly motivated by concern for his well-being or was there a touch of adventure-seeking to it as well?

3. During the ambush, both Ry and Josie took great personal risks in order to save the other. Did you find this brave and believable? Or foolhardy and over-the-top? Did you think either was more heroic than the other? Why or why not?

4. After the ambush, Ry was torn between his duty to Belle and his duty to Josie, and frustration that he was not in a position to help either of them. Have you ever been caught between two equally urgent needs and forced to make a choice? How did you finally decide?

5. Josie's desire to travel and see the world stemmed from a childhood admiration for a favorite aunt and a wish to follow in her footsteps. Have there been people in your life who helped shape your dreams? In what way?

6. Josie was certain that the heavenly Father was arranging matters to help her achieve her long-held dream of traveling the world. Do you think she was wrong to believe

this? Do you think God uses situations such as these to help us see matters more clearly?

7. Did the fact that Ry struggled so much trying to figure out where he wanted to settle down make him seem indecisive, torn or thoughtful?

8. Both Ry and Josie thought Viola's sudden insertion into Ry's life made it imperative for him to find a wife, but they each had a different take on who that wife should be. Do you think they were both being true to themselves in their thought process, at least at first? How about later?

9. Josie felt very strongly that holidays were a time for gathering with family and friends, and couldn't understand Ry's seemingly more impersonal take. How big a part of your holiday experience is having your family and friends around to help you celebrate?

10. There was a disconnect between Ry and his siblings. While he didn't like it, he didn't know how to correct it. Have you ever been in a similar situation? How did you get through it?

11. Did you feel that Cora Beth was doing a bit of matchmaking of her own? If so, how effective do you feel her efforts were?

12. Viola and Audrey formed an immediate and very strong bond. How realistic do you think this was? Do you think children form these sorts of attachments easier than adults?

13. Did you feel Josie's emotional about-face the morning after the kiss was in character for her? Were her reasons

and thought process logical given her personality and long-term dreams?

14. Was it unreasonable of Ry to ask Josie to make do with the one taste of travel she had and then settle back down in Knotty Pine? Or was he being perceptive in understanding what would truly make her happy and fulfilled?

15. Was Josie's ultimate recognition of what was most meaningful in her life a believable transformation?

When a young Roman woman is wrenched from the safety of her family and sold into slavery, she finds herself at the mercy of the most famous gladiator in Rome. In God's plan, a master and his slave just might fall in love....

Turn the page for a sneak preview of
THE GLADIATOR
by Carla Capshaw
Available in November 2009
from Love Inspired® Historical

Rome, 81 A.D.

Angry, unfamiliar voices penetrated Pelonia's awareness. Floating between wakefulness and dark, she couldn't budge. Every muscle ached. A sharp pain drummed against her skull.

The voices died away, then a woman's words broke through the haze.

"My name is Lucia. Can you hear me?" The woman pressed a cup of water to Pelonia's cracked lips. "What shall I call you?"

Pelonia coughed as the cool liquid trickled down her arid throat. "Pel...Pelonia."

"Do you remember what happened to you? You were struck on the head and injured. I've been giving you opium to soothe you, but you're far from recovered."

Her eyelids too heavy to open, Pelonia licked her chapped lips.

Gradually her mind began to make sense of her surroundings. The warmth must be sunshine, because the scent of wood smoke hung in the air. Her pallet was a coarse woolen blanket on the hard ground. Dirt clung to her skin and each of her sore muscles longed for the softness of her bed at home.

Home.

Where was she if not in the comfort of her father's Umbrian villa? Who was this woman Lucia? She couldn't remember.

Icy fingers of fear gripped her heart as one by one her memories returned. First the attack, then her father's murder. Raw grief squeezed her chest.

Confusion surrounded her. Where was her uncle? She remembered the slave caravan, his threat to sell her, but nothing more.

Panic forced her eyes open. She managed to focus on the young woman's face above her.

"The master will be here soon." A smile tilted Lucia's thin lips, but didn't touch her honey-brown eyes.

"Where...am I?" she asked, the words grating in her throat.

"You're in the home of Caros Viriathos."

The name meant nothing to Pelonia. She prayed God had delivered her into the hands of a kind man, someone who would help her contact her cousin Tiberia.

Her eyes closed with fatigue. "How...how long have I...been here?"

"Four days and this morning. You've been in and out of sleep. I'll order you a bowl of broth. You should eat to bolster your strength."

Four days, and she remembered nothing. Tiberia must be frantic wondering why she'd failed to attend her wedding.

She opened her eyes. "I must—"

"Don't speak. Now that you've woken, Gaius, our master's steward, says you have one week to recover. Then your labor begins."

"My cousin. I must..."

"You're a slave in the Ludus Maximus now. A possession of the *lanista,* Caros Viriathos."

Lanista? A vile *gladiator* trainer?

"No!"

Lucia crossed her arms over her buxom chest. "We will see."

Heavy footsteps crunched on the rushes strewn across the floor. The new arrival stopped out of Pelonia's view.

The nauseating ache in her head increased without mercy. What had she done to make God despise her?

Focusing on Lucia, she saw the young woman's face light with pleasure.

"Master," Lucia greeted, jumping to her feet. "The new slave is finally awake. She calls herself Pelonia. She's weak and the medicine I gave her has run its course."

"Then give her more if she needs it."

The man's deep voice poured over Pelonia like the soothing water of a bath. She turned her head, ignoring the jab of pain that pierced her skull.

"You mustn't move your head," Lucia snapped, "or you might injure yourself further."

Pelonia stiffened. She wasn't accustomed to taking orders from slaves.

Lucia glanced toward the door. "She's argumentative. I have a hunch she'll be difficult. She denies she's your slave."

Silence followed Lucia's remark. Would this man who claimed to own her kill or beat her? Was he a cruel barbarian?

She sensed him move closer. Her tension rose as if she were prey in the sights of a hungry lion. At last the lion crossed to where she could see him.

Sunlight streaming through the window enveloped the giant, giving his dark hair a golden glow. A crisp, light-colored tunic draped across his shoulders and chest contrasted sharply with the rich copper of his skin. Gold bands around his upper arms emphasized the thickness of his muscles, the physical power he held in check.

Her breath hitched in her throat. She could only stare. Without a doubt, the man could crush her if he chose.

"So, you are called Pelonia," he said. "And my healer believes you wish to fight me."

Her gaze locked with the unusual blue of his forceful glare. For the first time she understood how the Hebrew, David, must have suffered when he faced Goliath. Swallowing the lump of fear in her throat, she nodded. "If I must."

"If you must?" Caros eyed Pelonia with a mix of irritation and respect. With her tunic filthy and torn, her dark hair in disarray and her bruises healing, his new slave looked like a wounded goddess. But she was just an ordinary woman. Why did she think she could defy him?

"Then let the games begin," he said, his voice thick with mockery.

"You think...this...this is a game?" she asked faintly.

The roughness of her voice reminded him of her body's weakened condition—a frailty her spirit clearly didn't share. Crouching beside her, he ran his forefinger over the yellowed bruise on her cheek. She closed her eyes and sighed as though his touch somehow soothed her.

Her guileless response unnerved him. The need to protect her enveloped him, a sensation he hadn't known since the deaths of his mother and sisters. As a slave, he'd been beaten on many occasions in an effort to conquer his will. That no one ever succeeded was a matter of pride for him. Much to his surprise, he had no wish to see this girl broken either.

"Of course it's a game. And I will be the victor."

Defiance flamed in the depths of her large, doe-brown eyes. She didn't speak and he admired her restraint when he could see she wanted to flay him.

"You might as well give in now, my prize. I own you whether you will it or not."

He gripped her chin and forced her to look at him.

"Admit it," he said. "Then you can return to your sleep."

She shook her head. "No. No one owns me...no one but my God."

"And who might your god be? Jupiter? Apollo? Or maybe you worship the god of the sea. Do you think Neptune will rescue you?"

"The Christ."

Caros wondered if she were a fool or had a wish for death. "Say that to the wrong person, Pelonia, and you'll find yourself facing the lions."

"I already am."

He laughed. "So you think of me as a ferocious beast?"

Her silence amused him all the more. "Good. It suits me well to know you realize I'm untamed and capable of tearing you limb from limb."

"Then do your worst. Death is better...than being owned."

Caros suddenly noticed Pelonia had grown pale and weaker still.

He berated himself for depleting her meager strength when he should have been encouraging her to heal. He lifted her into his arms.

She weighed no more than a laurel leaf. Had he pushed her to the brink of death?

Holding her tight against his chest, he whispered near her ear. "Tell me, *mea carissima*. What can I do to aid you? What can I do to ease your plight?"

"Find...Tiberia," she whispered, the dregs of her strength draining away. "And free me."

* * * * *

Will Pelonia ever convince Caros of who she is and where she truly belongs? Or will their growing love bind her to him for all time?

Find out in
THE GLADIATOR
by Carla Capshaw
Available in November 2009
from Love Inspired® Historical

HEARTWARMING INSPIRATIONAL ROMANCE

Get more of the heartwarming inspirational romance stories that you love and cherish, beginning in July with SIX NEW titles, available every month from the Love Inspired® line.

Also look for our other
Love Inspired® genres, including:

Love Inspired® Suspense:
Enjoy four contemporary tales of intrigue and romance every month.

Love Inspired® Historical:
Travel to a different time with two powerful and engaging stories of romance, adventure and faith every month.

Tacy Jones had come to
Mule Hollow to train
wild horses—but
Brent Stockwell doesn't
think *ladies* belong in
the pen. So Tacy will just
have to change his mind!
But when she learns his
reason, she's determined
to show the handsome
cowboy that taking a
chance on your dream is
what life is all about.

Look for

His Cowgirl Bride

by
Debra Clopton

*Available November
wherever books are sold.*

Steeple
Hill®
LI87563

REQUEST YOUR FREE BOOKS!

2 FREE INSPIRATIONAL NOVELS
PLUS 2
FREE
MYSTERY GIFTS

Love Inspired.
HISTORICAL
INSPIRATIONAL HISTORICAL ROMANCE

YES! Please send me 2 FREE Love Inspired® Historical novels and my 2 FREE mystery gifts (gifts are worth about $10). After receiving them, if I don't wish to receive any more books, I can return the shipping statement marked "cancel". If I don't cancel, I will receive 4 brand-new novels every other month and be billed just $4.24 per book in the U.S. or $4.74 per book in Canada. That's a savings of over 20% off the cover price. It's quite a bargain! Shipping and handling is just 50¢ per book.* I understand that accepting the 2 free books and gifts places me under no obligation to buy anything. I can always return a shipment and cancel at any time. Even if I never buy another book, the two free books and gifts are mine to keep forever. 102 IDN EYPS 302 IDN EYP4

Name _____ (PLEASE PRINT)

Address _____ Apt. #

City _____ State/Prov. _____ Zip/Postal Code

Signature (if under 18, a parent or guardian must sign)

Mail to Steeple Hill Reader Service:
IN U.S.A.: P.O. Box 1867, Buffalo, NY 14240-1867
IN CANADA: P.O. Box 609, Fort Erie, Ontario L2A 5X3

Not valid to current subscribers of Love Inspired Historical books.

Want to try two free books from another series?
Call 1-800-873-8635 or visit www.morefreebooks.com

* Terms and prices subject to change without notice. Prices do not include applicable taxes. Sales tax applicable in N.Y. Canadian residents will be charged applicable provincial taxes and GST. Offer not valid in Quebec. This offer is limited to one order per household. All orders subject to approval. Credit or debit balances in a customer's account(s) may be offset by any other outstanding balance owed by or to the customer. Please allow 4 to 6 weeks for delivery. Offer available while quantities last.

Your Privacy: Steeple Hill Books is committed to protecting your privacy. Our Privacy Policy is available online at www.SteepleHill.com or upon request from the Reader Service. From time to time we make our lists of customers available to reputable third parties who may have a product or service of interest to you. If you would prefer we not share your name and address, please check here. ☐

LIH09

Love Inspired.
HISTORICAL

TITLES AVAILABLE NEXT MONTH
Available November 10, 2009

GINGHAM BRIDE by Jillian Hart
Buttons and Bobbins
The last thing Fiona O'Rourke wants for Christmas is an arranged marriage. Yet a pretend engagement to her rugged betrothed Ian McPherson will keep her safe from her cruel father—and give her time to earn her freedom. But in a season of unexpected miracles, Fiona and Ian will soon risk everything for the most precious gift of all.

THE GLADIATOR by Carla Capshaw
He won his fame—and his freedom—in the gory pits of Rome's Colosseum. Yet the greatest challenge for once-legendary gladiator Caros Viriathos comes to him through a slave. *His* slave, the beautiful and mysterious Pelonia Valeria. Her secret brings danger to his household...and offers Caros a love like he's never known.